THE EMIGRANTS

Gilbert Imlay (1754?–1828?) was a man of many trades and talents, few of which were within the confines of what is conventionally regarded as legally and morally acceptable behavior. A self-styled "captain" in the American Revolutionary army, Imlay set out to try his luck across the Allegheny Mountains in the Ohio Valley soon after the war ended. In Kentucky, he became involved in various shady activities, including land speculation schemes and dubious secessionist politics. Having accumulated more debt than he could handle while successfully eluding sheriffs' summonses and court writs, Imlay quietly left the West (as the Ohio Valley was considered then) and America sometime in late 1786. He reappeared in London in 1792, the year in which his first and highly influential book, *A Topographical Description of the Western Territory of North America*, was published. This was followed, in 1793, by his only other known publication, the epistolary novel *The Emigrants*. During much of 1793 Imlay was in Paris, where he associated with the group of intellectuals and revolutionaries who gathered around the notorious radical Tom Paine. It was here that he met the writer and feminist Mary Wollstonecraft, with whom he began a tempestuous and ill-fated love affair. After he abandoned Wollstonecraft, little is known of Imlay's life. A grave believed to be his is found on the Channel Island of Jersey, dated 1828.

W. M. Verhoeven teaches at the University of Groningen (The Netherlands) in the Department of English and is cochair of the American Studies Program. An editor of *Post-War Literatures in English* and *The Dutch Quarterly Review Studies in Literature*, he has published essays on a wide array of topics, including Gothic literature, epistolarity, canonization, the idea of the wilderness, postmodernism, and multiculturalism. He edited *James Fenimore Cooper: New Historical and Literary Contexts* and *Rewriting the Dream: Reflections on the Changing American Literary*

Canon, and coedited *Making America/Making American Literature: Franklin to Cooper.*

Amanda Gilroy teaches at the University of Groningen, in the Department of English. She works mainly on women writers of the late eighteenth and early nineteenth centuries. Her current projects include a book of essays on travel writing entitled *Romantic Geographies,* and an edition (with Keith Hanley) of the work of Romantic poet and dramatist Joanna Baillie.

Together, W. M. Verhoeven and Amanda Gilroy have coedited the special issue of the journal *Prose Studies* on nonfictional letters, and *Cultural Correspondences: Essays on Epistolary Writing* (forthcoming).

THE EMIGRANTS

GILBERT IMLAY

WITH AN INTRODUCTION AND NOTES BY
W. M. VERHOEVEN AND
AMANDA GILROY

PENGUIN BOOKS

PENGUIN BOOKS

Published by the Penguin Group
Penguin Putnam Inc., 375 Hudson Street,
New York, New York 10014, U.S.A.
Penguin Books Ltd, 27 Wrights Lane,
London W8 5TZ, England
Penguin Books Australia Ltd, Ringwood,
Victoria, Australia
Penguin Books Canada Ltd, 10 Alcorn Avenue,
Toronto, Ontario, Canada M4V 3B2
Penguin Books (N.Z.) Ltd, 182–190 Wairau Road,
Auckland 10, New Zealand

Penguin Books Ltd, Registered Offices:
Harmondsworth, Middlesex, England

First published in Great Britain 1793
This edition with an introduction and notes by W. M. Verhoeven and Amanda
Gilroy published in Penguin Books 1998

1 3 5 7 9 10 8 6 4 2

LIBRARY OF CONGRESS CATALOGING IN PUBLICATION DATA
Imlay, Gilbert, 1754?–1828?
The emigrants/Gilbert Imlay; with an introduction and notes by
W. M. Verhoeven and Amanda Gilroy.
p.   cm.—(Penguin classics)
ISBN 0-14-043672-3 (pbk.)
1. United States—History—1783–1815—Fiction.
2. British—Travel—United States—History—18th century—Fiction.
I. Verhoeven, W. M.   II. Gilroy, Amanda.   III. Title.   IV. Series.
PR3517.I44E45   1998
823'.6—dc21   97-34617

Printed in the United States of America
Set in Bembo

ACKNOWLEDGMENTS

In preparing the introduction to *The Emigrants,* we greatly benefitted from the previous scholarship of William Clark Durant, Ralph Leslie Rusk, and, especially, John Seelye, whose original and highly informative writings on Gilbert Imlay and his cultural-historical context inspired us throughout and are a model for all scholars working in the field of early American studies. We would very much like to thank Sandy Stelts, at the Rare Books Room at Pennsylvania State University Library, and Jaime Jamison, of the microforms department there—two of the most efficient library researchers we have ever had the pleasure of working with and who were able to trace and retrieve various documents by and related to Imlay for us, in some cases at a moment's notice. We also thank Nancy Armstrong at Brown University, Dorothy McMillan at the University of Glasgow, and Saree Makdisi at the University of Chicago for having carved out time in their own busy academic lives to find materials for us. We appreciate the assistance of Morgan Love, and the comments of students on our "Revolutions & Watersheds" course. We gratefully acknowledge the commitment and patience of our editor, Kristine Puopolo. Finally, we would like to thank our friend Carla Mulford for her support and advice throughout the preparation of this edition.

CONTENTS

INTRODUCTION

I

The American Gilbert Imlay is best known to readers of British Romanticism as the cad who abandoned Mary Wollstonecraft, the founding mother of modern feminism, and whose philandering drove her to attempt suicide (twice). Wollstonecraft's *Letters to Imlay* (first published posthumously in 1798) and her travel book *Letters Written During a Short Residence in Sweden, Norway, and Denmark* (1796) detail the ups and many downs of their affair, while William Godwin, in his *Memoirs* (1798) of his late wife, set the tone for subsequent criticism in deeming Imlay, after Othello, a man who could, "like the base Indian, throw a pearl away, richer than all his tribe."[1] Scholars of American literature and history, on the other hand, have long been familiar with another side of Imlay, that of the entrepreneurial author of one of the most influential and successful travel books of the late eighteenth century, *A Topographical Description of the Western Territory of North America* (first published in London in 1792). Few readers of either British or American literary history, however, are familiar with Imlay's novel *The Emigrants*, published in England in July or August 1793, a few months after the start of his affair with Wollstonecraft. This epistolary novel, which combines a sentimental plot of impeded love with episodes of travel and adventure (including a capture by Indians), acts as a type of fictional companion to the travel text: Both books, aimed at a British audience, function as practical guides for emigration to the Ohio Valley and map out a geopolitical future for the New World across the Allegheny Mountains.

In addition, *The Emigrants* provides a salutary alternative to the distinct absence of feminist ideals in Imlay's checkered personal life, for it "espouse[s] the cause of oppressed women" (Letter XIII), especially the rights of women in marriage, which it ties to an anticolonial agenda. The novel exposes marriage in England as a type of cultural captivity for women, and makes a plea for more liberal divorce laws. The treatment of women also serves as the most affecting example of the differences between Britain and America, as Imlay uses the issue of domestic politics to construct a utopian vision of American national character. *The Emigrants* thus makes a claim for consideration as a Jacobin novel—a document of the transatlantic revolutionary movement. However, there are contradictions in the revolutionary rhetoric of personal liberty that support *The Emigrants'* valorization of America over England (or Europe), and women continued to be seen as possession or spectacle.

In order to understand the novel's politics of geography and of gender, we need first to know something about Imlay's *Topographical Description* and the revolutionary era in which and of which he wrote, as well as something about the contradictory and charismatic character of the man himself, whom Edith Franklin Wyatt described as "unscrupulous, independent, courageous, a dodger of debts to the poor, a deserter, a protector of the helpless, a revolutionist, a man of enlightenment beyond his age, a greedy and treacherous land booster."[2]

II

Very little information is available about the earliest period of Gilbert Imlay's life or, indeed, about his life after he broke up with Mary Wollstonecraft—the known facts of his life covering roughly the twenty-year period from 1777 to 1797. Imlay was born on 9 February 1754, probably in Upper Freehold, Monmouth County, New Jersey, where the Imlay family had been established since the early decades of the eighteenth century. Apart from a brief reference to a Gilbert Imlay in a will drawn up in 1761, nothing is known about him until his name appears in the military service records of the American Revolutionary army. These records indicate that Imlay served in Forman's Additional Continental Regiment from 11 January 1777 to July 1778, and that he had enlisted for the duration of the war. Although he commonly styled himself "captain" (as on the title page of

A Topographical Description), there is no evidence that Imlay ever rose beyond the rank of first lieutenant.

At the close of the Revolutionary War, Imlay, like so many other decommissioned officers of the American army, set out to try his luck across the Allegheny Mountains in the western territories of the Ohio Valley. The settlements along the shores of the Ohio River, in what is now the state of Kentucky, were at the time the farthest outposts of the westward expansion of America. This was the age of legendary frontiersman Daniel Boone, who first visited the area in 1769 and whose adventurous rambles through the sublime wilderness and constant tussles with the Indians in what the latter called the "dark and bloody ground" later earned him the status of national mythic hero (as well as the honorary title of "colonel"). This was the age, too, of Boone's first biographer and fellow Pennsylvanian John Filson, who had crossed over into Kentucky in 1783 in search of fame and fortune, and who a year later published *The Discovery and Settlement of Kentucke*, one of the most influential accounts of what Filson described as "the best tract of land in North America, and probably in the world."[3]

According to his own account of the trip in *A Topographical Description*, which borrows heavily from Filson's book, Imlay arrived in Kentucky in March 1784. Although as a veteran officer of the Revolutionary War he would have been able to claim automatic land rights in the western territory, in March 1783 he had already bought a tract of land in Fayette, one of the three counties into which the District of Kentucky was divided at the time. Soon after his arrival in Kentucky, Imlay became deeply immersed in land speculation deals, leaving a long and complex trail of legal entanglements, according to Kentucky county court records. In Louisville in April 1784 he was sworn in as a deputy surveyor of Jefferson County, a position which must have been of considerable commercial advantage to him: As "a Commissioner for laying out Land in the Back Settlements" (as he styled himself somewhat inflatedly on the title page of *A Topographical Description*), he could play a modest role in publicly furthering the cause of the "probable rise and grandeur of the American empire" (Letter III in *Description*), while lining his pockets on the side.

It is not known how long Imlay retained his surveying job, but there is plenty of evidence to suggest that before long lining his pockets was his main, if not his sole, preoccupation. However, the records of the various county courts also indicate that he was not always very successful in his business deals. Continually incurring debts and breaching contracts, Imlay was soon forced into a life of constant county-hopping in an attempt to elude sheriffs' summonses and court writs. At one point, in August 1784, a warrant for Imlay's arrest was issued by the Jefferson County Court, but, of course, he had taken to his heels by then.

Among Imlay's business associates in Kentucky was the notorious General James Wilkinson. A veteran of the Revolutionary War and a man with a lust for wealth and power, Wilkinson had survived the siege of Boston and was present at the siege of Quebec, after which he served under Washington at the battles of Trenton and Princeton. Wilkinson later showed up in Kentucky, where he was soon involved in large-scale land speculation schemes. What earned Wilkinson the sobriquet "Washington of the West" was his plan to establish relations between the western territories and the Spanish authorities in Louisiana, with the ultimate aim of bringing about the secession of the western regions from the United States. While ostensibly backing the federal government in its dispute with the Spanish over boundaries and navigation rights to the Mississippi, Wilkinson was actually an agent in the pay of Spain and secretly campaigning for an independent state west of the Alleghenies and, ultimately, for his self-aggrandizement.

Sharing Wilkinson's commercial self-interest as well as his unruly, rebellious western pride, Imlay became an admirer and a supporter of his double-tongued patriotism. Thus it is quite possible that the staunchly patriotic and expansionist 1788 petition to the United States by "the people of Kentucky in convention," which is quoted at length in the preface to the first edition of *A Topographical Description*, was actually composed by General Wilkinson, who appears in *The Emigrants* as the avuncular character of "General W——," the kindly godfather of Imlay's secessionist utopia. In May 1785 Imlay asked Wilkinson to look after his business interests in Fayette County, no doubt because the place had become too hot for Imlay himself. In November 1785, soon after he had joined an ambitious investment project aimed at erecting an ironworks (later known as the "Green River Company"), Imlay absconded from Kentucky, leaving his business associates to figure out what had happened to their money. For years after his departure, sheriffs' summonses continued to be posted on church doors and published in newspapers, but Imlay was no more to be seen or heard of in Kentucky.

At the end of 1785 Imlay was in Richmond, Virginia, where he continued to speculate in Kentucky land. Thus in December he acquired a patent for over twelve thousand acres of land in Jefferson County, Kentucky, which he sold in Philadelphia in September 1786 to a Silas Talbott for a dollar an acre. In November 1786 Imlay was back in Richmond, presumably to receive letters of patent issued to him for a large tract of land in Fayette County, Kentucky. Very shortly afterward, Imlay's trail on the North American continent abruptly terminates, and it is generally assumed that he left the United States in December 1786, leaving behind legal entanglements that were to keep the courts busy for more than a decade. (Indeed, one case—that of Isaac Hite, one of Imlay's fellow investors in the Green River Company— dragged on until October 1799, when, though Hite had died in the meantime, the plaintiff's inheritors finally savored the taste of a legal victory over Imlay, although of course no money was forthcoming.)

As for Imlay's reasons for silently departing from the United States, we can only speculate. It has been suggested that he may have been involved in a French conspiracy against Spanish Louisiana. It is known that French agents were active in Kentucky as early as 1785 and that many of the settlers there were frustrated with the federal government for not settling with the Spanish the ques-

tion of the navigation of the Mississippi, and were therefore
threatening to appeal to a foreign power to intervene on their
part. However, it seems more likely that Imlay's trip to Europe
(if that is where he went) was motivated by his own troubles in
America rather than by any concrete plan to plot against the
United States. It is, for one thing, hard to imagine that the *ancien
régime* would recruit a small-time land speculator from Kentucky
as an *agent provocateur* against the Spanish interests in Louisiana and
the southwest. Still ahead were the two developments needed to
change this situation and put Imlay at the center of a cabal that,
had it been successful, might have changed the map of the United
States and the course of American history: the emergence of a
more radical, expansionist foreign policy in France under the national assembly, and the publication of Imlay's highly successful *A
Topographical Description* in 1792, which won him the reputation
of being a geopolitical expert on the western territories of North
America.

III

Following the example of Crèvecoeur's *Letters From an American
Farmer* (London, 1782), *A Topographical Description* presents itself
as "a series of letters to a friend in England," but internal evidence
suggests that the book was written (at least in part, but probably
in its entirety) long after the author had left both Kentucky and
America, most probably in England from 1791 to 1792. Again
like Crèvecoeur's *Letters, A Topographical Description* is aimed at a
European, particularly British, audience, and, as may be concluded
from its format (a cross between an epistolary correspondence and
a travelogue), it asks to be read as an authentic, eyewitness account
of the American social experiment as a "real life" application of
a long tradition of progressive, utopian, Enlightenment thinking,
which could be described as radical pastoralism. Thus, in the Introduction, the English "editor" of the letters describes his American friend "Imlay" as a "man who had lived until he was more
than five-and-twenty years old, in the back parts of America,"

where he had become "accustomed to that simplicity of manners natural to a people in a state of innocence." Having since traveled to Europe, his friend "must have been powerfully stricken with the great difference between the simplicity of [the New World], and what is called *etiquette* and good breeding in the [Old]." Being a man of unspoiled manners and morals, his American friend, the "editor" believes, "is better calculated than ourselves to judge our manners." Besides being an eclectic account of the American horn of plenty and a practical "how to emigrate to Kentucky" guide, Imlay's *Topographical Description* thus becomes a comparative analysis of, in the words of Imlay's Kentuckian Noble Savage, "the simple manners, and rational life of the Americans, in these back settlements" and "the distorted and unnatural habits of the Europeans," which, Imlay's narrator reminds us, "have flowed no doubt from the universally bad laws which exist [in Europe], and from that pernicious system of blending religion with politics, which has been productive of universal depravity" (Letter I).

It is worth noting that Imlay chose the same epistolary form for *The Emigrants*, and, as in *A Topographical Description*, he mixes in stirring amounts of travel and adventure. Though *The Emigrants* is relatively unsophisticated in its use of epistolary techniques and devices (apart from the duplicitous letter written by Caroline's sister that causes some misunderstandings between the lovers, there is nothing of the complexity of a Samuel Richardson or even of a Hannah Webster Foster), it is appropriate to consider the ideological resonances of this particular textual form at this particular historical moment. During the 1790s, the sentimental novel, and especially the epistolary novel—paradigmatically represented by Jean-Jacques Rousseau's tale of illicit love, *Julie; Or, The New Heloise* (1791)—came to be seen especially in conservative circles as supporting a trend toward dangerous, individual excess at a time when national political consensus was thought to be paramount. Parallel to this development, the familiar letter, traditionally seen as an authentic document of the self, moved more and more into the sphere of public critique: The letter was revolutionized, so to speak, and came to be regarded as an agent of conspiracy. Significantly, the increasingly reactionary British government began to view the burgeoning networks of radical correspondence (such as the London Corresponding Society), which were dedicated to political reform, with great suspicion, and ultimately imposed legislative gagging to suppress them. *The Emigrants* entered this ongoing cultural correspondence on the side of revolutionary writers.[4]

Imlay's *Topographical Description* made a strong impact on all those radical minds in Britain who considered their society to be hopelessly corrupt and their civil rights under serious threat from an outdated and despotic government. First published at a time when tensions were rising between the French and the British (with war between them eventually breaking out in February 1793) and when the violent revolution was expected to cross the English Channel into Britain any minute, Imlay's book was seized upon by many as the promise for a Rousseauesque return to nature in the pristine wilderness of the New World. The decision of the radical scientist and philosopher Joseph Priestley (1733–1804) to settle on the banks of the Susquehanna in Pennsylvania and build an agrarian utopia not too long after a reactionary mob burned down his Birmingham house and laboratory in September 1791 initiated a widespread emigration movement to America among progressive European idealists in the 1790s, many of whom were thrilled by Imlay's description of the Kentucky paradise.

One of the best known of these utopian emigration schemes was Samuel Coleridge's pantisocracy—an experiment of human perfectibility which was to be created in pastoral seclusion, and which would be run on the principle of sharing property, labor, and self-government equally among all of its adult members, both men and women. Coleridge thoroughly researched the possibilities of an American pantisocracy, and enthusiastically read several of the recent reports on the country's topography, including Brissot de Warville's *New Travels in the United States* (1792), Thomas Cooper's *Some Information Respecting America* (1794), and Imlay's *Topographical Description*. It is probably not a coincidence that Kentucky was the first suggested site for Coleridge's pantisocracy, only some time later to be superseded by the site that most people nowadays tend to associate with pantisocracy—the idyllic Pennsylvanian hinterland on the banks of the picturesque Susquehanna River, which was the region Thomas Cooper (a business associate of Priestley's son in the Susquehanna project) recommended to potential emigrants.

It was apparently common knowledge in the 1790s that Imlay and Cooper were interested in more than the mere sale of their books. Thus, in January 1795, an article appeared in the *British Critic* discussing the activities of American and British land agents in London at the time, particularly the rival emigration schemes for Kentucky and the Susquehanna that were being promoted by Imlay and Cooper respectively. The article was highly critical of the dealings of both men, referring to "Messrs. Imlay and Cooper as two rival auctioneers, or rather two show-men, stationed for the allurement of incautious passengers; 'Pray ladies and gentlemen, walk in and admire the wonders of Kentucky.'—'Pray stop and see the incomparable beauties of the Susquehanna.' "[5] Similarly, in the supplement to its 1794 issue, the *Gentleman's Magazine* published what it claimed was an authentic letter from an actual emigrant who had settled in Pennsylvania, hoping that its contents might "help to check the spirit of emigration so prevalent in [the] country," and that it "might serve as an antidote to the poison so generally diffused by writers, who scruple not to injure their native country by the grossest misrepresentations."[6] It was generally acknowledged that there was a growing popularity of American emigration schemes among Quakers, Unitarians, and other idealist freethinkers. By 1796 it was calculated that some two thousand people had set out for America—though many returned disillusioned.[7]

Even though it is not known whether at that time Imlay himself still held any land rights in Kentucky, land-jobbing was certainly one of the activities that kept him occupied during the six-year interval between his departure from America in December 1786 and the publication of *A Topographical Description* in 1792. Soon after the appearance of the book, however, Imlay found himself launched on a rather different career, and one that some have considered to be an unlikely occupation for a former "captain" in the Revolutionary army and western confidence man: that of a successful writer. The popularity of *A Topographical Description* soon led to the publication in 1793 of a second, expanded English edition (strangely, under the name of *George* Imlay) which added, in an appendix, Filson's *The Discovery and Settlement of Kentucke* and his *Adventures of Colonel Daniel Boone*. In the same year further reprints appeared in New York and Dublin, and a German translation was produced. *The Emigrants*, which also appeared in 1793, marked Imlay's initiation into the realm of creative fiction, although the novel was probably meant to be a fictional companion piece to his *Topographical Description*—an attempt to jump onto the bandwagon of the then-popular Jacobin novel, a short-lived genre of radical fiction that was inspired by the early popularity of the French Revolution in Britain. An even more expanded edition of *A Topographical Description*—which included such texts as the treaty with Spain on the free navigation of the Mississippi, the Plan of Association of the North American Land Company, and Thomas Hutchins's *Historical Narrative and Topographical Description of Louisiana and West Florida*—appeared in London in 1797, testifying to the book's continuing popularity in Europe. The book was not reprinted in North America after the 1793 New York edition.

Although it has been claimed in the past that Imlay's *Topographical Description* is closely modeled after (or even concocted from) earlier topographical classics—notably Thomas Hutchins's *A Topographical Description of Virginia, Pennsylvania, Maryland, and North Carolina* (1778); Jonathan Carver's *Travels Through the Interior Parts of North America* (1781); Thomas Jefferson's *Notes on the State of Virginia* (1784–85); Comte de Buffon's *Histoire Naturelle* (1749–1804); Jedidiah Morse's *American Geography* (1789); Brissot de Warville's *New Travels in the United States* (1792); and, especially, John Filson's *The Discovery and Settlement of Kentucke* (1784)—a closer look at Imlay's text reveals that, unlike its predecessors (with the exception of Jefferson's *Notes*), Imlay's book constitutes a sustained geopolitical doctrine. It does not merely describe the western territories as a new Canaan for the prospective emigrant; it also provides the physiocratic rationale for the opening up and development of the western territories.

A doctrine developed by political economists in France in the eighteenth century, physiocracy is characterized chiefly by the belief that government policy should not interfere with the operation of natural economic laws and that land is the source of all wealth. In contrast to Enlightenment thought in general, physiocracy holds that liberty is not so much a precondition for universal prosperity as the *consequence* of prosperity. In other words, liberty follows trade and commerce, not the other way around. Accordingly, Imlay's attitude toward the natural environment of the western territories is not that of an idealist pantisocratist seeking refuge from oppression and persecution, or of a romantic, Wordsworthian "lover of the meadows and the woods, and the mountains," but that of a staunchly rationalistic, pragmatic Enlightenment real estate developer. Thus, when he describes the area around Lexington, Kentucky, as the "finest and most luxurious country in the world" (*Description*, Letter III), Imlay is not transported by "aching joys" and "dizzy raptures," but is rather thinking of the richness of the soil, the navigability of the rivers, and the wholesomeness of the climate.

Roughly speaking, Imlay's topographical description of the western territory of the United States, as well as the geopolitical vision based on it, centers around just two natural phenomena: mountains and rivers—more particularly, the Allegheny Mountains and the Ohio and Mississippi rivers. The Allegheny Mountains, which until the 1760s caused the colonization of America to be contained within the relatively confined coastal strip bordering on the Atlantic, undergo a crucial metamorphosis in Imlay's *Topographical Description* as well as in *The Emigrants*. Rather than an impregnable obstacle for further westward expansion, the Alleghenies are presented to us in both texts as not so much a physical but a *moral* watershed, separating the pastoral innocence of the western settlements from the social evil, political corruption, and religious blindness that dominate life in the eastern states. As stated in *The Emigrants*, the virtuous "region of innocence" lies to the west of the mountains, while vice runs rife in Bristol and the East. This symbolic geography underlies the distinction between European depravity and American innocence made in both of Imlay's books. As described in *A Topographical Description*, the Arcadian utopia of pastoral bliss that presents itself to the emigrant to the Ohio Valley reminds one of a blend of Samuel Johnson's Enlightenment "Happy Valley" in his Eastern tale *Rasselas* and an Old Testament view of the promised land from the top of Mount Sinai. Imlay's mountaintop prospect of the western Canaan occasions one of the few moments in the book in which he indulges in uncharacteristic "rhapsody" (reminiscent of similar outbursts in *The Emigrants*):

Everything here assumes a dignity and splendour I have never seen in any part of the world. You ascend a considerable distance from the shore of the Ohio, and when you would suppose you had arrived at the summit of a mountain, you find yourself upon a extensive level. Here an eternal verdure reigns, and the brilliant sun of lat. 39%, piercing through the azure heavens, produces, in this prolific soil, an early maturity which is truly astonishing. Flowers full and perfect, as if they had been cultivated by the hand of a florist, with all their captivating odours, and with all the variegated charms which colour and nature can produce, here, in the lap of elegance and beauty, decorate the smiling groves. Soft zephyrs gently breathe on sweets, and the inhaled air gives a voluptuous glow of health and vigour, that seems to ravish the intoxicated senses. The sweet songsters of the forest appear to feel the influence of this genial clime, and, in more soft and modulated tones, warble their tender notes in unison with love and nature. Every thing here gives delight; and, in that mild effulgence which beams around us, we feel a glow of gratitude for the elevation which our all bountiful Creator has bestowed upon us. Far from being disgusted with man for his turpitude or depravity, we feel that dignity which nature bestowed upon us at the creation; but which has been contaminated by the base alloy of meanness, the concomitant of European education, and what is more lamentable is, that it is the consequence of your [his British friend's] very laws and governments. (Letter III)

But Imlay knew well enough that even a promised land is a worthless land if it is not easily accessible. The northern route to Kentucky—by wagon from either Philadelphia or Baltimore across the Alleghenies to Pittsburgh and then down the Ohio River on flat-bottomed barges—was an onerous one, and no matter how smooth Imlay makes the journey appear, it would continue (as Filson had already noted in his book) to render produce dear in the western settlements. The key to reaching the the back settlements lay in the navigability of the Mississippi and Ohio rivers, and it is not surprising that, in his *Topographical Description*, Imlay (following earlier authors like Carver, Filson, and Jefferson) dwells at length on the unique transportation potential of the West's interlocking rivers and lakes, which effectively turn the region into a physiocratic paradise:

> You will observe, that as far as this immense continent is known, the courses and extent of its rivers are extremely favourable to communication by water; a circumstance which is highly important, whether we regard it in a social or commercial point of view. The intercourse of men has added no inconsiderable lustre to the polish of manners, and, perhaps, commerce has tended more to civilize and embellish the human mind, in two centuries, than war and chivalry would have done in five. (Letter V)

And, once the problem of upstream navigation was solved with the help of steam (and Imlay was confident that this would be only a matter of time, given that experiments with steam-powered boats were already under way in Virginia), dwellers on Kentucky's green and fertile fields would be able to open up communication and trade with the settlements on the Pacific coast and in Canada. Seeing that "[a]ccording to the present system, wealth is the source of power" and that "the attainment of wealth can only be brought about by a wise and happy attention to commerce," Imlay proudly concludes that the western regions, far from being an outpost of civilization on the margins of America, were actually at the heart of the North American experiment and were mankind's best bet to realize even the wildest, most extreme notions of physiocratic idealism and neoclassical perfectibility.[8]

The Emigrants in many respects simply puts into fictional form the ideological concerns of the earlier text. While downplaying any overt commercial angle, the plot nevertheless emphasizes the ease with which the emigrant may travel west and how an elaborate infrastructure of roads and waterways is at his disposal once he arrives there. With its sentimental interest frequently being put to the service of its geopolitics, *The Emigrants* not coincidentally reads at times more like a travelogue than a novel. Thus the opening letters make much of the heroine's insistence on walking much of the way across the Allegheny Mountains—more like a picturesque tourist than a pioneer—in sharp contrast to her lethargic brother, George, who prefers to be moved around on a wagon, along with the old people in the company. But even more significant is Arl——ton's unstoppable wanderlust, which first takes him from Pittsburgh down the Ohio River to Louisville, and later, in what John Seelye calls "a fit of expansionist pique,"[9] farther west, via St. Vincent (Vincennes) toward St. Anthony's Falls and the sources of the Mississippi, from which he plans to travel down the river to Kaskaskia, then up the Missouri, back again to Kaskaskia, down the Mississippi to New Orleans, and back to Baltimore (see map on pp. lviii and lix. Further details are provided in the Explanatory Notes). Even though Caroline's captivity by the Indians forces Arl——ton to prematurely abandon his frantic wilderness trip, the reader gets the distinct impression that moving across vast tracts of the rugged American landscape is not more arduous, and only slightly more risky, than a journey in rural England or a promenade in London, and certainly much more thrilling—sublime or picturesque sights being available at every twist and turn of the emigrant's tour. As Caroline puts it, "here is a continual feast for the mind" (Letter VIII).

However, Imlay was not merely mindful of the economic, so-cial, and aesthetic significance of the western landscape, especially its elaborate network of waterways: he was also very sensitive to its political significance. Blending the region's rivers with its mountains, soil, climate, and natural resources into a physiocratic, geopolitical doctrine of progress and universal prosperity, Imlay in effect creates a prototype of the doctrine of Manifest Destiny, albeit with at least one significant difference: Imlay's physiocratic millennium does not have its origin in the early colonial experi-ments in Virginia and New England, nor even in the ideological energy released by the American Revolution; instead, he envisages the cradle of his physiocratic utopia to be in the West, more particularly in Kentucky, and the ideological forces that rock it to be generated by the French, rather than the American, Revolu-tion. Indeed, underlying Imlay's dream of America is a fervent plea for a secessionist utopia across the Alleghenies, whereby "the Mountain" (as he refers to them) creates an ideological dichotomy between two distinct Americas: between the eastern states, which he regards as an outpost of an earlier, Puritan exodus and whose original energy had petered out and become permeated with the social evils of the Old World, and the "true," trans-Alleghenian America in the West, which was radically discontinuous with the earlier European colonization of North America. Imlay's separatist agenda leads him to reformulate the notion of a federal America as a nation whose political power is not centered in the East— not in the "federal city" that has just been established in the Dis-trict of Columbia—but in the West:

The federal government regulating every thing commercial, must be productive of the greatest harmony, so that while we are likely to live in the regions of perpetual peace, our felicity will receive a zest from the activity and variety of our trade. We shall pass through the Mississippi to the sea—up the Ohio, Monongahala and Cheat rivers, by a small portage, into the Potowmac, which will bring us to the federal city on the line of Virginia and Maryland—through the federal rivers I have mentioned, and the lakes to New York and Quebec—from the northern lakes to the head branches of the rivers which run into Hudson's-bay into the Arctic regions—and from the sources of the Misouri [*sic*] into the Great South Sea. Thus in the centre of the earth, governing by the laws of reason and humanity, we seem calculated to become at once the emporium and protectors of the world. (*Description*, Letter V)

Imlay's physiocratic dream of an independent western state governed by the laws of reason and humanity is fulfilled in the utopia founded by Arl——ton toward the end of *The Emigrants*. Arl——ton confirms that he turns to the western territory as the site of his new community, named Bellefont, "as its infancy affords an opportunity to its citizens of establishing a system conformable to reason and humanity" and it is thus able to "extend the blessings of civilization to all orders of men" (Letter LXVII). The community is situated on the banks of the Ohio near Louisville and constitutes in total an area of about 256 square miles, parceled out to men who served with Arl——ton in the Revolutionary War (presumably because they are most likely to be men of honor and common sense). These men and their families live in an idyllic, enchanting spot, against the background of the impetuous Ohio River, the gushing fountain that gives the community its name, fertile meadows, whispering breezes, and warbling birds. The days follow a regular routine of agricultural cultivation and rural relaxation, including much dancing to rustic music.

Bellefont is no doubt the type of insular Arcadia promised by Imlay to prospective emigrants as part of his land-jobbing activities. The society is organized along radical, Godwinian notions of social and political justice; each man owns the section of land that he occupies, and all males over the age of twenty-one are entitled to vote for members of a house of representatives, who, in turn, elect a president. The members are to meet every Sunday throughout the year to discuss issues of agriculture, arts, government, and jurisprudence. The subversive, antiecclesiastical Sunday meeting as well as the structure of its government confirm that

Arl——ton's community is to be a secessionist state, independent of the government of the United States, rooted in a tradition of French physiocratic thought, and turning south (*not* east) toward Louisiana, and beyond, toward revolutionary France, for guidance and support.

No problems are foreseen for the fictional Bellefont, but in *A Topographical Description*, Imlay is somewhat more pragmatic: He recognizes that if Kentucky had the potential to become the center of the New World—indeed, the center of a New World millennium, thanks to its strategic position at the junction of the waterways of the future—then control of those waterways threatened to undermine Kentucky's position in Imlay's geopolitical master plan. He was acutely aware that "whoever are possessed of this river [the Mississippi], and of the vast tracts of fertile lands upon it, must in time command that continent, and the trade of it, as well as all the natives."[10] In the early pages of the book, Imlay recounts with evident disgust the attempts by the French in the course of the seventeenth and eighteenth centuries to put the western settlements in a stranglehold with an "insidious" plan to first occupy the mouths of the St. Lawrence and Mississippi rivers and subsequently to secure the communication between Canada and Louisiana by erecting an elaborate network of fortresses. But this "colossian plan" is very much attributed to the *ancien régime*, notably to Louis XIV ("that voracious tyrant"), and emphatically *not* to the new, revolutionary administration in France (Letter I).

By the time Imlay was composing his *Topographical Description*, the French sphere of influence on the North American continent had been drastically reduced at the close of the French and Indian Wars, when, via the Treaty of Paris of 1763, Louisiana and control over the mouth of the Mississippi had been seceded to Spain. Although the United States, as the inheritor of the Treaty of Paris, had formally retained the navigation rights to the Mississippi, the Spanish had more or less blockaded the river so as to frustrate the westward expansion of the United States. With the federal government showing only little sympathy with the plight of the western settlers, it is not difficult to see why, in the early 1790s, the rebellious Kentuckians should be ready to make overtures to the French, whose territorial ambitions toward Louisiana and the Mississippi Valley had been rekindled by the revolution of 1789. Nor is it hard to see how Imlay, as the author of one of the most recent popular treatises on the western settlements, was about to start rubbing shoulders with prominent Girondist politicians in France and get involved in French foreign affairs.

IV

In March 1793 Thomas Cooper (1759–1839)—an English radical holding French citizenship—recommended Imlay to Brissot de Warville (1754–93), leader of the Girondists (also known as Brissotins), who in turn introduced him to senior members of the French administration as an expert on the western territories of the United States. Imlay's *Topographical Description* undoubtedly provided him with the right sort of credentials for access to the intellectual and political circles in Paris, one of the best known of which was the group of intellectuals and revolutionaries that gathered around the notorious radical and author of *The Rights of Man*, Tom Paine (1737–1809), and which included General Francisco de Miranda, Thomas Christie (1761–96), Joel Barlow (1754–1812), and Mary Wollstonecraft (1759–97). Brissot, too, was a regular visitor at Paine's house in Saint-Denis, just north of Paris.

Brissot, along with Charles-Edmond Genet, minister plenipotentiary of the French Republic to the United States, had been campaigning to spread the French Revolution to the North American continent—more particularly, to "liberate" Spanish America, open the navigation of the Mississippi, and trigger a rebellion against British rule in Canada. The French plot against Spanish Louisiana was not unattractive to the United States (indeed, it had Secretary of State Thomas Jefferson's tacit approval), who saw in it a cheap and easy way of reopening the Mississippi to American navigation and possibly gaining control over Louisiana and the southwest. The French considered the political sentiments in Kentucky to be of strategic importance in their

Louisiana plan, and this no doubt explains why Imlay suddenly found himself deeply involved in the French-American cabal against Spain.

In 1793 Imlay, at Brissot's instigation, prepared two reports on the West for the French government—"Observations du Cap. Imlay, traduites de l'Anglois" and "Mémoire sur la Louisiane, présenté au Comité de Salut public par un Citoyen Américain"— which were duly presented to the notorious Committee of Public Safety (which formed the actual French government between 1793 and 1795 and which instituted the Reign of Terror under its Jacobin leader Robespierre). In the former document, Imlay expresses his willingness to act on behalf of the French in a military expedition against Spanish Louisiana, archly pointing out that involvement in the plan by American citizens was sure to bring the United States into the war against Spain. In the second, much longer document, Imlay sets out in detail what the political and economic benefits would be of a French conquest of Louisiana, and how such a conquest might best be effected. A letter dated April 1793 from Brissot to Le Brun, the French minister of foreign affairs, which was personally delivered by Imlay, suggests that the American was on the point of setting out on a mission to Louisiana with an unknown number of other agents.

But the mission was never to be carried out. In the course of May 1793, the Girondists were ousted from power and Brissot ultimately went to the guillotine. With Genet being recalled as ambassador to the United States and Jefferson discreetly withdrawing his covert support of the plan, the projected conquest of Louisiana was quietly abandoned. With it, Imlay's short-lived career as an agent provocateur and warmonger abruptly came to a close. By that time, however, Imlay was already launched on the amorous adventure that, more than any cabal or business deal he was ever involved in, would determine his reputation and public image to the present day.

V

Imlay met Mary Wollstonecraft for the first time at the Paris home of Thomas Christie, a Scottish businessman and writer on the French Revolution whose wife, Rebecca, was later to become one of Wollstonecraft's most intimate friends. Wollstonecraft had traveled to France (her second visit there) in December 1792, partly because she was interested in seeing the French Revolution in action and partly because she was trying to recover emotionally from her unrequited love for the Swiss painter Henry Fuseli (1741–1825). Having become acquainted with Imlay through a mutual friend (the writer Helen Maria Williams, who also may have been Imlay's mistress), Wollstonecraft initially took a strong dislike to the American and for a time avoided meeting him. However, since they frequented the same American expatriate circles in Paris (notably the one that had formed around Paine), it was probably hard to avoid meeting him altogether. Thus, when Wollstonecraft was having some difficulty procuring a passport to travel to Switzerland that spring, it was Imlay who offered to help her (as an American citizen, he would have been able to intercede for her with the French authorities).

Instead of going to Switzerland, however, Mary settled at Neuilly, just outside Paris, but her feelings toward Imlay had distinctly changed. Romantically inclined as she was, and yearning for a life in the kind of pantisocratic utopia on the idyllic banks of the Susquehanna that Coleridge had propounded earlier, Wollstonecraft was impressed by the charms of what she regarded as an unspoiled child of nature—an incarnation of Rousseau's Émile. They started their "affair of the heart" in the middle of April 1793; by late summer their liaison became public knowledge after they had started to live together in a house in Faubourg St. Germain. When the Franco-British war, which had started in February, led to the arrest of some 400 British citizens (including Tom Paine and Helen Maria Williams) in Paris on the night of 9 October 1793, Imlay registered Wollstonecraft at the U.S. embassy as his wife, which made her, in effect, an American citizen and thus eligible for protection. Soon after, however, Imlay went off alone to Le Havre on business, leaving Wollstonecraft to her pregnancy, to the book she had begun working on in Neuilly—*A Historical and Moral View of the French Revolution*—and visiting friends in prison.

Imlay stepped up his business activities in response to the defeat of the Brissotins—when it became clear that the Louisiana plan had been shelved indefinitely—and he suddenly found himself without a likely source of income. His expressed, immediate ambition, as Wollstonecraft informs us in her *Letters to Imlay*, was to accumulate a thousand pounds, which would have been "sufficient to have procured a farm in America" (Letter XXXVI). Wollstonecraft's brother Charles, who was an associate to Coleridge in the latter's pantisocratic utopian plans, actually went out to find a suitable site for the farm. But before long Wollstonecraft began to feel that "crooked business" was Imlay's true motive and that there was no legitimate reason for him to abandon her for so long (Letter XXX). "Beware!" she wrote to him in January 1795, "[Y]ou seem to be got into a whirl of projects and schemes, which are drawing you into a gulf, that, if it do not absorb your happiness, will infallibly destroy mine" (Letter XXXII).

Wollstonecraft joined Imlay in Le Havre in either January or February 1794, and their daughter Fanny was born in the following May. They were not to be together for long, though. In September Imlay set out for London, again "on business," sending Wollstonecraft back to Paris. Although he had promised her that he would return to France in a couple of months, Imlay kept postponing his departure from London. Then, in April 1795, he sent a missive to Wollstonecraft urgently requesting her to join him in London, presumably to help him "extricate [himself] out of [his] pecuniary difficulties" (Letter XL). Soon after her arrival in London, Wollstonecraft found out that apart from having become involved in business entanglements, Imlay was also amorously involved with an actress of a strolling theatre company. Wollstonecraft responded with bitter recriminations and an abortive suicide attempt. Partly because he was anxious to distract her, and partly because he must have sincerely trusted her talents in looking after his financial interests, Imlay asked Wollstonecraft to sail to Gothenburg, Sweden, to sort out the problems that had arisen between him and his Swedish business partner, Elias Backman (1760–1829)—a task that turned out to involve the pursuit of a stolen treasure ship. Wollstonecraft revised the letters that she wrote to Imlay on her trip to Scandinavia to form the narrative thread of *Letters written during a short Residence in Sweden, Norway, and Denmark* (published in 1796).

On her return from Scandinavia and finding Imlay living with another woman, Wollstonecraft again attempted suicide. She subsequently offered to live with Imlay and his new mistress; characteristically, however, Imlay evaded all complications by taking his mistress off to Paris. The last Imlay and Wollstonecraft saw of each other was when they met by accident on the New Road in London—an encounter that apparently passed "without producing in [Wollstonecraft] any oppressive emotion."[11]

What emotions Imlay felt upon the occasion, we do not know: The trail of Imlay's life abruptly ends on that day in the spring of 1796 when he parted from the woman to whom he became one of literary history's most notoriously nasty footnotes. He disappeared into the obscurity on which his dubious trading ventures thrived and which enabled him to elude his legal responsibilities in America and the vindictive, xenophobic mood of Jacobin-controlled France. We hear of him again through the burial record of the curate of St. Brelade's, on the Isle of Jersey, which informs us that "M. Gilbert Imlay fut enterré le vingt quatriéme jour de Novembre mil huit Cent vingt huit, âge de 74 ans."[12] Even Imlay deserved a better epitaph than that by a minor poet which at one time adorned his tombstone—though he probably would have been pleased to be posthumously acknowledged as a man who had helped promote "the social advances of the day."[13]

VI

The Emigrants, or the History of an Expatriated Family was published in London in July or August 1793, a few months after the beginning of Imlay's affair with Wollstonecraft. The title page claims that the novel was "written in America"; however, this seems to be an advertising gimmick: The novel was most likely written in London in 1792, and is clearly directed toward a British audience. Significantly, there is no evidence that the novel was read in America, and it was first published there in a facsimile edition in 1964.[14] On the other hand, the novel is more of a transatlantic affair than may be deduced from its claim, made on the title page, that it is a "Delineation of English Manners," for alongside its critique of English social mores, the novel proudly celebrates the achievements of the American social experiment, notably in the realm of its enlightened marriage laws. *The Emigrants* is set partly in post-Revolutionary America—the action extends from September 1783 to July or September 1785—and partly in pre-Revolutionary Britain (though, of course, it was published in a Britain already at war with France). The plot turns on the fate of an English family that emigrates to America. Central to the novel's concerns are two episodes of "cultural captivity" which demonstrate the novel's key theme that "There is no reciprocality in the laws respecting matrimony" (Letter IX). Both episodes—the inset narrative of Caroline's uncle about his relationship with the married Juliana, and the story of Caroline's sister Eliza—take place, for the most part, in Britain.

The first of these stories runs for almost one fifth of the novel, indicating just how important the issue of marital legislation is to the text as a whole. According to his heartrending account, Caroline's uncle, P. P——, is smitten with the tender Lady B—— (Juliana), a "beauty . . . in tears" who is victimized by her tyrannical husband and whose dignity is constantly violated by the raucous behavior of her husband's friends, the insolence of the domestic servants, and, not least, by Lord B——'s predilection for drunken sex. During a particularly moving rendition of

Othello's "put out the light" speech, Lady B—— faints into
P. P——'s arms in a secluded alcove in the garden, as witnessed
by the footman. In what turns out to be a setup (for reasons of
finance and fertility, Lord B—— wants to divorce his wife and
marry someone else), Lord B—— takes out an action against
Caroline's uncle for "a criminal connection" with his wife. Refused entry to her parental home, Juliana takes refuge with her
old nurse in London, and a jury awards damages of £10,000
against P. P——, which he cannot pay. He spends the following
decade in prison for debt,[15] during which he marries the charming
Juliana after her divorce and fathers seven children. Lord B——,
his fortune dissipated by his new wife, finally makes a settlement
for damages of £500 and P. P—— is released.

This plot line speaks to the ongoing cultural debates about the
status of women, frequently couching its critique in the language
and rhetoric of other contemporary debates, especially the
language of abolition, of Enlightenment rationalism, and debates
about the nature of political authority. Abolitionist rhetoric in the
1790s is by no means easy to describe; indeed, the modern critic
Deirdre Coleman talks of its "general murkiness."[16] While the
cause is generally associated with feminism, some women, such as
Mary Ann Radcliffe, in her 1792 tract *The Female Advocate*, plead
for the cause of middle-class Englishwomen over the interests of
illiterate slaves. Imlay, working at the close of the heyday of protest (1789–92) and on the cusp of the moment when antislavery
becomes associated with revolutionism, makes use of the powerful
analogy between enslavement and the position of women, in
which marriage is represented, in the words of the anonymous
author of *The Hardships of the English Laws in relation to Wives*, as
"a *State* of *Captivity*."[17] The legal position described by William
Blackstone in 1765—i.e., that "the very being or legal existence
of the woman is suspended during the marriage, or at least incorporated and consolidated into that of the husband"—remained
in force in the 1790s in both Britain and America.[18] In Imlay's
novel, Lord B—— thinks of a woman merely as "a domestic
machine," but Lady B—— nonetheless considers herself as

"bound" to her disagreeable lord by the ties of matrimony (Letter XXIII). Observing their marriage, P. P—— has an insight into the "state of degradation and misery" to which "thousands of amiable and sensible beings" are "reduced" (Letter XXV). There is a parallel attack on the slave trade itself: The father of Miss R—— (who is herself captured by a marriage plot), speaks out against slavery, using the familiar trope of the disruption of family. His daughter concurs with his condemnation of the traffic in slaves, and hopes that an "enlightened government" will punish such "Monsters" (Letter XVI).

The Emigrants also adapts the language of political libertarianism for a feminist position. Like the rhetoric of enslavement, this contemporary debate provided a conceptual language from which to attack the tyranny of "custom." As Mary Robinson puts it in her *Letter to the Women of England on the Injustice of Subordination* (1799), "The barbarity of custom's law in this *enlightened* country, has long been exercised to the prejudice of woman."[19] The novel privileges a discourse of natural rights, which Caroline's uncle—in one of his explanatory/exculpatory letters to her about the Juliana affair —calls "those absolute rights" which are "antecedent to the formation of states" and which justify resistance to inhuman laws (Letter XXVI). Caroline replies with the Burkean argument that in order to enter society, men relinquish part of their liberty in order to secure their most important rights. She initially presents the antidivorce case, arguing that "the laws respecting matrimony" may transgress "the codes of nature," but that "the tranquillity, safety, and happiness of society" depend on them (Letter XXVII). Thus, she describes her uncle's "principles" as "dangerous" (or revolutionary): They "strike at the root of domestic quiet." This is an argument that is used again and again by conservative writers after 1793, when the fears engendered by the French Revolution retarded reform in any field for over three decades (by the time of Wollstonecraft's *The Wrongs of Woman* [1798], such principles were explicitly described as "French"). Yet the reprehensible Lord B—— argues, in almost identical language, that the *"tranquillity of society"* rests on the control of women, or

what he calls *"tyranny"* (Letter XXII). The reader is encouraged
to make the link between individual and institutional oppression,
between beastly husbands and "brutish legislators," both of whom
invite rational resistance.

Sympathizing with the sufferings of Juliana and her uncle,
Caroline is won over—from custom, or prejudice—to a belief in those "principles" based on "unalienable rights" (Letter
XXXIX).[20] She reflects on the inequities of the contemporary
matrimonial institutions, and her thoughts dwell on the fate of
Princess Matilda of Denmark, whom she deems the victim of both
political tyranny and gender oppression.[21] The reader, like Caroline, is presumably similarly enlightened by such radical "moral
instruction," as is promised in the novel's preface.

The novel's second story of an unhappy marriage, that of Caroline's sister Eliza, recapitulates many of the ideological points
raised by the first story, reinforcing the connection between Britain and gender oppression. Eliza is disgusted that, while living in
a state of "voluptuous richness," her husband, Mr. F——, withholds any financial assistance from her impoverished family. She
observes the contrast, made throughout the novel, between the
simplicity and sincerity of the American way of life and the studied
ceremony of European manners, and laments that she, too, is not
in the arcadian regions inhabited by her sister. Eliza's husband
neglects her, indulging in all sorts of extravagances (by implication
sexual as well as financial), until his finances are, as Il——ray puts
it, completely "deranged" (Letter LXVIII). His shocking solution,
"to propose to Mrs. F—— the prostitution of her own person,"[22]
is the most despicable example in Imlay's critique of the economic
basis of marriage and sexuality. We are explicitly reminded that
in British law women are "considered in the light of property"
and that a separated wife may "be subject to lose the very fortune she may have carried her husband" (Letter LXXII). Both Mr.
F——'s proposed sexual/financial transaction and Juliana's husband's action for "crim. con." (criminal conversation) are markers
of a commercial society that contrasts with the chivalric one that
the text supports.[23]

The figure of prostitution is a crucial one in the novel: Juliana, for example, refuses the "most ignominious prostitution" of continuing to sleep with her brutal husband (Letter XXIII). Ultimately, what is indicted is "[t]he prostitution of principle" in British political life, a public prostitution that poisons private life.[24] Motivated only by commercial desires, the body politic is enervated.[25] What turns out to be at stake is Britain's gender identity: The "unmanly" behavior of Mr. F—— and his supposed impotence parallel the emasculated state of his country. Britain's commercial interests have "contaminated" British hearts, producing "[e]very species of luxury" while "Effeminacy has triumphed." P. P—— "blush[es]" for the degeneracy of [his] countrymen," calling Mr. F—— "a being," not *a man* (see Letters LXIV–LXX). In *A Topographical Description*, Imlay argues that the American legislative system explicitly "prevents the prostitution of principle" (Letter VIII), while the novel offers emigration as the alternative to British sexual/political impotence. The novel further proposes that the present British government's resistance to reform may hasten its destruction, and that a third revolution may follow that of 1688 and the more recent American Revolution (Letter LXXII).

The watershed event that is left out of this revolutionary genealogy is the French Revolution, which, of course, postdates the period in which the novel is set but not the period in which it was written and published, and which clearly influences the boundaries of gender that Imlay maps out. The debate about Britain's failure in the masculinity stakes has to do with a triangulated set of national relations between Britain and France and between Britain and America. Especially in the years after 1789, Britain defined itself as a manly nation in sharp contrast to France, whose effeminacy (including such national traits as emotionalism and sensual indulgence, and the prevalence of "improper" women—both those sexually available and those who "manned" the barricades) supposedly had dragged it into revolutionary chaos. However, Britain's status as an "enlightened" and "manly" nation (Preface) is threatened by the institutional oppression of women in marriage. Imlay offers women a place in the new manly nation of America, thus both inverting and transferring the gender distinction from a cross-Channel to a transatlantic one. In this way, America demonstrates a superior manliness while Britain languishes in a state of effeminate impotence.

The Eliza episode includes a long disquisition into the difficulties of separation or divorce—an issue fraught with national as well as gender implications. Sir Thomas Mor——ly informs Il——ray that Eliza could not obtain a divorce without proving Mr. F——'s impotence or infidelity, which, as Il——ray observes, would be "mortifying to women of sensibility" (Letter LXVIII). This case substantiates Imlay's assertion in his preface about the great difficulty of obtaining a divorce in England—a process, as the novel makes clear, substantially more difficult for women than for men because of the sexual double standard. In fact, male infidelity would not have been grounds for a divorce, and proving impotence in order to obtain a nullity was almost unheard of.[26]

The Emigrants exploits the analogies between familial and international politics that pertained during the American Revolutionary period. As Jay Fliegelman argues, there is a close ideological connection between easier divorce laws and the political separation of the United States from Great Britain that was institutionalized in the Declaration of Independence.[27] Certainly to some people the freedom to pursue life, liberty, and happiness seemed to involve the right to be liberated by divorce from an unhappy marriage. Moreover, the belief in contractual relationships—by definition open to dissolution—was "[c]entral to the rationalist ideology of the American Revolution."[28] Divorce statutes passed by colonial assemblies were contrary to English law and hence invariably vetoed; thus, Pennsylvania's Divorce Act of 1773 was disallowed by the Privy Council and so came to play a modest part in the independence conflict. In the years after the war, the sentimental rhetoric of affectional and voluntaristic marriage was crucial to the affirmation of national character, and many texts, such as Royall Tyler's popular 1787 play, *The Contrast*, combine antipatriarchal and patriotic sentiment. Perhaps most relevant here is the rhetoric of a pamphlet published in Philadelphia in 1788, *An Essay on Marriage or the Lawfulness of Divorce* (apparently the first such pamphlet in America). The anonymous writer defends divorce and permission for remarriage, quotes Milton on "domestic liberty," and draws an analogy between an unhappy marriage and slavery. The pamphlet argues that America's (self-promoting) reputation as a freedom-loving land means that it should extend the "same spirit of indulgence" to those constrained by marital "bondage."[29] Personal sympathy for the distressed (the occasion of the pamphlet was the suicide of an unhappily married woman) is conjoined with republican sympathy. *The Emigrants* explicitly offers emigration as the solution to marital inequity and as a means of validating sentimental experience that has no outlet in Britain: "Put yourself under the protection of Mr. Il——ray," Caroline advises Eliza, "and fly immediately from bondage to a land of freedom and love" (Letter LXX).[30]

As we might expect, there is a gap between the rhetoric and the reality of revolution, and the women of the new republic remained constrained. Before the American Revolution, divorce was legal only in New England states (with Connecticut most liberal), but post-Revolutionary America in fact retained most features of British laws on domestic relations. As Linda Kerber has documented, though "[t]he rhetoric of revolution, which emphasized the right to separate from dictatorial masters, implicitly offered an ideological validation for divorce, . . . few in power recognized it."[31] Only in Pennsylvania was a new divorce law adopted as a part of republican renovation. Elsewhere, divorce required a private bill in the state legislature, which took both financial and political clout to achieve. The situation in America differed from that in other modern revolutionary governments which made divorce reform a priority; in France, for example, a system of civil divorce was instituted in 1792 as an explicit part of the Jacobin program (this system was restricted by the Code Napoleon of 1804, but it was not eliminated until the Bourbon Restoration in 1814).

Although *The Emigrants* is rightly seen as a feminist critique of gender and national identities, the sexual-political agenda of the novel remains somewhat limited, as demonstrated by Il——ray's words: "the charms of fine women can only be relished by men who have not been enervated by luxury and debauchery" (Letter LXVIII). The novel's revolutionary critique of Britain's marriage and divorce laws rests on a potentially conservative (indeed, Burkean) rhetoric of chivalry—that is, the manly protection of beauty and virtue in distress.[32] This is the attitude that Il——ray puts into practice in his treatment of Eliza and that motivates P. P——'s response to Juliana (as well as his outrage at the sacrifice of the lovely Princess Matilda to state politics). The community established at the end of the novel is made up solely of military men who served in the Revolutionary War and who are idealized in order to serve this paradigm of gender relations. There are constant references to women's "delicacy" and "sensibility"; they are "helpless beings . . . whose weakness demands [men's] most liberal support" (Letter IX). The novel enlists support for a "liberal system" that would give "reciprocity to conjugal engagements" (Letter XXVIII), but such a system would be predicated on male protection of women, a protection enacted most dramatically in Arl——ton's rescue of Caroline from her Indian captors.

The novel's captivity narrative takes up only a few pages yet is a significant cultural-ideological marker as well as one of the earliest examples of its kind in American fiction.[33] While Arl——ton, suffering the pangs of disappointed love, dashes off into the wild zone west of Louisville, Caroline makes her own unintentional wilderness trip: Attempting to view the falls at Louisville, she crosses the Ohio River into Indian country and is carried off by a band of marauding natives. In line with his chilvaric code, Il——ray anxiously envisions the palpitations of Caroline's "sensible heart," wondering "How will her tender limbs support the fatigue of being hurried through briary thickets?" (Letter

LVII). Remarkably well, one is compelled to answer. Though she marches nearly four hundred miles before Arl——ton, having come coincidentally upon Caroline and her captors on the Illinois River,[34] rescues her, her tender limbs are positively enhanced by her experience and her wounds are eroticized (the lacerations making her "more lovely than ever" [Letter LIX]). Arl——ton describes how he finds "the most divine woman upon earth, torn into shatters by the bushes and briars, with scarcely covering left to hide the transcendency of her beauty"—beauty in a state of distress and undress is surely the most affecting beauty! The text allows for a kind of Gothic voyeurism, making of Caroline an erotic spectacle, especially in the moment when Arl——ton hangs over her sleeping body, quite "distracted" by the sight of her "half naked" bosom. Eventually, in a playful reversal of Enlightenment rhetoric, he is "obliged to extinguish the light, to preserve [his] reason" [Letter LXIX]. When the text shifts from a metaphoric captivity to a literal one, the bedrock of essentialism that lies beneath the novel's support for oppressed women is exposed. The female body is objectified in precisely the way that the novel critiques elsewhere. Indeed, we might note that the captivity narrative codifies Caroline's status as a possession: Il——ray refers to the Indians' act as "robbery," and there is much talk of Arl——ton "retaking" Caroline and much play with the notion that Caroline is now his "fair captive."

The captivity narrative also points to the limits of the rhetoric of revolution as it regards the American Indian. Despite Caroline's enterprising desire, on encountering a peaceable band of Indians early in the novel, "to become better acquainted with their nations" (Letter XIII), neither this group nor the one that takes her captive later are described in any detail or differentiated by nation (in contrast, *A Topographical Description* lists tribes by name, giving their numbers and location [see Letter XI]). Government policy affecting the Indians from the revolution through the presidency of Andrew Jackson has been described as displaying "a pattern of rhetorical liberation and political subjection" that parallels the experience of postwar American women.[35] Imlay's own opinion, expressed dispassionately in his *Topographical Description*, was that Indians should assimilate or be annihilated (see Letter IV). *The Emigrants* implicitly justifies imperial expansion, and Indians are not represented in Arl——ton's ideal community.

   In terms of gender politics, the novel proposes that the unhappy marriages produced by English inequality will be countered by the conjugal happiness that it makes central to America's destiny. By the end of the novel, all unsatisfactory husbands have indeed been disposed of and, in good sentimental form, everyone is with their proper partner. But these happy marriages sublimate the questions about the oppression of women that have preoccupied the novel. We know that in the history of the new republic, the language of natural rights proved less powerful than the republican conception of womanhood which privileged woman's place in the home. Women remained disenfranchised while being assured that "The solidity and stability of the liberties of your country rest with you."[36] Likewise, the novel concludes with a vision of woman's subaltern role in civil society: While Arl——ton is sorting out the government of his secessionist utopia (in which every *male* over twenty-one is entitled to vote), Caroline is in a separate domestic sphere, visiting the wives and "instruct[ing] them in various and useful employments, which must tend not a little to promote their comfort." As well as domestic instructress, she is a civilizing force in the wilderness (she does a lot of gardening) and a symbol of the virgin land she inhabits. The novel is thus, in the final analysis, fissured by the contradictions of the Enlightenment in the sense that "the rise of feminism was the premise and occasion for newly fixed models of sexual difference."[37]

   Mary Wollstonecraft argued that "the laws of her country—if women have a country—afford her no protection or redress from the oppressor."[38] *The Emigrants*, for all its critique of British laws, shows that the new nation did not necessarily offer women a country of their own. If the cultural captivity endured by women in Britain threatened to unmoor the fixities of gender, the new nation secured its difference from Britain by resecuring gender differences. The novel's espousal of the rights of women is predicated on the stereotype of feminine weakness thriving within the strong, manly arms of America. On 31 March 1776, Abagail Adams wrote to her husband John of her longing to hear about "independency" and her hope that the rejection of British rule might entail the rejection of gender subjection. John Adams not only laughed at this thought, but even more disastrously for women's rights, strategically exalted women's confinement: "We [men] are obliged to go fair, and softly, and in Practice you know We are Subjects."[39] Likewise, Arl——ton, the gentle colonialist entrepreneur, goes softly with women, granting them "home rule" but not independence.

VII

While Imlay's *Topographical Description*—published only a year before *The Emigrants*—had been widely reviewed in the British press, there were, so far as is known, only three contemporary reviews of *The Emigrants*. The Anglican journal *British Critic* provides little more than a brief notice of the novel's "flowing and easy style," which, the reviewer believes, marks it as a sentimental novel, and hence, we gather, as a species of writing not to be taken seriously.[40] The *Critical Review* finds sporadic "strokes of local description which are entertaining," but generally the reviewer dismisses the style as "intolerably inflated, and at the same time very incorrect."[41] The reviewer is not impressed by either of the novel's apparent two aims—that is, "to recommend the government and manners of America, in preference to those of [Britain]" and "to recommend divorces." As for the former, the reviewer finds there is nothing among the "tastes and morals" of the Americans of which the British need to be particularly jealous; the second aim he brushes aside with equal ease, arguing that the introduction of more liberal divorce laws would "inevitably degrade [the female] sex from the honourable companions of men, to the instruments of their looser pleasures, and slaves of their transient liking."

If these two reviews are anything to go by, it would appear, then, that *The Emigrants'* reformist radicalism did not go down well in increasingly anti-Jacobin Britain, where the start of the Reign of Terror in France (January 1793) and the outbreak of war between that country and Britain (February 1793) had triggered a backlash against revolutionary ideas in general. By contrast, the Whig *Monthly Review*, which consistently supported liberal causes, provided a glowingly positive critique in the fall of 1793. The anonymous reviewer hails Imlay as an "intelligent and lively author" and praises him for pouring forth "high and almost idolatrous encomiums on the fair sex" and for depicting "the rise and progress of love with all the ardour of youthful sensibility."[42] But, the reviewer goes on to argue, the novel's ambitions far exceed the level of the merely sentimental; indeed, the reviewer boldly states, in the novel's reflections we may "discover a mind inured to philosophical speculation," while on the general subject of politics, Imlay can be observed to express himself "with the freedom of an enlightened philosopher." The reviewer is impressed most, however, with Imlay's rendering of "the present state of society with regard to marriage":

> It is an opinion, which this writer seems to think of great importance to communicate and support, that the female world is at present, in consequence of the rigour of matrimonial institutions, in a state of oppressive vassalage; and that it would greatly increase the happiness of society, if divorces could be more easily obtained.

Although ultimately appearing to put the blame for the matrimonial oppression of women more on the "depraved manners of the age" than on the institution of marriage itself, the reviewer does not hesitate to claim that Imlay's novel is "so perfectly consonant to the present state of manners, that we can easily credit the writer's assertion, that the principal part of his story is founded on facts."

What is perhaps most striking about the novel's contemporary reception is that none of the reviewers picked up on Imlay's geopolitical scheme to build an agrarian utopia on the banks of the Ohio, while that was the very aspect that elicited such favorable reviews for his *Topographical Description*. Apart from the obvious explanation for this (namely, that a novel was less likely to be taken seriously as a guide for emigration to the New World than a topographical description), what probably played a significant role here is the fact that, as one commentator in the *Gentleman's Magazine* put it, "the rage for emigration," notably to Kentucky, was "nearly over," not just in Britain but in America as well. It is therefore perhaps not surprising that the novel did not even come close to becoming a popular success—even though a cheap, one-volume reprint (with minor corrections) appeared in Dublin in 1794.

Nor did *The Emigrants* attract much attention from critics during the nineteenth century; if its author was remembered at all, it was because of his ill-fated relationship with Mary Wollstonecraft and, occasionally, as the author of *A Topographical Description*. *The Emigrants* basically disappeared from view until the beginning of this century, when critics such as Ralph Leslie Rusk, William Clark Durant, Richard Garnett, J. W. Townsend, Edith Franklin Wyatt, and Oliver Farrar Emerson began to acknowledge Imlay's novel usually as a candidate for that rather dubious palm of "first American novel." In 1964, in the wake of Robert R. Hare's facsimile edition (the first edition to be published in the United States), interest in Imlay and his novel became more widespread. Unfortunately, Hare is also largely responsible for the persistent misconception that *The Emigrants* was in fact not written by Imlay but by his lover Wollstonecraft (whom Hare in his introduction also credited with having written *A Topographical Description*). Hare's argument is for the most part weak, misinformed, and suggestive, and sometimes downright wrong or simply emotive. Let it suffice, then, to just observe here that there is no evidence whatsoever that Wollstonecraft contributed in any way to *The Emigrants* (nor to *A Topographical Description*, for that matter), except perhaps indirectly through her emancipatory tract *A Vindi-*

cation of the Rights of Woman. The very chronology of their affair makes it almost impossible for Wollstonecraft to have (co-) authored any of Imlay's work.

Now, just over two hundred years after its first publication, *The Emigrants* is poised for critical revival as part of the contemporary reading of the pivotal decade of the 1790s—an era of cultural and political anxiety, both in Europe and America, during which the plots of sensibility got mixed up with the plots of revolution and counterrevolution. Thus, while *The Emigrants* was for the Wollstonecraft biographer Claire Tomalin, writing in 1974, still "a wholly atrocious piece of work," John Seelye, writing in 1988, deemed the novel "a unique accomplishment" that deserves a place in the tradition of the Anglo-American Jacobin novel.[43] Now that we have begun to recognize that the sentimental novel, and especially the epistolary novel, came to function as both the document and agent of the transatlantic revolutionary movement, *The Emigrants* is likely to achieve new significance for today's cultural and literary critics.

NOTES

1. William Godwin, *Memoirs of the Author of "The Rights of Woman,"* reprinted in Mary Wollstonecraft, *A Short Residence in Sweden, Norway and Denmark* and William Godwin, *Memoirs of the Author of "The Rights of Woman,"* ed. Richard Holmes (1798, 1796; reprint, Harmondsworth, England: Penguin Books, 1987), 246.

2. Edith Franklin Wyatt, "The First American Novel," *Atlantic Monthly* 144 (October 1929), 466.

3. John Filson, *The Discovery and Settlement of Kentucke* (1784); reprinted as *The Discovery, Settlement, and Present State of Kentucky* in Gilbert Imlay, *A Topographical Description of the Western Territory of North America* (1792), 2nd ed. (London: J. Debrett, 1793), 276.

4. For a detailed account of the fate of the letter in this period, see Mary A. Favret, *Romantic Correspondence: Women, Politics and the Fiction*

of Letters (Cambridge and New York: Cambridge University Press, 1993).

5. *British Critic* V (January 1795), 27.

6. *Gentleman's Magazine* Supplement (1794), 1170.

7. See Richard Holmes, *Coleridge: Early Visions* (New York: Viking, 1990), 89.

8. Gilbert Imlay, *A Topographical Description of the Western Territory of North America* (1792), 3rd, expanded ed. (London: J. Debrett, 1797), xii.

9. John Seelye, *Beautiful Machine: Rivers and the Republican Plan, 1755–1825* (New York and Oxford: Oxford University Press, 1991), 156.

10. Imlay, *A Topographical Description*, 3rd ed., xi.

11. Godwin, *Memoirs*, ed. Holmes, 254.

12. From Ralph Leslie Rusk, "The Adventures of Gilbert Imlay," *Indiana University Studies* X (March 1923), 25.

13. From William Clark Durant, ed., *Memoirs of Mary Wollstonecraft Written By William Godwin* (1927; reprint, New York: Haskell House, 1969), 246. The full text of the epigraph reads:

> Stranger intelligent! should you pass this way
> Speak of the social advances of the day—
> Mention the greatly good, who've serenely shone
> Since the soul departed its mortal bourne;
> Say if statesmen wise have grown, and priests sincere
> Or if hypocrisy must disappear
> As phylosophy extends the beam of truth,
> Sustains rights divine, its essence, and the worth
> Sympathy may permeate the mouldering earth,
> Recal the spirit, and remove the dearth,
> Transient hope gleams even in the grave,
> Which is enough dust can have, or ought to crave.
> Then silently bid farewell, be happy,
> For as the globe moves round, thou will grow nappy.
> Wake to hail the hour when new scenes arise,
> As brightening vistas open in the skies.

14. Robert R. Hare, ed., *The Emigrants (1793) / Traditionally Ascribed to Gilbert Imlay / But, More Probably, By Mary Wollstonecraft* (Gainesville, Fla.: Scholars' Facsimiles & Reprints, 1964). This edition reproduces the second (Dublin, 1794) edition of the novel (with minor corrections). For comments on Hare's introduction, see section VII of the present introduction.

15. Imlay's account is quite accurate, for, as Lawrence Stone notes, "especially in the period 1740–1820, the damages awarded were so much beyond the defendant's capacity to pay that the verdict was tantamount to a sentence of life imprisonment for debt" (*Broken Lives: Separation and Divorce in England, 1660–1857* [Oxford and New York: Oxford University Press, 1993], 23).

16. Deirdre Coleman, "Conspicuous Consumption: White Abolitionism and English Women's Protest Writing in the 1790s," *English Literary History* 61 (1994), 341–62 (the quote is on p. 341).

17. *The Hardships of the English Laws in relation to Wives* (1735), in Vivien Jones, ed., *Women in the Eighteenth Century: Constructions of Femininity* (London and New York: Routledge, 1990), 219.

18. From Jones, *Women in the Eighteenth Century*, 224.

19. Extract in Jennifer Breen, *Women Romantics 1785–1832: Writing in Prose* (London: Dent, 1996), 123 (Robinson, like Imlay, compares "Mahometans" and British husbands in the treatment of their wives; see Breen, p. 123, n. 1).

20. See also Letter LXVI. Imlay deals more fully with the issue of "the natural and imprescribable rights of man" in Letter VIII of *A Topographical Description*.

21. As do many other writers of the period, Wollstonecraft memorably sympathizes with Matilda in Letter Eighteen of *A Short Residence*.

22. This episode is much extended in Wollstonecraft's later novel, where we see the husband berating the purchaser for his sexual timidity (see, *The Wrongs of Woman; Or, Maria* with *Mary, A Fiction*, ed. Gary Kelly, [1798; 1788; reprint, Oxford: Oxford University Press, 1976], 158–63).

23. As Lawrence Stone notes, the "shift from physical violence against, or challenge to duel with, one's wife's lover to a suit for monetary damages from him" is a "sign of a change from an honour-and-shame society to a commercial society" (*Broken Lives*, 23).

24. Early in the novel, Miss Laura R—— worries that she may have to marry Mr. S——, a man who turns out to be tainted with all the vices of the Old World, and she fears the "prostitution" of her feelings (Letter VI). See, too, Mary Wollstonecraft's use of Daniel Defoe's phrase to describe marriage as a "legal prostitution" (*Vindication of the Rights of Woman*, in *Political Writings*, ed. Janet Todd [1792; reprint, Oxford: Oxford University Press, 1994], 130 and 229).

25. Ironically, Imlay's critique of the detrimental effects of the commercial spirit sounds very like Wollstonecraft's complaints about him in her *Letters to Imlay* and her anxieties about commercial society in *A Short Residence*. She argues that the "interests of nations are bartered by speculating merchants" (*A Short Residence*, 195).

26. See Lawrence Stone, *Road to Divorce, England 1530–1987* (Oxford: Oxford University Press, 1990), 428.

27. Jay Fliegelman, *Prodigals and Pilgrims: The American Revolution Against Patriarchal Authority, 1750–1850* (Cambridge: Cambridge University Press, 1982), 137.

28. Ibid., 123.

29. Ibid., 125.

30. See, too, Mrs. W——'s exclamation to Miss R——: "Come to these Arcadian regions [west of the Alleghenies] where there is room for millions" (Letter VII). It is possible that the character of Eliza owes something to that of Mary Wollstonecraft's sister of the same name, whom Wollstonecraft persuaded to leave her husband, the brutal Mr. Bishop, and for whom she cared during 1782.

31. Linda Kerber, *Women of the Republic: Intellect and Ideology in Revolutionary America* (Chapel Hill: University of North Carolina Press, 1980), 184.

32. The novel does make pragmatic suggestions to improve the condition of women, especially in its support of female education. Wollstone-

craft argues that women are kept in the educational dark to prepare them for "the slavery of marriage" (Todd, *Political Writings*, 237), a slavery the novel explicitly wishes to banish. Writing to her sister, Caroline cites the "injudicious . . . education of women" as circumscribing their understanding and constraining them to "colloquial charms . . ."; her uncle advocates the moral reform of male education, which would lead to the "amelioration" of female education (Letter XXVI). See also Letter XIX.

33. Christopher Castiglia cites Ann Eliza Bleeker's *The History of Maria Kittle* (1793) as the first, and he argues that women writers "popularized the wilderness of fiction" and exploited the possibilities of "gender critique" offered by the captivity narrative (*Bound and Determined: Captivity, Culture-Crossing, and White Womanhood from Mary Rowlandson to Patty Hearst* [Chicago and London: University of Chicago Press, 1996], 112). Imlay's novel was published well before those by Brockden Brown and Fenimore Cooper, which are credited by traditional literary history with bringing captivity, and the American "wilderness," into fiction, and is contemporaneous with the women's writing analyzed by Castiglia.

34. Arl——ton goes to the rescue of what he perceives only as a "female prisoner" (Letter LIX); he does not know until afterward that the prisoner is Caroline.

35. Castiglia, *Bound and Determined*, 158 (with reference to the work of Michael Paul Rogin).

36. Columbia College commencement oration of 1795 entitled "Female Influence," from Kerber, *Women of the Republic*, 230.

37. Felicity A. Nussbaum, *Torrid Zones: Maternity, Sexuality, and Empire in Eighteenth-Century English Narratives* (Baltimore and London: Johns Hopkins University Press, 1995), 21.

38. Mary Wollstonecraft, *The Wrongs of Woman; Or, Maria*, 159.

39. L. H. Butterfield, et al., eds., *Adams Family Correspondence, December 1761–May 1776* (Cambridge, Mass.: Harvard University Press, 1963), 370, 382.

40. *British Critic, A New Review* I (May–August 1793), 341.

41. *Critical Review; Or, Annals of Literature* VIII (1793), 156. Subsequent quotations are from pp. 155, 156, and 158.

42. *Monthly Review; Or, Literary Journal* XI (May–August, 1793), 468. Subsequent quotations are from pp. 468 and 469.

43. Claire Tomalin, *The Life and Death of Mary Wollstonecraft* (New York and London: Harcourt Brace Jovanovich, 1974), 145; John Seelye, "Charles Brockden Brown and Early American Fiction," *Columbia Literary History of the United States*, ed. Emory Elliott (New York: Columbia University Press, 1988), 175.

SUGGESTIONS FOR FURTHER READING

GENERAL STUDIES

Armstrong, Nancy. *Desire and Domestic Fiction: A Political History of the Novel.* New York and Oxford: Oxford University Press, 1987.

Barker-Benfield, G. J. *The Culture of Sensibility: Sex and Society in Eighteenth-Century Britain.* Chicago and London: University of Chicago Press, 1992.

Benson, Mary Sumner. *Women in Eighteenth-Century America.* New York: Columbia University Press, 1935.

Bloch, Ruth H. "The Gendered Meanings of Virtue in Revolutionary America." *Signs* 13 (1987): 37–58.

Brown, Herbert Ross. *The Sentimental Novel in America, 1789– 1860.* Durham, N.C.: Duke University Press, 1949.

Castiglia, Christopher. *Bound and Determined: Captivity, Culture-Crossing, and White Womanhood from Mary Rowlandson to Patty Hearst.* Chicago and London: University of Chicago Press, 1996.

Cott, Nancy. *The Bonds of Womanhood: "Woman's Sphere" in New England, 1780–1835.* New Haven and London: Yale University Press, 1977.

Davidson, Cathy N. *Revolution and the Word: The Rise of the Novel in America.* New York: Oxford University Press, 1986.

Eckert, Allan W. *That Dark and Bloody River: Chronicles of the Ohio River Valley.* New York: Bantam Books, 1995.

Elliott, Emory. *Revolutionary Writers: Literature and Authority in the New Republic, 1725–1810.* New York and Oxford: Oxford University Press, 1980.

Fliegelman, Jay. *Prodigals and Pilgrims: The American Revolution Against Patriarchal Authority, 1750–1850.* Cambridge: Cambridge University Press, 1982.

———. *Declaring Independence: Jefferson, Natural Language, and the*

Culture of Performance. Stanford, Calif.: Stanford University Press, 1993.

Hansen, Klaus P. "The Sentimental Novel and Its Feminist Critique." *Early American Literature* 26 (1991): 39–54.

Hoffman, Ronald, and Peter J. Albert, eds. *Women in the Age of the American Revolution.* Charlottesville: University Press of Virginia, 1989.

Jehlen, Myra. *American Incarnation: The Individual, the Nation, and the Continent.* Cambridge, Mass., and London: Harvard University Press, 1986.

Jones, Vivien, ed. *Women in the Eighteenth Century: Constructions of Femininity.* London and New York: Routledge, 1990.

Kerber, Linda K. *Women of the Republic: Intellect and Ideology in Revolutionary America.* Chapel Hill: University of North Carolina Press, 1980.

Lawson-Peebles, Robert. *Landscape and Written Expression in Revolutionary America: The World Turned Upside Down.* Cambridge: Cambridge University Press, 1988.

Lee, A. Robert, and W. M. Verhoeven, eds. *Making America/Making American Literature: Franklin to Cooper.* Amsterdam and Atlanta, Ga.: Rodopi, 1996.

Looby, Christopher. *Voicing America: Language, Literary Form, and the Origins of the United States.* Chicago and London: University of Chicago Press, 1996.

May, Henry F. *The Enlightenment in America.* New York and Oxford: Oxford University Press, 1976.

Norton, Mary Beth. *Liberty's Daughters: The Revolutionary Experience of American Women, 1750–1800.* Boston and Toronto: Little, Brown, 1980.

Parker, Patricia L. *Early American Fiction: A Reference Guide.* Boston: G. K. Hall, 1984.

Pattee, Fred Lewis. *The First Century of American Literature.* New York: Cooper Square Publishers, 1935.

Patterson, Mark R. *Authority, Autonomy, and Representation in American Literature, 1776–1865.* Princeton: Princeton University Press, 1988.

Petter, Henri. *The Early American Novel*. Columbus: Ohio State University Press, 1971.

Rendall, Jane. *The Origins of Modern Feminism: Women in Britain, France and the United States, 1780–1860*. London and Basingstoke: Macmillan, 1985.

Rogin, Michael Paul. "Nature as Politics and Nature as Romance in America." *Political Theory* 5.1 (1977): 5–30.

Salmon, Marylynn. *Women and the Law of Property in Early America*. Chapel Hill: University of North Carolina Press, 1986.

Seelye, John. "Charles Brockden Brown and Early American Fiction." In *Columbia Literary History of the United States*, edited by Emory Elliott, et al. New York: Columbia University Press, 1988, 168–86.

———. *Beautiful Machine: Rivers and the Republican Plan, 1755–1825*. New York and Oxford: Oxford University Press, 1991.

Silverman, Kenneth. *A Cultural History of the American Revolution: Painting, Music, Literature, and the Theatre in the Colonies and the United States from the Treaty of Paris to the Inauguration of George Washington, 1763–1789*. New York: Thomas Y. Crowell, 1976.

Spengemann, William E. *The Adventurous Muse: The Poetics of American Fiction*. New Haven and London: Yale University Press, 1977.

Stone, Lawrence. *Road to Divorce, England 1530–1987*. Oxford: Oxford University Press, 1990.

———. *Broken Lives: Separation and Divorce in England, 1660–1857*. Oxford and New York: Oxford University Press, 1993.

Thompkins, J. M. S. *The Popular Novel in England, 1770–1800*. London: Constable, 1932.

Todd, Janet. *Sensibility: An Introduction*. London and New York: Methuen, 1986.

Tompkins, Jane. *The Cultural Work of American Fiction, 1790–1860*. New York and Oxford: Oxford University Press, 1985.

Watts, Steven. *The Republic Reborn: War and the Making of Liberal America, 1790–1820*. Baltimore and London: Johns Hopkins University Press, 1987.

Ziff, Larzer. *Writing in the New Nation: Prose, Print, and Politics in the Early United States.* New Haven and London: Yale University Press, 1991.

STUDIES RELATED TO GILBERT IMLAY
AND *THE EMIGRANTS*

Béranger, Jean. "Emigration et communauté utopique dans *The Emigrants* de Gilbert Imlay (?) 1793". In *Annales du Centre de Recherches sur L'Amérique Anglophone*, Nouvelle série, no. 11 (Séminaires 1985), eds. Jean Béranger, Jean Cazemajou, Jean-Michel Lacroix and Pierre Spriet. Talence: Presses Universitaires de Bordeaux, 1986, 21–35.

Durant, William Clark, ed. Supplement to William Godwin, *Memoirs of Mary Wollstonecraft.* 1798. Reprint, New York: Haskell House, 1969.

Ellison, Julie. "There and Back: Transatlantic Novels and Anglo-American Careers." In *The Past as Prologue: Essays to Celebrate the Twenty-Fifth Anniversary of ASECS*, eds. Carla H. Hay and Syndy M. Conger. New York: AMS Press, 1995, 303–24.

Emerson, Oliver Farrar. "Notes on Gilbert Imlay, Early American Writer." *PMLA* 39 (1924): 406–39.

Garnett, Richard. "Gilbert Imlay." In *Dictionary of National Biography*, vol. X, 1891–92, 417–18.

Godwin, William. *Memoirs of the Author of "The Rights of Woman."* With Mary Wollstonecraft, *A Short Residence in Sweden, Norway and Denmark*, edited and introduced by Richard Holmes. 1796, 1798. Reprint, Harmondsworth, England: Penguin Books, 1987.

Hare, Robert R. Introduction to *The Emigrants (1793) / Traditionally Ascribed to Gilbert Imlay But, More Probably, By Mary Wollstonecraft.* 1793; second edition, 1794. Reprint, Gainesville, Fla.: Scholars' Facsimiles & Reprints, 1964.

Rusk, Ralph Leslie. "The Adventures of Gilbert Imlay." *Indiana University Studies* X, no. 57 (1923): 3–26.

Seelye, John. "The Jacobin Mode in Early American Fiction: Gilbert Imlay's *The Emigrants.*" *Early American Literature* 22 (1987): 204–11.

Wollstonecraft, Mary. *A Short Residence in Sweden, Norway and Denmark.* With William Godwin, *Memoirs of the Author of "The Rights of Woman,"* edited and introduced by Richard Holmes. 1796, 1798. Reprint, Harmondsworth, England: Penguin Books, 1987.

———. *Letters to Imlay*, edited and introduced by C. Kegan Paul. 1879. Reprint, New York: Haskell House, 1971.

Wyatt, Edith Franklin. "The First American Novel." *Atlantic Monthly* 144 (1929): 466–75.

A NOTE ON THE TEXT

This edition reproduces the text of the first edition of *The Emigrants*, printed for A. Hamilton in London in 1793 (duodecimo, 3 volumes, at 9 shillings, sewed). In order to preserve a flavor of late eighteenth-century language usage, we have throughout adhered to a principle of minimal editorial intervention, silently correcting typographical errors or inserting and deleting words only where these would impair comprehension of the text. We have retained other typographical inconsistencies, errors, and idiosyncracies—thus "farewel," "develope," "rout," (as well as "route"), "to loose" (as well as "to lose"). We have also retained the original punctuation and spelling, including the spelling of geographical names, such as "Pittsburg," "Allegany" and "Alligany." However, the text prefers modern usage for quotations; that is, whereas in the eighteenth century printers used opening quotation marks at the beginning of each line containing quoted material, this edition uses only a single set of opening and closing quotation marks for each separate quotation. In addition, the eighteenth-century long *s* has been replaced by the modern *s*.

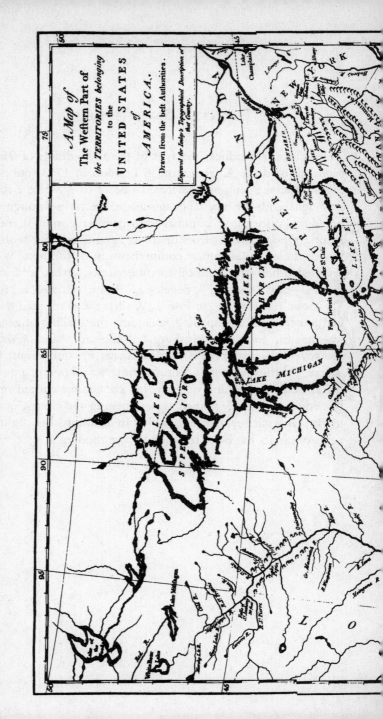

A Map of
The Weſtern Part of
the TERRITORIES belonging
to the
UNITED STATES
of
AMERICA.

Drawn from the beſt Authorities.

Engraved for Imlay's Topographical Deſcription of
that Country.

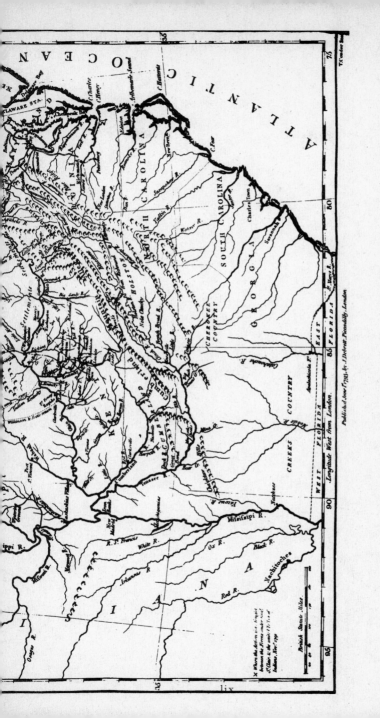

Published June 1st 1795 by J. Debrett, Piccadilly, London.

THE

EMIGRANTS, &c.

OR THE

HISTORY

OF

AN EXPATRIATED FAMILY,

BEING

A DELINEATION OF ENGLISH MANNERS,
DRAWN FROM REAL CHARACTERS,

WRITTEN IN AMERICA,

———————

By G. IMLAY, Esq.
AUTHOR OF THE TOPOGRAPHICAL DESCRIPTION
OF ITS WESTERN TERRITORY.

VOLUME I

PREFACE

HAD I not been flattered in the accounts my friends have given me of the favourable reception, which my letters regarding the western territory of America received in England,[1] perhaps I should not have been bold enough to offer a work of this kind to the world.

In this history I have scrupulously attended to natural circumstances, and the manners of the day; and in every particular I have had a real character for my model. The principal part of the story is founded upon facts, and I was only induced to give the work in the style of a novel, from believing it would prove more acceptable to the generality of readers.

Perhaps it is the most effectual way of communicating moral instruction; for when the vices and follies of the world are held up to us, so connectedly with incidents which are interesting, it is most likely they will leave a more lasting impression than when given in a dull narative.

How far I have succeeded in my object, must be left to the world to determine; for I have neither the vanity to expect, nor the arrogance to claim any other merit, than having endeavoured to prompt many readers to turn their thoughts toward the important political questions now agitated throughout Europe;[2] for upon the fate of which, doubtless, materially depends the happiness of mankind.

These important principles have been treated of by so many authors of the most consummate penetration and talents,[3] that it would only be a presumption in me to attempt to say any thing new upon the subject; for I beleive it is only possible to place the same ideas in different points of view.

Men of understanding, who are not biassed by selfish considerations, entertain nearly the same sentiments upon political sci-

1

ence; and contemplate the progressive improvements in arts and government, as striding to that perfection, which limits the human capacity; and it is only the errors of education, that have caused many persons to reason upon a practical polity, deduced from false principles, grounding their arguments upon the examples which the ancient states of Greece and Rome afford us, without recollecting those existed, when society was in an infant state—when knowledge was monopolized,—when superstition supplied the place of reason, that the imperfections of their own systems made them an easy prey to the surrounding barbarians; and that the cloud of ignorance which overspread Europe for many centuries past, totally eclipsed the rays of truth, while the government of men was a mere trick of state, and that thus it happened, the ill digested systems in modern Europe have been productive of so many miseries to mankind.

Printing and navigation have compleatly changed the complexion of Europe; they must change that of the whole GLOBE: and the dissemination of knowledge, must mould the minds of men into a more social texture; and when reciprocality constitutes the basis of politics, protection will be extended to every description of persons; and not untill that is done will the great object of philosophy be answered.

As to the form of a government, provided its constituent principles are good, and the executive part has efficiency, it is all that is required; and certainly, the more simple the springs it acts upon, the greater will be its unity, and the more extensive its protection.

It is not in the least extraordinary, that the generality of men should be divided in their political sentiments, nor that Englishmen should believe that their political system is the model of perfection; since Great Britain for many centuries, was the only country upon the earth where the advantages of freedom have been properly ascertained; and if they are intitled to the merit of having shewn to mankind the radiance of its form, and laid the foundation by their manly efforts for its extension, and thus illumined the reasoning faculties of half the WORLD, it is perhaps time to place a mirror to their view, that they may behold the decay of those features, which once were so lovely.

It is not altogether fair, to infer from the prosperity of a country, that its ministry is equitable, and its government salutary. That is a consequence of the improvements in arts and manufactures, the progress of agriculture, and the accumulations of capitals employed in trade.

But it is necessary, to look into the miseries of individuals; for it was the object of man, when he entered into a state of society to secure his comfort and happiness, and not to aggrandize one citizen, at the expence of another; and every benevolent and generous man must pronounce that an imperfect or unjust system, which suffers the innocent and unfortunate, to become victims to its policy.

I have no doubt but the many misfortunes which daily happen in domestic life, and which too often precipitate women of the most virtuous inclinations into the gulf of ruin, proceed from the great difficulty there is in England, of obtaining a divorce.[4] Those who have paid a superficial regard to this subject, will be of a different opinion.

Should it be asked for what reason I withold my opinion, if I have formed one, respecting what ought to be the nature of law upon this subject, I should answer, that this is not altogether a proper work for a business of that importance; nor have I the presumption to attempt to legislate for the world; for my object is confined to induce them to reflect upon the unhappy consequences which flow from the present practice, and that they may take into their consideration, the establishing, by a more manly and enlightened policy, laws that will in future prevent the sacrilege which the present practices of matrimonial engagements necessarily produce.

It was no small surprise to me when I was in England, to find a man, who had been first minister, in a neighbouring kingdom,[5] and who had fled from his country, to avoid being punished for a robbery actually committed upon the property with which he was intrusted, not only obtain an asylum in Great Britain, but to be caressed and closetted repeatedly both with the minister and his master: after the notoriety of his peculation[6] was as flagrant as the action was dishonourable, appeared truly astonishing; and I was satisfied, while such were the moral sentiments, at what you call the fountain head of justice, it must be something like a miracle that can prevent depravity from becoming general.

INTRODUCTION

Mr. T——n was an eminent merchant in the city of London, part of whose family having been extravagant, ruined his fortune, and obliged him to seek an asylum in America.[1]

His whole family, which consisted of an only son, and three daughters, the youngest of whom was Caroline, followed his fortune.

Whether the character of the old man had been that of a fair trader, or not, I never gave myself any concern about; as I have ever felt myself superior to receiving any unfavourable impression against an innocent progeny, for the depravity of their parents.

It is, however, certain that the old gentleman upon his arrival in Philadelphia, thought it most prudent to remove into the back settlements of the country, and there in obscurity endeavour to preserve that tranquillity, to which the follies and dissipation of Mrs. T——n and his son had made him a stranger.

There would have been some virtue in that determination, had it been uncontaminated with that miserable selfishness, which ever characterizes little minds; for it seems that the old man's principal object, was to avoid the importunities of his creditors, who might have followed him to Philadelphia.

The departure of this unfortunate family from Philadelphia, exhibited a most pathetic scene.

Eliza, the eldest daughter, had been married to Mr. F——, who had been passenger in the ship which conveyed them across the Atlantic, and who having settled his business, was about to return to England; and while she was preparing to resume her rank in the gay circles of London, decked with all the elegance of a splendid fortune, and to move in the radiance of courtly lures, this dejected family was preparing to traverse a region which they had been taught to believe was inhabited mostly by wild beasts and savages;[2] unattended, except by the driver of the waggon, they had hired for the purpose of transporting the small hoards they had preserved from the wreck of that opulence, they once so prodigally squandered.

The lovely Caroline's face diffused the the soft effulgence of an opening rose when heaven impearls it with the morning dew:— and as you have seen the æther of a western sky brighten the horizon in the evening showers of June, so shot the æthereal sparks from her half-closed eye.—With her heart beating high in the transports of nature her lovely bosom seemed to palpitate with emotions which threatened the confines of her delicate frame; and when she was severed from the arms of her more fortunate sister, it appeared as if the fibres of her tender heart would burst with the agonies of sorrow.

Every spectator caught the flame of sympathy, and in that querulous moment,[3] we appeared like the mourners of Adonis surrounding the Queen of Love.[4]—The hasty hours upon the rapid wings of Time hurried on the moment of their departure.—Language then was mute.—As when a shipwrecked crew, who are entombed in the boisterous waves, and whose murmurs cease, and you no longer hear aught but the scolding winds;—as such was that *luctiferous* schism.[5]

LETTER I

MR. IL——RAY TO CAPT. ARL——TON.

Philadelphia, Sept.

MY DEAR ARL——TON,

THE English family which I have so often mentioned in my letters to you, and who appear to be reduced to extreme penury, left us this morning for Pittsburg.

I was present at their departure, and such were the sensations I experienced at that interesting scene, that I am sure it has made impressions too lasting for time to eraze.

Whatever may have been the cause of their present wretchedness, is of no consequence,—intrepid generosity never waits to enquire into causes which lead to such lamentable events; but eagerly seeks for an opportunity to alleviate the pangs of human misery.

Figure to yourself two beautiful girls, possessed of all the graces of person and mind, which nature and the embellishments of education can furnish—born to prospects, the most flattering—arrived at that age when the human heart begins to thrill with ardent expectations for the possession of those social pleasures, and matured raptures, which diffuse a mild lustre over the dignity of our nature; and which so amply compensates for the tedious æra of juvenile mortifications;—now torn from the bosom of their friends and dear relatives,—banished from their country into the wilds of a desert,[1] and in the gloomy atmosphere of sorrow, perhaps they have not enough of paltry gold to procure sustenance; and I am sure that your motions will be accelerated, in order to overtake them, that you may administer some relief to their distracted minds.

I know you are a soldier, which is a sufficient warranty to me for the practice of that delicacy which ever distinguishes the gentleman, and real generosity from an ostentatious benevolence.

There is a manner in doing every thing, and I have too much confidence in your friendship, to suppose you will deprive me of the pleasure of having contributed to the relief of those amiable girls.—The plan rests between us.—It shall never be promulged by me.—Draw upon me at sight.[2]

Adieu,

G. IL——RAY

LETTER II

CAPT. ARL——TON TO MR. IL——RAY.

Baltimore, Sept.

I Received your letter two days after date, my dear friend, and have with the greatest alacrity prepared for my journey.

I hope to set out in the course of tomorrow, and as your fair friends will only have had five days the start of me, I expect to overtake them at the foot of the mountain.[1]

You shall hear from me on my arrival at Pittsburg.—But let me beg that in our future correspondence, nothing may be said of pecuniary matters; as I had flattered myself that you had known your friend better.

J. ARL——TON

LETTER III

MRS. W—— TO MISS R——.

Pittsburg, Sept.

WE had but just arrived here my dear R—— when a circumstance whimsical enough happened. Among the gentlemen of the army who have retired to this country,[1] is a Dr. K——, an old acquaintance of Mr. W——'s.[2] The Doctor is a man of facetious manners, grotesque figure, and of an amiable disposition, and with a very sensible heart, which ever makes him a dupe to the artifices of designing woman.

Mr. W—— whose greatest foible, and which is a very dangerous one, is that of laying schemes to promote his mirth at the expence of his friends, induced him to suggest to the Doctor the idea of paying his addresses to a buxom young widow, who is said to be possessed of considerable property.

The Doctor consulted his friend Capt. C—— upon the business, when he said to the Captain, that though his figure was aukward, yet, he thought (stroaking his face at the same time) that his countenance was that of a gentleman; in that opinion C—— did not fail to flatter him, and encouraged his intention, by assuring him, that his address was irresistible.

Such is the vanity of men, my dear R——, that there is not one among them, however deformed and emaciated, but think, they have only to direct their artillery against us, to make us surrender at their mercy.

The Doctor had scarcely commenced his attack, when the widow upbraided him for his folly, and as C—— is a man who cannot resist his propensity to expose every thing which is pleasant, we had the story with all the particulars one day at dinner, in the Doctor's presence, as having happened to a person of C——'s acquaintance; but which appeared so pointed to the Doctor, (though by the bye, not a soul would have enjoyed the thing except Mr. W——,) that he could not contain himself, and burst into a most vehement passion, which produced a general laugh at the ridiculous manner in which he had exposed himself: and what made it the more agreeable to the Ladies present was, that the Doctor has always declared a repugnance to matrimony.

You see R—— that genius is every where the same, and that when it is embellished by education, and enlivened with good humour and fancy, the happiness of rational and social beings, is as secure in these wild regions, as in the most populous cities of the universe.

The comedy of human life is exhibited every day upon the great theatre of the world, as well as upon the theatrical stage, and only people defective in sensibility, are obliged to have recourse to such arts to be amused.

You must not infer from such sentiments that I am an enemy to the stage, for I am very far from it, I assure you.

In every great country there will always be a number of pre-posterous characters, whose absurdities can only be generally ex-posed upon the stage; and as it may, under proper regulations, be made the censor of public manners, the terror of vice, and at the same time encourage virtue, I think it one of the most brilliant contrivances for the promotion of human felicity that ever was devised. Adieu my dear R——; mention both Mr. W—— and myself kindly to your affectionate father, and assure him how very much we lament his infirmities.—I hear that we are to have an addition to our little society of two English Ladies of whom I shall not fail to give you an account.

I am your's affectionately,
MARIA W——

LETTER IV

MRS. W—— TO MISS R——.

Pittsburg, Sept.

THE untimely pleasantry of Capt. C—— was very near having been attended with disagreeable consequences. But as there is something irresistible in reason united with humour, the Doctor was so forcibly struck with his absurdities, after he received C——'s answer to a challenge which he had sent him,[1] and which he now shews and laughs at as a good thing, that he asked C——'s pardon in the most gentlemanlike terms, and acknowl-edged that the folly originated on his part, and of which he was now so sensible, that he wished to make his concessions as ample as possible.

This affair has been altogether so ludicrous my dear R——, I think if it was promulged to the world, with all the particulars, and C——'s manner of treating affairs of honour, that it would place the practice of duelling in so ridiculous a point of view, that the greatest advocates for that unmanly and barbarous custom, would appear equally as much ashamed of their opinions, as the Doctor was of his conduct. However as you have some knowledge of the two men, and know the celebrity which the Doctor acquired in the unhappy affair between him and Mr. B——, I will send you a copy of C——'s answer, as I think there is not the smallest ground to suspect the Doctor's courage; particularly, after the many mortal proofs he has given of the most heroic firmness.

COPY OF THE ANSWER TO THE DOCTOR'S CHALLENGE.

"SIR,

"WHEN a man commits an absurdity, he must expect to be laughed at; for which reason, a man of sense will cautiously avoid doing any thing that might render him ridiculous in the eyes of the world: but as no human being is destitute of foibles, it is the business of rational men, when they feel their sensibility wounded, to reflect upon what was the cause of it; and I am sensible whenever a brave man is convinced that his own folly was the reason of his being ridiculed, that instead of being hurt, he would be convinced he ought to thank his friends for laughing him out of his inconsistencies.

"Suppose for a moment you had not felt the force of ridicule, and should have renewed your attention to the widow, who I think is about five and twenty, and you are nearly fifty, possibly the widow might have appeared more pliable, and your fondest wishes might have been crowned with success; but in all probability it would have completed your shame.

"You have had at least thirty years experience in the world, and from your profession as a Physician, you must have acquired some knowledge of the human constitution, and which knowledge I apprehend must have convinced you, that it is almost an impossible thing for youth to be attached to old age.

"No man can be a warmer advocate for the fair fame of women than I am; but I should call myself a monster, if I could expect from them a forbearance so repugnant to the genial current of human felicity—a forbearance which strikes at the first and most important principles of our holy religion, which is to increase and multiply, and saps the very sources of that population which is so necessary to lead to our aggrandizement and future prosperity. Besides, what can be so unmanly as to expect the exercise of a temperance on the part of women, for which our conduct affords such bad examples?

"When you have brought these considerations to your view, I think you must be made sensible, that in case you were to marry the widow, you would become a cuckold; and whether that is a crime or not, is of no consequence, for it never fails to fix an obliquy upon men who are so unfortunate, which renders them infinitely more contemptible in the eyes of the world, than the most atrocious and nefarious felons.

"I shall leave you to your own reflections, and to judge, whether or not your friends do not do you a favour by making such of your weaknesses a subject for their merriment, and thereby prevent you from becoming an object of ridicule to an invidious public.

"If I encouraged you to court the widow, it was done with the purest of motives; that of not checking the ardent expectations of a romantic man, which I know, judging from the human heart, is always dangerous; and if you did not discover the irony in my manner of speaking of your address, you must have been inebriated with the most foolish desire, and which alone, could have prevented your seeing a thing so palpable and pointed.

"Perhaps you may consider this as an elaborate apology; but for fear that should be the case, I must inform you, it is not intended as such; for as you were the aggressor in the first instance from a breach of good manners, and that too, in the presence of Ladies; and in the next for challenging; I must insist upon your asking my pardon for the double offence. But in case you are not willing to concede to these terms, I have a right to demand that you fight me in my own way, it being my privilege as the party called upon.

"But as I am addressing myself to a man of sense, I shall first take some notice of the original way of settling points of honour; and as I am sensible that you are a man of the purest delicacy, I flatter myself you will agree with me, when I say, that the present vulgar manner of fighting duels, is a deviation from the *sublime ideas of ancient cavilliers, and so far a derogation from that heroic institution.*[2]

"Whether or not a person having been engaged in a personal combat be a disgrace to him, I will leave you to determine; but it is however certain, that it proves he is either a brute, a fool, or has been in bad company; and whether it was by chance he was thrown into the society of ruffians signifies not in the least, as a quarrel with such creatures is equally an impeachment upon a man's understanding.

"Montesquieu says 'that among the barbarians the offended person began with declaring in the presence of the judge, that such a person had committed such an action; and the accused made answer that he lied; upon which the judge gave orders for the duel.' The same author observes 'that gentlemen fought on horse-back, and armed at all points; and that none but villains fought on foot.'[3]

"Now as you are in every respect a gentleman, *and an enemy to all kind of innovation, I demand that the venerable and sacred practice of duelling, be restored by our example, and that this wise and gallant system be renovated, that it may acquire its ancient splendour, which has been so materially sullied by the vulgar manners of the unpolished moderns.*

"I shall wait impatiently for your answer, and in the mean time I shall prepare for the combat, and shall leave it to your discretion, whether we shall erect a monument to immortalize our folly, or your prudence. I have the honour to be with every due consideration.

Yours, &c.

Signed P. C——"

The Doctor was so forcibly stricken with C——'s good sense and his own vanity and madness, that he went instantly to thank him for thus having rallied him out of his false and ridiculous opinions, and giving him a proper sense of those absurd men who first commit a breach of good manners, or by the most preposterous conduct excite the laughter of their friends, and then assassinate them for having corrected the former or ridiculed the latter.[4]

The English family arrived this evening attended by our old friend Capt. Arl——ton.—My first object in the morning will be to call upon them.

It is now past one in the morning, and Mr. W—— is importuning me to retire,[5] and begs I will leave off the practice of writing so late at night; but it is from these lucubrations alone I can receive the smallest solace for that poignant dereliction which I find from the absence of my dearest friend, and who I wish again to clasp in the arms of her most tender and affectionate

M. W——

LETTER V

CAPT. ARL——TON TO MR. IL——RAY.

Pittsburg, Sept.

I Set out on the day I mentioned for this place, my dear Il——ray, and though I posted upon the wings of the most ardent expectation, still I did not overtake the charming T——ns until they had ascended some distance up the mountain.

Whether it was owing to the impetuosity of my disposition or not, I will leave you to determine; but it is however certain, that I had travelled some distance on the west road before I recollected the rout from Philadelphia to this place was through Lancaster,[1] which put me more than a day's journey out of my way.

The people every where at the inns gave me tidings of the lovely emigrants, in whose fortune every heart seemed to be interested.—They deprecated that phrenzy which prodigally squanders the substance that is so necessary to support the delicacy and elegance which so admirably characterizes the youngest of the Miss T——ns.

My anxiety increased every foot I moved in that ratio which so rapidly multiplies beyond the powers of comprehension.—As I approached the mountain I expected every moment to get sight of the waggon which transported them, and such was my fervour, that I continued my journey without intermission the last four and twenty hours before I overtook them.—It was after travelling all night, and just after the sun had risen, and was gilding those immense plains, extending on either hand at the foot of the mountain, I first caught sight of Caroline—she was resting upon a large stone on the road side, when I came upon her by surprize,—was leaning with one hand upon her cheek, and held a handkerchief, which I thought had been applied to her eyes, that were glimmering like the rays of the sun through the mist of an April shower.

My appearance was so sudden that she started from her seat, when I threw myself from my horse, and instantly informed her who I was.—Her fears were soon allayed, and she endeavoured to put on an air of chearfulness. Sir, said Caroline, you must have travelled with wonderful expedition, for your friend Mr. Il——ray said, you would not set out from Baltimore until the 15th, and wished very much my father to delay our journey, alledging, that as we were strangers we might meet with inconveniencies which it would be in your power to obviate, as you were better acquainted with the modes and customs of the country.

She had risen from her seat at this time, and as my servant had taken my horse, we walked slowly on together after the wagon.

Gracious heaven! said I, Miss T——n you must have encountered many difficulties; and I lament that my motions have been so tardy as to prevent my overtaking you sooner.—Caroline thanked me for my solicitude; but assured me they had met with no inconveniencies whatever; for as they knew, they were not to expect such accommodations as are general in England, they had been most agreeably disappointed; for what the honest people on *travel &c* [handwritten annotation in top margin]

the road wanted of the necessary articles to accommodate travellers, they had made most ample compensation in their disposition to please.

All this time it appeared to me not a little strange, that Caroline should be alone, and walking.—When we had arrived at a steep part of the mountain, I begged that she would accept of my arm, as it would assist her in ascending a height that was almost perpendicular.—But which she declined, with observing, that the waggoner had provided her with a walking stick, and she thought in such an uneven road it was more easy to walk unassisted.

We had now got sight of the waggon, which had stopped to know what had become of the fair pedestrian; when to my utter astonishment the brother was still sleeping, or rather had not risen.

You will please to understand, that it is not an uncommon practice for people who are travelling over this mountain, to sleep at nights in their waggon or carriages.

I was introduced by Caroline to the family, the brother excepted, and when the waggoner had stopped to bait his horses at a hovel on the road side,[2] we began to prepare for breakfast. My sumpter mules came up in good time,[3] and while my servants were unpacking and preparing the tea apparatus, of which hitherto I had made no use, Caroline requested that I would breakfast with them, to which I told her I should readily assent, but I begged she would not fatigue herself, for my men would very soon prepare it; she answered with a most fascinating smile, and said, that it was quite ready.

George (for I find that is the brother's name) had by this time roused himself from his pillow, and like a torpid beast which takes shelter in some cavern during the inclement season of the year, insensible to every thing passing, which when the genial spring has again warmed into life the vegetable world, saunters out and eagerly devours whatever falls in his way; so came the drone from his lethargic bed.[4]

He entered very familiarly into conversation with me. Superciliously apologized for the style in which I was invited to breakfast—reprobated with pointed wit the uncouth figures of the people on the road, who he said, with the affectation of civility wanted that polish of manners necessary to make men bareable— wondered that our legislative body had not thought of introducing turnpike roads,[5] and seemed to think it would have been impossible for him to have had a comfortable morning sleep, even if he had been in one of those coaches described by Baron Beilfield,[6] as being so convenient and elegant when you are obliged to travel day and night.

And is it possible, said I to myself, that a man who is not deranged can talk such absurd nonsense?

Caroline saw I was quite amazed, and with the most charming vivacity, turning her head at the same time to the right, and pointing to some venerable firs, between which and upon the side of a high and rocky precipice grew several mountain laurels, depicted in the most animating colours the beauties of wildness.

Breakfast being over the waggoner let us know that he was ready to proceed; the old people and George took their seats in the waggon, Mary being indisposed had taken her bowl of tea without having risen, and Caroline still persisted in her wish to walk.

I had ascertained from the waggoner the place he intended to reach by the evening, and had accordingly dispatched my men, in order that we might be better accommodated there on our arrival. And travelling in this kind of way, we arrived here on the fourth day, after I had joined this extraordinary family.

I have the pleasure to inform you that Caroline's spirits are connsiderably mended, and that she is quite enchanted with the situation of this place. Mary has recovered from her fatigue, and is in other respects perfectly well.

They know that I am writing to you, and have requested that I will assure you, that the family are not insensible of your many kindnesses.

Farewell. I will give you Caroline's reasons for walking in my next. I am obliged to conclude for the present, for fear of loosing the chance of sending this.

I am your's truly,

J—— A——

LETTER VI

Miss R—— to Mrs. W——.

Bristol, Sept.

MY DEAR W——,

I Am still importuned upon the subject of matrimony by Mr. S——, and urged to accept of him by my father, who certainly has no idea how repugnant such a connection would be to my feelings, otherwise I am sure his paternal regard which has ever been of the most tender kind, would not permit him to reiterate his importunities upon the subject.

I cannot love him though I cannot always resist his powers of persuasion.—That torrent of eloquence by which he fascinates would be exercised in the senate to more advantage—for with an understanding so accute, a wit so brilliant, and a delivery so happy, it is impossible, but such talents would prove an acquisition to any body of legislators in the world.

The female heart admires every thing which is refined and brilliant;—but the attachments of the soul are of a higher and more pure nature. They are generated in the celestial elements of desire, and emanate from bosoms congenial to each other.

Love is the food of the heart, which invigorates the mind, and it must lead to rapture in every situation in despite of the vicissitudes of fortune, whilst it gives a lustre to human nature transcendently pleasing.

How very cautious ought we to be my dear W—— in precipitating ourselves into a situation which may make us eternally miserable? And how very cautious ought parents to be in urging a dutiful child to give her hand to a man when it is not an act of volition?

Whether or not the great number of miserable connections of this sort, which we see are owing to the inconsistency of the laws of matrimony, perhaps, would not become a person of my youth

and inexperience to give an opinion upon; but with all due sub-
mission to the Lords of the *creation,* I should suppose it the height
of wisdom to organize this part of the system of jurisprudence, as
conformable to the code of nature as possible—particularly as it
is a subject that more materially concerns, than any other, their
felicity as well as ours.

Forgive my friend this retrogade digression, and attribute it to
the effusions of sensibility, and not to vanity. It is not my business
to arraign the customs of the world; but it was impossible to avoid
it under the influence of the present state of my mind.

You have only to take a view of the many instances of misery
of this kind that have come under your notice, to feel the greatest
abhorrence of the profanation which is every day marked with
such distressing circumstances—circumstances which depict with
more energy, the absurdity of their cause, than could the most
laboured animadversions.

You are perfectly happy, my dear friend, and I am sure you
are better qualified to judge of my situation than I am myself.

Mr. S—— it is said is very opulent; but you know that men
of experience say that the fortunes of speculative and enterprizing
persons are always precarious; but such are the pecuniary distresses
of my father, that I apprehend it will be impossible for me to
avoid becoming a victim to his misfortunes.

It was this necessity which gave rise to my reflections upon the
customs and laws of matrimony. Mr. S—— is a most agreeable
man; but then I do not love him. Now in case I should marry
him, it is very possible I might in time feel for him a more tender
regard; but if he should prove less agreeable, I should, you know,
be condemned to perpetual misery; and certainly of all the different prostitutions those of the feelings are the most ignominious.
And according to the present system, it is impossible for a woman
of delicacy to be separated from her husband.[1]

Not a line have I received from you since your arrival at Pittsburg, and I have only oral testimony that you are alive.

How has it happened that two beings who were once inseparable should be so long silent? If there is a fault, it must be on

your side; for I did not know where to direct my letters. However I will forgive you upon the score of your lively attachment to the General, which I always thought would continue to increase, untill your mind totally absorbed in your solicitude for him, would insensibly drown in oblivion the remembrance of your friends. But that heaven may preserve it, though I should be forgotten by my charming W—— is the most ardent wish of your affectionate
L—— R——

P. S. Miss G—— who returned from Philadelphia a few days since, says that the whole city talk of nothing but an English family which have emigrated to your country, in whose fortune every body appeared interested. Caroline the youngest daughter is spoken of as the most interesting creature that ever decorated our terrestrial orb—you will of course see them, and I pray that I may have your account of those amiable beings.

LETTER VII

MRS. W—— TO MISS R——.

Pittsburg, Sept.

MY DEAR R——,

I Have this moment returned from my visit to the English family—I shall pass over the whole of them except the two girls, for as I can say nothing in their favour I think it most charitable to be silent.

The eldest of the Miss T——ns appears to be about twenty, is handsome, possesses a great share of vivacity, which I was not a little surprised at, considering her change of situation; particularly after so fatiguing a journey as they must have had over the mountain—She possesses all the external accomplishments of a fine woman, and is in short, that kind of being which is rather an ornament to a drawing-room, than an useful piece of furniture.

But as the best criterion for us women to judge how far we are interesting objects, is that of the conduct of gentlemen towards us, I shall only remark that Arl——ton, who you know is a fine fellow, and who is perfectly domesticated in the family, while he treats her with the utmost politeness and attention, it is very observable it is without any other regard than what is due to every lady.

But what shall I say of the youngest, Caroline? How shall I find words to convey to you an adequate idea of so much perfection and loveliness? O that I had the talents of that poet who said of his mistress

> *"That she was all that painters could express,*
> *Or youthful poets fancy when they love."*[1]

Caroline appears to be about seventeen, is rather above the middle height, and is formed with that proportion which would have served for a model for even Praxillites, or any one of the Grecian Statuarists[2]—She has light hair, fair and vivid complexion, an oval face, her nose is in the line of beauty, and long, full, blue eyes

> *"Of whose sweetness, no pencil's power,*
> *The expression can declare;*
> *Their beams are gathered from her soul!!"*[3]

But above all what makes her so very interesting is the peculiar elegance of her manners. There is a blandishment which accompanies every word she utters that goes directly to the heart; and when she listens to the conversation of others, there is a lustre and benignity in her face which warms into animation the most torpid; but when she moves the Graces seem to direct her every motion,[4] and the radiance of her features express a divinity of soul, which makes her altogether the most interesting being I ever beheld.

From this description of so delightful a woman, was I a man, you might naturally conclude I was in love; for indeed it would be reasonable, as it would be impossible to be otherwise.

As far as I can learn their intention is to settle on a farm in the neighbourhood of this place; but as it is Mr. W———'s intention to go down to Louisville in the spring, I shall dissuade them, if possible, from settling in this country, and which I shall do from two motives; first, that of an interested one, as I should be happy to have near me such an amiable creature as Caroline—The next is more generous; for I find that most of the emigrants who arrive into this remote part of the world, proceed down the river to settle, on account of the greater fertility of the soil, and a more genial climate; which are reasons sufficient to prove that country is the most eligible for this family to live in.

What a cruel consideration it is my dear R——— that all sub-lunary happiness has its alloy. In following the fortune of a man who I am attached to by every tie of which the human mind has a conception, that of mutual tenderness, affinity of manners, age, and in short, the *tout en semble* which constitutes the food of love,[5] and which alone can give a zest to its raptures, I am removed so distantly from my next dearest friend.—And if I have found some consolation from so painful a circumstance in the delicate and affectionate manners of Mr. W———, who soothes my sorrows, by telling me, that for all my inquietudes he will amply compensate by his care and attention, I hope you will believe me when I assure you; that you are the second object of my heart.

Gracious heavens! when I reflect upon the distance which sep-arates us, and contemplate the probable time before we meet again, how agonizing is the thought?

Could I but receive a letter from you, the prototype of my friend, it would once more brighten a prospect which will ever constitute a principal part of my happiness or misery; and in rec-ognizing your animating sentiments I should still know you lived and loved your W———.

I know the distance between us, and the want of opportunities to forward letters are such that I cannot expect to hear often from you; but still I think the present interval the greater, as Capt. Arl———ton has informed me there are frequent opportunities of sending from Lancaster, and that by forwarding your letters by post to an acquain-tance in that place, we might receive them regularly.

But *apropos,*[6] I recollect you half promised you would pay a visit to me when I should be settled: now as I am settled for the present, I claim your promise; and the more earnestly, as if we go down to Louisville in the spring, the distance will be so great and the difficulty of returning so hazardous, that I could not expect you would fulfill your engagement.

The fatigue of travelling to this country is merely imaginary, and I am sure if you were to hear Miss Caroline T——n's description of the mountains and the beautiful landscapes upon the Susquehanna, you would be quite enchanted with the idea of taking such a journey.

I confess, though I had been highly delighted with the romantic and sublime scenes which were continually presented to my view as I came along, still I did not receive a just impression of their various beauties, untill this amiable girl depicted them in such glowing colours as made me think I must have been stupid not to have noticed them, and always with this delicate preface, you recollect such and such a place, which, confirmed my dulness, I had in many instances entirely overlooked.

However, sometimes I believe R——, when we have the prospect of our most substantial joys before us, we do not find those beauties in romantic scenes, nor feel those rapturous pleasures which many describe *when the pale light of the moon which shot through the spreading branches,* impending over the terrace walk, seems to sleep upon the couch of night; while planetary worlds moving in their different orbs with such wonderful harmony emit their twinkling rays, as if to cheer disconsolate lovers, or to assuage the sorrows of that bosom which pants to clasp some absent friend; nor do we find the same interest in the wonderful display of beauty with which the œconomy of nature every where abounds.

The theme is always elegant; and whenever I meet with genius capable of describing them, I am always delighted; but when a person has become a wife and mother, I think it is much more material to confine herself to real and substantial matters. Not that I disapprove of the indulgence of fancy in young minds; for I do not know of any thing which adds so much to the vivacity of youth, as it naturally tends to expand the heart and intellect, and ultimately produces a comprehension of ideas which renders the mind competent to engage in the most brilliant and copious conversations; and what makes such acquisitions the more estimable is, that colloquial talents are the most desirable accomplishments a woman of fashion can possess.

That accomplishment Miss Caroline possesses in a most eminent degree. And could I prevail upon my R—— to join our society which promises to become a charming one from the number of officers who are daily arriving, I think I should deserve a monument from the people for the happiness I had occasioned them.

Mr. W—— joins me in prayers for your happiness, and flatters himself you will not be able to withstand my importunities. He thinks it is a place of all others that both you and Mr. R—— would be pleased with, and he means to write to him shortly upon the subject.

Several of your friends have already arrived here, and more are daily expected; and there are a far greater number of objects to amuse an intelligent mind than either at Bristol or Philadelphia. Adieu! adieu! my charming friend, I expect every moment the Miss T——ns who promised to do us the honour to dine *en famille*.[7] I am as usual,

Your's affectionately,
M. W——

LETTER VIII

CAPT. ARL——TON TO MR. IL——RAY.

Pittsburg, Sept.

MY DEAR IL——RAY,

MY anxiety was such to inform you of the safe arrival of the charming T——ns at this place, that I embraced the first opportunity to write to you on the subject, at which time, I was so hurried that I scarcely knew what I wrote.

Caroline, said I, it gives me much pain to see you walking over these rugged mountains, for surely you must find yourself very much fatigued; She replied no,—it was always a great pleasure for her to walk. You mean said I, interrupting her, when you have passed the laughing hours

> *In groves where chirping birds, in wantonplay,*
> *Attuned to love, in frolic pass the day.*

But that walking here was materially different from the pleasurable walks in shady groves, or the promenades of London. True, answered Caroline, it is very different; one has a continual sameness which insensibly produces *ennui,* and the others are generally so crowded, that it is quite impossible either to enjoy the charms of conversation, or the pleasure of walking. But here is a continual feast for the mind—every rock, every tree, every moss, from their novelty afford subject for contemplation and amusement. Look but at yonder towering hills, (pointing at the same time at a rocky ridge considerably above the others,) whose summits appear to prop the heavens, and then view the various symbols which their chasms produce, and what a sublime imagery does it afford?—What can more resemble the ruins of a great city?—That grand division which rises higher upon the right, has the form and figure of a superb mosque—the left and various other divisions, that of palaces, temples, churches, streets, and squares, and you would suppose, if Pope had ever travelled this road, that he must have had the center division in his imagination, when he so beautifully described his temple of Fame.[1]

Caroline might have proceeded in this way to eternity, and I should not have interrupted her; for such was my astonishment at the fertility of her imagination, that I heard her with amazement, and gazed at her with the most ineffable transports!

What, said she, observing my silence, have I been talking ab-

surdly? Though indeed I apprehend that there is something very
je-june and romantic in such fancies. No, by heavens! Caroline,
said I, there can be nothing uninteresting, much less absurd in any
thing that you can say; and if you have indulged your fancy, the
theme was sublime, and your imagination highly poetical. But
when I recognize the delicacy of your frame—reflect upon those
vicissitudes of fortune that have exposed you to these hardships,
and attend to the amiable cheerfulness which gives a most lovely
lustre to your beauty, I am lost in admiration.

Ha-hah! cried Caroline, stepping briskly forward at the same
moment, we have lost sight of the waggon, and we must accelerate our movements, otherwise we shall not overtake them before the evening.

At that instant our ears were assailed with the tingling of bells,
which the country people who pack their goods upon horses, to
transport it over the mountain, put at their heads, to prevent their
being lost in case they should stray out of the road.

In a few minutes a number of packers came in sight,[2] when we
stepped on one side of the road to leave them at liberty to pass.
However they stopped, and after a short conversation had taken
place, I told those honest people we were travelling to their country with a view to live among them. They answered, that they
always were glad to have gentlefolks come among them, and that
there had been many first and last; but the frequent Indian wars
had always frightened them back again.[3]

Pray, said Caroline, hastily, there I hope are no Indians in these
mountains? No, no, good Lady, said the countrymen with one
voice, there are not any within two hundred miles of us,[4] and if
there were, they should not hurt you, for we would guard and
protect you at the hazard of our lives.

You are very good, replied Caroline, some of you perhaps have
lost a wife, a mother, or a child; for I am told that savages have
no regard for age or sex?

A venerable old man whose countenance commanded respect,
and who had all this time been viewing Caroline with great at-

tention, now with a heart overflowing with sorrow, and with the big tear starting in his eye, said we have all cause to mourn the havock of their depredations; but it is in looking forward that the human mind finds alleviation from the pangs of the afflicted bosom, and not in the retrospect, of the destruction of the tender blossoms of our fondest hopes. But when we behold the horizon of sorrow, (looking in Caroline's face,) gilded by so bright a sun, the tears of sadness will be exhaled, and the heaven of our hopes will be brightened into the meridian of joy. Forgive my charming girl this untimely effusion, continued the old man, seizing Caroline's hand, for I once was blessed in the possession of a woman, whose image is brought afresh to my recollection, by the recognition of that divinity which sparkles in your eyes; and if you will permit me sometimes to see you when I recross the mountain, it will make me happy, and I shall think myself highly honoured.

Caroline immediately gave him her name, which appeared to excite fresh emotions, and then informed him that she expected to be at Pittsburg, where she should be most happy to see him.

The old man took a most affectionate and respectful leave of us, when a young jolly lad of about eighteen years old, asked Caroline if she was my wife, and upon my answering in the negative, he requested also that he might be permitted to see her.

The packers cracked their whips, and went dancing on to the music of their bells, and we proceeded after the waggon, which they told us was near a mile ahead.

We had walked some distance without speaking one word, for we both seemed to be absorbed upon the adventures of the day, when Caroline said, do you not think Sir, this one adventure fully compensates for all the fatigue of walking? Indeed, said I, Miss Caroline, you are perfectly in the right; and I would rather walk one thousand miles than to have missed so interesting a circumstance. There was something, she replied, which bespoke the manners of a gentleman in the conversation of the old man, and said she should like to be made acquainted with the history of his life. I answered that I was of the same opinion, and recommended her to cultivate his acquaintance when he should return; for that both his address and language bespoke him a man of talents and education.

It was evening before we overtook the waggon, and to my great surprize, not one of the family expressed any joy at finding Caroline had arrived safe—which I am obliged to attribute to insensibility, for I am sure a more interesting being never existed.

During supper George complained of the accommodations, and thought it would be a wise plan in the government of America to establish great Inns at regular distances upon the mountain, which would be an inducement for people to emigrate and consequently tend to inhance the value of the waste land belonging to the federal empire. To which Mrs. T——n added, she thought his idea of turnpike roads ought to be first attended to:—true, replied George, but that is a matter of course.

Caroline during the course of the evening, endeavoured to relate the adventure with the packers, but not a soul would listen to her; and George having sarcastically observed, that it was not possible for her to have seen any thing but bears and wild animals, she was not a little affected by his contumely; and as I observed at the same time her emotions, I took an opportunity to relate how much I had been entertained with the beautiful ideas with which Caroline's imagination had furnished me, from her manner of describing the impending cliffs of Chesnut mountain;[5] and upon my attempting to relate them, he stopped me short, by saying he never knew before, that the Aborigines of America had been Mahometans, for that mosque was a Turkish temple.

This last attempt at wit quite disconcerted me, and as I felt myself not a little harrassed from having travelled two days and a night without rest, I apologized and retired.

Such my dear friend is the folly of a man, who I think you told me had received a courtly education.

That your social pleasures may be made perfect by the zest of fine women,

Is the wish of your's sincerely,
J—— ARL——TON

LETTER IX

MR. IL——RAY TO CAPT. ARL——TON.

Philadelphia

MY DEAR JAMES,

I Had the pleasure of receiving your favour dated Pittsburg this morning, and found my anxiety much removed by hearing that you had overtaken and arrived safe with the T——ns.

I confess that I am much at a loss to guess what reason Caroline could have had, for undergoing so great a fatigue as it must have been to her to walk across the rugged Appalachean mountains,[1] —except that it was compassion for the horses, which must have been greatly harrassed in climbing those hilly roads; and as I know her sensibility is exquisitely fine, I should have determined that to have been the cause of it, if there was not something extremely enigmatical in the manner in which you tell me that you will inform me in your next,—until I receive which my curiosity will be quite awake.

I did not wonder in the least at the manner of your describing George's indolence; though I confess there is something very ludicrous, in the idea of a man's complaining of not being able to sleep, when travelling over the roughest road for a carriage perhaps upon the whole globe. But such is the insensibility of men educated in the manner that young man was; and as he appears so extraordinary a character to you, I will give you some of the particulars of the family, and his former life.

Mr. T——n as I told you in a former letter was an opulent Merchant in London, and Mrs. T——n being a woman of fashion, had induced Mr. T——n to reside at the west end of the town, that is the court end,[2] where she indulged in all the gaities and extravagance of that great metropolis.

The idea of trade shocked her delicacy, and when she recognized the vulgar address of a citizen, she felt the most lively in-

dignation at the thought that Mr. T——n's profession fixed such
a stigma upon the family; and when the honest people to the east
of Temple Bar used to call upon her,[3] she was always denied being
at home; and the more effectually to risque the name from the
odium of being trade's-people, she determined that George should
have a commission in the Horse Guards,[4] which she supposed
would lead her into the first and most fashionable circles.

Thus after having prodigally squandered in the indulgence of
that kind of vanity the whole of Mr. T——n's estate, and entirely
destroyed his credit among his city friends; but after George had
for some time been enjoying that rank which gratified her ideal
consequence, and indulging in all the folly and dissipation ever
characteristic of the juvenile absurdities of young officers, they
were reduced to the miserable situation in which you have seen
them; George having been obliged to sell his commission some
time before he left London to pay a debt, for which he had been
arrested and confined.

Such my friend are the substance of those follies that have reduced a man whose business it has been said by unquestionable
authority, was at one time worth ten thousand pounds annually.[5]
With a family beggared, and two amiable girls suffering all the
tortures of disappointment, with the accumulated evil of being
exiled into a wilderness—forgive me for repeating this idea; but
when I reflect upon the vanity of a woman who regards more
the allurements of variety, and the pageantry of fashion, than the
future welfare of those beings whom she has brought into the
world, my indignation is for a time suspended by my wonder at
such unnatural vices.

View the whole catalogue of crimes which degrade the human
heart, and I defy you to fix upon one that is attended with such
lamentable consequences as the profligacy of an unprincipled
woman.

They commence their career like the felon who first steals trifles, and which he presumes will not be missed; but as he becomes
hardened he not only plunders promiscuously the necessitous, but

he feels no compunction for having committed the most atrocious sacrilege.

Thus when a woman gives loose to her desires, and no longer finds any charms from social intercourse, but eagerly looks for gratifications in the midnight orgies of female extravagance, what bounds can be fixed to their licentiousness?—a sacrilege against nature is the worst of sins.

Though there can be no extenuation for such unnatural folly, yet, let us in justice to female virtue examine into the cause productive of it, for their hearts are naturally formed for tenderness—there is a delicacy belonging to their nature that is peculiar to the softness of their sex—the lively animation which beams in their eyes at the tales of sorrow, or swells the pouting lip when the soul in the agonies of sympathy beats high to the calls of nature,—and the generous enthusiasm which kindles into rapture the coldest hearts, when they espouse the cause of the oppressed or unfortunate—all tend to prove that there is no turpitude belonging to them—and where shall we look for the cause of this depravity but in our institutions?—institutions the more ungenerous and tyrannic because the oppressed are not represented.

Unfeeling man! blush at that meanness which disgraces thy name and makes thee no better than a monster.

When heaven ordained for the particular purpose of carrying into execution the sublime object of the *Creator,* that there should be a difference of sex, how bountifully was the *goodness of Providence* displayed in the formation of woman—formed with all that beauty, with all that softness, with all that tenderness, and with all that brilliancy of sentiment, and vivacity of mind which is necessary to polish our manners, and sooth us in the lap of elegance and love, to a forgetfulness of all our mortifications

> *Beauty awakes, expands the glowing heart,*
> *And prompts the soul to act its noblest part;*
> *Warms it with pure Affection's kindling fire,*
> *Gives zest in love, and animates desire;*

Leads on to rapture, wakes Ambition's flame,
And crowns the lover's brow with deathless fame.

This tenderness entitles them to our protection and utmost care—It is not sufficient to say that while they demean themselves in a proper manner, they receive this protection—I deny it in toto.—Is it right for a man to insult a woman of spirit in the grossest manner with impunity?—Is it pardonable for a man to trample every day upon the sensibility of a delicate woman? What colour of excuse can be framed for condemning millions of them to suffer under the tyranny of the drunken or beastly caprices of men, or else forced into a life of prostitution, as ignominious as it is baneful to their health and constitution?

I should be glad to know what other alternative they have, according to the existing laws of all countries upon the face of the globe?

There is no reciprocality in the laws respecting matrimony. A man who is not comfortable at home, seeks abroad for those amusements which alone can compensate for domestic feuds; and should he transgress the bounds of that faith which he plighted at the alter of his religion, who is to call him to an account for his cupidity? *Scoundrel!*

I beg that I may not be answered that the law in such cases has provided for the woman. That is of no avail in the argument. Every institution which is of a nature to act partially, is more odious than the most flagrant despotism.

But what is most inhuman, is that when a woman of honour and delicacy has been driven to seek for some mitigation of the sufferings of an afflicted bosom, in the friendship of an ingenuous heart, and when that friendship has led to more tender ties—ties which spring from the finest feelings, and which characterize the most humane and exalted souls, that she should be branded with contempt, and condemned to live in poverty, unnoticed, and unpitied.

Look but at the numerous instances of this sort which disgrace the courts of Great Britain,[6] and you must be shocked with the

idea, that the most enlightened nation in the world, exercises the
most inhuman and barbarous tyranny over those helpless beings,
who have a claim upon our gratitude for our very existence, and
whose weakness demands our most liberal support.

I have been so insensibly drawn into this length upon this very
interesting subject, that I must take my leave of you for the present
my friend, begging that you will commend me to the T——ns,
and to General and Mrs. W——. Assure them that I wish much
to visit them in their retirement, and as I have it in agitation to
make a journey as far as the Illinois,[7] in case I should perform it,
I shall certainly take Pittsburg in my way.

Let me hear from you as often as you can meet with opportunities, for I find myself much interested in the welfare of the
society with whom you are living. God bless you my dear James,
Farewell.

LETTER X

Miss R—— to Mrs. W——.

Bristol, Oct.

MY DEAR W——,

I Have at length had the pleasure of receiving two of your
letters dated Pittsburg which convinces me you must be there;
otherwise the vivacity with which you write would have induced
me to believe you could not have changed your situation from
the elegance that surrounded you in Philadelphia, to that sequestration in which you must now live. However it proves to me
that you are perfectly happy, at which, believe me when I say, I
rejoice.

Not a word have you said of your journey, or of your situation;
nor in short of any one thing concerning yourself.

How amiable do you always appear? the changes of fortune
seem not in the least to affect your spirits—but you are the same

charming creature in retirement, that you were when you graced
the fashionable parties of our metropolis.

Every thing you can write must always prove interesting to me;
but when my heart overflows with tenderness, at the recollection
of the many hours that have so rapidly glided away, when we
together in youthful pastime cemented the most lively friendship,
and which was prolonged by your ever endearing virtues, I feel
an indifference at the absurdities of Dr. K——, however ludicrous
they may have been.

It is a misfortune that a man who possesses so many good qualities as the Doctor is said to do, and with abilities so eminent,
should be so very eccentric.

I have heard of many extravagant things of his committing
which at first used to excite my wonder, but I have been told
they were the result of affectation, when they excited my abhorrence and disgust.

The follies of young men, and the oddities of fools deserve
great allowance; for while one proceeds from an injudicious education, the other is the effect of weakness which ought to be
pitied;—but when a man who has a knowledge of the world, and
is acquainted with good manners, in contempt of the rules of
society violates every principle of decorum, merely because he has
the reputation of being an odd man, I think he ought to be banished from genteel company, however brilliant his wit; for I know
of no compensation that can be made for rudeness.

Capt. C———'s humour I have always understood was irresistible; but I think there was a breach of confidence in relating a
private conversation that passed between him and his friend, and
which I cannot conceive it was necessary to expose in order to
laugh the Doctor out of the folly of wishing to marry the widow.

There appears to be something so sacred in a confidential conversation, that nothing short of the danger of a man's country, or
a wicked conspiracy, ought to prompt any person to expose it.
Indeed to repeat trifles which have passed between two persons,
who are in the habits of intimacy, that have been uttered at an
unguarded moment, or when we have been indulging those little

weaknesses which are gratifications to the mind, is always a proof
to me, that the person who does it wants delicacy of sentiment.
But when a friend has laid open his little vanities, or expressed
his weakness, perhaps when his heart was overflowing in the effusions of his philanthropy, and has had those social feelings made
a subject of merriment for his friends, I declare I think such a
breach highly reprehensible. Capt. C——'s motive may have
been laudable, but I cannot perceive how it was auxiliary to the
purpose.

One of the greatest pleasures, perhaps, which can be derived
from the emanations of friendship, is the satisfaction we experience when we lay open, naked as it were, our very hearts to the
inspections of those we love; and if weakness or vanity was a very
uncommon thing, I should not wonder when people laugh at such
expositions; though it is rather extraordinary, nay, it is mean, to
be merry at circumstances, which were they brought home to
ourselves would make us angry.

However the misfortune is, that Voltaire was in the right, when
he said, that

"friendship is a tacid contract between two sensible and virtuous
persons; I say sensible, for a monk, a hermit, may not be wicked,
yet live a stranger to friendship: I add virtuous, for the wicked
only have accomplices; the voluptuous have companions, the designing have associates, the men of business have partners, the
politicians form a factious band; the bulk of idle men have connections, princes have courtiers:—but virtuous men alone have
friends. Cethegus was Cataline's accomplice, and Mæcenas was
Octavius's courtier; but Cicero was the friend of Atticus."[1]

Every day brings me fresh and additional cause to lament the
loss of your society my charming friend. Enveloped as I am with
difficulties, my mind is almost distracted—I see nothing but prec-
ipices on every side of me—with a mind labouring to act right,
I have not energy left to act in any manner or shape; and I begin
to tremble at the thoughts of what I foretold in a former letter

was just; i.e. of falling a victim to the misfortunes of my affectionate father. The rapid hours which used to gild my every wish,
now bring nothing but tidings of sorrow and wretchedness; and
the period is advancing with colossian strides, when my aged and
unhappy parent will be arrested for a debt which it will be impossible for him to pay; and that is another of the miseries brought
upon himself by his over generous support of a worthless brother.

What would I give could I but have the advice of my beloved
W———, in this delicate posture of affairs? But I cannot bear the
thoughts of my dear father lingering in a prison; and that gratitude
I owe him for his many kindnesses, independent of the ties of
nature, I begin to think will oblige me to accept of the hand of
Mr. S———. Great God! I shudder at the thought:—for though I
am sensible I can make him a prudent wife, yet I confess I am
shocked at myself, for even thinking to marry a man from necessity, whom I would not think of under any other circumstances;
and which I conceive would be treating him ill. But such is the
infatuation of some men, that they cannot see the most glaring
truths.

However, I am determined if he should continue to urge me
upon the subject, that I will candidly tell him, nothing could
induce me to have him but the situation of my father; and I think
after such an ingenuous declaration, if he should still persist in his
wish to marry me, he will never afterwards have a right to upbraid
me for duplicity.

I cannot help making a reflection here upon what is termed
generosity. When a man has prodigally squandered his property,
and has been frequently supported by his friends, and has as frequently involved himself in fresh trouble, it is so far from being
generous in them to support him, that it is a weakness, nay, criminal, when it eventually may intail misery upon a rising progeny,
who certainly are intitled to the first care of their parents.

Such you know my dear W——— has been the conduct of my
father, that all his disappointments in life have flowed from the
source of his brother's extravagance.

Adieu W———, forgive me for troubling you with so tedious

an account of my distresses; but I promise if ever I regain my cheerfulness, to make you amends for this dolorous epistle.

Commend me to the General, and assure the English family, that I envy you the pleasure of their society; and if I had been so fortunate as to have met them, I should have used my endeavours to have induced them to settle at Bristol. God bless you my friend, and believe

I am sincerely yours, &c.

L—— R——

LETTER XI

CAROLINE T——N TO MRS. F——.

Pittsburg, Oct.

MY DEAR SISTER,

FROM the recollection of our infancy, and recounting the joys which have flowed from our kindred nature in our infant pastimes and pleasures, how afflicting is it to a bosom which still retains the most animated recollection of those fleeting moments, and which finds from so severe a dereliction, not a ray of hope ever again that I can embrace my Eliza—the companion of my youth, the partner of my sorrows;—but above all the tutelary guardian of my unsuspicious nature.[1]

The fates,[2] who are said to preside over our fortune and lives, seem to have acted in our destination as if prodigally sporting with the feelings of humanity—we are placed almost at opposite sides of the globe, and when I stand most in need of your consolation and advice, I apprehend I have lost you for ever. The thought is too poignant, I must give vent to my sorrow!—O could I see but one vista through which the rays of hope could shoot her golden beams, as you have seen the orient sun pierce through the avenue of a beauteous grove, and gild the distant plains, I should not have this sadness which oppresses my heart, and makes me feel a *pre-*

sentiment that—but I will not name it—for whatever may be the fate of your Caroline, be assured she will never err but in judgment.

Forgive my dear Eliza this incoherent preface, and I will endeavour to regain my recollection, and then I will give you some account of our journey, reserving the particulars of it for a journal which I shall send you as soon as I have finished it, with an account of our present situation.

After leaving Philadelphia, passing Lanchaster, a place that would be considered as a large inland town in any part of Europe, untill we arrived at the Susquehanna, we found the country well settled, with little variation. The roads were much better than they had been represented to us, and the Inns every where, were supplied with the greatest plenty of provisions of all sorts, which were very cheap, and the people remarkably civil.

The Susquehanna is one of those immense rivers with which this large continent abounds. From its sources which are in the Apalachean mountains, it traverses great part of Pensylvania, and then stretching to the southward empties itself into the bay of Chesapeak. Where we crossed it, which it is said is nearly fifty leagues from its mouth,[3] taking its meandering course, it is about twice the width of the Thames at Westminster-bridge, with high impending banks that rudely seem to threaten its limpid stream, as though they were jealous of such attracting beauty; and first gives you an idea of the savage wildness of that region you are obliged to travel through in your way, from thence to this place.

After journeying for ten days we arrived at the foot of the mountain, where we rested for part of a day; and laid in at the same time provisions to supply us untill we should arrive on the opposite side; for we were told, it would be very difficult to procure them, after we left the flat country; and as we were under the direction of our waggoner, who was something of a despot, we were obliged to proceed almost at evening, and had ascended but a few miles when we stopped at a cabin on the road side, where we slept that night.

I had previously made up my mind upon walking over the mountain, which is about fifty miles across, from the opinion that

there must be many interesting views on the way, as I should
loose them in case I kept my seat in the waggon, which was not
only uncomfortable from being crowded with our little furniture,
but the roughness of the road made it very unpleasant to ride;
besides, I could not bare to see the poor horses tugging up the
almost perpendicular hills, a load that was almost too great for
them, when I was so capable of walking; and regardless of any
consideration but these objects, after the waggon had proceeded
the next morning, which was immediately after the break of day,
I followed, and after having travelled about two miles, finding
myself fatigued I had sat down upon a rock that was covered with
green moss to rest, when I was alarmed by a gentleman who
appeared to be a cavillier,[4] who had thrown himself from his
horse, before I had time to recollect myself; and announcing the
name of Arl——ton, I instantly remembered that our friend Mr.
Il——ray, had mentioned that such a person was going to Pittsburg, and that he was a particular friend of his, whom he should
take the liberty of recommending to us.

At this time the waggon had got some distance a-head, but I
did not stand to look much about me, for fear Capt. Arl——ton
would believe me romantic. We soon recovered the lost distance;
and after travelling a little farther we stopped to breakfast, at which
time our fellow traveller, I apprehend, gave orders to his servants,
who went forward to make the necessary preparations to accom-
odate us; for we ever afterwards found the most ample supplies
of provisions at every stage, and every thing arraigned in the most
comfortable manner the nature of things would permit.

When I came to the spot which was made memorable by the
defeat of the gallant Braddock[5] how did my heart beat at contemplating the sepulchres of so many brave Englishmen!—How rapidly did my imagination traverse back again the immense distance,
and to the period of time when so many mothers mourned for
the loss of a son! When the son grieved for the loss of a father—
and when perhaps the tender sentiments of many beautiful and
fond girls, which had been fostered by the persuasive insinuations
of elegant manners, and a suavity of disposition, were withered in

the bud, and those fantasies of pleasure that warms into enthusiasm the ardency of youth, then changed into luctiferous complaints, from those deadly schisms?

Gracious heaven! thought I, how wonderful are the vicissitudes of our fortune? But how much more wonderful must be the versitality of the human heart, to be enabled to bear up against the repeated disappointments, which we meet with in this world?

I had began to philosophize when my fellow traveller, (for Capt. Arl——ton persisted in walking with me,) who had been giving me an account of the action, observed the situation of my mind; said, as the wars were all over, it was not a time to look at human distresses, and that the season of our happiness was too much abridged by our very nature, to suffer us with impunity to make a wanton sacrifice of time; and repeated at the same instant those beautiful lines out of Tasso,

> "In vain the spring returns, the spring no more,
> Can waning youth to former prime restore;
> Then crop the morning rose, the time improve,
> And while to love 'tis giv'n, indulge in love."[6]

Taking hold of my hand as he continued, said he, Caroline I am afraid, seeing the effect which this spot has had upon your sensibility, that you must have lost in that unfortunate battle some relation or friend.[7] I told him none that I knew of, and I then informed him of our misfortune in the loss of our uncle. He seeing the tears start afresh in my eyes, took his handkerchief and dried them, saying, that it was probable he might be still living, as we never had a confirmation of his death; and then endeavoured to console me, by observing we should arrive in a short time at Pittsburg, when there would be an end to all my fatigues, and hoped to all my sorrows: but, said he, Caroline, was it not compassion for your delicate limbs, I should wish the journey had been twice as long.

I must give you some account, my dear sister, of this very interesting young man; for I am sure did you know how much we are obliged to him for his very great and many civilities, I am

sensible you would join with me in his eulogium, though nature
has been so bountiful to him, that he stands in no need of it.

His parents were Europeans, but he was born on the shores of
Columbia; and when the late unhappy war commenced,[8] I have
been told by General W—— he was not then sixteen years old;
but that his father could not prevent him from entering into the
service of his country, and as his youth did not intitle him to a
commission, for it was not here as it is in England, *officers were
wanted for actual service,* he was obliged to enter a cadet,[9] in which
capacity he distinguished himself upon several occasions, and in
the course of a very short time he was made an officer of dragoons,[10] which station he filled with the greatest honour, and in
the course of his second campaign he arrived at the rank of Captain, when he was not eighteen; and was ever afterwards looked
upon as one of the most heroic soldiers in the American army.

He appears now to be about two and twenty, has a ruddy
complexion, with full blue eyes, which are always very animated—his countenance is open and manly, and when he talks
to men he appears perfectly frank and ingenuous; but when he
addresses a lady he does it with the greatest diffidence, and distant
politeness; except it is those with whom he is very intimate, when
he is occasionally highly facetious and entertaining.

His figure is very graceful, it being about five feet nine or ten
inches high, well proportioned, and he seems to possess surprizing
activity. But he has a delicacy of manners and ideas that exceed
all praise, which in pecuniary matters reflects the highest lustre
upon his munificence.

Such my dear sister are the material circumstances that attended
our journey, which we finished in about fifteen days from the
time we left Philadelphia;[11] and as I shall have an opportunity of
writing again in a few days by George, who returns I have just
been informed for the little gold my father left in a bank at Philadelphia, I shall reserve my account of this place and its inhabitants
for my next. In the mean time if this should get safe to your
hands, you will know that we are in perfect health, and are in
other respects as well as possible, every thing considered.

We all wish to embrace you, Eliza, and once more experience that supreme joy which flows from the endearments of kindred souls! Farewell! You will naturally conclude that as George returns to Philadelphia for the money, that it is my father's intention to purchase a farm, when Mary and myself, I conclude, will appear clad in the garb, and with the habiliments of milk maids,[12] and I flatter myself we shall act our parts much better, than the feigned milk girls who often appear at masquerades. God bless you: Eliza, and remember your affectionate,

CAROLINE
P. S. Mention us kindly to
Mr. F———.

LETTER XII

MRS. W—— TO MISS R——.[1]

Pittsburg, Oct.

IN the changes of fortune, in the disappointments of our lives, but above all in that delicate and perilous situation which the letter of my dear R—— tells me that she is in, how much do we stand in need of the advice and solace of our friends?

The vivacity of unthinking youth sometimes dissipates in the allurements of variety all its mortifications. Hurried on by the splendour of pleasures, the warmth of their imaginations continues to search for that elysium, which recedes from their avidity to grasp it, as the ignis fatuus diverts the benighted traveller.[2]—But the sensible mind feels too poignantly the various ties of nature to be able soon to forget its former attachments; and though such affections may give much pain to the heart that possesses them, still it is the only esteem which is worth preserving.

We are by nature sociable beings, and the only permanent pleasure we can enjoy is by our conduct, first to deserve the love of our friends, and then to be sure that we possess it. In which situation it is impossible to be miserable—when our joys—when our pains—when our comforts,—and when our fortunes are reciprocally experienced, they are necessarily heightened or mitigated by the specific influence which a cordial sympathy has upon human actions. It is thus, that I feel all the horrors for your situation, as effectually as if I was myself the devoted victim.

I know your heart well, my charming R——, I know what were your sensations when I was in less danger—I remember (great God! the thought still chills my whole frame) when it was reported that Mr. W—— was killed at Saratoga.[3]—Who could have taken a more sensible interest in another's fortune and wretchedness than you did in mine?—Your gentle and endearing behaviour then made impressions which time or circumstances can ever expunge from my heart.—Fly then my beloved R—— to this place, and let me clasp you to my arms, and soothe you to a forgetfulness of all your past miseries.—Come and add one to our little society, who all wish for the addition of you to make their circle compleat.—I have said so much of you that Miss Caroline T——n is quite delighted with your image.—Come to these Arcadian regions where there is room for millions,[4] and where the stings of outrageous fortune cannot reach you—recollect our girlish pastimes,[5] for I now appeal to that friendship which was cemented at so early a period of our lives, and which you have touched upon so pathetically in your charming letter.—I conjure you by all the sacred ties which bind two hearts, that are in unison with each other.—I conjure you by the principles of pride, and the ties of honour, which I know you would preserve even at the expence of your life.—Remember that you have made the subject of our friendship your peculiar boast, and that after such declarations you cannot violate its sacred fire with impunity; and dreading that delays might prove dangerous Mr. W—— will send this post by his trusty old servant Terpin, for fear that in the hour of desperation you may be driven to an extremity which it would not be easy to remove; and to assure you of his cordial regard, he has insisted upon finishing this letter.

Mrs. W—— had written thus far my charming Laura when I requested I might be permitted to finish her letter.

I shall not repeat her importunities; but I well know the obligations I am under to you; and as you profess ever to deal upon
terms of reciprocity, I demand that her request be complied with;
and the more readily to carry it into execution, and at the same
time to return in a very small degree the obligations I am under
to you for your support and care of Mrs. W—— when she suffered so much on my account, and for which I have ever since
been your debtor, I beg that you will take no other notice of the
inclosed than to appropriate it to the purposes necessary to make
your generous and affectionate father easy as to his penal engagements; and if it is consistent with his safety, considering his infirmities, which I know are considerable, to remove him to this
country, where I will take care that every thing is provided against
his arrival.

Let me warn you against being fastidious, or governed by the
notoriety of some of my past follies, which has led the world to
believe that I am necessitous.[6]

I am not rich it is true;—but what I offer I can spare without
any disadvantage to my family.—You know my dear Laura, that
my attachment for your friend was always of the most lively nature, and if during the ebullitions of a heated imagination, which
hymeneal raptures produced in my fond attachment for my dear
Maria,[7] exceeded the bounds of moderation, still I was ever too
tenderly alive to her delicacy and honour, ever to suffer my indiscretions to transgress those limits, when fortune is almost irretrievable, and which never fails to lead to servility and contempt.

As I never was a man of large fortune, and as I had squandered
much of what I possessed in the service of my country, I always
looked upon this country, as an eligible retreat for such people,
whose pure and refined sense of their own dignity, would not
permit to brook the arrogance of supercilious upstarts, and purse-
proud knaves. And knowing that Maria was formed for domestic
happiness, there seemed to be nothing wanting to carry my plan
into execution but the difficulty of tearing her from her friends.
It was a severe task;—but the prosperity of my family, and the
support of her delicacy, as well as my own sensibility, demanded

my exertions. You my friend recollect the struggles she had to part from your arms, and in that recollection I presume you will find as lively a pleasure in the thoughts of returning to them, as you then experienced pain.

When the fate of two people are so nicely interwoven as yours and Maria's appears to be, it seems to me, that no argument can resist the energy with which this demand is made.

I have put myself out of the question in order that I may be considered a more faithful steward to Maria, and flattered in the hope, that you cannot make any resistance to a requisition which is an emphatical call upon the sincerity of your friendship for us, I shall begin immediately to make such arrangements, as will secure us all that felicity, which can flow from a society that will be made perfectly lovely, by the acquisition of a being so amiable.

Mrs. W—— has mentioned to you the English family—never was there a more interesting creature than the youngest—you have a pleasure to come in being made acquainted with her. In short, you will find every thing here, that a mind like yours wants to make it perfectly at ease. Such are the prayers, intreaties, and demands of your

Sincere and affectionate friends,
JAMES AND MARIA W——

LETTER XIII

CAPT. ARL——TON TO MR. IL——RAY.

Pittsburg, Oct.[1]

I Have at length had the pleasure to recognize my dear Il——ray, those sentiments in your favour dated —— which ever characterizes the warmth of your philanthropy.

Caroline is above the affectation of tenderness to dumb creatures. She thinks that the exercise of those feelings and not the parade of them, the only criterion by which we can form an adequate idea of a lively sensibility; and that however much we may attempt to acquire a surreptitious reputation for goodness, it only amounts to deceiving ourselves; for the discerning part of the world will always see through the veil, and consequently never fail to expose the hypocrisy.

I think it was an expression of the celebrated Rochefoucauld, "That persons are never so liable to be deceived as when they are endeavouring to deceive others."[2] But I am convinced Caroline was never obliged to recollect that reflection, to put her upon her guard. Her goodness is innate, and emanates from a soul which is as pure as the snow that covers the regions of the polar circle, but as warm as the genial clime of the torrid zone.[3]

I confess I admire your sentiments respecting the laws of matrimony, and have often wondered that an enlightened world permitted such barbarous codes to exist; for while the aggrandizement of families, has been relevant to the continuation of the institutions of the Goths and Vandals,[4] the sacrifice of human victims has been considered as necessary to the security of states. Great God! how preposterous is the thought?

The inconveniencies that have been felt by society, emphatically call for a reform in those institutions, which so materially concern our felicity in this world. But while I deprecate their continuance, I lament that the amelioration of manners is so extremely slow, that the tendency of this pernicious system, will yet poison the happiness of some millions of human beings, who possess all the social virtues necessary to enliven sublunary joys. And which instead of making the world a scene of gloom and sadness, would give a cheerfulness to mortals of every description, that would add a lustre to the dignity of man, of the most captivating kind.

You have touched upon the subject with such pathos and candour, that I never shall cease to admire the warmth with which you espouse the cause of oppressed women.

When I reflect upon their delicacy and tenderness, and recollect their oppressions, I feel the keenest indignation against brutish legislators, who have trampled upon sentiment, gratitude, love, and every other quality of the human soul, which has given to man the rank he enjoys in the link of the creation; and which they dared not to have done, but from the impunity power has given them, and which makes it the more base and dastardly.

To what a state of degradation is the human heart reduced, when it is obliged to have recourse to all the cunning and stratagem that it can devise, to obtain those gratifications not only essential to the existence of our species; but which flow from the essence of the human soul, and of which, were we deprived, it would place us upon a level with the brute creation.

> *Come my friend! and enjoy this delectable spot,*
> *Where Peace spreads her mantle to shelter my cot,*
> *Where Health on the wings of Zephyrus resorts,*[5]
> *To deal us those raptures unequal'd in courts;*
> *While the East beams effulgent as Time wakes the morn,*
> *To cheer my brown reapers, breast-high in the corn.*
>
> *Where at noon, O! for words to express the serene,*
> *The pencil of Claud had improv'd from the scene,*[6]
> *Where the rills blithe meandering chequer the plain,*
> *And Paradise lives for its mortals again:*
> *Where ten thousand bright objects, combin'd swell th' whole,*
> *While the music of Nature enraptures the soul.*
>
> *To this peaceable spot my dear friend come away,*
> *Leave the artful in towns on each other to prey:*
> *Here fair Liberality cultures the farm,*
> *As the sonnets of Reason she warbles to charm;*
> *Come haste and partake of this fund of delight,*
> *And friendship shall season the goblet at night.*

Here you may appropriate your talents for the benefit of mankind, and not waste them in idle speculation—here you will find a new creation bursting from the shades of wildness into a populous state;—and here is the country were the foundation must be laid for the renovation of those privileges, which have decayed under the influence of the most capricious and violent despotism. Nay which have been trampled upon, while the softer sex have lost half of that loveliness in losing their sincerity, which so peculiarly inhances the value of life.

I have mentioned to Caroline your intention of passing this place on your way to the Illinois. She was quite delighted at the thought of seeing you, and hopes that you will so contrive it, as to be able to spend some time with us.

Let me advise you to bring with you some fishing tackle, for I was in so much haste when I left Baltimore, that I did not procure an assortment by any means equal to the variety of fishing the rivers of this country afford—you will be in good time for the trout season, and Caroline is much flattered with the expectations of those pleasures which such recreation will produce her, particularly with the addition of your company.

You know that Mary is too much of a fine lady to move, except when she is compelled to do it, and as Mrs. W——'s mornings are continually occupied with her domestic concerns, Caroline has been obliged to look out for a female companion to attend her in her little excursions in the neighbourhood, in order to view the various prospects and wild beauties with which it abounds.

In one of these peregrinations in the course of this day,[7] and in which she was attended by her female companion Capt. C—— and myself upon the banks of the Allegany river, just as we were viewing some laurels that garnish an impending rock hanging over the river, two Indian men and an Indian woman came suddenly upon us.

I was at that moment pointing at a chasm in the rock which resembles the cell of a hermit; but Caroline catching a glance of them first, screamed out, and fainted.—C—— and the other lady was at that instant not in sight. I had only time to catch her in my arms before she fell.

In that situation was your friend for some minutes, regardless of every consideration, but protecting so much beauty and innocence.

Cowards are ever brave when there is no danger; but if you will forgive me, I had determined they should first pierce my body before they should profane the holy rights of humanity, in the sacriledge of murdering so much divinity.

Here I felt all the torrent of emotions which at once confounds the imagination; but intent upon nothing but shielding this fair creature, and watching for signs of returning life, I had not discovered that the men had approached close to us; and I was first apprized of it, by their asking me if they could be of any assistance to Caroline, and saying they were very sorry they had alarmed so pretty woman, for that was their expression. And then saying to me, Brother, if we have been your worst foes in war, we will be your best friends in peace, and that they were going to Pittsburg for the purpose of burying the hatchet,[8] that white people and Indians might live together like brothers.

Caroline began now to recover, and as she saw there was no danger, she immediately resumed her cheerfulness, and apologized for having been so weak. I told her it was very natural, particularly after the adventure with the old man in the mountain; and as there was not yet a peace between the Indians and us,[9] that at first, I had my apprehensions.

It was at that moment when after her animal spirits had ceased to flow, and when they were returning with accelerated quickness, that the mild lustre of so much beauty and conscious innocence, warmed the celestial fire of love into the most unbounded admiration. I felt for the first time in my life, my powers of utterance suspended—I felt in the returning pulsations of her hand, the high beating tones of Nature vibrate through every part of my frame; and in this ecstatic moment, when language was mute, and when Caroline's eyes spoke the most ineffable things, I was lost in the elysium of intoxicated desire.

At length recovering, said I, Caroline, had it been possible to have gazed upon your various charms with indifference, this interesting minute would have fixed my fate for ever. Then pressing her hand with both mine—and going to proceed, C—— and the other lady came up. I took an opportunity of relating to them the effects the seeing the Indians had upon Caroline, which I flatter myself appeared a sufficient cause for the confusion I was in. The

Indians bore testimony for the truth of what I had said, and repeating their concern for what had happened, when we all posted
together for town; assuring our new company that the fright proceeded from the lady's not being accustomed to such sights; and
Caroline added, that, she hoped to become better acquainted with
their nations, and which she should the more eagerly wish, as their
motives appeared to be so conciliatory.

Such, my dear friend, have been the consequences of my acquaintance with this charming girl. God knows were it will
end!—I dread the approach of winter, as it will prevent our walks
in future; and it will be almost impossible from the situation of
the family, for me to have an opportunity to enjoy the only pleasure of which my distracted mind is susceptible.

As you esteem your friend, fix an early period to set out upon
your intended journey, that I may have the pleasure of the conversation of a man who I have so long regarded. Hasten to this
interesting place—we all wish for you, and shall think the hours
sleep on their way untill you arrive. Adieu my friend, it is now
past three A.M. and I have no thought of repose—indeed it will
be impossible for me to sleep after so interesting an event—an
event on which hangs my future fate, until I have seen the lovely
Caroline, and heard the sweet music of her voice.

> I am truly yours, &c.
> J—— ARL——TON

LETTER XIV

MISS CAROLINE TO MRS. F——.

Pittsburg, Oct.

MY DEAR SISTER,

AS George sets out this evening for Philadelphia, I embrace
with the greatest pleasure the opportunity of complying with my
promise.

Every season has its charms, and every pleasure its alloy; but I shall ever feel the sensations of sorrow when I look toward the east, particularly as it will always afford me the image of my kind Eliza, in a distant prospective; and while my heart eagerly pants after the substance, I shall be tantalized with the shadow.

O cruel fate! how hard is the situation of poor Caroline?—Every day brings fresh proofs to her that the loss of her Eliza is irreparable.

There is something in the decrees of heaven which forbids us to examine too nicely into the object of Providence; but how can I forbear complaining, when I seem to stand insulated and deserted, at a time I want most the advice and support of my once kind protectress?

O Eliza! how shall I tell you?—my innocent heart diffuses the crimson over my face at the very thought—There was something too interesting, at the first sight of Capt. Arl——ton, for me, not to feel the most lively emotions;—but the time and place of his overtaking me, and his manner of assisting our helpless family, so conspired to make impressions upon my fond foolish heart, that it has ever since caused me considerable uneasiness; but what I have most cause to lament is of a very recent date.

Walking has hitherto formed my principal amusement, and as I had been taking a view of some of the picturesque scenes of this romantic country, accompanied by a female companion, Capt. Arl——ton and his friend, on our return I was alarmed at the sight of three of the natives, which quite overcame me; and when I recovered I found myself in the arms of Capt. Arl——ton, and frightened as I was, I could discover all the signs of solicitude and anxiety, so strongly pourtrayed in his countenance, that it was impossible for me to mistake the emotions of his heart.—His full eyes seemed to have caught the flame of sympathy, and emitted such a radiance of expression and tenderness, that I am afraid my feelings, which were in unison with nature, and ever true to the dictates of gratitude, which I felt anew for his attempt to preserve me against the fury of the sanguinary Indians, betrayed the situation of my heart; for he scarcely allowing me time to recover, he declared in the most ardent manner the existence of his passion.

Heavens! how was my soul agitated between hope and fear? but fortunately our company coming up before I had time to have spoken, which would have been impossible, my embarrassment in a degree subsided: and in that situation I returned home, and have ever since, more from anxiety than from any harm I experienced from my fright, been obliged to keep my room. He has been several times to enquire after my health, and has sent his servant much oftener.—He came this morning and insisted upon seeing me, and told Mary that it was unkind to deny him that satisfaction, after the intimacy which had for some time subsisted between him and our family; particularly since he had been my fellow traveller.—But recollecting himself he begged pardon if there was an impropriety in the request, and said he presumed I was not confined to my bed; and as Mary formally assured him that provided I was better in the evening he should be permitted to see me; I am afraid, it gave him offence. For she says he departed with signs of displeasure.

Mary is at a loss to know what to make of such rudeness, for such she terms it, and you know, my dear Eliza, that there is so little affinity of disposition between us, that it is impossible for me to communicate to her the real cause of his importunities. However, you know that she possesses all that kind of penetration which is necessary to develope such mysteries—I both fear and wish for the *rencontre* this evening,[1] but as Mary will be sure to be *present* I hope to be collected.

I find, as usual, I have wandered from the subject I intended to have began; but I know you will forgive the egotism after so ingenuous a confession; but not to have made it to you, my Eliza, would have been criminal.—Would to God it could have been oral! and when I again clasped you to my tender heart, you would be sensible how much I love you—but avaunt,[2] treason!—I will not doubt your confidence in that; but let me pray that you will continue to love your Caroline as usual.

Now for Pittsburg and its inhabitants.—How shall I talk of things which are inanimate or indifferent?—But I will rouse my senses from their torpor, for every thing here is interesting, and many of the citizens are amiable, and possess the most exalted virtues.

Pittsburg stands in the fork of the Allegany and Monongahala rivers, which intermingle their waters, and form the Ohio—Ohio, in the Indian language signifies fair,[3] and perhaps nothing can be more applicable than the name of this beautiful river.

The Monongahala is about the breadth of the Thames at London,—its current gentle,—its waters limpid,—and its banks on the opposite shore are high and steep, which are said to be a body of coal, and for many years were on fire, which exhibited the image of a Volcano.

The Allegany is not so broad as the Monongahala, but its current is much more impetuous, and from the fierceness of its aspect, and the wildness which lowers over its banks, it appears to be what it really is, the line between civilization and barbarism.[4] So that you see, my dear Sister, I have passed from the most populous city in the world—a city embellished with all the beauty that art and ingenuity can furnish, and which the accumulated industry of ages have produced, to the remote corner of the empire of reason and science.

But here are charms as well as at masquerades, operas, or the dusty rides in Hyde Park.[5]—Here is a continual feast for the imagination—here every thing is new, and when you contemplate a frowning wilderness, and view the shades or gradations of the polish of manners, which the blandishments of science has produced, and then compare this scene with what must have been the state of Great Britain, and the manners of the Aborigines of that island, when it was first invaded by the more polished Romans,[6] what a comprehensive and sublime subject is it for the human mind? How familiar does it make you with the appearance of things at an event so remote, and to form an adequate idea of which, requires a scene like this? and in what an estimable point of view does it place those geniuses, who by their labour and talents have produced the astonishing contrast?—I must pause for a moment at the stupendous thought.

On one side of us lie the wild regions of the Indian country; on the other our prospect is obstructed by the high banks of the Mo-

nongahala, beyond which lies a beautiful country that is well peo-
pled and cultivated—behind us a considerable plain that is laid out
in orchards and gardens, and which yields a profusion of delicious
fruits,—and in our front the Ohio displays the most captivating
beauty, and after shooting forward for about a mile it abruptly turns
round a high and projecting point, as if conscious of its charms, and
as if done with an intent to elude the enraptured sight.

From the various picturesque scenes with which this country
abounds, I have derived the most lively amusements; and perhaps
they have been made more agreeable from my having been continually attended by Capt. Arl——ton, which gave a zest to them,
without my being sensible of the cause.

I will not fatigue your attention by repeating the whole history
of this place; but you may recollect it was a fort erected previous
to the last war by the French called fort Du Quesne, and was
taken by the British forces in the course of that war—since which
period it has been a garrisoned town by the name of Fort Pitt, or
Pittsburg, in honour of the splendid virtues and talents of that
great man, during whose administration it was taken.[7]

The Americans keep a considerable force at this place, and as
it is the rendezvous for a great number of emigrants, who are
continually passing down the Ohio, it affords a great variety in
our society.

But I must tell you of two accomplished and amiable beings,
whose virtues and goodness would serve as a patron for half the
world. General W—— had felt a juvenile tenderness for his lady,
and had given every proof of it during his services in the army,
and after having acquired much honour at Saratoga in actions
fought against our brave and unfortunate forces,[8] he returned with
his brows incircled with laurels, to repose in the bosom of love,
after the fatigues and perils of three campaigns.

During his first overtures which were made upon the eve of
that ill-fated war, she wrote a sonnet, in which she chided him
in so delicate a manner, yet so pathetically, that I will transcribe
a part of it, as it will afford you an opportunity of estimating the
qualities of this charming woman.

"Full well dear youth,
I know thy truth,
And all thy arts to please;—
But ah! is this
A time for bliss,
Or things so soft as these.—
Whilst all around
We hear no sound
But war's terrific strain,
Our martial bands,
The drum commands,
And chides each tardy swain?"

They continued for some time after their marriage to be the admiration of the gay circles of Philadelphia; but, finding that the dissipation which the English and French manners had introduced during the late war, and knowing that their fortune was not equal to a continuation of that extravagance, which the times and their rank in society had made unavoidable, they came to a resolution of retiring to this country, which seems to be the asylum of all unfortunate people; but at the same time it has a large proportion of rational characters among them; which to be sure, is not often the case with such persons as have been the cause of their own troubles. But in the case of the disappointed persons who find their way here, the most of them are men of high spirit, who have consumed their estates in the service of their country.

The General has in addition to the graces of person, those of the mind—he is an accomplished gentleman, an affectionate husband, a fond father, a cheerful and pleasant companion; but above all he is a good and useful citizen.

Mrs. W—— appears to be about five and twenty, which may be two or three years younger than the General; and is one of those happy women whom we seldom meet in England, i.e. to derive her greatest pleasure from the General's attention, the care of her children, the free intercourse of her friends, and from sharing her hospitable board with strangers.

As to her character as a mere woman, I cannot give you a

better idea of it, than adopting that, which Cardinal De Retz has given Madam De Longueville; who he said, "had a great store of natural wit, and which was more, took great pains to refine and give it a pleasing turn.

"Her capacity which was not helped by her laziness, could never reach so far as state affairs. She had a languishing air that touched the heart more than the vivacity even of a more beautiful woman—she had even a certain indolence of mind which had its charms; because she was now and then awaked out of it by starts of fancy surprizingly fine."[9]

George is hurrying me to finish my letter.—O my dear Eliza! how does my poor heart beat? How powerfully do the ties of nature call upon me to tell you how sincerely I love you? and at the very moment when I expect—O my kind sister, George must write you from Philadelphia respecting the family. I can only say that we are all well. Adieu! I was very near omitting to mention, that Capt. Arl——ton and myself had a curious adventure with an old gentleman as we were crossing the mountain; for such he proved himself by his manners and conversation, though his garb and employment was that of a yeoman.[10] He promised to call upon me when he should return, and I assure you, such are my expectations of the pleasure I shall derive from this curious character, that I am quite impatient to see him.

God bless you.
Caroline

LETTER XV

Miss R—— to Mrs. W——.

Bristol, Nov.

HOW shall I express, my dear W——, my gratitude to you and the General for your most affectionate conduct to me and my unfortunate father?

I have read in romance, tales of the most lively and heroic friendship, and I have heard professions when the imagination has been warmed into enthusiasm equally disinterested; but I hope you will pardon me, my friend, when I say, that there is a delicacy in anticipating the wants of others, which was never more beautifully characterized than in the letter I received by Terpin.

As the wretch who is condemned to suffer for a supposed crime, after making his peace with heaven, and after having taken leave of his friends and drawn over his eyes the veil which hides from him the radiance of the world he loves, and shews to his imagination that chasm between our existence here and eternity in a manner more emphatical than words can express, and who has knelt to receive the fatal stroke, hears the sound of pardon, which he at first mistakes, conceiving it to be a seraphic voice from heaven, starts in wonder and amazement to find that he still lives, and may again enjoy the felicity of seeing some fond girl or beloved acquaintance; such was the frantic spirits of your R——— before she had half finished your dear letter.

It seems as if heaven ever meant to to punish those persons who would prodigally sport with her precious gifts. I find that my felicity is not to be compleat, and that the golden prospects which you so kindly held out to me, are banished into air—my father shedding a profusion of tears occasioned by the present, and a recollection of the many past kindnesses he has received from you, and fearing that the General's liberality might subject him to some inconvenience, determined to summon the different people to whom he was indebted, and to lay a state of his property before them, which he meant they should divide; and then, in despite of his infirmities, to remove to the country that has so much celebrity for its being the asylum of the victims of poverty; and which has all the charms that nature can produce, since it contains James and Maria W———.

But what was our astonishment when the creditors sent word that they had no demands, for that they had been paid? and desired at the same time that my father would make no interrogations, for they had received their money upon condition, that they

would never promulge to the world, who was the author that
cancelled his engagements.

Who could have done this exclaimed my father? By heavens!
these are transactions which overwhelm me! It is impossible for
my shattered frame to bear that torrent of emotions which is imposed upon a heart still alive to all the sentiments of honour and
gratitude, by so much generosity on the part of my friends the
W——s, and this friendly incognitum.[1] Come, said he, to my
arms my child, which though feeble will press you to a bosom
that is warm in philanthrophy, and beats high with manly sentiments. Perhaps Laura this is the last effort of nature; for I feel my
sensations too powerful, and I am apprehensive that my afflicted
heart will not be able to propel, that mass of vital fluid with which
it has been overwhelmed from every extremity of my emaciated
frame. But as I know you love and honour my name, let me
conjure you to find out this man, who would have been *unique,*
had there not been two W——s. Let them know that he was
sensible of the obligations he was under to him, and that he had
but two wishes to live. The first, for the sake of his only child,
whom he lamented had not a friend, but who was a long way
distant from her; and the next to make his benefactors sensible
how much he esteemed their worth and unparalleled goodness.
Here he ceased, and then pressed me to his bosom—I perceived
that nature by an effort had outdone herself, and while the hurry
of my spirits were almost in tone with his, I found before I had
time to make any answer, that the chill of death had fastened upon
his cheeks, which rested upon my distracted breast. Here let me
pause for a moment to contemplate the peculiar operations of
nature.

When a sensible heart vibrates in the ecstacy of joy or grief,
how wonderful and exquisite must be the pleasure or pain? and
how admirably are distributed those various fibres and filaments
which operate with such peculiar harmony? and how essentially
does it prove, that the finer the organs of the human body the
more delicate the feelings, and consequently the sense of honour?[2]

This may appear to you at first a strange digression; but when

I was confounded with three events so extraordinary, and when I felt a composure at this last circumstance, which made me think upon reflection that I was deficient in filial tenderness, I was induced to turn my thoughts to the operations of pleasure and pain; and I could only account for my indifference, from that equilibrium which so many sudden shocks upon my feelings had produced.

Such, my dear friend, have been the events within two days past; and as I begin to recover from the effects of that hurry of spirits which for a time left me without the power of acting, I must take leave of you in order that Terpin may return, to prevent the General putting himself to an expence and trouble for nothing.

You see my dear W—— the important task which my dear father has imposed upon me. Heaven only knows how I shall acquit myself—but be assured, that I never shall forget the obligation I owe to your happy and worthy husband. Farewell, you shall hear from me the first opportunity I can find to write.

I am your affectionate, but afflicted friend,

Laura R——

LETTER XVI

Mr. Il——ray to Capt. Arl——ton.

Philadelphia, Nov.

I HAVE this moment, my dear Arl——ton, met with General W——'s old servant Terpin, who has acquainted me with the sudden death of old Mr. R——, and that he is to set out in the morning on his return, post to Pittsburgh with the melancholy news.

This circumstance has affected me anew in the most sensible manner—you know what an amiable creature Miss R—— is? and what a series of disappointments she has met with to mar her hopes, and corrode her every felicity?

The failure of her uncle first involved her father, whose high sense of honour would not suffer the creditors to take a compromise; but it was from his frequent and generous actions that he beggared his fortune, and in the solitary wretchedness which penury produces, I had often reflected with the greatest concern upon the fate of a man, whose benevolence had so often warmed into rapture the frozen face of poverty, and turned the gloom of sorrow into a luminous cheerfulness.

It was under such reflections I determined to visit him in his retirement at Bristol, where I knew I should meet from his social heart a most honest welcome; and as I have always enjoyed the most lively pleasure from the exhilarating spirits of the charming Miss R——, I expected to spend a most agreeable fortnight in their neighbourhood, as I should be most of my time with them. But judge what were my feelings when I entered the door of that good old man. Instead of finding the same lovely Laura in the bloom of life, who used to gladden the laughing hours while her fancy was as vivid as the lustre of her eyes, now pale—her spirits quite evaporated, and sadness so marked on her cheeks, that it was not in her power, with all her exertions, to resume her former cheerfulness.

The kind old man received me with open arms. It was in the evening, and he was conversing with his usual sprightliness, when I had for some time missed Laura; and having repeatedly asked for her, I saw that it affected him. But when I entered into the supper room and found the table covered with all the usual elegance of Miss R——, and her little supper the exact emblem of her mind, I felt my heart leap with joy, at the idea that things were not so bad as I at first had conceived them.—But when the affectionate old man took Laura's hand and pressed it tenderly to his bosom, and softly said, are you not fatigued my dear girl, and after seating himself observing the tears start in his eyes, by heavens! I could not stand it.—The fire which had been kindling in my breast, now burst into a flame.—I threw down my knife and fork, and though Mr. R—— collected himself, and Laura seemed to have regained from exercise part of her former animation, still it was impossible for me to divest myself of those feelings, which this interesting evening had produced.

Come, said the friendly old man, taking hold of one of my hands, we are very happy to see you, and as you know that things are altered with us, then taking hold of Laura's hand with his other, I will candidly inform you, that my dear child has been employed preparing her little supper, for we are not in a situation to keep a maid. But said he, continuing, we are always glad to see our old friends, and when they do us the honour to brighten our lonely evenings, which as the autumn advances become long and tedious, the least we can do, is to make their time as agreeable to them as possible.—Do not suffer, my worthy friend, the sympathy of your feelings to throw a damp upon those joys which are so short lived.—For when I recollect how many millions of human beings, who at this moment are suffering not only under the most devouring poverty, but who are, perhaps, also shut out from all intercourse with their friends, nay, who never see daylight, but live unseen and unpitied; I have reason to rejoice at my comparative felicity.—But said he, as he still continued, when I take a view of the unfortunate African who is torn from his home—from his family—and from that independence when he laboured for himself, and when he enjoyed the fruits of his toil, which he kindly shared with a smiling progeny, whose infant faces, when lisping to their sire, taught him to feel that unbounded bliss flowing from the affectionate soul; now living in a state of captivity, suffering under the most tyrannic and inhuman sacrilege,[1] how much more reason have I to consider my situation happy than miserable?

Miss R—— and myself listened with profound attention to this harangue; but however forcible the moral truths it contained, they were not sufficient to cheer the gloom that had overcast the evening.

Laura at length broke the silence which had continued for some minutes, by saying, how very much was the system of slavery to be reprobated, and lamented, that the depravity of the world was such, as not to fix the most flagrant odium upon those concerned in a traffic, which disgraced human nature. And who could not be looked upon in any better light than homicides; for, that she had ever understood, the most inhuman murders had often been committed upon those unfortunate, sable beings, who were degraded to a situation no better than that of brutes; and, that cruelties even to brutes were highly reprehensible; and she hoped, some enlightened government would one day set the example of punishing Monsters of every sort.—The supper still remained untouched.

After an evening past in this way, my dear James, it was impossible for me to reflect, without feeling the most lively concern, upon the vicissitudes of the fortune of this amiable and once opulent family.

It appeared to me that inactive benevolence was little better than misanthropy; and, that my merely staying a fortnight, or even a year in their neighbourhood, could very little tend to alleviate the sorrows of a people which required a specific remedy.

It was under such considerations that I wrote a note to Miss R——, apologising for not having it in my power to breakfast with her the next morning, as business of consequence, and which had occurred since I left town, obliged me to return immediately; which I gave to the Porter of the Inn with instructions to deliver it early in the morning, and instead of going to rest, I instantly set out on my return.

After my arrival in Town the next day I sent for Mr. S——, who you know is very intimate with the family, and who, it has been said, had pretensions to Miss R——, to call as early as possible upon me, for that I had some particular business with him which did not admit of delay.

Now as Mr. S—— was one of the umpires in the settlement of the brother's accounts, it naturally occurred to me that he must be acquainted with the penal engagements of Mr. R——, who had been taken as security for his brother.

I was in the right. Mr. S—— knew every thing concerning the business, and upon enumerating the amount of those engagements, I found they were something less than the inconsiderable sum of Two Thousand Pounds.

I then told Mr. S——, which I thought was an innocent fraud, that previous to the death of young Mr. R——, and which had happened before he arrived in this country, that there was an honorary account between us, which had never been settled, and that in looking over some memorandums it appeared to me, I must be his debtor upwards of Two Thousand Pounds; and I thought if I could contrive to cancel those bonds which threatened Mr. R—— with immediate destruction, without his knowing any thing of the matter, I should be very happy; and at the same time I did not wish to appear in the business, for fear, that if it ever should be discovered it would seem like aiming at the reputation of benevolence, by first doing a good action by stealth, and then promulging it in order to acquire lustre to its celebrity from the *particular and delicate manner in which the thing had been done.*

There was something in Mr. S——'s answer, which appeared affected. Said he, this is being over fastidious. If you are debtor to the estate of Mr. R—— junior, why not pay it without cere-mony? But without giving me time to answer him, he continued with observing, that he supposed I wished the matter to be kept secret, as I had not come forward earlier in the business, which he did not doubt was adventitious, as it was very likely, that the documents or memorandums had been mislaid, and that gentle-men did not always wish to bring to light their juvenile indiscre-tions: however, said he, I will undertake it for you with the greatest pleasure, and will pledge my *reputation as a man of honour, that your name shall never be mentioned in the business.* And then said, still persisting to be heard, as old Mr. R—— was at that moment in a most perilous situation, which he knew, and that he would be arrested in a few days, there was no time to be lost.

I was quite disgusted with this loquacity;[2] but as I had broken the ice I was obliged to proceed, though I wished it had been managed by a better hand.

This man has the reputation of possessing great talents, and as I never saw so much of him before, I confess I had been deceived by the general opinion; but he appears to me a mere supercilious coxcomb, with all the pedantry of a classic,[3] without the erudition;

and with all the pomp and ostentation of a fine gentleman, he wants suavity of manners, and that civility which consists in suffering other people to have part of the conversation; and which was the more rude, as the subject agitated, concerned myself solely.

However I gave him a draft upon my banker, and left the business wholly to his management, which he has since, proved to me, was done, by assuring me the bonds were cancelled and burnt, and shewing me the receipts that he had taken; and which was a superfluous precaution, when a bond is cancelled.

You see, my dear friend, that when I expected the father of my late companion and friend would be made happy, I find he is no more. I shall write immediately a consolatory letter to Miss R———.

I begin to be impatient to know how your amiable society goes on, and whether or not your heart is in danger from the enchanting Caroline. Tell her how much I wish to be with you at Pittsburg. You know you are never to omit to mention me to General and Mrs. W———.

> Farewell.
> G. Il———ray

LETTER XVII

Capt. Arl———ton to Mr. Il———ray.

Pittsburg, Nov.

MY DEAR FRIEND,

HOW transitory are all our joys, and how vain are all our expectations? How miserable is that man whose breast is warm with the keenest desire, and receives in return, but cold civility? But how much more miserable is your friend, who had vainly believed that Caroline felt for him a tender predilection; and when he was calculating upon seeing the mistress of his heart in that elegant *dishabille,*[1] when the roses of her cheeks from confinement, blending so with the lilly, as to give that soft effulgence to her beauty which is all divine, and when the heaven of her eyes would warm into transports, feelings, already ecstatic;—then to receive a cold note that was scarcely civil?—Enclosed I send it to you, that my eyes may never behold the cruel sentence again. By heaven it is too much!—Forgive me my dear Il——ray; but it is by laying open to you the wounds which rankle my heart, that I find the pain in a degree mitigated.

A COPY OF THE NOTE

"Miss T——n presents her most respectful compliments to Capt. Arl——ton, and has the honour to assure him, that she communicated to Caroline the nature of his visit this morning, and she is very sorry to add, that Caroline was much surprized at such familiarity; and desired Miss T——n, to inform him, that when she was ready to see company, she should be glad to see Captain Arl——ton the same as any other friend. Mr. and Mrs. T——n desire to express their thanks to Capt. Arl——ton for his enquiries concerning Caroline's health."

Bower Row,
Tuesday Morning.

My mortifications at this extraordinary rebuke were such, that I was not out of my lodgings untill yesterday, when Andrew informed me, I was engaged to dine with General W——.

I will leave you to guess what were my feelings, when I had scarce entered the General's house, when the two Miss T——ns arrived, attended by Dr. K—— and C——. I involuntarily rose to hand Caroline to a seat; but as I thought she appeared as if she wished to avoid me, I turned short upon my heel, not knowing what I did, and told the General I had thoughts of taking a trip to Louisville before the winter set in. But before he had time to make me any answer, Miss T——n wondered what had been the reason they had not had the pleasure of seeing me for some time

past? upon which C———, who you know is ever aiming at pleasantry, observed, that he believed the Captain must be in love, for
all his friends had the same cause to wonder; and said he, continuing, my friend, you are in the right, a trip to Louisville, doubtless
will be of service to you, for I am told that absence is an infallible
cure for a tender passion.

This wit of C———'s, which was meant as mere pleasantry,
touched me so closely that I felt in the most sensible manner the
aukward figure I must appear in the eyes of the whole company;
and was ridiculous enough in reply, to say, what a misfortune it
was to the world, that he had not lived in those times, and in
those countries, where jesters had made such considerable
figures.——For certainly a man so facetious would have been an
acquisition to courts, *where buffoonery was mistaken for wit.*

My solemn tone would have made the whole company serious;
but C——— running immediately to Caroline, and seizing her hand,
and then placing himself in the precise attitude in which I was,
when he came suddenly upon me, at the time which I mentioned
Caroline was alarmed at the sight of the Indians; and affecting to
make love to her, then appealed to me, to know if such was not my
manner when he surprized me; but he was not satisfied here, for he
told the whole story of my embarrassment, and related my apology
with such irresistible humour, as to throw the whole company into
a roar of laughter. Caroline hung down her head; but I thought I
saw her bite her lips, to prevent her from tittering out.

This was altogether too much, and had it not have been for
the amiable Mrs. W———, I believe I should have been ridiculous
enough, to have left the company to have continued their merriment by themselves.

Well James, said she, I dare say this is not the first time you
have made love; and I declare I should have thought it very extraordinary, if a man of your gallantry could have taken those
sequestered walks, which you have done with Miss Caroline,
without in some degree having experienced the influence of the
little wanton deity, who always was the attendant of beauty.[2] And
continuing, she said,

That commerce through stormy elements was blown,
And the ruby made to shine in wat'ry zone;—
Love storms, &c.

Madam, said I. Dinner was at this instant announced. Sir, replied she, be so good as to hand Miss Caroline to the dining-room. I then endeavoured to rally my spirits, and stepping briskly to Caroline, I begged that I might be permitted to have the honour, &c. She gave her hand. Here I experienced new emotions. It was the same hand I once had pressed so tenderly; but Caroline was more lovely than ever. She was dressed in a plain white muslin gown,—her light hair hung in loose ringlets down her back, which without powder gave additional luxuriance to her neck, which was covered with a thin handkerchief; but through which the transparency of her bosom displayed ten thousand beauties. There was only a tinge of that rose left which formerly had covered her cheeks; but it was still sufficient to give animation to beauty, and which contrasted with the crimson of her lips, produced the most enchanting softness, and bespoke a soul as gentle as the dove,

Whose plaintive cooing, renovates desire,
Warms ev'ry pulse, and kindles genial fire,
Which leads to ecstacy without alloy,
Drowns ev'ry sense and consummates the joy.

I made several attempts to speak as we were passing through the passage on our way to the dining-room, without effect: at length, said I, Miss Caroline, I hope you have recovered from the fright you received when I last had the pleasure to walk with you. Sir, replied she, what could have induced you to believe that I was so much flurried at that trifling affair, as to think I was not yet recovered? I hope you will pardon me, Miss Caroline, said I, for I meant only to make a civil enquiry. Sir, she answered, with considerable vivacity, I never presumed that you meant any thing more.

We had now reached the dining room, and as the General had seated Miss T——n upon his right, I handed Caroline towards the head of the table; and at Mrs. W——'s request, seated myself upon her left hand, which was very fortunate, as it gave me an opportunity to be very officious in assisting in doing the honours of the table, which was an excellent cloak for my embarrassment, and a shield against the unmerciful attacks of C——.

I made a variety of flourishes with my knife and fork, and as often had my plate changed; but eat not a morsel.

In this kind of way I got through an hour or two; but the period was advancing when I expected fresh difficulties; for Mrs. W——, during dinner, had said to me aside, she intended we should have a dance in the evening, and that Colonel B—— had been so obliging as to promise to send the band of music belonging to his regiment; but begged I would not betray the circumstance, as from being unexpected, it would, perhaps, be the more agreeable.

If she had known the state of my mind, I dare say she would have thought her precaution needless; for I was too much taken up with the most corroding reflections to think of dancing, music, or any thing else, but the fate of my foolish passion; which I found every moment was increasing, as every look from Caroline went directly to my heart; though I could discover that they were casual glances, and made with no other difference, than those to any other person. But how silly is this expression after the note I received?

We were all about to retire at the same time, (for Mrs. W——'s parties are so composed, that the gentlemen never wish for amusements separate from those of the ladies,) when the General took hold of my arm, and said, James I want to talk to you for half an hour, for which detention I hope the ladies will be so obliging as to forgive me. Mrs. W—— gave one of her complacent nods of assent, when we were left alone.

Though I lament, said the General, that we are going to loose you, yet I rejoice that you are about to undertake a journey, which I flatter myself will afford you so much pleasure; and which will only separate us for a time. But this joy is far from not being selfish, for, said he, I have it in contemplation to remove to Lou-isville in the spring, and wish to have an account of the country from a person whom I can depend upon.—I thanked him for his good opinion.

Though I first mentioned my intention of going down the river in a moment when I knew not what I said, I had already made up my mind to pursue it without delay, in order to avoid the indifference of Caroline, which I found I could not support.

The plan of my rout was settled, and the General was expati-ating, in his usual way, upon what would be the brilliancy and extent of the empire which is forming in this part of the world; which he said would eclipse the grandeur of the Roman dominion in the zenith of their glory, when he was stopped short by Mrs. W———, who said, that we had taken an hour and a half, and which was three times as long as he had requested.—The General thought the time had been short.—I thought it had been an age.

Well, said he, my dear, taking hold of her hand, and with a tenderness which so admirably characterizes his manners to Mrs. W———, will you pardon the transgression when I assure you, that we have been planning for the promotion of your future felicity. It is always for me you know, my dear, she replied with the most charming vivacity; but if you please, I will take Capt. Arl———ton with me.

During our stay we had finished two bottles of old Madeira and had begun upon the third; so that my spirits by this time were not a little exhilarated; and in that situation I entered the ball room with more vivacity, than I had possessed during dinner.

I had called to my recollection how often the fate of states and empires had been determined by the charms of women, and how inglorious it would be, for me to abandon an enterprize, pregnant with so many visionary and inflated schemes of grandeur, for a foolish passion, that had no reciprocality; and which could only subject me to contempt, and make me an object to promote the merriment of my acquaintances. With such reflections I entered the ball room.

Where the nymphs and the swains to the pipe and the song,
  While the mirth moving dance claim'd the innocent kiss,
I saw my sweet Caroline join in the throng,
  Like a seraph just flown from the regions of bliss.

The graces had lavished their pow'rs on her form,
  Not Hebe surpass'd her, the goddess of youth;—[3]
Her smiles might the breast of Decrepitude warm,
  As her toe to brisk time beat the measures of truth.

But her eyes, ah! her eyes—recollection forbear;
  There a band of soft Loves their sharp arrows let fly;
Not a swain caught a glance from my delicate fair,
  But languishing fell like a lover to die,

Full Discord ne'er dealt her an atom of strife,[4]
  Jove gave her a charm to subdue even care,—[5]
With such worth I would finish the thread of my life,
  For the rest must be heav'n were Caroline there.

In that intoxicated situation, and with such artificial spirit, I danced alternately with different ladies, and, thus by affecting an air of indifference, and with the hilarity of the company at supper, I retired with the idea, that the whole party must be convinced the affair with Caroline, was the mere effect of gallantry, and not what is termed a love fit; and in this opinion I retired with considerable composure.

O my friend! what were my reflections this morning? How much did I reprobate a conduct so disingenuous? How much did I repent that a hasty and unguarded expression should exile me from all that my soul holds dear? But the mandate is signed, and I must obey.—All my fond wishes are withered for ever—I am going to traverse regions which are almost unknown, and hope in my solitary wretchedness to forget the object of my misery—but that is impossible—I shall wait your arrival at Louisville, and will then attend you to the Illinois—my baggage and horses are embarked. Farewell my friend. That the God of love may be more propitious to you, is the wish of your's sincerely,

J. ARL——TON

P. S. I see from my window that the boat I embark on board is under way, I shall follow in a barge, and in all probability in seven days I shall be seven hundred miles distant from the lovely Caroline.[6]

LETTER XVIII

CAROLINE T——N TO MRS. F——.

Pittsburg, Dec.

AS heroes have their defects, and as a celebrated philosopher has said, that the great Prince de Condé "with the most brilliant wit in the world, did not enter enough into particulars, nor weigh things together";[1] I flatter myself that my dear Eliza will not wonder when I inform her, how much my credulous and silly heart was imposed upon by the professions or gallantry of Capt. Arl——ton; for his subsequent conduct has proved that it was nothing more.

For when I felt the most lively expectations of seeing him, and after he had solicited, seemingly, with the greatest earnestness for such an indulgence, what was my astonishment, when for three days I saw no more of him untill we accidentally happened to meet at a dinner of Mrs. W——'s, where he behaved with the greatest indifference, and indeed, seemed rather confounded for having said so much as I repeated in my last?

But judge what were my emotions, when I heard him say to General W——, he intended to take a trip to Louisville before the winter set in—a journey I never knew he had in prospect.

Whether his friend who attended us on that day, heard what

he said to me and laughed at his folly, or not, I cannot positively say; but it is certain, that previous to dinner at Mrs. W——'s, he appeared to be very much hurt at his friend's raillery, and which gave me the most exquisite pain, as I then still believed his sensibility was too much concerned to have it made a jest of; but at which, every person present, Mrs. W—— excepted, laughed most immoderately, while his humorous companion was holding my hand, and mimicing his ardour;—this was the more torturing to me, as I abhor buffoonery of every sort, and at that moment it gave me such indignant anguish, that it was with difficulty I could keep from forcing my hand away, and which nothing but delicacy could have prevented.

He remained with the General after dinner, and did not join a little dance that Mrs. W—— had, most unexpectedly to me, prepared, for nearly two hours after we had left the dining room, when I was told by the General, by way of apology for being so long absent, and which he lamented, that it was occasioned by settling the plan of Capt. Arl——ton's journey, who would set out the next day for Louisville.

O my dear Eliza! this was too much for your Caroline. The General saw that I was pale, when he with that elegance that anticipates our distresses, conducted me to Mrs. W——'s apartment, where I was afterwards informed, I fainted. But as I found Mrs. W—— when I recovered, who told me the General had attributed my illness to dancing in the weak state I appeared to be in, occasioned by my late confinement; and insisted upon my not fatiguing myself any more; it proved to me, he had not discovered the real cause of my indisposition, as I at first had apprehended.

When I returned to the party Capt. Arl——ton was dancing with Mary, and appeared to possess the most animated spirits; for after they had passed to the bottom of the dance, and Mary was seated, he flirted with several of the ladies with all the gaiety of a man of fashion.—In short, he seemed to be perfectly at his ease, and only formal to me; for when he asked me to dance, which he was obliged to do out of politeness, it was, "Miss Caroline will you do me the honour," &c? and when I told him I felt myself fatigued, and begged he would excuse me, he replied with great briskness, by all means, Madam, for he did not doubt it, as I had not been accustomed to exercise; which you know, my dear Eliza, was the very reverse; and was the more cruel, as it brought fresh to my recollection the pleasure I had experienced when travelling over the rugged Appalachean mountains.

Heavens, said I to myself! can there be any thing in nature so barbarous as to tantalize the feelings of sensibility; and from a man who was all gentleness when I treated him with deference only; and who has now become the very reverse when I have betrayed signs of my fondness? but, said I, pride, the antidote of all human sorrow, will stand my friend and be my auxiliary—come then to my aid thou charming partner of my most sensible mortifications, and let poor Caroline rest in thy friendly bosom, for she has no protector or council but thee,—my heart overflowed, I was again obliged to retire, where I remained in the most agonizing sorrow untill the company sat down to supper; for so insensible was Mary, that it was impossible for me to persuade her to permit me to leave the company and go home. She remonstrated, and said, that it would look like affectation, and moreover it would be treating Mrs. W—— with disrespect, who had given the *ruelle* in honour to us.[2]

You know, my dear Eliza, that Mary never was remarkable for her generosity; but lately there has appeared so much distrust and caprice in her conduct towards me, that I have every cause to make me miserable, and not one to make me happy; but the persuasion when you, my charming sister, know of your Caroline's sufferings, will shed a tear of sympathy as you read over these pages, which are made quite wet with the profusion of mine.

Even my walks I apprehend would no longer appear to have charms, since I have lost the companion of my journey, and the guide to my rambling excursions. But he is gone!—and the *sombre* heaven shuts out from me every ray of comfort.

When ruthless frost with unrelenting hand,
In icy fetters binds the mourning land,
Seals up the murmuring river at its source,—
And marks with sadness all its winding course:
Kind heav'n indulge me with one generous friend,
The choicest boon, that heav'n itself can lend;
The social virtues of whose kindred heart
Can banish gloom, and cheerfulness impart;—
Expand the soul, reanimate the frame,
And give celestial bliss to mortal's name.

I then think, Eliza, I could unbosom my heart, and experience from the charms of conversation and free intercourse, some consolation and relief to my wretchedness.

Mrs. W—— is the most amiable creature alive; but she has already formed her attachments, and her heart is compleatly occupied by the General and a Miss R——, who lives near Philadelphia, and who she tells me, it is most likely will become an addition to our society at this place.

However ridiculous it may appear to you, it is true, Eliza, that I am calculating very much upon the pleasure I shall receive from the society of the old man I mentioned to have met on the mountain; and who I have been informed this morning by a young man who was with him at that time, has returned, and sent word to me, by him, that he would be at Pittsburg as early as the fatigue of his journey would permit.

Such, my dear sister, have been the rapid changes of my fortune in the perilous field of sentiment and love; and as I would not suffer you to remain ignorant of a circumstance, that concerned your Caroline, I embraced this opportunity to inform you of the whole.

I begin to think it time I had heard from you,—though I know the distance is so great between us, as to forbid my being too sanguine in a matter that must always give me the most lively pleasure; and should I be so fortunate, and you promise still to love me, I will then recover my spirits.

I write this unknown to the family, who are all well, and who only wait for George's return to take possession of the farm, after having complied with Mrs. W——'s importunities, to permit me to remain with her at this place during the winter; which I confess, though it once had so many beauties, no longer affords me pleasure; for I am constantly mortified with the projecting headland, that obstructs my view down the river.

God bless you, Eliza.

CAROLINE

LETTER XIX

MISS CAROLINE T——N TO MRS. F——.

Pittsburg, Dec.

MY DEAR SISTER,

I HAVE just time to inform you of a circumstance of the most extraordinary kind. The old man came according to his promise —and the moment he recognized my mother, who was sitting at the fire side, he exclaimed, and is it possible! she trembled—there was something in his voice that was familiar to her, but which she had not sufficient recollection to know. I entered the room at that moment, for he had enquired for me at the door—Madam, said he, behold your brother—yes! my dear sister, the uncle who we have long believed was no more, and who it was said had fallen a victim to his indiscretions, still lives, and is the same open and ingenuous hearted man as he has always been represented.

He embraced my mother, and told her that no past feuds should be related by him, for he had buried in oblivion a recollection of those personal injuries, which once had caused him so much uneasiness.—He then embraced me, and asked if he might be permitted to adopt me for his daughter.—My mother appeared as if she was in a dream, and while he first prest me to his breast, and bathed my cheeks with his tears, I felt all the joy which a long absence of two friends inspires when they suddenly meet. My mother's astonishment caused her to continue silent, untill her sensibility, like Niobe, appeared to have formed her into a statue.[1]

Strange events, said our dear uncle, at the same time seating me by his side, and taking me by the hand, chequer the path of this life; but this meeting is too unexpected for me to inquire into the particulars which were the cause of bringing you to this wild country. However, continued he, my dear girl, the pleasure I have in meeting you is considerably lessened, by knowing that misfortunes alone could have been the cause of your migration to this new world.

My father now entered the room, and as Mary had been informed of the strange recognition, she came down from her apartment, and here my dear sister, I must leave you to judge what were the sensations of the whole party. They are easier to be conceived than to be transcribed—I shall only say, that he remained with us for several days, and has promised to furnish me with the whole of the particulars respecting the affair with Lady B——; for which you know, he has been so severely censured, and which as soon as I am made acquainted with, I will transmit you.

I now despair of having my anxiety removed by hearing from you before the spring, for the winter winds now howl abroad, and the bear in caverns sheltered, neglects to feed.

> *Not a bird is heard but the whistling quail;*
> *Nor squirrel seen to sport his brushy tail.*

You know, my Eliza, that the bear is a torpid animal which sleeps throughout the winter season; but I do not know, whether you are so well acquainted with the natural history of this country, as to know that the squirrels of America, of which there are several sorts, are much larger than those of Europe, and that they have most beautiful tails, that wave over their backs in a most meretricious manner, as they leap from branch to branch in the forests, industriously collecting nuts for their winter's provender, which is carefully laid up in the hollow part of some tree, where they retire upon the approach of cold.

The quail is entirely different from those of Europe. In size they are something larger than a dove, and their plumage very much like the English partridge, from which circumstance they are called by many people in America partridge; but I should suppose they cannot be of that species, as they migrate, and are birds of passage; and what is more remarkable, they are in a degree domestic, for our long lost uncle informs me, when this country was first settled, not a quail was to be seen; but as it became inhabited, they crossed the mountain, and are now in the greatest plenty.

They resort farm yards, and all places where they can find grain of any sort; and when all other birds keep close within caverns, you hear their melancholy whistle in every part of the groves and orchards; for nothing but bad weather prevents their being abroad, when they take shelter in some thicket, and affectionately huddle so close together, that the inhuman and unsportmanlike fowler, will at a single shot destroy a whole brood of them, which always continue together until their season of love commences, when they separate in pairs, and every incubation produces a new and distinct family.

One thing I have not been able to reconcile, which is, as they are aboriginal to this continent, and are now found only in cultivated countries, how they existed when America was altogether a wild.

You see, my charming sister, that I have been getting on at a most rapid rate; but I know you will forgive the presumption of my touching upon subjects, which should be left to the sublime Buffon, or the more accurate Pennant.[2]

However, I do not know, why a person should remain ignorant of a subject that affords so much matter for admiration? and if the education of women have generally been so injudicious, as to prevent their extending their understanding beyond the common limits that custom has prescribed, doubtless it has been the material cause, why illiberal men have estimated our talents at so cheap a rate. For while we have been taught to talk of dress and the things of the day, and which have constituted the extent of our colloquial charms, few women have had strength of mind equal to burst the bands of prejudice, and soaring into the regions of science and nature, have shewn that comprehension of mind which gives a lustre and dignity to the human understanding.

You must not think this a short letter for the distance between us, when I assure you that I am hurried for time.

Tell our friends that I often reflect upon our past pleasures, and assure Mr. F—— of our respect and esteem.

I am your affectionate sister,
CAROLINE

LETTER XX

P. P——, ESQ. TO MISS CAROLINE T——N.

Laurel-mount, Jan.

MY DEAR GIRL,

I Shall not repeat the joy our unexpected meeting gave me; but I beg leave to add, that finding a niece in this remote part of the world, in an image so fair, has heightened that felicity I thought at the time was supreme. But we can only judge by comparison, and feel according to the tone or elasticity of the nervous system. And it is thus, my charming Caroline, while the youth and vigour of your constitution, which will make you experience the most exquisite pains and pleasure, I have arrived at that period of life, when the animal spirits are more tranquilized. However, I am still sensibly alive to every thing in which you can have an interest—I participate in the sorrows, the derelictions you have been compelled to make, caused you; and which at present seem to agonize a frame, that like the aspin, is tremblingly alive to every breath; and which wants the balm of consolation, to prevent its tender heart from receiving a dangerous mortification.

I have watched your emotions with an eye long accustomed

to the world, and I know that you will forgive me, if I say, I have
seen the contending passions of pride and love, agitate your tender
bosom, like a rude northern wind opposed to some limpid stream,
which ruffles its gentle current, when it seems to wish, to pay its
tribute to nature.

Stoicism is a virtue only in the estimation of fools—it is a
contemptible philosophy,[1] because it never was practised but by
men without sensibility, or when they have been hardened by
vice—because it aims at the destruction of social pleasures, and
because it saps every rational sentiment, by sacrificing real for
imaginary good.

But why should I preposterously talk of philosophy to youth
and beauty, which eagerly pants for the acquisition of joys flowing
from the current of nature?

It is from the solace of friendship that we first receive an alleviation to those pains, which the sensible and virtuous heart finds from
the losses to which it is subject. Our passions are not unlike the element in which we live, deviable;[2] and though governed by springs
that move the whole creation, they appear capricious. It is right
they should be so; otherwise our lives would be full of sameness and
gloom. Recollect that mirth and cheerfulness were the peculiar attributes of Venus.[3] Milton has said in a pleasant strain,

> *"Come thou Goddess fair and free*
> *In heaven y'clep'd Euphrosyne,*
> *And by men heart-easing mirth,*
> *Whom lovely Venus at a birth,*
> *With two sister graces more*
> *To ivy-crowned Bacchus bore.*
> *Haste thee, nymph, and bring with thee*
> *Jest and youthful Jollity."*[4]

I know how difficult it is to be cheerful when the heart is ill
at ease, but as you have taken so much interest in my history as
to request that I will communicate to you, from time to time, the
circumstances of my life since I abandoned my friends, or if you

will forgive me, rather since my friends abandoned me, I must deprecate the continuance of that latent melancholy in you, which embitters my every bliss; for it would be the height of apathy on my part to proceed in a narration that concerns myself, untill I had first removed the sadness from your bosom.

If you will add to the ties which already connect us, those of friendship, you will impose upon me an obligation, that shall be the pride of my life to support with honour.

I am growing old it is true, but I would still be alert in the service of my friend. The ties of consanguinity have their influence; but there is something too interesting in you, my dear girl, not to influence a man of feeling at first sight; and it would be impossible for the most callous, with indifference to behold the tear of sympathy beam in those eyes which are as brilliant as that torch which led to the illumination of the Grecian world in the destruction of Troy.[5]

In the struggles which beauty makes for the preservation of its virtue, that celestial gem which adds a mild lustre to feminine charms, how ineffable are the transports of a manly heart when it recognizes such a divinity of soul? How effectually does it arrest the consideration of every brave and generous man? and if there have been cowards or base betrayers, who have ravished from it that inestimable gift; what an odium has it placed upon our generosity, for suffering such paltroons to triumph in the spoils of innocence, and vainly boast of the blackest villainy with impunity?

Tell me all, my charming Caroline, for I am still strong in the feelings of honour; and if aught has been offered to you which is incompatible with your delicacy or sentiments, my feeble arm shall chastise the wretch who has dared to suspect the honour of an insulated and lonely orphan.—I must again deprecate your forgiveness—I cannot disguise my feelings, though I know they formerly laid the foundation of my ruin.—I am obliged to consider your family as cyphers.

If you will deal candidly with me, and judging by the benignity of your countenance, I know you are incapable of doing otherwise, you will ever find me consistent. Pardon this egotism—my age and experience intitles me to the privilege of being frank and open.

I send this by my mountain companion, who always seems delighted with the thoughts of seeing you; and as I know your goodness I mention it, for fear you might unintentionally put it out of his power.

It has ever been an observation of mine that much appropriate pleasure has been abridged by the forms and customs of the world; and how very unfeeling is it in those people who have it in their power to give others pleasure without any trouble to themselves, but will not do it, under that selfish idea, that there is no reciprocality; though I should suppose that genuine benevolence always found a pleasure in making others happy.

However, I believe, my dear girl, that a fine woman never was accused of depriving men of the pleasure of gazing at her beauty, let them be ever so uncouth or uninteresting.—This indulgence, I know, has been generally attributed to vanity; but I confess I have a better opinion of the tenderness of the female heart, or at least of your's, my dear, not to attribute such indulgences to more generous motives.

I shall be impatient untill I hear from you.

> Believe me to be,
> Affectionately your's, &c.
> P. P——

LETTER XXI

Miss Caroline T——n to P. P. Esq.

Pittsburg, Jan.

MY DEAR FRIEND,

THE manner in which you demand my confidence is such, as to draw from me the most candid declarations; and while I admire your sentiments as a gentleman, permit me to reprobate the cause of your misfortunes.

If Telemachus wanted a Mentor to conduct him with safety through the perilous search for his father Ulysses,[1] how much more is a friend and guardian necessary to me in my present situation? And as you have in the most ingenuous way, proferred your council and support, I shall only tell you how very much I consider myself fortunate, in an event that affords me the greatest consolation.

I acquainted you with every particular respecting the family since you left them, and if I omitted taking any notice of the material cause of the emotions you observed agitated my heart, it was not from any disrespect to you; but it was the effect of that modesty, which is not the least ornament of our sex, and of which, it is impossible for a delicate mind to divest itself.

While education has continued to fetter the human mind, untimely attachments on the part of women have been considered as criminal; and while we have been obliged to secrete our feelings from those who ought to have been our consolers and friends, we have been compelled in many instances, to search for relief from sources, that have led to our disgrace or destruction; and thus has flown great part of our juvenile miseries.

I had experienced in the conversation and company of Capt. Arl——ton, the most animated pleasure, and while I had fondly listened to his gentle solicitude for my comfort and happiness in travelling to this country, my heart was sensibly touched with that tenderness for him, which his manly behaviour had justly inspired; and when I heard the declaration of his attachment for me, which he made, and which was like the sweet music of heaven, I believed his soul was beating with the same transports, and in unison with mine.

Something has intervened I apprehend, that made it necessary he should not repeat any thing upon the subject; for it is most likely, under the existing circumstances that governed his conduct, and to which it was his duty to attend, it would have been incompatible with his honour, and the object of his noble pursuits;—for I have understood, from a casual conversation with General W——, that his object of visiting Louisiana is of the most patriotic kind.[2]

His sudden departure from this place gave me the most poignant chagrin, and nothing but a previous, and which was a feigned indisposition, could have prevented me from having discovered the real situation of my heart.

It is thus by candidly laying open to you the wounds my sensibility has experienced, I expect to dissipate sensations the most painful, and to consign to oblivion the recollection of a period the most delightful that my imagination can paint; though it was at a time, that promised me nothing but fatigue and misery.

Since you very facetiously concluded your letter with a compliment to the female heart, let me assure you, that I think it best not to examine too nicely into the motives which prompt us to acts of kindness; for, whether it proceeds from vanity or benevolence is of no consequence, while the effect is precisely the same.

Will you give me leave also to ask, since you began this sort of pleasantry, and which I think will not be *mal-apropos*,[3] what moral the good archbishop of Cambray meant should be drawn from his representing Mentor, as so very watchful over the emotions of Telemachus, when Calypso discovered her tender anxiety,[4] from the fears she had of his intended departure?

Is it that love is incompatible with patriotism or glory?—or was it that the allurements of artful women are dangerous to inexperienced youth, and that they cannot too cautiously avoid the snares which are continually laid for them?

Thomson has said,

> *"And let the aspiring youth beware of love."*[5]

Now there appears something so repugnant to nature in this idea, that I confess from deference to so great a man, I am willing to attribute such an apparent inconsistency to my own dullness, in not having a just comprehension of his ideas.

If you will not think me too philosophically inclined, I will just venture to promulge my opinion of the matter, or rather will analyze the subject.

Patriotism is supposed to be, or is called the love of your

country, and the love of glory it is said emanates from heroism. Now it is impossible for a man to love his country who is incapable of loving a woman:—and as tenderness is the concomitant of bravery, it seems, as if it would be impossible for a brave man to avoid being in love. And as genuine love is nearly allied—indeed is inseparable from honour; it also appears that a man cannot deserve celebrity for patriotism or courage, who never had an attachment for a woman.

You must forgive this rhapsody of ideas, and proceed with your history as you promised, as I now have complied with your request; and give me leave to assure you, my honoured friend, how much I am gratified in the pleasure of your correspondence. Farewell.

I am affectionately your's, &c.
CAROLINE

LETTER XXII

P. P. Esq. TO MISS CAROLINE T——N.

Laurel-mount, Jan.

MY DEAR GIRL,

LOVE is not incompatible with patriotism or glory, nor was there ever a brave or virtuous man who was not attached to women.

The construction you have put upon the opinion of the ingenuous Fenelon is just, and if Thomson has cautioned youth against the danger of love,[1] it was because he knew from the experience of his own feelings, how fascinating are its charms.

Your letter has quite relieved my anxiety. I was apprehensive, my friend, that you had been insulted by some wretch, who unlike a man had taken advantage of your unprotected situation, and offered you an indignity, because he expected to avoid chastisement.

There is something however mysterious in the conduct of your friend Captain Arl——ton; and I have my suspicions that your delicacy and partiality, has induced you to convey the circumstances in the most favourable terms. But let me tell you, my charming girl, that it was not like a man of spirit, to declare his attachment, and then to leave you without coming to an eclaircissement—a gentleman would have done it for his own sake,[2] and if his passion had been an honourable one, he would have requested it from pleasurable motives.

However, I will not add one word more, since you have made so candid a declaration of the cause of your latent sorrows—I rejoice that I have been able to draw them from you; for I know of nothing that is so corroding as the secret emotions of the heart, when we have not a friend to whom we can unbosom ourselves, and I hope you will now resume your wanted cheerfulness.

But to begin a story, the recollection of which, brings to my mind the idea of so many pleasures and pains—so many mortifications and vicissitudes, with a circumstance at the close of my life so extraordinary, that my whole faculties are for a time suspended.

That part of my life which was dedicated to the service of my country, in the army that acted under the command of General Wolfe,[3] you are acquainted with; and when you recollect, as I informed you, the corps in which I had the honour to serve was disbanded, and the officers put upon half pay, I had only that pittance to subsist upon; and as I had from habit, and from the connections I formed, fallen into a way of living far beyond my income, I experienced every pecuniary distress, of which a mind attached to integrity is susceptible.

My Lord M—— who had served in the same army, was pleased to say, my services had merited the thanks and rewards of my country, and said, he would take every opportunity of recommending me to the notice of his Majesty;[4] and he assured me so gracious a Sovereign, could not fail to distinguish me according to my talents.

Flattered with such expectations, I continued to keep up my connections, and appeared as usual at court. But after being tantalized by such promises, for upwards of three years, and after having involved myself considerably in debt, I experienced that the promises of my Lord were nothing more than the cant of courtly hypocrisy, which gilds the horizon of your hopes like a setting sun, and then leaves you in darkness to lament the loss of its enchanting rays.

In this situation, treated with coolness by those whom I thought had been my friends, I felt that disgust for the depravity of the human heart, which is natural to a mind uncontaminated with servility.

It was under such sensations I sold my half pay, with a motive to pay my debts, and retire into some part of the country where I should not be known, and there, by some kind of labour, endeavour to procure an independent subsistence, and avoid the contumacy of obligation.[5]

But as if the destinies had taken cognizance of my actions, I was diverted from that salutary resolution by meeting with Lord B——, who had known me at court, and whose estate lay in the neighbourhood to which I had retired. He seemed quite astonished to see me in the garb in which I was clad; and after many assurances of his regard and wishes to serve me, he begged that I would make his castle my home, untill he should have it in his power to do me those favours I so much merited. I thanked my Lord B—— for his kindness and hospitable invitation; but I told him I had been so often disappointed, and had been reduced to such a state of degradation and wretchedness, that I had come to a determination, by the exercise of those powers which nature had given me, and by a life of industry, to avoid in future those rocks and quicksands upon which I had been so lately wrecked; and that animated by a love of virtue, I could never again consent to fall into that state of apathy, which indolence produces, and which, when indulged to a certain length, never fails to end in certain destruction.

Lord B—— appeared to admire my heroic sentiments, and said, that it would be a misfortune, *the King should loose the use of talents so splendid and appropriate;* and if I would rely upon his zeal, he should consider himself bound to secure to me the possession of my most sanguine hopes.

Though I had determined not to suffer such allurements to divert me from my object, yet there was something too flattering

in such apparent disinterested promises, for me to be able to withstand them: and whether it was, that I found my vanity gratified
by his eulogium upon my abilities or not, I will leave you to
determine; but I *thought at that moment, he was the most graceful
orator and finished gentleman I had ever known.*

I immediately sent to London for my baggage which I had
deposited with a trusty housekeeper, and after putting myself into
my former garb, I waited upon Lord B—— at Lilbourn House,
the place of his country residence, where I was received in the
most obliging and affable manner by Lady B——.

Lady B—— after having been the toast of the town, and the
admiration of the fashionable circles, had married Lord B——
about two years previous to that æra, and still possessed all that
radiance of beauty, that gaiety of youth, and that irresistible grace,
which were the peculiar attributes of Venus.[6]

It was at that season when nature in all her glory wore her
gayest attire, when pleasure seemed to be spontaneous—It was in
that season when the animal spirits receive a glow from the genial
warmth of the voluptuous winds, which were perfumed with the
aromatic fragrance of the groves through which they had passed,
and when every thing animate seemed to be impregnated with
the seeds of love.

The piercing brightness of her eyes communicated a mild effulgence to her animated features, which bespoke a divinity of
soul, commanding at once, both reverence and esteem.

I was sensible of my danger, and said to Lord B——, that though
I considered myself much obliged by his proferred friendship and
support, and highly gratified in the pleasure of his society, yet it
would be impossible for me, to be able to endure a life of such in-
activity; and if he would not attribute my leaving him to disrespect,
I would prosecute my former resolution, which alone could secure
me that tranquility I had so long desired, and which I was convinced I could never receive, but from a state of independence.

To such reasoning Lord B—— answered, that he thought I
was actuated by the most capricious folly; for that the summer
would soon pass over, when he should return to town, and then

there would be no doubt of his obtaining for me every thing which I could expect.

This remonstrance diverted me from my resolution; but at the same time I determined to rise early, and by that means I should avoid breakfasting with Lord and Lady B——, which would prevent my being of Lady B——'s morning parties, for I ever considered those with fine women, the most dangerous; and by walking in the garden, which was very extensive, I hoped to pass my mornings in solitary study, and thus elude the shafts of love.

I continued this plan for some time; but it was impossible for me to remain ignorant of the domestic bickerings that agitated the tender heart of Lady B——. I had frequently observed her bosom palpitating with contending passions, and had as often seen the tears of sorrow, like the lustres in heaven, eradiate the divinity of her charms.

These scenes were too pathetic for me, not to feel the most lively concern for the cause of her inquietude. I found the air of gaiety which she had been used to put on, was entirely forced; and as her chagrin appeared daily to increase, it was impossible for her any longer to hide the poignancy of her sorrows.

Beauty is never so formidable as when in tears—It is then that every charm receives additional lustre, and when the heart is softened to pity, the arrows of love are mortal at every shot.

Great God! how ineffably painful is that scene when a sensible and beautiful woman, with the most delicate feelings of honour, finds herself injured, and has no appeal for justice?

Was that exquisite sensibility given to them that they should be mortified and made miserable? Can folly, or arrogance, or the presumptive madness of man conceive that the master-piece of nature —the perfection of the immense designs of the DEITY, could have been formed to become the sport of unfeeling contumely, and to fall a victim to matrimonial tyranny?—a virtuous man cannot.—

Or rather does it not prove how much they are entitled to our protection and support? and I pronounce that man a paltroon who would suffer any consideration under heaven, to weigh with him, when the feelings of an unprotected woman have been violated, and she insulted, for having pretensions to a delicacy to which a brute is a stranger.

It was under such ideas that I did not hesitate to say to Lord B——, that there appeared to be something in Lady B—— that indicated an uneasiness of mind, and I hoped it was not of such a nature as to be lasting. I begged that he would forgive me for the interest I had taken in their reciprocal happiness; but that it was impossible for me to see any person, much less a virtuous and amiable woman, miserable, without endeavouring to alleviate their distress.

Lord B—— said with great coldness, and with a sarcastic air, that it was impossible for some women to be otherwise than unhappy—for they were under the most ungovernable caprices; and that was Lady B——'s misfortune, or rather his, and which had made him apprehend for some time past, that they would lead to their mutual wretchedness.

I again remonstrated, and told him that she appeared to me to be of the most amiable disposition; and wondered if she was so different as he had represented her, how it would be possible to be so compleat a counterfeit?—He said in answer, that it was quite the fashion of the times for fine women to have fine feelings; and that it was now looked upon as quite *brutish* for a man to go to bed to his wife in a state of *intoxication, which was at once endeavouring to destroy all our social pleasures,* and rendering a man's life as insipid as the amusements of women—In short, said he, it is a direct attack upon our *prerogatives, which if we surrender, we should become the most abject and contemptible animals in the creation.*

I still attempted to reason with him, but it was all in vain, for he was decided in the opinion, that the *tranquillity of society depended upon the tyranny* which should be continually exercised over them, otherwise a female *empire would destroy every thing that was beautiful, and which the talents of ages had accumulated.*

To such absurdities no arguments were of any avail. I told him I differed so compleatly from him in my opinions, that it was impossible for me to witness the exercise of such a tyranny with indifference; and as it appeared not to be possible for me to afford any relief to either of them, he must forgive me, when I told him I should depart the next day.

Lord B—— would not hear a word upon that subject, for whether or not it proceeded from shame or design I cannot decidedly say, but it is however certain, that he was more strenuous than ever, in preventing my departure; for he said, he had expected much from my society, and had not been disappointed.

Such, my dear girl, was the prelude to all my subsequent miseries, and which I never recapitulate, but I reprobate customs of the world, that are entirely repugnant to nature; particularly those which diabolically oppress the weak. Farewell, my dear friend, you shall hear from me by the next opportunity.

I am affectionately, your's, &c.
P. P——

LETTER XXIII

P. P. ESQ. TO MISS CAROLINE T——N.

Laurel-mount, Jan.

MY DEAR FRIEND,

WHEN virtue is united with beauty, and love with firmness, they ultimately will lead to the alleviation of those distresses, in which the peculiar circumstances of fortune may have placed them.

I had made up my mind to depart in the morning, though Lord B—— had signified his disapprobation of such a measure, and even went so far, as to say, that, after his friends had understood I meant to pass the summer months with him, my sudden departure would be considered unfavourable to his hospitality and good name. But as it would have been highly improper I should have gone without acknowledging to Lady B——, how very much I felt myself honoured by her politeness, and how much I lamented the cause of that necessity, which compelled me to return to town, which I intended to have made as an excuse, I had risen as usual, and after walking for some time in the garden, I returned to the breakfast-room, where I expected to find both Lord and Lady B——; when I meant to take my leave of them —but I was disappointed. My Lord was at breakfast by himself.

I inquired after Lady B——'s health, and expressed my alarm at not finding her down. My Lord said that she was in one of her blessed humours, and as he had become so used to them, they had ceased to have any effect upon him; and then added, that he was going to have some fish-ponds drawn,[1] which would be his amusement for the day, and that he did not doubt but Lady B—— would be recovered by the evening.

I still determined not to depart without making my acknowledgments to Lady B——; and as I thought it was very likely she would be confined the whole day to her bed-chamber, which was frequently the case, I made up my mind to wait until the next day.

I had generally been of my Lord B——'s parties; but upon that occasion I declined it, alledging, I had some letters to write, which required my immediate attention.

Going into the garden, where I intended to have amused myself until Lord B—— should return to dinner, which he said would be as usual at six o'clock; I was agreeably surprized to find Lady B—— was sitting in an alcove at the farther end of the ground —I stepped immediately that way, and on my approach she seemed quite absorbed, and did not at first take notice of my advance. I halted for fear of interrupting her, and was about to turn back, when she observed me, and said, Good morning to you, Sir, I understood that you had accompanied my Lord——, who, Sophia told me, had gone upon a fishing party. I then entered the alcove, and said, that I had excused myself to my Lord, and begged that I might not interrupt her studies, for she was sitting with a book in her hand.

A deep sigh escaped her, and I felt every wound in my heart bleed afresh. She had been drying up her tears; but nature must have vent—and when the torrent of emotions have been checked, they generally accumulate in such force as to overturn the barriers of pride, and it is when the divinity of the soul floats in tears, that it creates a sensibility, which like an electrical shock, rouses into action the most dormant animation.

Her whole faculties were for a time suspended with the proud idea, that her rank and virtue would shield her from the animadversions of an invidious world; and that by concealing her wrongs, the dignity of her name would escape the obliquy of censorious fools, who spend half their lives in disseminating scandal, and calumniating their neighbours; which constitute the *primum mobile* of their colloquial vivacity,[2]—is the food of their envy, and the spring of their every felicity.

Her labouring emotions at length so agitated her tender bosom, that every returning swell appeared to threaten her with immediate destruction; but when her tears began to flow, the inward storm subsided into a serene calm, and her soft azure eye gave a mild radiance to her charms, which was love itself, robed in all its celestial splendour.

The die was cast—I stood upon the banks of the Rubicon.[3] I must either have retreated like a coward, and have abandoned the empire of the world, or by a stroke of manly courage, cross the limits of despotism, and risque from oppression and tyranny the most lovely creature upon earth.

Who is so base as to say they would have hesitated?—What, desert the perfection of beauty in distress,[4] and suffer virtue to mourn without offering it protection?

No, by heavens! when a degenerate world stands by, and beholds every day with indifference, their privileges trampled upon, and make sport of the miseries of unfortunate woman who have been driven over the brink of perdition, by the injustice of nefarious codes; shall no man dare to take their part? Who is so insensible as to be moderate when reprobating a conduct so infamous and contemptible?

No, Caroline, I did not hesitate—I fell upon one knee, and seizing her hand at the same time, I exclaimed, here will I for ever rest until I know the cause which makes you unhappy? I have no claim, to your confidence, but as a man of honour, and if you will permit me to profer you my friendship, I here pledge myself by the sacred ties of a Gentleman, in the presence of that luminary which warms into life the whole creation, but which in future will not effect me, only, as the smiles again resume their empire in your face.

Ten thousand thoughts appeared to rush into her imagination—honour, candour, and pride, seemed to contend for dominion; but the innocence of her heart, betrayed the sentiments of her mind.

I attempted to relieve her perplexity by saying, I knew the cause of her misery; and as my Lord had done me the honour to converse with familiarity upon his domestic concerns, I begged that I might be permitted to represent to him, to what a dangerous length her unhappiness had increased. She replied, that it was in vain; for his Lordship had for a series of time been in such habits of life, that it would be next to impossible for him to lay them aside. And it was from their influence, that his mind and manners were become so vitiated, that nothing short of regeneration would effect a change; for she had used every persuasion and entreaty, to divert him from the practice of drinking, without producing any other end, than having herself abused—adding, that his Lordship was one of those extraordinary men, who considered women merely as a domestic machine, necessary only as they are an embellishment to their house, and the only means by which their family can be perpetuated.

"And is it possible that your friends my Lady," replied I, "can suffer you to become a sacrifice to the tyranny of absurd customs, and the vanity of nonsensical grandeur? Is it possible that they can behold the roses fade upon your cheeks, and the spring of youth overcast with the *sombre* reflections of a heart, labouring in the elements of virtue, pride, and inclination, and not attempt to rescue you from a situation so repugnant to your nature, and so dangerous to your health and constitution?"

"How is it possible," answered she, "for my friends, in my present situation, to remove my distresses? I am bound to my Lord by the ties of matrimony, which it is not possible to dissolve, but under circumstances which are as repugnant to delicacy, as they are remote from my thoughts; and which make situations like mine the more deplorable, as there is no retreating from them with honour; and to endure them, is a thought too painful for a

quick and lively sensibility to support:" and continued, with saying, that she had made up her mind upon the subject; which was
to be as little with Lord B—— as possible, and to seek in study
for that amusement she had been taught to expect from the attention and conversation of a husband; adding, that when she was
married, she was so young that it was impossible for her to have
had an adequate idea of the nature of so solemn an engagement
—that her family had made the match from motives of convenience, in which her heart never had any concern, and that she
had been induced to accede to their importunities, from considerations of filial tenderness and duty, *without having the most distant
idea of what fatal consequences might flow from such an acquiescence.*

She then begged I would not think she slighted my friendship,
for that she regarded the candour which marked my conversations
with his Lordship, and assured me, that when I was not better
engaged, she should be happy to see me in the alcove; the place
she intended should become her summer's retirement and study;
alledging that company began to be disagreeable to her, as it
brought to her mind the innocent pastimes of her youth, and the
recollection of those dreams of pleasure, which a lively and credulous imagination had furnished.

I then told her of the determination I had taken to leave Lilbourn House, and recapitulated the conversations which passed
between his Lordship and myself; cautiously avoiding to repeat
such parts as could tend to strengthen the difference between
them, and which was the real cause why I had not attended my
Lord that day. She said it would give her concern if I should put
myself to any inconvenience on her account; and told me by way
of proof, that those disagreements would not happen again; for
the struggle I in part had witnessed, was the cause of the agitation of
a mind sensibly alive to every sentiment of duty and honour, then
labouring in the event of a determination, which she had made, and
which was, never to enter the bed of my Lord B——again; for his
conduct to her that morning, after coming to her two hours after
midnight in a state of intoxication, was too gross for a woman of
spirit and delicacy to forget; adding, that he had every chance given

him from time to time to shew his compunction, and to reform; but that he had proved, by a series of contempt and indifference, no such change was to be expected; and that she would sooner sacrifice her life than her delicacy; which would be, after the treatment she had received, a most ignominious prostitution.

In this kind of manner we passed a most melancholy day, but as I observed that Lady B—— was firm, and seemed to become more and more collected, I again relinquished my design of departing from Lilbourn House, and upon my Lord's return, which was not untill considerably after six o clock, we returned to dinner.

Permit me, my dear Caroline, to assure you, how much I love and esteem you.

Adieu,
P. P——

LETTER XXIV

Miss Caroline T——n to P. P——, Esq.

Pittsburg, Jan.

MY DEAR FRIEND,

I HAVE only time to thank you for your last favour, by the return of your Mercury,[1] and to assure you that I am trembling for your honour—I dread the studies at the alcove—I could almost wish you had flown as you had determined—I will not anticipate you; but I cannot see how it was possible for you to acquit yourself with credit in the state your heart was in—certainly it was imprudent to trust yourself, and as there was no probability of your being of any service to Lady B——, you was not only inconsiderate, but you do not appear to have had that regard for her honour, which a delicate sensibility would have inspired; for however manly and pure your motives might have been, it must have given occasion for the servants to talk of Lady B——, which never fails to spread, and thus, what might have been the effect of politeness to you, as my Lord B———'s guest, is turned by their conjectures into a disposition to intrigue; and thereby the reputation of an innocent woman is destroyed, and that peace which you wished to restore is for ever blasted by the resentment of a man, who thinks that his wife has dishonoured him with the very person who was supported by his hospitality, and who had found an asylum in his castle against poverty and wretchedness.

The severity of the winter, and the depth of the snow upon the mountain, has shut out all intercourse between this and Philadelphia, which has prevented our hearing from George, who my father has been anxiously expecting for some time past, but it is almost impossible, at present, to traverse those frosty regions, so that when I recollect George's fondness to indulgence, I think it is most likely that we shall remain in this place till the approach of spring, and

> *Until Cancer reddens with solar beams,*[2]
> *Unbends the ground, and thaws the weeping streams.*

We pass our time as agreeable as possible, considering the events that have happened.

Mrs. W——— is the most engaging woman alive, and so continually varies the few amusements of which this place is susceptible, when there is hardly such a thing as moving out of doors, that it is impossible not to find our animation cheered—I wish I had the addition of your society, and then I think I should be happy; but I will not complain if you will relieve me from the anxiety your last has produced.

We all join in wishing for a continuation of your health and spirits; but believe me no one so cordially as your friend

CAROLINE

P. S. We have not yet heard a word respecting Capt. Arl———ton. I wish he may have arrived safe at Louisville, for I am told the Indians are still at war with the low country.[3]

END OF THE FIRST VOLUME.

VOLUME II

LETTER XXV

P. P. Esq. to Miss Caroline T——n.

Laurel-mount, Jan.

MY DEAR GIRL,

MY Lord entertained us at dinner with a long account of the amusements he had experienced during the day, and seemed in no way solicitous on the score of Lady B——'s uneasiness; for indeed he treated the circumstance with the greatest *sang-froid,*[1] by saying to her, he hoped she had passed an agreeable day? to which she answered, *it had been the most tranquil she had experienced since she had the honour to be his Lady, and flattered herself, that the lesson he had given her that morning would prove the most salutary she had ever received.* My Lord replied, that he hoped it would, and said he rejoiced he had unintentionally been the instrument of doing so much good.——

Lady B—— had hitherto appeared serene and firm, but this raillery of my Lord's brought tears into her eyes, which when I had perceived, I told her, that was not consistent with the assurances she had given me; and by turning the conversation, my Lord became hilarious, and when Lady B—— retired, I confessed to him my reasons for not attending him that day.——He said, with seeming indifference, he thought if I had been with him I should have enjoyed much sport, and upon my attempting to renew the conversation, he begged I would not take any notice of Lady B——'s humours,[2] for, she certainly was the most capricious woman alive, and if he had nothing else to mind, he should be continually pestered with her temper.

I begged him not to treat with so much levity a subject in which his honour, his humanity, his felicity, and his name as a gentleman were so materially concerned.

I then told him that Lady B—— had promised from that day,

she would endeavour to resume her cheerfulness, and in future
would not suffer her mind to be agitated by domestic feuds;—
but without mentioning what concerned his bed; as that would
have been highly indelicate as well as improper; and after depre-
cating the consequences which might flow from his indifference
and inattention, I conjured him by all the ties which a gentleman
holds sacred, to recollect, that the violation of any one of those
principles would fix an indelible stain upon his name, which in
the eyes of virtuous men, would never appear to be removed.

After moralising for some time in that kind of way, my Lord
burst into a fit of laughter, and said, he believed I had been a man
of more spirit, than to be affected by things which were so ridiculously nonsensical.

I was convinced by this last stroke, that Lady B——— was in
the right, and that his Lordship must be incorrigible; and in that
opinion I was as cheerful as the impressions which the adventures
of the day had produced, would permit.

We sat as usual after dinner;—Lady B——— having sent our
coffee from her dressing-room. And as my Lord was a *bon compagnion* over a bottle,[3] I should have drowned in wine the recollection of misery, if it had been possible to have forgotten, that
at the very moment, when we were indulging in all the extravagance of that selfish amusement, Lady B——— was brooding over
those unpleasant thoughts, which had been generated in consequence of my Lord's contumely—and who was left to pine in
secret—lost to all those social pleasures, for which the hearts of
amiable women are so admirably formed,—and whose mortifications are consequently so much more poignant.

It was under the influence of such reflections, abstracted from
more tender sensations, that I passed a most unpleasant afternoon.—

It was late before we retired to Lady B———'s dressing-room,
and not until the servants wanted to lay supper. When we entered,
she was sitting reading the Moor of Venice, and at that moment
the passage where Iago says,

"Trifles light as air
Are, to the jealous, confirmations strong
As proofs of holy writ."[4]

And as she was much struck with the idea, she appealed to my Lord, to know, if he did not think in that instance Shakespear, that great master of nature, had indulged his imagination, and exceeded the limits, to which the most wicked design, and the most credulous, are carried by their jealousy. My Lord answered in the affirmative; but in such a manner, as proved he did not attend to what had been said, and without farther ceremony threw himself down upon the sofa, and in less than a minute he was sound asleep. In that situation I was left with Lady B—— until supper was announced, which was nearly an hour after we had entered the room.

I found that she was perfectly tranquil, and that the exercise she had received from the several turns we had taken during the day, upon the grass walk, and the calm which had succeeded in her bosom, tended to make her countenance more than usually animated.

"One brilliant eye-ball shot a beam of fire,
Another languished blue as æther's light:
Here dignity and heav'n his touch inspire,
There dimpling, laughing beauty charms his sight."[5]

I felicitated her upon her firmness;—for which she thanked me with a most complacent affability; and then entered into a conversation with me, upon the subject of the Moor's suspicions of Desdemona's virtue, when she appeared decidedly of opinion, that it was not possible, there ever could have been such a monster as Iago.

Such was the innocence of a heart, which unhacknied in the ways of the world, and incapable as she was of dissimulation, I could not enforce upon her mind, a belief that such base arts were

frequently practised upon men of warm passions for the most atrocious purposes; and which had frequently been the cause of driv-
ing women of honour to extremes, that ended in the most
lamentable consequences; and which was a most emphatical call
upon all men of sentiment and delicacy, to be extremely cautious,
not only how they yield to such insinuations, but which proves
how necessary it is to prevent their tempers from discovering such
suspicions; for it is not possible for a woman of spirit to brook
reflections injurious to the purity of her honour.

After my Lord was roused from his slumber, and had arrived
in the supper-room, he began with his usual volubility to expatiate
upon the excellence of his dogs, the breed of his hunters, and the
various pleasures that were to be derived from such manly amusements as coursing and hunting: and while the most interesting
being in the world was again reduced to a cypher, if it is possible
for love itself to be a cypher, I was forcibly struck with the contrast
of ideas, between what was passing, and those of a charming
woman, who added to a most lively sensibility, the most brilliant
wit and captivating vivacity, which kindled into rapture the admiring senses; for she seemed to breath sentiment, talked like Minerva,[6] and looked like the Queen of Beauty;[7] so that my wonder
was for a time suspended by my indignation, excited by the
thought, that the prevalence of manners, should not only strike at
the root of the colloquial happiness of rational beings, but which
substituted the practice of *je-june,* and anomalous conversations,
in the place of brilliancy of thought, and elegance of expression,
and which imperceptibly, when fine women have their share of
it, gives the most lovely polish to manners, and zest to the charms
of society.

When I speak of wit, my friend, I do not mean that flippancy
of expression, which is too often mistaken for it. And as that great
man Frederic II. king of Prussia,[8] has given a definition of wit,
which ought to be written in letters of gold, and for fear that you
may not have met with it, I will transcribe it for you as well as
my memory will permit.

"When the wit is too pert it makes us guilty of folly, but when its ardour and rapidity are under the guidance of reason, when it is prompt to conceive, quick in combining, and brilliant in reply, the man of wit in the general opinion, is superior to other men."[9]

Lady B—— retired a little before twelve o'clock, and as my Lord had drank much during the day I presume, besides what he had taken after dinner, he was unable to sit so long as usual; so that I was relieved from that *ennui* which proceeds from being compelled to attend to the conversation of a person, when it is not in the least interesting; and particularly so, when the mind is totally absorbed with considerations of the most sensible kind.

Heavens, said I to myself, when I had got into bed, to what a state of degradation and misery, have the manners of the world reduced thousands of amiable and sensible beings?

When I contemplated the graces of the spring, which yields so many sweets, when impregnated with the fragrance of the riches which fair Flora,[10] in all the effulgence of her reign diffuses. When I brought to my imagination the blooming rose that converts the morning dew into sparkling nectar—when I figured to my mind the gay scenes of a luxuriant verdure which gives enchantment to the mild evenings of the vernal season, when universal love seems to pervade the whole creation.—While I admired the myriads of orbs that decorate the heavens, and revolving in perfect harmony, shoot their mild beams, and illumine the vault of the high empyrean regions in their infinite progression; how ineffably beautiful and sublime, said I, are the works and operations of nature? and how preposterous have been those manners, which have destroyed the pleasures that flow from the benign goodness of a bountiful *Creator?* and, what a shameful sacrilege have we committed against heaven, for having destroyed those exquisite joys which are spontaneous?

Judge, my Caroline, what were my sensations in my then state of mind, after I had just been the spectator of the most animated beauty retiring in sadness, through the gloom of night, to reprobate that despotism which surrounds you with all the variety and elegance nature and art can produce, and then interdicts its appropriation? It was too cruel—And when the vigils of the night warned me of the approach of day, which peeping through the curtains of the dark, lighted my apartment; I rose to revisit that alcove where I had passed the preceding day in all the transports, the emotions of love, honour, pity, sorrow, and indignation can excite.

I had passed a long and solitary morning without a thought about breakfast, when I observed Lady B—— approaching the alcove, attended by Sophia, who was carrying her books—she appeared to be perfectly tranquil and composed; and after I had enquired how she had rested, she began to converse with more than her usual vivacity upon the subject of the honest Moor, as she called him, and still seemed to think it was impossible there ever could have been such a character as Iago. Pray, said I, did you never read Othello before? Oh yes! often, she replied; but confessed never with attention; and could not give a reason why she had never admired a tragedy which was one of the most celebrated that Shakespear ever wrote; for no person could have a higher opinion of his genius and beauties. I told her there appeared something in the character of Iago so inhumanly wicked to an ingenuous mind, that even disgusted it with the man who represented the character upon the stage, and every thing which is so unnatural, certainly must give pain, instead of affording pleasure; but that it was not from a superficial view we could form an estimate of a work of such an exquisite nature as the play of Othello;—and with her permission I would begin and read it through, and if she would watch the incidents, and observe how wonderful are the concatenation of circumstances which work upon the credulous and honest heart of the Moor; and that when she entered into the designs of a wicked man, and noticed the nice gradations by which the secret springs of the human mind is moved when impassioned by love and jealousy, she would not only see how perfectly Shakespeare understood the human heart, but she would discern the probability of the effects which the designs of Iago produced. Lady B—— thanked me, and promised to attend—I went on—she became so absorbed with the story, that when Othello said "put out the light and then—put out the light"—she fainted as compleatly as though the circumstance had been real and present to her view.[11]—I had caught her in my arms when a footman started upon us, and said, that my Lord sent his compliments to me, and wished I would take an airing with him in his curricle.[12] I desired him in answer, to tell his Lordship that I was reading for Lady B——, and begged that he would excuse me;—For it would not only have been a breach of politeness to have broken a prior engagement, but it would have been inhuman to have left her even when she had recovered.

Upon Lady B——'s recovery I told her I was extremely sorry for having induced her to have been so very attentive to so interesting and pathetic a tale, but if she would forgive me, I would atone for my fault by reading more cheerful subjects, and as I was going to take up Don Quixote,[13] which was among the books that Sophia had brought, she said, I had not been to blame, for she had taken such an interest in the fate of the unfortunate Desdemona, that she thought she beheld the Moor ready to commit the fatal deed: and if I would excuse her, she would take a few turns upon the grass walk and endeavour to recover her spirits.

The circumstance of the message I had forgotten to mention to Lady B——, and as her cheerfulness by degrees returned, we conversed upon a variety of subjects without hinting, in the most distant way, at the preceding day's conversation.

Never, my friend, was I more charmed—never did a mind discover a more sacred regard for all the principles of honour and humanity—never was there a soul more replete with that celestial fire which glows with purity and virtue—I was intoxicated with admiration, and in that ethereal element of bliss, which gilds the fleeting moments as they pass, I thought the sun had scarcely passed its meridian,[14] when Sophia came to inform Lady B—— that as dinner would be on table at six o'clock, there would be very little time for her to dress, and that Sir J—— C——, and the Hon. W—— H—— were to dine with my Lord.

Such, my charming Caroline, were the events of the second
day of the alcove, which the letter I have this moment received
from you tells me has excited your fears; and if you will permit
me, I will answer it first, and will then proceed agreeable to my
promise. I am,

Your affectionate friend,
P. P——

LETTER XXVI

P. P——, Esq. to Miss Caroline T——n.

Laurel-mount, Feb.

I Experienced the most lively pleasure, my dear girl, to find by
your last favour, that your spirits are in a degree tranquillized, and
that you are so tremblingly alive to the feelings of honour and
the sacred ties of hospitality.—

But while I admire your extreme sensibility, I must assure you,
that there could have been nothing on my part, which appears
like a breach of confidence.

I had communicated to Lord B—— my sentiments respecting
the distresses to which women of honour and delicacy are subject,
from the tyranny of those customs which prevent a friend from
offering to mitigate their sorrows by attention, and that respect
which are so peculiarly soothing to the feminine mind. He must
have known it would be natural for me with such sentiments to
take an interest in Lady B——'s inquietudes.

I confess I did not attend to the prejudices of the world, as I
looked upon the happiness of Lady B—— superior to every other
consideration; and if I could not expect there would be a reciprocal pleasure in my attentions, I conceive that, however selfish
the object may appear, it was the more laudable.

"As to what is called honour, there is a material distinction
between that which is founded on the opinion of the world, and

that which is derived from self-esteem. The first is nothing but the loud voice of foolish prejudice, which has no more stability than the wind; but the basis of the latter is fixed in the eternal truths of morality";[1] which is regulating our actions according to the undeviable obligations that result from the nature of our very existence, and the relation of life, whether to our *Creator,* or to our fellow creatures; which principles appear to me to comprehend the whole of human virtues; and a strict regard to such, is the only criterion by which we are enabled to estimate the purity and judgment of any human being.

The instability and very genius of human nature has, to be sure, at all times made political laws necessary for the government of civil society. But unfortunately, while manners have been in a gradual state of improvement, individuals have been the sufferers; and thus it has happened that the weak have been continually oppressed by the caprice or tyranny of inhuman institutions; and untill laws are made more conformable to the principles of morality, and the unalienable privileges of our nature, the voice of the world will continually decry the conduct of those who are governed by the pure and celestial precepts of virtue, in contempt of that prejudice which has no rule or reason to direct it but the crude customs of a half-civilized world.

Let us for a moment take a view of man, artificial as he has been formed, imperious, sullen, and weak, ever aiming at the establishment of laws to suit his own immediate convenience: and if civilization and the polish of manners have in a degree smoothed the barbarous institutions of our forefathers, and given a due rank and support to women who have been happily married, in how many instances have their despotism reduced many women of exalted characters to a state of degradation which is shocking to delicacy, and which has placed an odium upon human dignity, as flagrant as it was shameful?

It is when laws or customs interfere with the duty we owe either to GOD or to our fellow creatures, that we are constrained, from a principle of honour, to resist their influence:—For thus it has happened, that having shamefully too long neglected to correct their despotism; what are called the factitious duties of society, have led to the most detestible sacrilege against nature, and call more emphatically aloud for an amelioration in such monstrous practices, than could the most brilliant dissertation upon the subject. The world has slumbered too long.

The first aim of society is to protect every individual in the enjoyment of those absolute rights with which they were invested at the *creation*—which were not only antecedent to the formation of states—which are not only paramount, but which are immutable, and cannot be revoked or abridged by any tribunal upon earth, farther than it is absolutely necessary that they should be surrendered for the order and benefit of society; and therefore it ought to be the business of every government, in the formation of laws, to regard both the dictates of reason and morality—indeed they are coexistent and inseparable—they are the gifts of GOD, of which no human power can deprive us; *but as we degenerate under the influence of a base jurisprudence.*[2]

> "*Ye tyrants entrusted with power,*
> *Who often the helpless oppress,*
> *'Tis yours to presume for an hour,*
> *It is their's to think on redress.*"[3]

I have been insensibly drawn into this length upon this subject, my dear Caroline, by that repugnance I feel to a system so very reprehensible and while I deprecate its effects, I fear, that nothing short of a total difference of education will be able to prevent them.

Will you forgive me if I digress, and offer my sentiments upon that important subject—a subject which there has been so much said upon by men of first rate talents; but unfortunately for the world, they have either been too fond of perfecting their theoretical systems, or of displaying their ingenuity—The subject yet requires to be simplified, and perhaps a few years experience, with the aid of the books already written upon the subject, will do more good than would the most elaborate production.

Rousseau, who went to an extreme in almost every thing which he wrote, so he did in his Emelius;[4] but, still I think the evil effects arising from bad education must every day tend to convince all rational minds of the necessity of teaching youth, however exalted their rank in life, or splendid their prospects of fortune, some appropriate art or employment which would not only accustom them to the habits of industry, but which might become useful to them in case of a change of circumstances. No human being can be exempt from the contingencies of fortune.

There should be play given to the genius and passions; for the greatest evils in life flow from too great a coercion upon the minds of youth—For which reason they should be made familiar with every thing that is not vicious.—

It is from too great a restraint upon the infant mind, that it is led to suppose something magical in whatever it may be prohibited; while mystery never fails to inflame the passions—prompts it to indulgences clandestinely, when the natural consequences are, the practice of tergiversation,[5] falsehood, perfidy, and the whole train of vices natural to a sanguine and vigorous constitution, if once it transgresses the bounds of a narrow and injudicious education.

Let youth be taught to distinguish between right and wrong,—virtue and vice, and their concomitant rewards and punishments—Let them be shewn the effects from certain causes, which are incidental to us as moral beings, and that it is first necessary to make themselves useful to society, before they can expect to be esteemed.

With such instructions it is most likely the world would regain that sincerity they have imperceptibly lost, from the influence of a system so much at variance with reason and morality; and which has been productive, at least, of half the evils to which we are subject.

I will say nothing of the education of girls, for the amendment of the one, would naturally lead to the amelioration of the other—And if women have in some instances discovered vices incompatible with delicacy, I am convinced they were foreign to their nature, and proceeded from the unnatural restraints under which they live in every country upon the globe.

Every thing has been perverted—and while the tyranny of custom has substituted duplicity for candour, the crude sentiments of cunning have destroyed that genuine felicity which flows from the genial current of the human heart; and thus the blandishments of our pleasures have lost that fascinating charm which so peculiarly enhances the value of our existence—

While we have been governed in our amusements by ridiculous forms, and directed by shameful insincerity and subterfuge in our manners and conduct, we have omitted to

> "*Mark how spring*
> *The tender plants, how blows the citron grove*
> *That drops the myrrh, and what the balmy reed;*
> *How nature paints her colours; how the bee*
> *Sits on the bloom extracting liquid sweets.*"[6]

And while tumultuous pleasures have continued to destroy that lively sensibility which characterizes the rational and innocent heart, a depravity has become so general, that it has commonly been mistaken for turpitude; and thus hardened, the world has become incapable of receiving that happiness in retirement which flows from innocence, virtue, and beauty; and which felicity is heightened with the transporting consideration, that it is not dependent upon the caprice of fortune, or the adventitious aids of art.

You must forgive, my dear friend, the length to which I have digressed; for whenever I touch upon a subject which brings to my mind the recollection of so many disastrous events, that were the result of the depravity of the times, I cannot help reprobating a degeneracy so baneful to the happiness we are by nature formed to experience. God bless you, my dear girl, and permit me to assure you, that I love you more than ever, if possible, for your attachment to virtue and honour.

Adieu,

P. P——

LETTER XXVII

Miss Caroline T——n to P. P. Esq.

Pittsburg, Feb.

MY DEAR FRIEND,

INSTEAD of allaying my fears your two last letters have increased them—I now fear that you were aiming at the practice of a virtue, that is not in the power of any human being to accomplish.

It was a strange omission not to inform Lady B—— of my Lord's message—it was leaving her ignorant of a circumstance which might lead to the most fatal consequences—consequences that might prove to her ruinous past redemption; and which situation, knowing my Lord's disposition better than you possibly could, she was better qualified to judge of the propriety of the answer you returned to Lord B——'s message. It was a strange punctilious regard to etiquette, in which you seem to have acted in contempt of the established opinions of the world—I know your refuge—you will plead the influence of your passions; but that in my opinion ought to have put you more upon your guard. How could you expect, or with what face to meet Lord B—— at dinner, after having spent the whole day with his Lady in rural and solitary study, and after his servant had beheld her in your arms, and with the cause of which, you did not deign to desire him to acquaint his Lordship; and of course it was leaving the servant to make his own animadversions upon, and suffering him to have an opportunity of insinuating to his Lordship things of the most wicked nature, and which are seldom omitted in cases of that sort.

I consider your last letter a mere piece of ingenious sophistry, wherein you have addressed yourself more to the passions than to reason; and by calling in the auxiliary aid of the privileges of nature, you appear to triumph in the advantage you have of the argument; without ever recollecting that when men entered into society, they gave up part of their liberty, the more effectually to secure their more important rights,[1] and thus it is, that every good citizen imposes upon himself the talk of *conforming to those laws which the community has thought proper to establish, and which cannot be violated without the utmost danger to society.*

However repugnant the laws respecting matrimony, may be to the codes of nature, is of no consequence, compared with the tranquillity, safety, and happiness of society; and if we compare the unnatural practices of the Egyptians, and the loose customs of the Greeks and Romans, with the stable practices of the moderns, how much more reason have we to applaud the wisdom of our legislators than to reprobate their folly?

Contrast the situation of a woman of honour now, with what it was when a man had nothing more to do to repudiate his wife, than to signify to her his intention.

It is true that this facility of being divorced was in the extreme among the Romans. But I apprehend the difficulty married people have of separating from each other according to the existing laws, must operate to induce them to be more anxious to continue agreeable to each other; for it is impossible for me to conceive that any prudent and rational man and woman would not attend to things, upon which must depend their future happiness or misery. No laws perhaps, are equal to correct the incorrigible habits of the depraved and wicked.

It is not a little surprizing that you, who have been accustomed to observe the fluctuations and caprices of the human mind, should not fear from a practice of less difficulty in obtaining divorces the confusion it would produce.—It appears to me, that it would have an effect equal to offering prizes to adultery, and instituting asylums for the incontinent.[2]

To be virtuous it is not sufficient to talk of it, or to define in what it consists.—It is practising those precepts which are deduced from those invariable morals you have so well described as the basis of all virtue, which constitutes the man of honor.—It is a talk imposed upon us from the very nature of our existence in a

state of society; and it is from the imperfections of human nature
and the extravagance of our desires, that virtue in the whirlpool
of passion, has an opportunity to triumph.—Divest us of these
desires or passions, and an equilibrium of animation may secure a
negative, but it never can an heroic virtue; and thus it has happened that while chastity in many instances has been celebrated
for its integrity, and admired for its spotless fame, benevolence,
the warmest of all the qualities of the heart, has passed unnoticed,
when it has been tarnished with the loss of that immaculate purity,
which every woman of pride and honour values as inestimable.

If society have experienced, or rather individuals, the inconveniencies which flow from the existing laws respecting marriage,
I am convinced that it has proceeded more from the manner and
depravity of the age, than from the nature of the institutions themselves; and as far as you think education would tend to ameliorate
the condition of women, I perfectly agree with you;[3] and when
I contemplate the situation of many of those unfortunate creatures,
whose miseries are too shocking to think of without feeling the
keenest emotions of sympathetic distress, I most fervently pray,
that something may be done to risque from desperation and infamy, those friendless beings, who, after they become hardened
in vice, and emaciated with age and disease—lost even to the pity
of the world, which to be in, is a situation for a human being the
most unfortunate; and not until it is done can I think the actions
of legislators are so humane and generous, as the wisdom and
magnanimity of a civilized and intelligent world requires.

It is impossible for me to quarrel with an amiable friend for a
mere difference in matter of opinion: but I think I behold in your
sentiments, principles the most dangerous to the safety of society
—principles which strike at the root of domestic quiet—principles
calculated to engender distrust, and to produce continual and use-
less separations, which would at once destroy all that harmony,
and that beautiful system, which has been productive of so much
decorum and blandishment to manners.[4]

The brutish behaviour of those men who neglect delicate and
sensible women, and suffer them to live insulated as it were, or

to seek a refuge in the society of others, are the greatest enemies to conjugal bonds: and from that source, doubtless, have flown the greatest inconveniencies; but that is the fault of men, and not the laws which respect matrimony; and proves how very necessary it is for parents to be particular, how they encourage their children to marry men, when there is not an affinity of age and disposition between the parties. It is an attention of the highest consequence, and nothing perhaps, can be more unnatural and wicked, than parents suffering their children to continue to live with men they have married, when they cease to treat them with respect and tenderness; but when the despotism of which you complain, has been practiced, it is inhuman to suffer a child to fall a victim to its influence.

Your opinions appear to me to be calculated to promote domestic feuds, rather than to alleviate, or reconcile the differences which may result from opposite dispositions; for when you should have been endeavouring to bring my Lord B—— and his Lady more frequently together, and shewing them the necessity of a mutual desire to please, for which purpose both sides must relax in that tenacity of opinion, which, when carried to a certain height, or under particular circumstances, becomes obstinacy, you determined to carry into execution a plan, the object of which you had already fixed your heart upon, and which was nothing short of making a conquest of Lady B——'s heart; for you say, that you "stood upon the bank of the Rubicon,[5] and that it would have been cowardly to have abandoned the empire of the world"; which is a virtual acknowledgment that you had already conceived a design, not so much to risque Lady B—— from oppression, as to indulge the influence of her beauty which so powerfully operated, that you could not resist its impulse, nor the power of those feelings, which told you she might be yours, if you would hear the tales of her misery, pity her distresses, and sooth by the influence of sympathy, the inquietudes of her tender heart.

It is in such moments, that the attraction of sympathy, like the magnet that touches certain bodies, draws it by its specific quality, and holds in bondage by magic, as it were, the whole powers of reason.

You could not have been so great a novice (pardon the expression) in the art of love, as not to have seen the dangerous and
slippery ground upon which Lady B—— was standing: and thus
seeing that she stood upon the brink of perdition, it would have
been more prudent, and more like a man of honour, if you had
conducted her back to that flowery plain from which she had
been driven by the tempest of resentment, instead of attempting
a leap, which was not in the nature of things for her to make
with safety. Besides, it was ungenerous;—for while the prejudices
of the world would forgive the rash action on your part, Lady
B—— must be condemned as infamous, which is more shocking
to a woman of honour than even death itself.

Such, my dear friend, have been the sentiments and reflections
your letters produced, and as they were too powerful to be suppressed, I was constrained to give them with all the candour your
good sense, but above all in a manner that friends are intitled to
expect one from another; and I have only to add, that I wish most
sincerely you may be able to justify fairly, without subterfuge or
mere ingenuity, a conduct apparently so very reprehensible. Believe that I feel the most lively expectations, and that I still am,
and wish to continue,

Your affectionate friend,
CAROLINE

LETTER XXVIII

P. P. Esq. to Miss Caroline T——n.

Laurel-mount, Feb.

MY DEAR GIRL,

I HAD scarcely answered one of your letters, before I received
another of the same complexion.——

How ineffably delightful are the sentiments which flow from
the purity of your heart? Quarrel with me! no by heavens, I would

sooner cherish your errors, in hopes that the maturity of your judgment would remove them, than I would loose the esteem of a heart so delicately alive to the sentiments of honour.

If I had drawn my conclusions, or formed my conduct upon an idle theory, which might have had a selfish basis, I should have considered my conduct as highly ignominious;—for I perfectly agree with you in the opinion, that it is not the fine precepts of moralists, or the elegant and patriotic declamation of the states-man, that constitutes the good or virtuous man; it is to be sure, a conduct of a more exalted nature than a mere profession of words; but it is founded upon the nature of man and things be-longing to him as a reasonable being, uninfluenced by prejudice, and divested of that littleness, which is continually under the con-troul of fear, the most degenerate and dastardly of all human passions.

Education and the habit of living and acting, have given a sov-ereignty to man which has long been exercised in contempt of those generous sentiments, which uses its power with more lenity, because it is superior.

Nature has given a superiority to man over woman in point of strength, and consequently an activity, that fits him, not only for the more difficult parts of sublunary duty, but necessarily promotes that ascendency of power, which the exercise of talents produces; *and it is thus that the barbarous codes of a savage world, have continued to oppress and restrain the acts of volition on the part of women, when the most licentious bounds on the part of men, have found impunity from the prejudices of the world.*

An ingenuous and liberal system would afford ample protection to their delicacy, and by giving reciprocity to conjugal engage-ments, it would interdict the practice of those cunning and base arts to which a timid prudence ever has recourse;—which first leads to an incontinency in the exercise of resentment,[1] that is frequently considered as retaliation; and then hurrying over every barrier of moderation, seeks in vengeance for a compensation of the deprivations which despotism has produced, untill every rad-

ical vice compleatly destroys that elegant softness, with which nature has so exquisitely formed the female heart.

The most amiable women must be susceptible of injuries;—
except we can suppose them inanimate, which would be paying
a most injurious compliment to that lively sensibility that alone
can lead to the practice of virtue, and which constitutes the brightest part of feminine excellence.

It is in that situation, when injured beauty, and insulted virtue
mourns in secret, that it is driven to extremes; and when the base
betrayer, seizes the opportunities which a brutish tyrant affords
him, that women of honour are hurried into the gulph of ruin.

When every indulgence and opportunity has been given to a
depraved man to reform, after he has shewn the most obstinate,
incorrigible, and insensible habits;—and after the health of a
woman has been materially injured by living in a state of continual
anxiety and uneasiness, and which has not been a little accelerated
by that oppression which is so corroding to a bosom, formed for
love and society, when they have not a friend to whom they can
unfold their hearts; it is then not only a weakness not to dare to
hear them, pity them, and protect them, but it is both cowardly
and inhuman.

The empire of the world is the dominion of beauty, enthroned
in the bosom of reason and virtue; and whether it is to be left, to
be destroyed, or decay in the atmosphere of sorrow, or to be
trampled upon by the rude dogmata of ignorance; or whether it
is to be guarded, and its fragrant blossoms made to disseminate its
odours, and extend its fair germ, are considerations in which no
rational man can hesitate to determine.

What, is beauty and innocence not only to be depressed, but
is it to be made to pine in secret, languish in solitude, and expire
unnoticed and unpitied, because a brutish or drunken man is insensible to its charms? or is it to be deemed infamous to feel the
influence of its radiance, while the purest sentiments of love, honour, virtue, dignity, and courage, should prompt you to protect
and assuage its anguish? No, my charming Caroline, it cannot be

dishonourable to insist on the side of the weak and oppressed, and the more exquisite the beauty the more lively will be the delicacy which governs the conduct of two virtuous beings; and when a mutual passion has been inspired by the æthereal spark of a glorious magnanimity of spirit, it is then that virtue and honour appears in all its lustre.

What, shall two beings who have justly inspired a confidence in each other, who feel an affinity of sentiment, and who perceive that their happiness or misery are so materially connected, that to separate them would prove fatal to both, not to consider themselves superior to prejudices which are founded in error, and which would lead them to ridiculously sacrifice a real and substantial, for an imaginary good; and when too no person can be injured by the unity?—

For how can it be an injury to a man to loose that upon which he sets no value, and which he has treated in such a manner as to prove it by his conduct? Or, is it possible that there can be a human being so preposterous as to think, a woman is a mere animal who it is necessary sometimes to immolate, in order to support the presumptuous and supercilious prerogatives of arrogant and inhuman men?

Terror is ever the attendant of guilt, and serenity that of innocence; and it was the purity of my motives, that enabled me to meet my Lord B—— at dinner with the most perfect composure.

As I found by your last favour, which I received this day, that your fears were increased, my dear friend, and that your mind seemed to be agitated with the subject, I immediately broke off from my narrative to answer it, as briefly as possible; but when I have the pleasure to meet you at Pittsburgh,[2] which I hope will be shortly, if you have any doubts remaining, I will endeavour to remove them. Adieu, my dear girl, and believe that every day increases my anxiety for your happiness.

I am affectionately your's,
P. P——

LETTER XXIX

P. P. Esq. to Miss Caroline T——n.

Laurel-mount, Feb.

MY DEAR CAROLINE,

I Found Sir J—— C—— and the Hon. W—— H—— with my Lord, to whom I was introduced, and then explained the nature of my engagement with Lady B——, and which, I said, had prevented my having the honour to attend his Lordship that morning; but hoped as he had fallen in with company, he had passed the day agreeably. He answered, very much so; and then related some mischievous adventures of the Hon. W—— H——'s, which he thought I should have been highly diverted with—he then attempted to be pleasant, and seemed to think, I was destitute of that spirit, necessary to enjoy such enterprizes, and turning to Sir J—— said, he thought I was better qualified to read for Lady B——.

I had watched his manner, but saw nothing which I thought appeared like an innuendo, and as they all seemed to be in a sportive mood, I did not think it would be prudent to mention the circumstance of Lady B——'s having fainted at the alcove.

Lady B—— now entered the drawing-room, and as dinner was almost immediately after announced, she was handed to the dining-room by Sir J——, and placed at the head of the table, where she sat as if she had been a mere automaton; whilst my Lord and his two friends appeared to feel all that tumultuous pleasure, which the luxury of a nobleman's table produces, when surrounded by his country friends.

I sat the whole time dinner lasted as if upon thorns, for though I continued to converse with Lady B——, it was upon subjects so remote from my feelings, and upon such common place matter, that my bosom glowed with new emotions—I was at one instant petrified with the indelicacy of the expressions which fell from

my Lord's noisy companions—at the next disgusted with the gross
attempts at wit; and when my astonishment would be for a moment suspended, by the horror I felt at the outrages committed
against every principle of decorum, I was afresh alarmed at the
tremulous tones, which seemed to be pronouncing anathemas
against what they termed,[1] enervated, and degenerated *petit maitres,*[2] *who appeared by wicked innovations, to be endeavouring to destroy
the old and wholesome manners of the country—manners which had given
a celebrity to English hospitality, as splendid as it was generous—and
which had been productive of those cordial amusements a plenty of old red
port and sparkling burgundy inspires.*

As soon as Lady B—— with common politeness could retire,
we were left by ourselves; and upon my rising off my feat, as she
rose, Lord B—— exclaimed, that was a notable proof of the just-
ness of his friend's apprehensions; for nothing could be so tiresome
as to be interrupted, or to have a good story destroyed whenever
a Lady chose to leave the room. As the Gentlemen agreed perfectly in that sentiment, it was unnecessary for me to make any
reply.

The dignity of a sensible and accomplished woman, will keep
under some degree of awe the most licentious and brutal. And
immediately after Lady B——'s departure, the gentlemen, who
began to be a little exhilarated, gave a loose to all the extravagance
of the most nauseous and offending conversation, which I was
obliged to bear with until coffee was ready, when my Lord desired
that it might be sent to us; but as my patience was quite exhausted,
and as I thought it would be a breach of common civility, to leave
Lady B—— to take coffee alone, I retired to the drawing-room,
leaving my Lord and his companions to indulge themselves in the
foul and depraved inclinations of noise and intoxication.

I was so rejoiced after my departure from that noisy company,
that joy appeared to throb in my veins, and courage to glow in
my bosom. I felt myself more than ever interested in the fate of
Lady B——, and determined to risk every thing that could be
relevant to extend her felicity, or assuage those corroding reflec-

tions, which a sacrifice of so many appropriate pleasures must occasion.

I told her on my entry, how much I had been disgusted during dinner, with the flagrant and indecorous manners of Lord B——'s companions; and said, I hoped that she was not often troubled with their company?—she told me they were my Lord's constant visitors, and that she never had known them so moderate—Great God! and is it possible, said I, that my Lord who can be a finished gentleman when he pleases, can be so lost, as to suffer your feelings, or rather to place you in a way to have your delicacy so shamefully wounded?

Lady B—— made no other reply, but declaring it was impossible for a woman of sentiment, to be able to endure for any length of time, such repeated violations of that dignity, which was so necessary for a woman of honour to preserve; and that my Lord's treatment had produced even a coldness towards her from the servants, which was insupportable; for except Sophia and the house-maids, all the others were insolent in the extreme.

This new information required all my firmness to enable me to keep within the bounds of the most passionate declarations. What, said I to myself, is a woman the most chaste, and with sentiments the most refined and delicate, to be insulted by wretches who have not the power to discriminate between virtue and vice, and is she thus to bear patiently with the contumely of her own domestics?

Lady B—— observed that I was agitated, and in the most affable manner changed the conversation; but she had scarcely recovered her wonted cheerfulness, when my Lord and his two friends entered the room accompanied by the footman, who had waited upon me in the morning at the alcove with his Lordship's message.

We that moment had taken a pack of cards with an intention to play at picquet.[3] My Lord's first salutation was; as I understand, my Lady, that you play with this gentleman, (meaning myself) at softer games, you will permit me to interrupt you.—He then desired the footman to relate every circumstance which he had told him in the dining room.

I had not at that time the most distant idea what all this could mean; but as the footman was proceeding, I discovered the nefarious design, and desired my Lord B—— to recollect himself, and instantly order the rascal to leave the room, when I would unriddle to him the true fact, which delicacy forbid me to do before, as I had not a proper opportunity: and though I lamented the cause, yet, by God, no man should dare to impeach the honour of an innocent and unprotected woman. At this my Lord and his three aids grew outrageous—he attempted to lay hold of Lady B——, when I stepped between them. Lady B—— was quite astonished, she exclaimed, what was the matter? what had she done?—and what did Lord B—— mean by so unprecedented a procedure?—I begged to be heard; but it was in vain—I prayed that Lady B—— might be permitted to retire while I removed my Lord's suspicions; and which I was surprised he should bring forward in such a manner—a manner so incompatible with his dignity and character—He exclaimed that she was a w——e, and he would proclaim it to the world.—There was no time to reflect—it was one of those gross and unmanly impeachments which confounds the imagination, and suspends every consideration of prudence—I put my Lord on one side to enable Lady B—— to retire, in order to prevent her delicacy being wounded with such foul expressions—her innocence had so animated her that she appeared totally divested of fear—I begged her to leave the room, at which moment, I was laid hold of by my Lord's two friends, and as Lady B—— had effected her escape, I no longer felt any restraint, and making use of my strength, I soon separated myself from them; at which instant I received a blow from the footman—I did not hesitate—but catching a stick the Hon. W. H—— had in his hand, I caned him severely; then turning to Lord B——, said I should leave his house immediately as he persisted in not suffering me to justify the conduct of Lady B——, and hoped he would not offer any farther indignity to her, untill I should inform him of the circumstances which laid the foundation of the story that it appeared the footman had told him, and which I would do in a note; adding, that Lady B—— was not only innocent, but ignorant of the whole business; for that I had not informed her of the circumstance of the message in the morning—I was not permitted to proceed any farther; and as I have ever considered noisy disputes disgraceful even to fish women, I instantly left the room, and went to a neighbouring Inn, from whence I immediately wrote the particulars of the whole affair, mentioning that I should expect an answer by the return of the bearer—but as I received none, I sent a servant to know from Sophia the situation of her Lady,—when horrid to recollect, I found she had been ordered by Lord B——, to leave Lilbourn House that very night, and that he had dispatched a servant with a letter to her father in justification of his conduct.

I was not personally known to Lord L—— the father of Lady B——, but I did not hesitate, for I wrote to him immediately, and related all the particulars respecting the matter, with a detail of the different conversations which I had had with Lord and Lady B—— upon the subject of their disagreements, and made at the same time some gentle animadversions upon the conduct of Lord B——, appealing to his good sense in justice of the part I had acted, not doubting, but his humanity and paternal affections, would induce him to suspend his opinion, untill the whole business could be properly investigated. To which letter neither did I receive any answer.

Under such circumstances I left the Inn, after waiting for two days to no purpose, endeavouring to find out, what kind of reception Lady B—— had met with from Lord and Lady L——.

I was then puzzled to know how to act in order to rescue that innocent being from a situation into which my imprudence had tended to place her.

Extraordinary cases require extraordinary measures. In this dilemma I determined to call first upon Lord B——, and remonstrate with him upon the violence and hurry of his conduct, appealing to his honour, to his justice, and if neither would have excited considerations in him, I had determined to appeal to his courage,[4] and to have made him expiate for the wrongs of an injured woman, at the risk of his life.

I went to Lilbourn House—Lord B—— denied himself—I knew he was at home; but it was impossible for me to have had any redress.

My next appeal was to Lord L——, I was again equally unsuccessful; for though he did not deny himself, he refused to see me, alledging as an excuse, that it was impossible for me to reconcile a conduct to him, which on my part had been so shamefully licentious, and wanton on the part of Lady B——, for that he had not only received the most unequivocal assurances from Lord B——, of Lady B——'s infidelity, but that his Lordship had sent the footman to him who had witnessed the sacrilegious transaction; and whose testimony was so clear, that it did not admit of a shadow of doubt.

Great God! and is it possible, thought I, that a father who has been bred in the school of honour, and who has educated his daughter in the path of virtue, and taught her the precepts of the purest sentiments, can be carried away in a belief of the commission of a crime which circumstances, time, and place, considered, must have made it of the most shameful nature.

I then tried to ascertain how I could convey a letter to Lady B——, in order that I might have an opportunity to acknowledge to her, how much I felt hurt for having been the innocent cause of her ruin, and to assure her, that every exertion on my part should be made to shield her against the reproaches of an invidious public; but judge what must have been my astonishment, when I was informed that Lord and Lady L—— had not only refused to see Lady B——, but had even denied her an asylum at Rose-hill, the seat of Lord L——; and as my Lord B——'s postillion had orders to return from Rose-hill, that Lady B—— had been compelled to depart from thence on foot; but where, or which way she had gone, no one could tell, for it was in the night that she was forced to wander from the castle of those *beings who were the authors of her existence*. I shall leave you, Caroline, to make your own reflections upon a conduct so unfeeling.

As soon as my frantic mind would permit me to think, I conceived it was most likely that Lady B—— had gone to London, as I had often heard her mention a kind old woman, who had been her nurse when an infant, and whose house was in St. James's-place, where she lived by letting appartments. Thither I repaired without delay—I was in the right—the good old woman had received her with all that kindness, which ever afterwards marked her conduct to both Lady B—— and myself.

Can you paint to yourself, my friend, a scene which could have been so interesting to me. All the emotions of gratitude, concealed love, honour, pity, contrition for my faults, indignation at the wrongs done to an amiable woman, rushed into my breast, and the increased influence of sympathy, that her sufferings had produced, and which diffused a torrent of sensations through my frame, laid me for some time speechless at her feet. Then imploring her forgiveness, I deprecated that distress which I had brought upon her by my inconsiderate conduct; and then begged that I might be permitted to atone for my faults, by dedicating my whole life in endeavouring to restore to her that peace, of which she had been so shamefully robbed. Here my eyes overflowing when gazing upon the divine face of beauty in distress, I intermingled my sorrows with hers, and in that celestial element of chaste sentiment, which emanates from the ingenuous soul, I experienced a kind of ethereal rapture, mixt with grief, which I have no language to express.

The bloom had faded upon her cheeks; but the empire of love had received additional enchantment from the mild lustre of her eyes, which eradiated the atmosphere of sorrow,[5] and as they shot their lucid beams "through a vista of tears,"[6] heaven seemed to approximate in the gleam of returning joy. I found myself in elysium—and while her soul, which stood trembling in her eye, expressed the most ineffable sweetness, my ravished senses in languid transports, for a moment seemed to have lost their energy; and while she continued to express her pleasure for my safety, and to applaud my conduct, there was an emotion which accompanied her mellifluous voice, that told me the secrets of her heart—I listened, and as I heard, forgot that I was a beggar, and believed I was in possession of the universe.

Here permit me to pause my dear friend—it was the most auspicious moment of my life. But the most critical for my honour.

Farewell.
P. P——

LETTER XXX

P. P——, Esq. to Miss Caroline T——n.

Laurel-mount, Feb.

MY DEAR CAROLINE,

AS you have seen the radiance of the morn when creeping upon the frowning night, suddenly obscured by dark and threatening clouds, and the lustre of fair Aurora eclipsed by the unruly elements—as you have seen Old Ocean lie,[1] unruffled and smooth as a mirror to the bounding sky, quickly agitated by the boisterous winds, and the calm changed into a raging hurricane—or as you have seen a rainbow in all its gaudy colours, and with the brilliancy of more than ten thousand dies,[2] illumine the horizon of the declining day, while its effulgence warmed you into admiration, imperceptibly vanish and leave you to lament that its rays were so transitory—such was the cloud that deadened the prospects of my hopes—such was the suddenness of the storm which succeeded the calm that had given rest to the bosom of Lady B——, and such was the momentary joy of those celestial raptures, which to use an idea of Rousseau's, would have been worth an eternity had they have lasted an hour.[3]

Scarcely had I unriddled to Lady B—— the cause which furnished Lord B——, with a pretext to proceed in the manner that he had done, when we learned from the friendly old woman of the house, that Lord B—— had instituted an action against me for a criminal connection with his Lady.[4]

Every evil was to be apprehended from such an action. For however innocent we were, circumstances, and which the world are too apt to judge by, were against us; and when you reflect upon the wound the thought must have given, to a delicate woman, that her name and virtue would be made the sport of a set of unfeeling advocates,[5] who have neither sensations of joy or sorrow, but as they are charmed with tissue of Plutus,[6] or palsied with the face of poverty—when you reflect that she must not only undergo the censure of the world, and the jests of fools, and when too she had no prospect of living with a man to whom she was attached by every sacred tie, except in a loathsome dungeon, those cells of misery, which reflect more disgrace upon a civilized country, and are more incompatible with the feelings and dignity of humanity, than the brutish tyranny of the Despots of the east;[7] it is then that you may figure to your mind, what were the change of our feelings.

The suit went on, and as I continued to visit Lady B—— at her appartments in St. James's-place,[8] it was considered as an aggravation of the first offence,—which if I had not done, and thus to have abandoned, from motives of prudence, an innocent, offended, and friendless woman, *I should have considered myself cowardly and ignominious.*

The evidence upon the trial, in the opinion of all men of delicacy and discernment, invalidated itself; yet in despite of the eloquence of my council, the Jury from the advice of the Judge, *brought damages against me of ten thousand pounds, when I was not worth so many shillings.*

Such were the unnatural proceedings of a court of justice in the most enlightened country in Europe. Such is the tyranny of laws which were formed by the influence of a Turkish despotism to produce fidelity among women, and such was the inhuman and nefarious mandate, that condemned me to live for upwards of ten years in a prison,[9] but which was the happiest period of my life, as I had the endearing consolation of my charming Juliana, (as I shall in future call her,) to soothe me in all my misfortunes.

Lord B——, anxious to perpetuate the name of his family, rejoiced at the opportunity of meeting with a man such as he conceived to be of my cast and disposition; and invited me to Lilbourn-house, with the hope, that by suborning his servants he would soon get clear of a woman,[10] who had not produced him an heir, when he wished to marry, not doubting, but another connection would be more propitious to his wishes:—and it was with such an object, and his great interest, that he soon obtained after the trial, an act of parliament divorcing him from his late Lady,[11] when he immediately married the Honourable Catherine H——, sister to the Honourable W—— H—— his friend; who was a woman of high spirit, and whose extravagant passion for gaming soon beggared my Lord's fortune, as opulent as he was; though indeed he had not a little accelerated his own ruin; for finding that he was reduced to a mere cypher at home, after several contests with his new Lady for dominion, in which she always triumphed, he was compelled to look abroad for those indulgencies and gratifications, which are so necessary to a man of his disposition and habits.

It was under such circumstances that he was obliged to fly over to the continent;—and to such a state was he reduced, that he sent an ill-looking Jew-like attorney to me in the King's-bench prison,[12] impowering him to compromise for the damages awarded him in his action against me.

I had married my loved Juliana soon after my Lord B——'s divorce bill passed, and as she enjoyed a jointure of three hundred pounds per annum,[13] left her by a maiden aunt, lately dead, we had lived as comfortably as our situation would permit; but as there is always a number of unfortunate and distressed objects in such places,[14] who it is impossible for a benevolent mind to see want, so long as it has any thing left for itself, and as our family had increased by the births of seven children, who were all living, and whose education was a considerable charge upon Juliana's little fortune, we had lived up to every penny of her income.

However as the attorney offered me a releasement from all future demands for five hundred pounds, Juliana did not hesitate, but went and sold, unknown to me, the few jewels she had left, and which she considered as baubles calculated to please children, and her wearing apparel, and brought me the full sum that was wanting to procure my emancipation;—and thus it happened that I obtained my discharge. Will you, my friend, drop a tear to the memory of my Juliana, when you read this act of her goodness? It was but one of more than ten thousand.

Lord B———'s plan to get rid of his Lady, was first suggested to me by the information of the very footman who had served as his principal evidence; and which information upon farther investigation I had every reason to believe was true.

That man I met after I was released, a common beggar in the street. I knew him, though disguised, and upon interrogating him upon the subject, he acknowledged all that he knew, and said, that he and Lord B——— having had a quarrel, his Lordship was afraid that he would injure his character by exposing the plot, and had ever after reprobated him as a villain; and by denying him a character,[15] which prevented him from getting into place,[16] he was reduced to the state of wretchedness in which I saw him.

I knew at any rate, that the man must be dishonest and wicked by his own story, and told him, that it was impossible to place any confidence in a person, who was capable of saying one thing at one time, and another at another; much less in one who acknowledged that he had perjured himself. However, if he would call upon me in a few days, I would do what I could for him, and in the mean time I would make what enquiry I could into the validity of his assertions. And as my Lord B———'s fortune was ruined, and his influence no longer dreaded, the truth appeared.

The man called upon me according to promise, when I told him, if he thought he could reclaim, and repent for his past atrocity, I would pay his passage to America, whither I was going, and where as he would not have temptations to commit acts of wickedness, he might live to become a useful citizen.

The poor fellow shewed the greatest compunction for his past

crimes, and acknowledged with the utmost contrition his gratitude, and seemed quite overjoyed in the redemption that was
offered.

How many miserable wretches have been left to continue habits of life, that are so dangerous to society, and derogatory to
human nature, when a little salutary advice would render them
useful members of the community? How inhuman are those men
who encourage them to the commission of crimes, and then ruin
them in the estimation of the world by an exposition of those
vices of which they have laid the foundation? And how much
more reprehensible is that system of government that rather promotes than discourages the habits of vice, by the impolitic practice
of interdicting the operations of justice, by the duties they annex
to its process, and which absolutely amounts to shutting its doors
against the whole of the indigent and friendless?

As soon as I had settled my affairs after my liberation, I determined to leave a country which gave me birth.—A country which
I loved as a Briton; but where I had been treated not like a
citizen—not like a stranger; but as though I had been a monster.

Cruel and inhuman are those laws and that government, exclaimed I, as we lost fight of the Land's-end,[17] which punishes the
innocent for the faults of the guilty; and how impolitic are those
institutions, that drive men of spirit to look for hospitality and
more humanity in foreign states who love the name of an Englishman, and who never hear the sound of Albion,[18] but every
nerve vibrates with the emotions of glory?

> Fair Science there, with her benignant smiles,
> As Dullness fled, began to wake the Isles;
> The lib'ral Arts with Commerce, hand in hand,
> Led up a thousand blessings for the land;
> Surpassing all the raptur'd eye could see,
> They led the mountain nymph, sweet Liberty!
> At her bold song the hardy natives chear,
> A song! that Gods might quit their spheres to hear.
> As new sensations fir'd the list'ning band,

They hail'd her guardian of their sea-girt land;
She smil'd consent, and all who lov'd her name,
Went forth with honour to immortal Fame!
Each foe astonish'd when her laws were known,
Burst his rude gyves,[19] *and claim'd her for his own,*
Exulting follow'd where her flag unfurl'd,
'Till Albion reign'd, the Mistress of the WORLD.

I had seen much of America during the last war with the French,[20] and as our family continued to increase, I determined to migrate to this Continent, and to live in these back settlements where land is cheap.[21] For I found that it was necessary for me to make every exertion, *as my youth had been spent in the service of my country, the prime of my life in a prison,* which time it was impossible for me to appropriate to any advantage, and at the decline of my days, I had to begin the world afresh, and to provide for a numerous and infant progeny.

Over and above such considerations my plan was perfectly suitable to the disposition of Juliana, who was formed for domestic life, and who took so much pleasure in fostering the minds of her children, that she, experienced no chagrin at the thoughts of living out of the world, as it was termed.

We all arrived in good health; and Juliana was so much delighted with the novelty of the country, and the grandeur of the prospects, that she was in every respect perfectly happy.

I had fixt upon the spot of land on which I now live, and had began some improvements; but while we were enjoying in prospect the probable satisfaction we should have of providing comfortably for our infant family, judge what was our consternation, when we were informed that a war had commenced between Great Britain and her then Colonies.[22]

That event was of the most alarming nature to us, as it was obvious, the communication between the two countries would be obstructed, and which would render it difficult, if not impossible, for Juliana to receive the remittance of her jointure.

But O my friend! my Caroline! how shall I impart to you the

sad! sad! events that followed? How can I tell you, my dear girl,
a tale which is so shocking? How can I expose a circumstance,
the recollection of which, still makes me shudder? and should it
be related, would fix an indelible stain, upon the authors of that
unnatural war, which no time could remove.

When the ferocious savages were let loose to crimson their
murderous weapons in the blood of the unoffending, and the
unfortunate subjects of an empire, to the remote parts of which
they had taken shelter against poverty, and in which the government of their country had encouraged them, who is so insensible
as not to feel the keenest indignation at the depravations of that
wicked and inhuman war? Would GOD its history could be ex-
punged from the records of my country! for I would gladly cast
a veil over events so inglorious; but sometimes exposition by producing shame, ameliorates the principles of the most abandoned
and wicked, and I would gladly believe that the ministry is not
so incorrigible, but were they to be rightly informed of the effects
of such inhuman murders, they would not encourage them in
future.

I was employed in my plantation when I was alarmed by a
neighbour, who told me that he had seen a body of Indians enter
my house, and advised me to return home to know what was
their business, for we knew nothing of the war they had commenced against us.—My neighbour attended me, but—my pen
had fallen from my hand, my friend—for the shrieks still vibrate
in my ears—my neighbour now advised me to retire; what, said
I, suffer my Juliana and children to be massacred and basely desert
them! and then rushing into the house and seizing my sword from
the hand of one of the Indians, who had taken it from its place,
and which had often borne me through the enemies of my country, I soon dispatched two of them; but being overpowered I was
left for dead, and scalped; in which situation I was taken by my
neighbours, who were alarmed, and came to my assistance, and
who conveyed me from a sight which must have proved the most
distressing:—and from that fatal morning, my Caroline, have I
never beheld my beloved Juliana, or one of those little cherubs

who once used with their infant prattle to gild the laughing hours of domestic joy, and taught me to believe that I possessed the most perfect felicity. O Caroline! what a damnable schism. It is impossible at present for me to add any thing more, for thus set for ever the sun of all my smiling hopes.

Farewell, my dear girl,
P. P——

LETTER XXXI

Miss Caroline T——n to P. P. Esq.

Pittsburg, March.

IN the multiplicity of sorrows which have overwhelmed the heart of your friend, still she has had sensibility enough left, to weep the whole day for the tragical end of your interesting story.

If at this immature age I have been doomed to witness so many miseries, and to look for consolation in the communications and sentiments of a philosopher which are generally so much out of tone with juvenile organs; and if I have learned from the lessons that your misfortunes afford me, to know, that mine hitherto have been merely nothing; what my dear friend may I expect to meet, judging of the horizon of my present hopes in the uneven journey through life?

It is impossible to make any comments upon the propriety of your conduct, after reading the barbarous treatment of Lord B——, and the more cruel and unnatural of Lord and Lady L——.

And can it be possible that sensible beings can be so unfeeling as to condemn and punish an unhappy object, who is araigned for a supposed crime, upon circumstantial evidence, particularly after the world has produced so many pathetic instances, when the innocent have suffered, and which are sufficient to rouse the feelings of the most obdurate?

How depraved must be that heart which instead of offering consolation and advice to a delicate and depressed woman, condemns her unheard, and consigns her name to infamy and contempt?

But who can help feeling the most exquisite anguish, when they recollect that the ingenuous heart of an amiable woman, who is formed for the soft endearments of domestic felicity, should be first imposed upon by a base and cowardly being, who ought to have been her guardian and protector, and who after having shocked her delicacy, and sullied her honour by his unmanly aspersions, should be condemned to eternal disgrace?

If virtue is any thing more than a name, certainly it must consist in administering relief to the unfortunate, and protecting the innocent; and if a mother, or any other woman, can behold a daughter or a friend, thus treated, and thus aspersed, and will not intrepidly step forward, and attempt to save them from being wrecked upon that coast which is inevitable destruction, is it wonderful that in so many instances, women of quality have disgraced not only their rank, but have degraded the name by a depravity, which is consequent to those sacrifices and distresses they are compelled to experience.

> *O! Enchantment airy sprite,*
> *Thou little wanton playful boy,*
> *With tuneful sounds inspire delight,*
> *And every sorrow change to joy.—*
>
> *Come gently touch the living lyre,*
> *And with thine artful wiles display*
> *The laughing raptures, which conspire*
> *To crown with bliss the fleeting day.*
>
> *To earth direct thy dazzling ear,*
> *Which with unrivalled lustre shone,*
> *When Venus charm'd the God of War,*[1]
> *And Love sat smiling on his throne:—*

And when the love-inspiring Queen,
Adorn'd the splendid court of Jove,[2]
And Beauty deck'd the radiant scene,
While earth re-echo'd songs of love.

I have a thousand things my friend to say to you; but I feel such a sadness at my heart, that was I inclined to be superstitious, I should apprehend, over me, some terrible event was impending. Can you not make a visit to this place. I think your company would make me cheerful; and I then would forego my anxieties. We have not yet heard a word from Captain Arl——ton;—and to add to my uneasiness, my father begins to be very impatient for George's return, as several people have arrived lately from the other side of the mountain. Indeed Mrs. W—— has received letters from Philadelphia.—Pray come, that I may embrace and tell you how much I participate in all your miseries.

Farewell,
CAROLINE

LETTER XXXII

MRS. S—— TO MRS. W——.

Philadelphia, March.

MY DEAR FRIEND,

THE sudden approach of winter, after I informed you of the exit of my worthy and lamented father, prevented my having an opportunity to write to you, since my last sent by the return of Terpin.

I have innumerable incidents to relate to you, that conspired to bring about the change which has taken place, both as to my name and situation; but the greatest part of them I shall reserve to detail when I have the pleasure to embrace you upon the banks of the Ohio, as I am now morally certain of having it in my power, in the course of the spring.—My dear W——, will you not guess what have been the material events before you have read thus far—I am—married—I am—am—how shall I mention it? But I am the wife of Mr. S——.

Let me briefly tell you how it so happened, for fear you will consider me the most inconsistent creature in the world.

You know W—— that my heart was always grateful, and it was the influence of the obligations imposed upon my unfortunate father, by the unparalleled generosity of Mr. S——, and my father's last request, that induced me to consent to a thing, which had ever been so repugnant to my feelings; but after I had considered the circumstances and the delicacy of Mr. S——'s conduct, I felt for him, both a reverence and esteem, that tended to make me view the idea of a connection with him, as less horrible than formerly. However, I must inform you of the material of those circumstances.

You recollect that I told you some bountiful being had cancelled my father's pecuniary engagements, and which had been done in such a manner, as to produce a glow of sensibility that quite overpowered him, and that he sunk under its influence.

The impression the pathetic scene made upon my mind, tended to place the image of the friendly stranger to my view, in the most exalted light; and I determined if it was possible, to discover who he was. For this purpose, I did intend to visit the different parties to whom my father had been indebted, in order to extract from them, some information, which might eventually enable me to trace out the munificent author. Chance, that often decides the fate of empires, was auspicious to me—Mr. S—— had paid me one of his friendly visits immediately after I had lost my dear and affectionate parent, when I told him of the disinterested conduct of the unknown person, and that I intended to call the next day upon Mrs. Finbourn, who was one of the party, and endeavour to draw from her the secret. Mr. S—— pleasantly replied, that he presumed I had determined to try the Lady, from the consid-

eration of the general opinion, that women cannot keep a secret
—I told him I really had not recollected that such were the
sentiments of the world; but that I was much obliged to him for
the hint. I was a little rallied upon the subject, and thus we parted
without his renewing his former overtures. Accordingly the next
day I waited upon Mrs. Finbourn, and before I had time to commence my interrogations, a servant entered with a letter from Mr.
S—— to Mrs. Finbourn, which had been brought by one of the
servants of Mr. S——. Fortunately the servant who brought the
letter in to the good woman, did not say how it came, and as
Mrs. Finbourn is unhappy enough not to be able to read, she put
the letter into my hand, and begged I would do her the favour
to read it, saying, that she had no secrets. Judge, my dear W——,
what must have been my surprize when I found by its contents,
that Mr. S—— was the generous benefactor, and that this letter
was written purposely to exhort her not to promulge the business
to me for any consideration; and to be particularly upon her guard,
for that my visit was for the purpose of drawing from her, whatever I could respecting the author, and the manner in which the
bond she lately had holden of my father's had been paid. The
good woman seemed much discomposed at the accident; but
upon my assuring her that no harm could possibly happen, and
begging that she would not give herself any uneasiness about the
matter, she became satisfied.

There was something so extremely delicate in this conduct of
Mr. S——, that my heart overflowed with gratitude, and immediately after my return home, I wrote to him, and mentioned
the whole circumstances of the day, and hoped he would be so
candid as to acknowledge that, which it was not possible for him
to deny with any face; and I assured him at the same time, his
goodness had made the most lively immpressions upon my heart;
and that it would always form the first object of my life to make
him some recompence for an action so truly disinterested. To that
letter I received a most polite and affectionate answer, assuring
me it was nothing but the purest tenderness for me, that had

prompted him to pursue the measures he had, and in which, generosity had no share; for though he had entirely, despaired of ever being blessed in the possession of the charming Laura R———, as he was pleased to call me, yet he could not bear to see a cloud gathering over my father's head, that appeared to threaten not only him with destruction, but which had it been suffered to burst, would have reduced me to extreme misery, and which he knew would be the consequence, from my very great and warm affection for my father. Adding, that it would have been little and base to have seen me wretched, when he could, by a sacrifice so paltry, secure my happiness; which he confessed was not a little selfish, for upon that depended his own; and as an accident had made me acquainted with the circumstances, he hoped, and which had been his principal reason for adopting the measures he did, it would not wound my pride, and thus ingenuously acknowledging the facts, he expected I would not accuse him of an ostentatious benevolence.

I was determined not to be outdone in sentiment and liberality. I informed him in return of the sentiments his solicitude for my felicity had inspired in me;—and that I should continue to foster a sensibility, which by keeping awake the sparks of gratitude, might one day enable me to make him a small return for his extreme kindness—this declaration produced a visit from him, when he renewed the subject of his former tenderness; and upon which my heart overflowing at the recollection of his late kindnesses, I could not resist its natural impulse, and in that situation I told him I was so alive to a just sense of his many virtues, that I found I was attatched to him by every tie but that of love; but I could not doubt, judging by what I conceived to be the qualities of my heart, that my esteem would prove as lasting as if more refined or delicate: at this confession he appeared enraptured, and taking me at my word, begged I would consent to an early day, to consummate that expected joy which was too fervent to admit of being delayed.

Such my dear W——— were the substance of those rapid in-

cidents that have happened since I last wrote to you, and which
I now consider as the more fortunate, as they will lead to the
ineffable joy of bringing us together; for Mr. S——, anxious to
give me every proof of his tenderness, consented, nay, immediately after our marriage offered to remove into the back country,
in order that I might live in the society of my friend, provided
that I wished it.—Wish it! exclaimed I—if it is not presuming
too much upon the goodness of the most generous man alive, I
should consider it as the most happy event of my life, except that
one which has put it in my power to experience a pleasure that
must prove so great, as embracing my dear friend W——.

Some few days before I lost my father we had a visit from our
friend Mr. Il——ray, who appeared to take much interest in our
then unpleasant situation. But his departure was so sudden, on
account of some unexpected business, that, if I had not known
how many virtues he possessed, I should have attributed his quick
return to the effect of caprice.

He has since written me a consolitary letter, that breathes all
the elegance and sympathy which so admirably characterizes his
life and manners. And I have since received many marks of friendship from an unknown person, or persons, and if I had not experienced the unbounded liberality of Mr. S——, I should have
concluded that Mr. Il——ray had been the author of them.

Assure the General how much I esteem his kindnesses, and that
I now consider my prospects of felicity the most flattering, and
the more so, as it promises me the supreme delight of living
near you.

Pray continue to mention me to the T——ns, for I expect
much from their society. God bless you my dear W——, and for
the first time permit me to subscribe myself,

Your friend,
LAURA S——

LETTER XXXIII

MR. IL——RAY TO GENERAL W——.

Philadelphia, March.

DEAR SIR,

THE last letter I received from my friend Captain Arl——ton, informed me of his immediate intention of going down the Ohio to Louisville, to which place I will thank you to forward the inclosed.

I promise myself the pleasure of seeing you shortly at Pittsburgh on my way to the Illinois; and if Mrs. W—— will consent, I certainly shall endeavour to prevail upon you to be of the party, as I have no doubt but the expedition will prove highly pleasant and agreeable.

Mrs. S——, whose marriage was as unexpected to me as it still appears extraordinary, has informed me that she has written to Mrs. W—— upon the subject.

I wish I could rejoice at the event.—But the deed is done, and I intend to accompany them to the Ohio as soon as the season becomes fine.

Mrs. S—— mentions their intended migration to her friends, as a proof of Mr. S——'s affection for her, whose wish was always to live near Mrs. W——. Unfortunate and deluded woman! How much is it to be lamented that so much innocence and virtue must fall a sacrifice to art. But can it be wondered at, when it appears he has imposed upon the whole city? Certainly he must be the most specious knave in existence.[1] For it seems that he fled from Dublin to St. Eustatia,[2] and by that circuitous rout to America he expected to elude the enquiry of his creditors. But since the war, his residence has been discovered, and a commercial gentleman informed me a few days ago, that was the real cause of his retiring to the Back Settlements, as it was very certain, was he to remain in this place he would be prosecuted.

Poor Laura! I had flattered myself there would have been an end to her troubles, as I understood that Mr. P——'s affairs were settled before his death; and there could have been no doubt, but so lovely and amiable a woman might have married to the greatest advantage.

You know my sentiments of men of this description.—It is only possible to make them contemptible in society, by keeping them at a distance. However, I cannot treat with marked disrespect, the man who is the husband of a virtuous friend; except her own distrust should lead her to dislike him, and there was not a prospect of their being made happy.

Under such considerations I shall make it a point to accompany them; and I have communicated these things to you, that you may be enabled to act accordingly upon our arrival.

It is too delicate an affair to meddle with, neither is it necessary, since there is no undoing what has been done, and from such circumstances, I am convinced, both you and Mrs. W—— will do whatever is in your power, that can tend to promote the happiness of your friend.

It is perhaps needless for me to add, that it must always be best to receive men with just impressions of their characters; for by too high an opinion either of their talents, virtue, or property, we are too apt, in a change of opinion to fall into the other extreme; and when this change may militate against the feelings of a delicate sensibility, it had better be prevented.

You know Mr. S—— has been considered a man of large fortune, as well as possessing splendid talents. I have described the nature of the first.—The general opinion of the latter is equally unfounded.

Give me leave to felicitate you upon the acquisition your society at Pittsburg obtained in the Miss T——ns. Doubtless, my friend Arl——ton told you the cause of their distresses.—I wish that it was in my power to entirely alleviate the sufferings of those charming girls—For at this moment, I blush at the depravity to which the human heart may be reduced, and feel the utmost indignation at the baseness of their unworthy brother.—Wicked and atrocious as it may appear, it is however certain, he has left this place with a phæton and pair,[3] and a servant mounted upon a third horse for New York; and is thus wantonly dissipating that small pittance, which was the only prop to his reduced family,— and whose destruction his former dissipation had been one of the material causes.

This is one of those circumstances that requires no exaggeration to confound the imagination, or to be related with embellishment and pathos, to shock every sentiment of humanity, gratitude, generosity, and honour.

If you can communicate the information to Mr. T——n, it is possible, by pursuing him, that he may save some part of the money; without which I am at a loss to know how the family will exist.

Forgive my adding, that this is a very delicate interference; but I have no objection to your shewing this part of my letter, and pray desire him to forbear mentioning it to his family, who I am apprehensive have more troubles than they can well support.

Do not omit to mention me to Mrs. W——, and Mr. T——n's family, and assure them of my utmost regard and respect.

I am your's truly,
G. Il——ray

LETTER XXXIV

Mr. Il——ray to Capt. Arl——ton.

Philadelphia, March.

MY DEAR JAMES,

THE communication between this place and Pittsburg having been closed from the immense quantities of snow, which has for some time past covered the mountains, is the reason I did not answer your last before this period; which I know you will have the indulgence to consider as a sufficient apology for my silence.

The affair with the lovely Caroline T——n appears to me very enigmatical; and I think that you ought to have judged better of her good sense, candour, and politeness, than not to have supposed there was *"something rotten in Denmark."*[1] At any rate it was not acting like yourself to leave Pittsburg when you knew that the family stood in need of assistance.

As to your saying, at a time when you did not know what you were doing, that you meant to take a trip to Louisville before the winter set in, and which imposed upon you the necessity of going according to your declaration, I think, that it was the most ridiculous thing in nature, to believe it would have been a derogation from consistency to have retracted.

Does not every man alive, propose to do things that intervening incidents may prevent their carrying into effect? and I cannot conceive you were bound to give an account to any person whatever for your motives for delaying your journey; particularly, as it would be undertaken at this season with more safety, and would be more pleasant. Besides, you ought from feelings of humanity, to have considered the care of these strangers, as paramount to every speculative object.

What would be your sensations if you were to hear that the imprudence of the brother had driven them distracted; and I should be glad to know, what guarantee they have against the imprudence and prodigality of an undisciplined man, who has given every proof of his contempt for the ties of honour and gratitude?

It appears to me, that when a man has been inspired with a delicate attachment for an innocent and virtuous woman, he would be governed by sentiments more heroic, than to abandon her in the hour peril and danger.—Instead of which, your conduct exhibits an instance of captious caprice,[2] that is so unlike the dignity of a man, that I confess I was not less mortified when reading your letter, than I was astonished at your precipitation.

As to Caroline's having been merry at your expence, it is the most boyish idea I ever heard.—Certainly you ought to have been a better judge of good breeding, and to have had a more just opinion of her gentleness, than to entertain suspicions so injurious to feminine charms.

In short, my friend, you have nothing to plead as an excuse for your impetuosity, but an excessive tenacity; a refuge, of which I hope you would be ashamed, as it is ever the characteristic of little minds. Forgive me, James, for expressing myself in such terms; for I wish you to feel the force of the absurdity that marked your conduct in the affair, in order that you may be induced to make for it some atonement.

I will not deceive you, by aiming at the reputation of being thought prophetic. For the brother, who you recollect was dis-patched to receive the money, Mr. T——n left in a bank in this place, is now indulging his former propensities with all the wanton extravagance of the most contemptible and prodigal spendthrift; and perhaps before he can be overtaken by his father, who I have desired General W—— to inform of his conduct, those charming girls—that enchanting woman, whom you seemed to consider as a divinity, will be reduced to beggary.

Such, my friend, is likely to be the situation of the woman you adored, and whom you deserted at a moment when you ought sooner to have forfeited your life.

You will not be permitted to say that there was no reciprocity in your attachment, for that being admitted, your conduct would have been the more noble and generous, for having been disinterested.

I expect soon to set out to explore those regions which all travellers, who have passed through them, agree are so delectable; and when I see you I shall say more than I can convey in a letter; —and when I hope you will be sufficiently temperate to reprobate your own folly.

The late Laura R—— has become Mrs. S——; Mr. S—— has agreed to settle upon the Ohio—more of this when we meet.—I shall attend them to Pittsburg.

I am affectionately your's,

G. IL——RAY

LETTER XXXV

MRS. F—— TO MISS CAROLINE T——N.[1]

London.

MY DEAR CAROLINE,

WE had a quick passage to England, for we flew before the wind, which blew a strong gale from the day we lost sight of the shores of America until our arrival at Falmouth, which was in eighteen days after our departure from Sandy-hook.[2]

We hurried up to town where I found Mr. F——'s house in Bruton-street newly fitted up to receive us,[3] and where we received the congratulary visits of our friends upon the events of our marriage and safe return.

In the splendid apartments of this superb residence, that have a voluptuous richness, altogether corresponding with the taste of Mr. F——, I cannot forget the separation from my family, and above all, from my tender and affectionate Caroline, which still gives a deadness to all my pleasures; without wishing I was in the wilds of America, participating in the hardships I know you must have encountered, there to enjoy the felicity the ties of nature, and the congenial sentiments of kindred souls experience through the vicissitudes of every change of fortune.

It is not in the power of enervating luxury, the grandeur of riches, the pageantry of a blazoned chariot, the golden tissue which decorate the hangings of a drawing room, the brilliancy of operas, or the eclat[4] of exciting admiration at tumultuous routs,[5] can ever compensate to me, for the derelictions fortune has compelled me to make.—No, my dear sister; for sadness often fixes upon my brows, and when Mr. F—— attempts to sooth my sorrows, I insensibly feel a disgust at that appearance of tenderness, that surrounds me with flowery prospects, while the vista through which I behold my solitary relatives, is penury and wretchedness.

In vain am I told that my misery will not alleviate their suffer-

ings. Such remonstrances only increase my anguish, for by attempting to convince me how much he is concerned for my
happiness, it proves to me equal to demonstration, that his
soothings are mere affectation, otherwise my wishes would be
anticipated, and my filial sensations would lead to a paternal par-
ticipation of that superfluous opulence with which I am at present
surrounded.

You recollect, my dear sister, how sanguine I was upon this
subject, before the ceremony of our marriage; and the least I expected, was that you would have been invited to return with us
to England. But as that was not done, I suspended my opinion of
Mr. F——'s generosity, and believed that he intended to do
something, which would have secured the comfort of my aged
parents in the country, where they now are; as it was impossible
for my father to return without Mr. F—— making a sacrifice I
could not expect.

Several of our former acquaintances have been to visit me, who
would wish to make me believe, that they feel the most *ecstatic
joy* at their good fortune, in having the honour of my being once
more joined to the circle of their society.

How little do we know of the human heart, until we have
experienced, in some degree, the changes incidental to us as sublunary beings? How strangely versatile are the opinions of those
Automatons,[6] who would wish the world to believe like

> *"The spider's touch which exquisitely fine!*
> *Feels at each thread, and lives along the line,"*[7]

that they are all sensibility, without really knowing, what is, either
joy or sorrow? But who exclaim in affected raptures at every trifling circumstance.

Such, my dear Caroline, have been the affectation of those
unworthy objects, who at the period of our most reduced state,
sometimes did not recollect us in the streets; and who when they
met us in company where they felt themselves inferior, used to
sympathise with us for my father's misfortunes, as they termed the

change of our situation; but which with all their disguise, discovered the secret satisfaction little minds are too apt to feel, at the reduced circumstances of those they call their friends.

The etiquette of visits, and the tumultuous amusements to which I am hurried almost harrass me to death; and when I contrast the simple and sincere manners of the people of your hemisphere, with the studied ceremony of European customs, I not only lament, that I am not with you enjoying the charms of those Arcadian regions,[8] but I assure you, my dear sister, I envy you that felicity which flows from the genuine sentiments of nature.

I do not send this by a regular packet, for hearing of a ship which will soon sail, I have snatched an opportunity to tell you how much my happiness is abridged in consequence of our separation, and to prove to you how affectionately I am alive to your wishes, by sending the books, &c. as you requested.

I am very anxious to hear from you, and have thought it not a little extraordinary, that none of your letters have yet come to hand. I wish this may reach you before the winter sets in, as the books will prove an acquisition to you, when it is not pleasant going out. But I fear the season is too far advanced for my wishes to prove propitious. Adieu, my dear Caroline, and assure the family of my duty, and that I am tenderly their

ELIZA F——

LETTER XXXVI

CAPT. ARL——TON TO MR. IL——RAY.

Louisville.

O! my friend, into what a state of wretchedness am I plunged? The horrors of my voyage to this place were dispelled by the more horrible sensations of my distracted mind. The nightly owl which skims through the airy regions, when nature seems awake only to such wretches as myself, with their solitary hollos,[1] which

were re-echoed through the sounding vallies, as I passed the uninhabited wilds that separate me from the lovely, but cruel Caroline, constantly warned me of the situation into which I was
launched. I remained upon deck, and while the towering forests
that hang over the brink of the river, and spread a gloom upon
the *sombre* curtains of the night, heaven appeared in all its lustre,
as if purposely to mortify me for having abandoned the object of
all my joys.

The weather continued fine, and as the stream, which is ever
true to the current of nature, imperceptibly approached the genial
clime of this delightful region, I felt in my glowing veins all the
tumultuous transports of love, contending with agonizing grief,
produced from the certainty, it was not in my power soon to
return.

The fragrance of the groves which on our way, Zephyrus
wafted across the river,[2] gave voluptuous delight; and as the evening breezes playing upon the surface of the water, danced to the
soft tones of enchantment, heavens! said I, was man made reasonable to occasion his own misery, while things inanimate appear
to frolic in all the raptures of congenial elements? And when the
sun had declined below the horizon, and Venus in her evening
car shone in all her eradiated charms,[3] I figured to my imagination
the various beauties of the sweet Caroline; but when I reflected
upon the attributes of the Queen of Love, my heart deadened at
the thought of my not being more accomplished in the school of
gallantry.

Such, my friend, were my lucubrations during the night of my
passage, when my tapers were the twinkling stars, for the sober
moon was then giving light to the Antipodes,[4] and such has been
my state of mind, that I have not been able to attend sufficiently
to the great object, which was my ostensible reason for coming
to this country.

However, I have made several excursions, and have seen so
much as to convince me, that those persons who wish to settle in
the western country, had infinitely better come here, than to stop
upon the upper branches of the Ohio. To which effect I have

written to General W——, and as you will pass through this district on your way to the Illinois, I know that you will forgive me for not being able, at present, to describe it.

Your letter that informed me of the death of Mr. R——, contained sentiments so truly disinterested, that while I applaud the generosity, I admire the delicacy with which you administered the relief.

Certainly benevolence is a most celestial virtue, and its generous offerings I should conceive, must ever afford a delight to the heart of a good man, to which ostentatious persons are strangers.

When I recognize the many instances which have characterized yours, I think you must be the most self satisfied man living. Yes! my friend, while you have been intent upon pursuing practical virtues, I have suffered my passions to transport me into the abyss of misery, where I am friendless, and without the power of being friendly.

My very faculties appear to have taken their leave of me, and when I take a view of myself, I am confounded at the thought of that folly, which accelerated me into this wilderness, where I am shut out from all social intercourse, and left to brood over the events which led to my solitary wretchedness.

In contemplating the various characters that constitute the groups into which men assemble, how very few do we find who possess that kindred sentiment, is so essential to soften the calamities to which our passions and the changes of fortune subject us?

The fault cannot be in nature—it must be more superficial—it must proceed intirely upon the first impressions that are made upon the mind, and to which it behoves parents to attend with the greatest nicety; for upon that depends the only charms of which the human heart is susceptible.

The rigid rules of moralists have tended to harden the human heart, and in many instances, the most virtuous inclinations have been condemned as of the most criminal nature; while the unfeeling prudence of some persons has been applauded, which merited at most, the consideration of a negative virtue.

Such have been the factitious duties of men,[5] that every thing mental appears to have been perverted, and while cold inanimate characters have been admired and carressed, a soul warm in social feelings, and glowing with the most heroic sentiments, has been left after his ardour has carried it a little beyond the bounds of prudence, to languish under the contempt of a misguided world.

You know, my friend, what was the clamour against the late unfortunate Mr. R———, who had so nobly stood forward not only on his brother's account, but who had given so many examples of his exalted sense of honour and friendship; and who was not only condemned as imprudent, but was neglected, and suffered by those that called themselves his friends, to experience every mortification a man of spirit must feel, from the contumely of the supercilious coxcomb, and the prosperous and arrogant squire.

It is from such considerations that I think your conduct toward Mr. R———, as the most glorious part of your life, which to adorn and set it off, has so many brilliants.

If I was less sincere in my general manners and actions, perhaps, you would suspect me of being adulatory in this due tribute of praise; but the brightest diamonds want no borrowed lustre, and when a man withholds his praise or censure upon the conduct of his friend he deceives him, and prevents his forming a just estimate of his own actions; and thus it frequently has happened, that men have fallen into errors, that have been the result of a superfluous delicacy on the part of those they were in the habits of consulting, and which errors, in many instances, have proved irretrievable.

The inflexible Cato was vanquished by the greatest soldier the world ever saw, the specious Julius Cæsar.[6] The manly and virtuous Brutus, by Anthony and the more fortunate Octavius Cæsar; —but how many equally good men, and they not deficient in understanding, have been ruined by a more dangerous and insidious foe to society—that of insincere friendship.

> *"A generous friendship no cold medium knows,*
> *Burns with one love—with one resentment glows;*
> *One should our interests and our passions be."*[7]

If mankind would be more candid with one another, certainly it would tend very much to correct that fallacy of opinion we are too apt to entertain of ourselves. For while we affect to be governed by tenderness, as to the foibles of our friends, the errors of education, and the vanity concomitant with youth become so fixed, that they constitute part of our nature:—and from that source flow one half of the difficulties which we meet with through life.

I have known a lady whose face had not a single beauty, who had been all her life surrounded by sycophants,[8] believe that she was as charming as an angel, and in consequence of that self admiration, loose many good offers, which was the cause of her living and dying a maid. The same vanity is not uncommon in men; and it has frequently happened, that many worthy and good characters have continued the sport of those flatterers, who produced such a belief; and if such things proceed from the weakness inherent in human nature, and if they are generally innocent in their effects, it is nevertheless true, that we too often meet with characters, who by mistaking their talents, have committed blunders which have led to ruin and contempt.

Men generally undertake things, which, according to the estimate they form of their talents, are likely to prove successful; and therefore it is the business of a friend, always to prevent by a delicate interference, an erroneous bias,[9] otherwise they do not perform the important office with sincerity; and which neglected, is the reason that when friends fall out, they generally become the most virulent and implacable enemies; for both parties having been in an error, in respect to the opinion they had formed of themselves, they mutually accuse each other, not only with insincerity, but with hypocrisy, and every vicious quality of the mind.

These reflections are not mere speculation.—I have seen the effects so often, that I am perfectly satisfied that they are just.— Indeed I have in some measure, been the dupe of insincerity myself; for if I had been told with candour, I did not possess that address necessary to inspire a fine woman with an attachment for me, or so much as to arrest their notice, so far as to become a favourite, I certainly should have turned my thoughts upon my-self, and if I could not have prevented the spontaneous sensations engendered by the fascinating charms of the divine Caroline, yet I might have checked them in their infancy, and at least have prevented my pride being mortified.

Forgive this egotism my dear Il——ray, and hurry to this place, that I may feel the consolation of knowing I am not lessened in your estimation.

As you pass Pittsburg assure Caroline that I enquired particu-larly after the health and welfare of the family; but for God's sake do not touch, even if you should receive an oblique hint of the affair, that you know a word of the matter. Excuse this weakness, and assure all my friends of my sincere regard.

I am truly your's, &c.

J. A——

LETTER XXXVII

Mrs. W—— to Mrs. S——.

Pittsburg, March.

HOW exquisitely delicate is the sensibility of my friend, and how amiable has she appeared through the various mortifications and sorrows which such a rapid succession of accidents could not fail to produce?

I am at a loss which to admire most, the generosity of Mr. S——, or your gratitude. What a lustre has virtue, and how tran-scendently lovely has its struggles rendered the most charming of women? How divinely ecstatic must be the sensibility of that heart, which gave such proofs of its filial tenderness while it shone with so much brilliancy in the agonies of that severe dereliction, when that celestial spark which animates the frame of a good man, was emanating from mortality to join the pure regions of eternal felicity? Yes! my dear Laura, your dear father must have flown directly to heaven, and in that certainty you ought to be happy.

I had no opportunity of writing to you after the return of Terpin, until I received your last, which informed me of your marriage—never was I more delighted than with the thoughts that you felt for Mr. S—— a more tender attachment than mere gratitude; and that his kindness would place you in the situation, where I again may enjoy all those pleasures, which flow from the interchange of those endearments that have marked the course of our lives.

You find, Laura, how much too high you had rated the common offices of a friend in Mr. W——; for while you were contemplating a conduct as munificent, which was only repaying those bonds that cement the ties of his esteem, when you experienced the effects of the most heroic generosity from a person, who from his manner of doing the action, proved that it was totally disinterested, and to the discovery of which, nothing could have led but accident.

Mr. W—— has received such extraordinary accounts of the country low down on the Ohio from Captain Arl——ton, who left us for Louisville before the winter set in, that he has made up his mind to remove there, and only waits for your arrival to make his arrangements, as we flatter ourselves, that such a plan will be perfectly agreeable to both Mr. S—— and you.

I have been using my endeavours, to prevail upon the English family to emigrate with us, and find that nothing is wanting to effect my success, but to prevail upon a relation, who they have discovered in a very strange manner. He is an elderly man, and possesses so much the manners of a gentleman, you would immediately conclude, that he had been a man of fashion, though he dresses in the plain garb of the country.

I know you will forgive this short epistle, when you know that I expect in so short a time to have the pleasure of embracing you, and when I can say ten thousand things which cannot be written.

Mr. W—— begs leave to felicitate both you and Mr. S——, upon the propitious event of your marriage, and to assure you how very much he is interested in every thing that concerns your happiness, and in which is blended, that of your affectionate friend,

MARIA W——

P. S. The Miss T——ns request that I will inform you of the joy they experience, at the thoughts of obtaining in you, so valuable an acquisition to our society. Poor Caroline! she droops and has lost her vivacity.—Indeed it is not to be wondered at, when we recollect the sacrifices a change of fortune must have compelled her to make, and which situation is the more cruel, as not one of the family have a disposition congenial to hers.

LETTER XXXVIII

GENERAL W——, TO MR. IL——RAY.

Pittsburg, March.

DEAR SIR,

Mrs. W—— had written a congratulatory letter to Mrs. S——, before your favour came to hand, expressive of our most unfeigned joy, at the event of her marriage.

Judging by the letter Mrs. W—— received from Mrs. S——, Mr. S—— appears to be one of the best men alive; and so totally different from the character you give of him, that I feel myself in the most unpleasant and aukward situation. Therefore I have transcribed such parts of it as concerns him, and send them inclosed to you, as they contain matter, which I presume you have not been made acquainted with, and in which, it seems there could not be a possibility of a deception, intended by that beneficence they describe.

However, I confess I have been so highly pleased with a man, who appears so transcendently generous, that I cannot help thinking you have been imposed upon by the invidious censures of a malevolent set of wretches, who take a pleasure in calumniating the fair fame of such men as experience a reverse of fortune; and if such has been the case with Mr. S——, I am heartily sorry for it; for a man who could have acted by old Mr. R——, in the manner the enclosed will inform you he did, must have a soul of the most exalted nature.

In this delicate affair I have been perfectly silent with Mrs. W——, for fear it might reach Mrs. S——, who would consequently be made unhappy, from a mistrust of things, which I hope have no foundation. Besides it is a maxim with me, to avoid touching upon opinions that may lead to domestic uneasiness, when it cannot possibly do any kind of good.

I have received such flattering accounts of the low country, that I only wait for your arrival to proceed down the river. In the mean time believe me to be sincerely yours,

J—— W——

P. S. I communicated without delay the unpleasant information to Mr. T——n, respecting his unworthy son, and with as much tenderness as I possibly could, who has in consequence set out in pursuit of him.

LETTER XXXIX

Miss Caroline T——n to P. P—— Esq.

Pittsburg, April.

MY DEAR FRIEND,

YOU had only parted from us, when my father received some unpleasant information respecting George, and set out almost immediately for Philadelphia in order to see him.—I have my apprehensions, but God forbid that they should prove true.

Permit me to assure you how very much I was charmed, during your kind visit, in the elucidation of those important subjects, upon which the happiness and misery of society depend; you have dispelled the mist, which had always darkened my understanding, and illumined the region between prejudice and reason; and I now think, I behold the fetters that have been so ingeniously contrived to subjugate the human mind; and clearly perceive the difference between principles, which have for their basis, our unalienable rights, and those which are grounded upon the opinion of the world. But I must lament at the same time, that the inconvenience society will experience from such a perversion, cannot be easily removed: and thus I fear many virtuous characters, will yet suffer under the influence of a system, which their honour will not suffer them to violate; for it is certainly better for a woman of spirit to forfeit her existence, than to excite the scorn and contempt of a supercilious set of beings, who have no regard for any thing but appearances.

In reflecting upon the various institutions that have been made, and the numerous laws which have been contrived to support the present practices respecting women and matrimony, my thoughts were imperceptibly turned upon the fate of the unfortunate Princess Matilda, late Queen of Denmark.[1]

When I brought into consideration many ideas which your admirable lectures have given me; cruel and inhuman I thought, must be the practice of that government, which banishes an amiable and beautiful Princess from her native country, from those to whom she was attached by the ties of congenial sentiment; from those gay scenes of juvenile pastime, which always have charms to a sensible mind; from not only the companions of her youth, but from those friends her social heart had fixed upon to be its associate in the hour of inquietude, and more corroding disappointment, and when too, such severe derelictions barely afford a chance to this victim of political tyranny, of being allied by one of those ties, which are the only compensations we can have for the many cruel mortifications we are subject to as mundane beings; and it is the more exquisitely torturing to a delicate woman, as she must shudder at that profanation of feeling, to which such alliances must subject her.

O despotic man! as the effusions of my heart continued, said

I, and is your understanding so contemptibly weak, as to oblige you to immolate the tender offspring of your sovereign, in order to secure your unnatural political system? wretched indeed, then said I, must be the situation of those who have the misfortune to be born a Princess.

Such, my friend, have been my reflections upon a subject, which perhaps my thoughts would never have turned upon, if I had not experienced the happiness of meeting you in these almost uninhabited wilds, where the mind naturally begins to look more into the nature of society, than when the objects which present themselves, are mostly artificial. I must therefore request, as you have been the material cause of my touching upon the subject, that you will be so kind as to correct my errors, and at the same time give me your opinion of the political necessity of such practices.

I have the pleasure to inform you, that General W—— has received dispatches from Capt. Arl——ton, which not only mention his safe arrival at Louisville, but he speaks of the security the present state of the country affords against any attacks from the natives.[2]

I have received a letter from my sister, and as usual, she expresses herself in the most affectionate terms; so that the opening spring has in some degree chased away the vapour which had thrown such a damp upon my spirits.[3] Believe me when I say, I am, your's sincerely,

CAROLINE

LETTER XL

P. P—— ESQ. TO MISS CAROLINE T——N.

Laurel-mount, April.

YOU have harrowed up my very soul, my dear Caroline, and opened afresh those wounds that have so often bled for the calamities the indigested practices of barbarians have produced; by bringing to my recollection, not only the sufferings of the unfortunate late Queen of Denmark,[1] but the horrors of that miserable catastrophe, which befel my own family, who had been nurtured under my own immediate care, who were learning to imitate the examples I set them, and who were not only the pride of my life, but would have been the comfort of its winter, which is now commencing; and was it not cheered by my amiable friend, I should be lost to that animating sensibility that warms the heart into rapture, and gives zest to the delights of social pleasures.

When I take a retrospective glance of the degradations and miseries that system of government produces which exiles its own Princesses, or condemns them to a life of celibacy, and thereby blasts the fair blossoms of their tender hopes, and shuts out from their glowing imaginations, the fascinating joys, emanating in all that luxuriance the sympathetic soul inspires, in such eradiated imagery, as to produce those divine sensations, when every place is converted into elysium, and every sense is feasted in the banquet of love; I cannot help feeling the utmost indignation for that system you so justly reprobate; and pity for those innocent sensible beings, who are made victims to that object of aggrandisement which has too long disgraced the courts of Europe.

It is not my business to make any comments upon the wisdom of monarchy, or the advantages it has over any other kind of government; but if it is obliged to resort to such means to support itself, it appears to me, to say the least of it, that it is inhuman.

Let any man of feeling and candour read the life and sufferings of the Princess Matilda, who not only suffered the severest mortifications in finding it necessary to be allied to a man she could not love; but who suffered the tortures of a shameful prosecution, in a strange dominion, unprotected, and unheard, and then say, if he can, that such practices are not nefariously inconsistent.

You have called for my opinion, my dear friend, upon this important subject; and if you will forgive me for being prolix, I will enter into it at some length.

The disputes between religionists had for a long time distracted the intellects of mankind,[2] and disturbed the repose of the world; so that the aera of protesting against the catholic creed,[3] was, perhaps the most important crisis for the extension of that mild philosophy, which tends to meliorate the condition of humanity, of any one period during the history of modern Europe; and when I recollect the sanguinary tumults, the different sects of christianity had occasioned, I cannot help admiring the wisdom of our ancestors, for taking effectual measures to check that spirit of bigotry that has fixed an odium upon its Priests, which no time or element will ever obliterate.

It was necessary to interdict, by statute,[4] the possibility of that intolerant system being revived, as it had so often disturbed the tranquillity of Great Britain, and endangered those liberties for which our ancestors had so nobly contended; and from the disposition of the faithless and unfortunate James II. it became necessary for the security of the protestant succession, and the extension of civil and religious liberty, to regulate the marriages of the royal family to protestants:[5]—and perhaps, when we recollect the state Europe was in at that period, it was not an unwise measure, to confine their marriages to royalty. But when those circumstances no longer existed, and after the radiance of reason had illumined the minds of men, it became highly oppressive in government to condemn the innocent progeny of their king to experience a coercion so repugnant to nature.

I confess I am totally at a loss to know upon what principle the statute is suffered to exist, when the danger that was apprehended for the safety of the Protestant succession is no more; and when too the government has obtained a stability from the affections of British subjects, *which nothing but its inconsistencies will he ever able to shake.*

The improvements in reason and science will continue to develope the fallacy of error, and in the progression of truth, the imperfections of every system will be discovered; and therefore it ought to be the moderation and wisdom of every state to make use of all appropriate knowledge which would effectually prevent those clamours, that are ever industriously raised by the indigent and factious; and which are suffered to gain ground from that weakness, that obstinately rejects every improvement or amelioration.

As to the popular principle of marrying the princesses to royalty in order to strengthen and extend by such alliances the political importance of Great Britain, nothing can be more chimerical and ridiculous; For whenever was the prosperity of England promoted by such connections? or indeed, when did ever a state or empire rise to fame and splendour but by the wisdom and magnanimity of its ministry? However I should be glad to know, what would be the sentiments of those immortal lawgivers, who erected monuments to perpetuate their fame, if they could be told that in the most enlightened kingdom among the moderns, that government sacrificed the most lovely woman in the world to state politics?[6]

Certainly such practices illy correspond with the gallantry of a brave and generous nation;[7] and while I most sincerely join with you, my friend, in those warm sentiments, you have so rationally promulgated, I feel the utmost solicitude for those unfortunate women, whose fair celebrity for beauty and accomplishments have arrested the admiration of every sensible heart.

If monarchy is the most eligible kind of government, and which some of the most celebrated men for talents that the world has produced, seem to have thought, it appears to me, that the only way by which it can be perpetuated, is to unite it by the ties of consanguinity to the people.

The absurd and stale idea that familiarity occasions contempt, has too long been the sole cause of the continuation of those forms, which have been mistaken for dignity; and they have induced many to believe, that all government is a mere trick, contrived by the cunning part of the community to answer selfish purposes; and while its ministers adroitly hoodwink the vulgar, they have had in the exercise of that omnipotence their places afford them, no other object in view but their own aggrandizement.

Men will no longer continue to be attached to forms, and

therefore it becomes a folly to reverence a system, that has not for its basis, reason and truth.

If a mixed government is better calculated to secure the happiness of mankind than any other,[8] and to give all that splendour to a state which is so necessary to amuse the bulk of them, in the name of God, why is it not continued upon rational principles? For certainly no person can be so preposterously absurd, as to say such is human weakness, that perfection in no one thing is attainable, and therefore it would prove a nugatory attempt to make improvements.[9]

Such opinions merit no consideration, and when I recollect how many splendid fortunes there are in Great Britain—fortunes more princely than many of those petty sovereigns of Germany inherit; and then reflect upon the depravations, the inhuman politics, which preventing a beautiful and amiable princess, who possesses all that sensibility which adds such wonderful lustre to female charms, from marrying any but a Protestant Prince; and after the cause that might at one period, have rendered such regulations necessary, no longer exist, and which restriction condemns them to deprecate the continuance of a life, that when robbed of all those delicious raptures, which so peculiarly enhances its value becomes burthensome; I confess every one of my faculties are for a time suspended in amazement at the thought, that any human creature, can be so unfeeling as to be an advocate for so crude a policy.

Such, my dear friend, are my sentiments upon the subject; and I have treated it more seriously, as I know, that it has been too much the practice with politicians to sacrifice every thing to their confined ideas; and while they continue to immolate the most lovely part of the creation to such a miserable system, every humane and thinking man, must be convinced that nothing can be more absurd and wicked.

Ah Caroline, my friend! When I contemplate the spontaneous sweets that spring up under our feet, and decorate the fragrant groves, which afford so many joys; and hear the melodious songs of the feathered creation tuned to love and nature, and then contrast them, with the mutilated pleasures of man, how poignant is the anguish which I feel at the idea of the imbecillity of such institutions, as are incompatible with reason and nature?

Perhaps when you desired me to give my sentiments upon this subject, you did not expect to be troubled with a disquisition so elaborate, nor indeed my dear was it altogether necessary that you should; but I have treated it in a political and religious point of view purposely; for in whatever light the world may hold the understandings of women, I hope my self ever to pay them the greatest deference, as I have always observed, that they judge from the elucidation of the most obstruse subjects, with as much precision as men; and if their ideas are not always so comprehensive, it ought in justice to them, to be attributed to education. Believe that I am, my dear girl, affectionately yours, &c.

P. P——

LETTER XLI

MRS. F—— TO MISS CAROLINE T——N.[1]

London.

MY DEAR CAROLINE,

SEVERAL of your charming favours have come safe to hand; all of which breathe the same tender sentiments that marked the sensibility of your heart.

While you continued happy, Caroline, there was always a vivacity in your manner of writing, which afforded me the greatest pleasure. But while I was admiring the animated account you gave me of your journey, I felt all the solicitude for you, the horrors of a savage wildness can produce.—I thought I saw you insulated, and liable to be carried off by those Indians, whose image was so forcibly impressed upon my mind by the story of the adventure with Captain Arl——ton in the mountain, that I have never been able to obliterate the impression.

Heavens, said I, to Mr. F——, involuntarily as I was hurrying over the contents of that epistle in which you mention to have seen the natives, Caroline is taken prisoner by the barbarous Indians!—Caroline is massacred—Caroline is dead—Mr. F—— caught me in his arms, and was going to read on, when I was soon electrified by that fluid,[2] which so suddenly rouses the senses of a woman, when a thought strikes her, in which her delicacy is concerned. I had discovered that your heart was not a little interested in the story you were telling, and in a moment I was so collected, as to prevent Mr. F—— from obtaining sight of those expressions which acknowledge your attachment for Captain Arl——ton—such was my delicacy towards you, Caroline, that had it been an affair of my own, I could not have been more alive to the danger.

Perhaps you may wonder how a woman can hide any thing from her husband?—I will briefly tell you. The caprices of the human heart are such, that whenever a weakness is discovered, it in a greater or less degree, lessens the estimation which we may have formed of the person so discovering their failings; except it is in the regard of our friends, or of those of open and ingenuous dispositions. And if you should wonder, why a husband is not the best friend a woman can have, I will also tell you, that it is a misfortune when it is not the case; for it is very certain, their minds are so delicate, and are so attached by the influence of social feelings, that if they do not find those congenial sentiments in the husband, they will certainly look for them elsewhere, which never fails ultimately to lead to an alienation of all affection.

If a woman should happen to be in love, and should afterwards marry to advantage, it is all very well. But if perchance her attachment should prove abortive, it is too apt to excite the pity of others, which is very little short of contempt. Doubtless these things proceed from a contractedness of mind; but while that is the case, it will be necessary for us to be upon our guard, how we make known the sentiments of our tender attachments.

If you will forgive a kind of pro-and-con style, I will state a case, which I conceive will illustrate the disposition of Mr.

F——, and nine tenths of the men with whom I am acquainted.

If you were to happen to be attached to a gentleman of eligible fortune, should marry him, and was then to return to this country, you would be caressed by all parties, as the most amiable, sensible creature that ever lived; but should it be known you were in love with a man, who did not care three straws for you, it would be considered as foolish, and your name under the affectation of pity, would be treated almost with contempt.

Ah! my dear sister, how effectually do I feel for your misfortune in loosing Capt. Arl——ton: Your account of him, and the delicacy of his manner in promoting the comfort of our helpless family, had produced in me the most lively gratitude; and when I was contemplating with peculiar satisfaction the expected felicity of hearing of a propitious event of your mutual sympathy, I experienced the most unpleasant chagrin, when your melancholy letter, by George to Philadelphia, which is the last I have received from you, informed me of his having left Pittsburg.

How pathetically do you describe the distresses of your sensible heart?[3] Ah Caroline! I cannot bear your complaints! I will risk every thing, once more to have it in my power to convince you how sincerely I love you. If you can obtain permission, for God's sake return to me without delay; you doubtless may meet with some compassionate traveller, who would protect you to Philadelphia, where I should suppose there may be always found good company returning to Europe, with whom you might associate in your passage, if not with pleasure, at least with satisfaction. Make no excuses; inclosed I transmit you the needful: and as I have told F—— that I shall be miserable until I regain you, and that I have given you an invitation to return, you cannot have any scruples upon that head.

Would God it was possible for me to do any thing for my aged parents and Mary; but you know their disposition too well to suppose, they will not resign you without hesitation. Come then Caroline! and let us by those mutual endearments, which at so early a period marked the conduct of our lives, try to forget the mortifications we have experienced. For it is impossible in the present situation of our minds, for either of us to be made happy while we continue separated.

Let me, therefore, beseech you not to endanger our felicity by an untimely delicacy and etiquette; for if the invitation is not immediately from Mr. F——, and which I know will startle your feelings,[4] it ought to have the same weight when you recollect, both your own happiness and mine depend upon your compliance; and if Mr. F—— knowing this, has not had consideration enough to make the request, he certainly ought not to receive so much deference from either of us, as to have his feelings consulted: —For I know of no tie, either in nature or matrimony, which makes it necessary to forego inclinations, that are perfectly pure and consistent with sisterly affection.

Yes! Caroline, I have experienced the influence of your complaint so poignantly, that I should think myself unfeeling if I did not make every sacrifice which could tend to alleviate your sorrows; and I am sure we know each other too well, to doubt the sincerity of this declaration.

Farewel, my dear sister, and assure yourself of my most unfeigned love. I have only to add that I hope the family will believe me, when I say how very much I lament the cause of our separation, and that I continue to pray for their health and happiness.

God bless you, Caroline, and come speedily to your affectionate but disconsolate sister.

ELIZA F——

LETTER XLII

MR. IL——RAY TO CAPT. ARL——TON.

Pittsburg, May.

I Have at length, my friend, reached the banks of the Ohio; and in contemplating the fierce Alligany, and the sublimity of the rock you was shewing Caroline when she was alarmed with the sudden appearance of the natives, I could not help reflecting upon the impetuosity of your passion, which it appeared to me must have been influenced by the current of that rapid river, which seems to be hurrying, to intermingle its waters with the more gentle Monongahala.[1]

Every idea of the most arduous passion came rushing into my mind, and when I beheld the gentle Caroline who attended our party to shew us the novel scenes of this place, whose sweet mildness seemed to create enchantment wherever she trod; and while her soft faltering voice, betrayed the symptoms of that very interesting scene, I was convinced how very much you have been deceived by the warmth of your imagination; and could not help condemning anew, the inconsistency of your conduct.

The emotions of the heart may for a time be stifled; but when nature has been labouring in the element of desire, that soul which is of a divine nature will emit its celestial sparks, and it is then that the dullest understanding must be illumined. Indeed my friend you must have been stupid not to have observed the lively attatchment which Caroline feels for you; she talks not of love, but when she describes her journey over the mountain, and when she speaks of her rambles about this place, the trembling tear, imparts a softness to her eye, which love alone can give.

You have bound me up in such a manner by your curious insinuations, that I do not feel myself at liberty to touch in the slightest manner upon the subject, otherwise I think I could find out more mystery in the business, than you have been aware of; and if you will give me leave upon our arrival at Louisville, to which place it is intended Mr. T——n and his family accompany our party, I will in the most delicate manner investigate the affair; when I think it will appear there has been some misconstruction in the business, and of which, I recommend you to think previously, as you will receive this sufficiently in time to make up your mind; for we shall be detained at this place a few days, in order that Mr. T——n may make his arrangements, for it was not determined they would go, until this day.

I attended Mr. and Mrs. S—— to this place, and we were

accompanied by Mr. T——n, who was on his return from the pursuit of George, and whom he was not able to overtake; for he had embarked on board the packet at New York, previously having squandered the whole of the money he was sent to receive: and which was every farthing his indigent and distressed family were worth in the world.

Such an instance of the depravity of manners, I confess has never before come under my notice; and when I reflect upon the effects of indolence, and that disposition to prodigality and dissipation, which has marked the conduct of that young man's life, I am led to believe if such instances of worthlessness are not uncommon, that there must be something radically bad in the present system of morals; for it is impossible for me to believe, that any man can be naturally so unfeeling, as to behold with indifference his family reduced to beggary and wretchedness, while he is indulging himself in all the excesses of the foulest banquets, and in all the stupefaction of the most enervating luxury; much less to accelerate their inevitable ruin, by a breach of confidence; by a sacrilege against nature and heaven; forgetful of the ties of consanguinity and filial affection,—forgetful of the feelings of a man, and the principles of a gentleman, and regardless of every honorary consideration which many highwaymen respect and reverence. But such are the diabolical effects of those habits, in which many men are educated, and so long accustomed to indulge, that they make every thing, moral, political, and divine, yield to their gratifications.

Our party will consist of General and Mrs. W——, Mr. and Mrs. S——, Mr. T——n's family, and perhaps the old gentleman you met in the mountain, who turns out to be the brother of Mrs. T——, the circumstances of which discovery I shall leave to be explained to you by Caroline after her arrival at Louisville; when I hope your spirits will be sufficiently tranquil again to enjoy all the charms of her modulated voice, when she so brilliantly relates anecdotes, details information, tells a story, or with glowing imagery pourtrays the beauties of nature.

The enigma of Mrs. S——'s marriage is explained. There has

been something so dark and infamous in that transaction that I
was petrified when I first got a clue to so disingenuous a proceeding. But from motives of delicacy, and a more sacred regard
for the comfort of the amiable and grateful Laura, I shall be perfectly silent upon the subject. Indeed I have been obliged to trim
a little with General W—— in consequence of the letter I wrote
him,[2] when I enclosed my last to you, and which I despise, but
from the purest considerations I was obliged. You shall have the
particulars when I have the happiness to meet you, which thank
God my friend will be in a few days. Farewell,

G. Il——ray

LETTER XLIII.

Miss Caroline T——n to P——P—— Esq.

Pittsburg, May.

MY DEAR FRIEND,

MY father returned two days since in company with some
friends of General W——'s, and Mr. Il——ray of Philadelphia,
who I have so often mentioned to you with so much pleasure.
He brought with him a letter from Eliza.

Come to us as early as possible; my father has determined to
remove to Louisville; my brother has abandoned us, and returned
to England, and Eliza in the most affectionate terms has invited
me to return, nay, has almost commanded it; but my friend, as
pleasing as such news would have been to me, previous to my
leaving Philadelphia, and as unbounded as my love is for her, I
have not at this moment, the most distant conception of complying with her requisition.

A thousand considerations now overwhelm my mind; but the
ties of nature, and the feelings of honour and duty conspire to
force me to accompany my parents, who are already made sufficiently wretched by the conduct of George; and before I would

consent to desert them in their present state of indigence, and fly to a state of ease and gaiety, I would dig, or cultivate the earth, which so faithfully rewards the industrious.

Forgive my friend, this effusion of self commendation, for my pride is wounded by the unmanly desertion of George.

Pray come to us, that I may enjoy the consolation, if I merit it, to have your approbation of the conduct of your affectionate and true friend.

CAROLINE

LETTER XLIV

P. P. ESQ. TO MISS CAROLINE T——N.

Laurel-mount, May.

I Have this instant hurried over your note of this date, my dear girl, which I perfectly understand, and I have only to assure you, that it is not possible for Caroline to deserve my disapprobation in any thing she can do,

I dispatch this by the return of the bearer of yours, and I will be with you early to-morrow.

God bless you, my dear Caroline, and rely only upon the care of yours, &c.

P. P——

LETTER XLV

MISS CAROLINE T——N TO MRS. F——.

Pittsburg, May.

AT a period when a combination of circumstances appeared to conspire to distract your Caroline, my dear sister, I received

your affectionate letter, directed to the care of our friend Mr.
Il——ray, who is now with us at this place, on his way to the
Illinois.

Never did I experience a period which seemed pregnant with
so many events—God knows what they will lead to—I am suspended as it were between Elysium and Tartarus—for while you,[1]
my Eliza, give me such proofs of your affection as your letter
contains, I again feel all those sensations your love has ever inspired. But when I take a retrospective view of the circumstances
that were the cause of all my inquietudes, and then look forward
to that goal to which every tie that I hold sacred obliges me to
advance, I confess my strength and spirits are overpowered.

Kindly and affectionate do I regard your invitation to return:
and was it possible for my love to be more lively for you, Eliza,
the tenderness and concern you express in that charming and ingenuous requisition, would have produced it; but your solicitude
for me upon all occasions, and the mutual endearments which
have been interchanged throughout our girlish pastimes, and cemented in our approach to maturity, had bound me to you by
ties that are indissoluble.

Yes! my dear sister, as fondly as I once would have embraced
a chance of again living with you, it is now impossible for me
ever to indulge such a thought. Every feeling of pride, filial duty,
moral, and honorary, tells me it would be base now to desert
those parents who gave me existence, when they have no consolation left but in the confidence of the esteem of that remnant
of a progeny, on whom they have lavished so many favours; and
who are now reduced to Mary and myself; for George has abandoned us, and sailed for England, in a manner, of which to think,
is shocking; and upon which I shall leave him to make his own
comments, as doubtless you will see him. It is an affair altogether
so disgraceful, that I am ashamed merely at the recollection.

I imparted to you in my last the manner our Uncle P—— was
discovered, and I now send you a copy of our correspondence
agreeable to promise;[2] which, should have been done sooner, but
my father not having returned from his pursuit after George, and

our destination being uncertain, I concluded I had better wait untill I could write more fully.

The enclosed copy to, and one from our worthy uncle will inform you of our preparations to embark for Louisville, which will be in the course of to morrow; from whence I hope to be able to continue our correspondence as usual.

I must now inform you how very much we are obliged to our honoured friend. His little plantation is upon the southern branch of the Ohio, about twenty miles above this place, which he has cultivated with all the care of an English farmer, and it produces him all the comforts of living in the most superfluous abundance: for this abundance there is always a generous market, as the emigrants who are continually passing through the country to form new settlements upon the Mississippi, after crossing the mountain want all kind of necessaries; but his munificence to us has been such, that instead of selling his produce, he has continued to send his own boat to Pittsburgh with such loads of provisions, that could you have seen our larder during the whole time since he has known us, you would have supposed, it belonged to one of the great Inns on the west road in England.

But two days since, when I informed him that my father intended to go down to Louisville, and take with him his family, he immediately, not only dispatched the note, which is enclosed, but in the course of the next day he arrived with a boat fitted up in the most commodious manner for our accommodation; and thus anticipating our wants, other boats have followed, bringing in them every kind of necessary for our voyage, with horses, &c. to enable my father to settle a farm upon our arrival in the low country.

However this is not all, for this friend goes with us—I remonstrated with him—I told him his age and the comfortable support he at present enjoyed, ought to induce him to reflect upon the hardships he might be compelled to undergo, in consequence of such an undertaking; and however much I might lament the necessity of parting with so valuable a friend, yet, I would sooner experience the pangs of such a dereliction, than I would recom-

mend him to launch again into a new settlement. I begged him
to recollect—here he stopped me.—O Eliza! how will your
tender heart melt when you read his tragecal history—I saw the
tears start in his eyes—The animation of his whole soul seemed
to have lighted again the torch of sorrow, and I trembled for
having bordered upon a subject, which has as potential an effect
upon him, as the unparalleled Sterne, said the name of Julia had
upon Slawkenbergius,

> "Harsh and untuneful
> Are the notes of love,
> Unless my Julia strikes the key,
> Her hand alone, can touch the part,
> Whose dulcit movements charm the heart,
> And governs all the man with sympathetic sway."[3]

For whenever the conversation produces a sentiment that brings
to his recollection his once fond Juliana and infant family, his
feelings quite overpower him, and his face pourtrays the most
lively sorrow.

He had paused for some moments to let nature take its course;
but perceiving that the power of sympathy had extended its flame
to me, and that my feelings were in unison with his, he took his
handkerchief, and after having dryed my eyes; said he, Caroline,
my friend, we have met here in these regions of innocence, where
there is no art to beguile and rob us of that felicity, which flows
from mutual sincerity; and while I discover in you all the warmth
of imagination peculiar to your animation and youth, and all that
regard for virtue which the ingenuous heart possesses, I feel that
I am growing old, and consequently I am governed more by my
principles than by my passions; and if you will permit me to say,
after the many proofs you have given me of your candour, that I
have not forgotten the affair with Captain Arl——ton, who you
know is at Louisville; but said he, still holding my hand, while I
felt a glow overspreading my cheeks, abstractedly from the obligations which consanguinity, and the ties of friendship have im-

posed upon me to be your guardian, I am actuated by all selfishness, which is too apt to be the spring of our every action —for I feel said he, continuing, that I cannot be happy where you are not; and I have learned to know better how to appropriate the joys of this world, than to sacrifice animated pleasures, to that sluggish inaction which merely affords comfort without zest.

Such, Eliza, has been the conduct of that man, whom we have heard so severely reprobated, and condemned as the most abandoned and unprincipled man alive; and what proves to me more satisfactorily than could the most brilliant display of oratory, that it is only sufficient for a man to govern his conduct by the principles of reason and justice, when they differ materially from the established sentiments of society, to receive that obloquy, which has tarnished that fame, that in my opinion, ought to be as fair as the unsullied purity of nature.

How shall I express to you, my dear sister, my regard, for the manner in which you sent what was enclosed in your charming letter?

If I have not appropriated it in the manner you expected, I am sure I have done it in a way that will prove agreeable to you— nothing could have come more opportunely; for though our friend has anticipated all our wants, which it was in his power to do, yet he had not the means of transmuting things into gold, when the only articles of that sort his little farm produces, had been already consumed in our family—and thus it has happened, that my father's penury has found in your generous remittance a most timely relief.

Farewell, I am obliged to finish, to assist in packing up for our embarkation. Be assured that you will hear from me by the first opportunity I can meet to send a letter. Direct yours as usual, to the care of Mr. Il——ray, Philadelphia.

O Eliza! I already tremble at the thought of seeing Captain Arl——ton. Will you pity your Caroline?—we all unite in prayers for your happiness.

God bless you my dear sister.
CAROLINE

LETTER XLVI

CAPT. ARL——TON TO MR. IL——RAY.

Louisville, June.

IT is impossible for me to see Caroline in the present state of my mind, and therefore I hope you will not look upon it in the least disrespectful, my friend, if I should happen to be absent when you arrive; for to be candid with you, I shall make a journey purposely to Lexington.

Your obliging favour from Pittsburg, which you meant should give me spirits, has had quite a contrary effect.

By attempting to soothe my mind, I discover that secret poison flattery ever contains, and which I consider the principal cause of my present wretchedness.

The image you have given of Caroline makes her appear to me more lovely than ever; and when you say that enchantment seems to spring up where e'er she treads, I feel the full force of all her charms, and conceive that I behold her in this season of fragrance and beauty, decorating those gardens which you passed through on your return from the fatal view upon the Allegany,

> *While the blushing rose, drooping hides its head,*
> *As Caroline's sweets more odorous prove,*
> *And op'ning lillies look faint, sick, and dead,—*
> *For things inanimate, feel the force of love.*

She is irresistible,—and it is only by absence that I shall ever be enabled to forget my misfortunes; and therefore, my dear friend, I must request that in your future letters, when you mention that divine woman, you will not appreciate that beauty which has ten thousand charms to fascinate and fetter the soul.

She has not only all the symmetry of form, the softness of love, and the enchantment of a goddess; but she can assume an ani-

mation and that surprizing activity of motion, that while you are
suspended in the transports of astonishment, you are lost in admiration at the gracefulness with which she moves—I have seen
her bound over a rock, and pluck a wild honey-suckle, that grew
upon the side of a precipice, and while I stood gazing at her in
amazement, she has brought it as a trophy of her exertions.

Believe, my friend, that if ever nature formed one woman to
excel another in personal charms, it must be Caroline.

As to the mystery of the note, it is not very conspicuous;[1]—
but my own credulity by vainly expecting to have excited a mutual sympathy, I believe to have been the only cause of my misfortunes, and therefore I must insist that you do not in the slightest
manner touch upon the subject.

I cannot say I am in the least concerned for the loss of the
brother; for he was so extremely inactive, that he would have
continued a dead weight upon the family.—

As to his conduct, certainly it is very reprehensible and inhuman, to say the least of it. However, that is a pleasant philosophy
which induces you to believe, every thing that happens is for the
best. I do not mean the sublime philosophy which Pope meant
when he said,

Whatever is—is right;[2]

for he clearly alluded to the great order of things; but there are
many people in the world, who let what will happen to them,
they believe it is all for the best; and I have no doubt myself, the
desertion of that young man, was the sole cause which induced
Mr. T——n to think of settling in this country; and certainly it
will prove a propitious circumstance, for this is a much more
eligible country in every respect for his family, than that of Red
Stone or Pittsburg.

I confess I have the greatest expectations in seeing the uncle,
who appeared to me, at the time we met, to be a very extraordinary man; and I flatter myself, that this infant settlement will
derive much advantage from talents so splendid as his appear.

It is perhaps needless for me to ask you, my dear friend, to write to me immediately on your arrival, and to let me know when you are ready to commence your tour of this country, for I will with the greatest pleasure attend you, as I have by my frequent excursions through its different parts, obtained a considerable knowledge of its geography, minerals, &c.

As I must suppose the family stand in need of pecuniary aid, I beg you will contrive to appropriate to their use the inclosed in such a manner, as not to offend their delicacy, and be particularly cautious, not to let it be suspected that I have any hand in the business, for should that be conceived, it would look like an attempt to lay Caroline under obligations to me.

You have quite alarmed me upon the subject of the charming Laura R——, now Mrs. S——, and I shall be all impatience, until I hear what you have to say upon the subject. Be so kind as to apologize to all our friends for my absence.

I leave this enclosed in a packet for General W——: I am this moment informed there are boats making round Diamond Island.[3]—Who knows but one of them contains the lovely Caroline?—ah! my friend, I feel every emotion of love and shame so powerfully, that I must instantly fly to avoid exposing myself —curse that mandate which banished me from the lovely tyrant of my heart—curse the vanity which exposed my weakness;—for damnable is that fate which compells a man to avoid the object of all others, which to him is the most interesting—I must this instant be off. O Caroline!—Caroline!—while my soul deadens at the thought, I abandon the spot which will be converted into elysium the moment you arrive. Forgive, my friend, this effusion of nature—this weakness, for it prepares us for those delicious raptures, that flow from the source of sympathy, and while it softens us to that tender texture, which is congenial to feminine charms, it invigorates our actions, and fosters every generous and noble sentiment.

The streamers of your vessels,[4] for it must be you, are playing in the wind, as if enraptured with the treasure over which they impend, seem eradiated with the charms of Caroline; while the gentle Ohio, as if conscious of its charge, proudly swells, and appears to vie with the more elevated earth, in order to secure to its divinity, upon which to tread at her disembarkation, the flowery carpet of its banks.

Adieu. I am off.
J. A.

LETTER XLVII

Mr. Il——ray to Capt. Arl——ton.

Louisville, June.

MY DEAR JAMES,

FROM the time we left Pittsburg untill our arrival here, which was ten days after our embarkation,[1] we were all appreciating the pleasure we should derive from finding you at this place.

I had expatiated largely upon the satisfaction we should experience from the information you would give us of the country; and no sooner were we in sight of the town than we hung out a flag of invitation; not doubting but you would observe it, and immediately come off to us in a barge; but judge what was the surprize of the whole party, and my mortification, when we learned upon landing, you had left the place not more than half an hour.

The letter you left enclosed for me in General W——'s packet, to be sure informed me of the cause of your absence; but it by no means justified the action. And I demand as a proof of your respect for your old friends, that you instantly return.

Remember, James, this is the command of a friend, who is anxious to restore you to a state of reason, which it appears you have not possessed for some time past.

Caroline was in tolerable spirits until within two days of our arrival, when she suddenly appeared to be pensive and in a state of extreme trepidation; and since we arrived she has been confined by indisposition.

If you have a delicate and tender regard for this charming girl, you will fly immediately to enquire after her health. But to put it out of your power to frame a shadow for an excuse, I inform you that it is my intention first to visit the Illinois, and to view this country on my return.

I waited during yesterday for an opportunity to send this, and as I could not meet with one, I send a person I have hired for the purpose, as my men are unacquainted with the country.

Believe me to be your sincere, but unhappy friend,

G. IL——RAY

LETTER XLVIII

CAPT. ARL——TON TO MR. IL——RAY.

Lexington, June.

YOUR express has this moment reached me: and to convince you, my dear Il——ray, that no man can be more alive to every sentiment of love and friendship, I shall not defer my return to Louisville a single hour; and I merely dispatch this by the return of your messenger, to let you know I shall be with you to-morrow in the evening; and that in my present distracted state of mind, I think it most adviseable to make my *entre* under the cover of the dark,[1] to prevent my being perceived, as I wish to devote the whole evening in sequestered converse with you my friend.

Caroline is ill! Ah! Il——ray I am wretched in the extreme. I am burnt up with a scorching fever—I am wrecked in the elements of every painful passion, and my every effort to reason is baffled by my reflections upon past occurences,

But I am your indissoluble friend,

J. ARL——TON

LETTER XLIX

MISS CAROLINE T———N TO MRS. F———.

Louisville, July.

MY DEAR SISTER,

WE arrived here about eight days since, and when we came in sight of the Rapids,[1] we expected every moment that Capt. Arl———ton would come off as Mr. Il———ray assured us, that he had informed him of the time we should leave Pittsburg, by which means he would be able to know nearly the time of our arrival. However every one of the party were amazed at learning he had left town immediately upon our appearing in sight; but which it seems was owing to some particular business up the country, and his not knowing our vessels.

Mr. Il———ray dispatched a messenger to inform him of the arrival of our party, and requesting him instantly to return. He came in the course of eight and forty hours; and after having spent the preceding evening with his friend they waited upon us the next morning.

I had been in such a tremulous state from the time I embarked, which increased to such a degree upon our approximation to this place, that I was unable to keep up my spirits, and at length became compleatly ill; so that when they arrived, as I had no previous intimation of Capt. Arl———ton's return, I was sitting in an undress,[2] in General W———'s *marquee* for the advantage of the air,[3] as the weather was extremely warm.

It seems they had inquired for me at our lodging, and hearing I was in the *marquee,* they came thither without any ceremony. I happened to be at that moment alone. Mr. Il———ray entered first, and said my dear Caroline, my friend has hastened from Lexington to enquire after your health, and to assure you of his solicitude for your happiness. He was leading him by the hand to present him to me, and had nearly approached me before I recollected him; for not expecting to see him, and the alteration which has taken place both in his person and his countenance, for he has become quite thin, and his face is very much sun burnt; so that I did not at first know him; but the instant I could think, I recognized the image of the same Arl——ton with whom I had crossed the Appalachean mountains; and when I had caught a glance from his piercing eyes my whole faculties were for a minute so confounded, that I was not able to speak. Indeed it was with difficulty I could keep from fainting.

Mr. Il——ray endeavoured to relieve me by the gentlest of all solicitudes, and by every tender effort to recall my powers of utterance; but it was not until my surprise was abated, that I was able to thank Capt. Arl——ton for his kindness, and to assure him of the pleasure it gave me once more to see him.

Mr. Il——ray then enquired after General W——, and said he would go and bring him to the *marquee,* when he left us alone.

O Eliza! what were the sensations of your Caroline? Harassed as my spirits were, by continual anxiety, and by this last effort to collect myself; still I felt a thousand emotions which succeeded each other with such rapidity, that I am incapable of forming a distinct idea of any one of them.

We were silent for near a minute after we were left by ourselves, when Capt. Arl——ton said, "Caroline it seems an age since I left Pittsburg," and then taking hold of my hand, said he, "I hope you passed your winter agreeably?" I told him it had been very tedious, and rather unpleasant. He then felicitated me upon the discovery of our uncle, and begged that I would do him the honour to introduce them to each other:—I told him I most certainly would do it with the greatest pleasure, and assured him, that he had often enquired after him with the most unfeigned concern.

His bosom now seemed to palpitate with the greatest fervency. Ah! said he, Caroline how much misery have I experienced in consequence of that note? But if I have lost so precious a season, and which can never be regained, it proves to me my charming

and enchanting girl, that every hour thus sacrificed, is worth an
eternity of a dull and tasteless existence.

The ardour of his expression, and the emotions of my heart,
which were then beaming in my eyes, induced me to hang down
my head, when said he, tenderly pressing my hand at the same
time, Caroline! will you not bestow one look upon me? Then
half leaning forward, as if to learn what was passing in my countenance, he said, pray Caroline! let me once more feel the influence of those eyes, which used to charm my every sense; and then
repeated these beautiful lines out of an ode of Thomson's:

> "O mix their beauteous beams with mine,
>   And let us interchange our hearts;
> Let all their sweetness on me shine,
>   Pour'd thro' my soul be all their darts."[4]

At that instant Mr. Il——ray returned with General W——,
and thus ended before it was well begun, the renovation of the
subject of his attachment.

Soon after our uncle entered they were introduced to each
other, and as General W—— invited the party to dine with him
in the *marquee,* I returned to our lodgings to dress, leaving the
gentlemen by themselves. Mr. Il——ray attended me, when to
my great surprize I found Mary already dressed, and which was
the more extraordinary, as it is not usual in this warm climate to
dress in the morning.

When Mr. Il——ray had taken his leave to return to the gentlemen, Mary asked me, if I had seen Captain Arl——ton, and
upon my answering in the affirmative, she thought it very strange
he should have called, and upon hearing I was not within, that
he should have left the house immediately; of which, at the moment, I took no other notice, than supposing the observation
proceeded from her very great tenacity to what she calls decorum
and good breeding.

Not long after Capt. Arl——ton attended by our uncle came

to pay his respects to the family. I was at the time occupied in dressing, for I was so flurried, and the day was so extremely warm, that I was obliged to be very tardy; and when I returned I found Capt. Arl——ton and our uncle were apparently very well acquainted, and seemed to be conversing with the greatest freedom. But the moment I entered Capt. Arl——ton rose and handed me to a seat, and with the most expressive tenderness, asked me how I did, and said he, "Caroline, as you have been indisposed, if you do not keep yourself very tranquil, the heat will most likely occasion a relapse."

At that instant I caught a look from him, which expressed all the animated tenderness the tear of sympathy, and which hung upon his long eyelashes, gives to the azure brightness of a living orb.[5] And as I was seated, he gently pressed my hand. It was too much for me, Eliza, my whole soul appeared to be rebelling against the despotism of restraint, and it was not possible any longer for me to controul its emotions. My worthy uncle, my friend, had been watching me, and said, Caroline my dear, I am apprehensive your weak state of health will not permit you with safety to make these exertions, and taking his handkerchief and drying my eyes, he begged I would sit perfectly quiet.

Ah! Eliza, never did your Caroline experience so much difficulty to command herself. Capt. Arl——ton was obliged to leave the room, while his face pourtrayed the most lively sensibility.

When we set out to dinner, Capt. Arl——ton took my hand, while Mary very officiously said, Caroline, my dear, take hold of my arm, for I am sure you can scarcely be able to walk. In this way we entered the *marquee*.

During the whole time of dinner and evening, for we took our coffee in the *marquee,* Capt. Arl——ton not only continued very attentive to me, but he did not omit any of those little elegant anticipations, which have such peculiar energy in love;—and it is possible I might have discovered symptoms of the great joy I experienced; for I found myself not only better, but I felt that supreme bliss which flows from the banquet of pure love, in the genial hours of sentimental rapture.

After we had retired, I received a lecture from Mary of the most extraordinary kind. She said my conduct during the day had been bold in the extreme, and that nothing could be more shameful, than to express the pleasure I had received from Capt. Arl——ton's attentions in the manner in which I had done; particularly as I had for so long a time been so very pensive, and which difference of my behaviour and spirits had been noticed by every one of the company.

O Eliza, what a stroke was this upon your Caroline? My fond imagination had flattered me with the idea, that there was nothing in my conduct, but what had been perfectly delicate and innocent.

I entered my apartment with the most agonizing reflections, and after a sleepless night, I found myself unable in the morning to rise, for after so many struggles both my frame and spirits were so harrassed that I believed, *as Mary assured me,* that my life depended upon my obtaining rest.

Mr. Il——ray and Capt. Ar——ton had called several times in the course of the morning to enquire after my health, and were told that the fatigue I had experienced the preceding day, had produced such an effect upon me, that it had confined me to my bed.

It was toward the evening, after a day passed in extreme anxiety, and which was very sultry, that our uncle requested to be admitted into my bed chamber; he came and found me in a high fever, and in that situation he thought it would not be prudent for me to rise: But assured me I wanted nothing but composure to restore me, and begged I would not suffer my spirits to be depressed, for he had watched the emotions of Capt. Arl——ton, and did not doubt the sincerity of his motives.

I then related to him every thing which passed in the *marquee* without the smallest reserve, and also the curious reprimand I had received from Mary. He started at the mention of the note. What did Capt. Arl——ton allude to by the note, said he Caroline? I answered him that it was entirely mysterious to me; when said he, this enigma puzzles me, but I have my suspicions, and if you will give me leave I will investigate them? I thanked him and asked what they were; to which he replied, that he would inform me the next day, and begged I would compose myself, for he would answer for it all would be well, and said he had much conversation with Capt. Arl——ton, and found him sensible, manly, and ingenuous.

In the course of the next day Capt. Arl——ton called frequently, but as my fever was not entirely abated, though I felt myself much better, our uncle, who visited me in the morning, thought it most advisable for me not to leave my room that day, and said in the course of it, he would find out the meaning of the note.

Accordingly he came; well said he, my dear friend, as he entered my apartment, are you any better? I told him I was; then said he, my dear I think in the course of to-morrow I shall be able to unriddle the mystery of the note, and said, from the whole of Mary's conduct towards me, he had long suspected there had been some unfair transaction; and he accordingly had asked her when they were by themselves, and at a moment when she could not expect any thing of the kind, what could have induced her to have written the note to Capt. Arl——ton at Pittsburg? Mary's face, said he, was instantly as red as scarlet, and though she affected to make a wonder at the interrogation, and meaning, yet he was confirmed in a belief in consequence of the blush which the question produced, that she knew something of the matter; and said he, with your permission, Caroline, I will to-morrow wait upon Capt. Arl——ton, and tell him that I am no stranger to what has passed between you and him, and ask what note he alluded to in the course of the conversation he had with you in General W——'s *marquee?*—I blushed and left the affair entirely to his management.

But—O my sister! he is gone again! For what is your Caroline reserved? I have been tossed between hope, expectation, love, and disappointment, while every one of my senses have been at war with fortune, and all my wishes have been palsied in their infancy.

I had risen the next morning, as I was considerably recovered, and every moment expected Capt. Arl——ton would call upon us, when to my great astonishment, Mr. Il——ray entered about eleven o'clock by himself. Caroline, my dear girl, said he, I lament that I am obliged to leave you immediately; but I promise myself the pleasure of making a much longer stay with you when I return. I hastily interrupted him, and asked if Capt. Arl——ton did not mean to attend him? He answered that it was on his account that it became necessary for him to set out so early. I was afraid to ask another question. "Sir," said I, "If you will excuse me, I will retire, for I find myself too weak to sit long up." He conducted me to the door of my apartment; when said he, "Caroline, shall I say any thing from you to Arl——ton, for he has already crossed the river to Clarkeville, and begged that I would mention him to you in the most affectionate terms?" I could not speak, but instantly fell, as though I had been shot.

When my recollection returned, I found I had been taken into my apartment, and that Mr. Il——ray had departed, leaving his servant behind him, to carry word when I should recover in what state he left me.

Such, my dear sister, has been the fate of your unhappy Caroline, and you must pardon me for writing you a whole letter concerning myself; but be assured, the moment I am able, I will fully compensate for this egotism, by sending you a full account of every thing in which you can be interested.

The family are all in good spirits and health, your Caroline excepted, who is not only unhappy, but wretched in the extreme. God only knows what will be my fate, Eliza.

Farewell,
CAROLINE.

END OF THE SECOND VOLUME.

VOLUME III

LETTER L

Clarkeville, Thursday, 8. A.M.[1]

TO what a state of misery am I reduced my dear friend? How have I been tantalized with idle hope? But you are to blame for the last mortification I received. However I know your intentions were sincere. But it certainly was very idle, to say the least of the matter, to renew my overtures, after I received the note at Pittsburg. But you know I did it, at your most earnest request. It was a sad experiment to prove your judgment erroneous. You must now, I think, be convinced that Caroline has no more regard for me, than she has for you, or any other acquaintance.

Never will I see her fair face again; it is impossible for me to live in the same place where Caroline dwells upon such terms. Again, has she affected to be ill merely to avoid me; for Miss T——n told me last evening, when I was impatient to know if her indisposition was in the least alarming, that nothing was the matter with her, and that keeping her room was entirely an air.

Never my friend was I so thunderstruck, every one of my faculties were suspended by grief, while I felt every torturing sensation, which disappointed love can produce.

Such were the considerations, that induced me to fly over the river. I could not last night explain myself, for I was wrecked in the element of the most agonizing and torturing frenzy. Cross immediately over to me, that I may hurry from the sight of that place, which contains the lovely, but dangerous Caroline. Let me look in the wilds of this extensive region for that peace of mind, which Caroline, I fear, has for ever destroyed. Come my friend, let us together explore the country until we find the sources of the Mississippi, and the limits of the more impetuous and extensive Missouri; for I will live in this uncultivated, and uncivilized waste, until my person shall become as wild as my senses.

O my friend! three days since, when we found Caroline half unzoned,[2] sitting in the *marquee* to receive the cool breezes,[3] which seemed to wanton in her bosom as if enraptured with its sweets, while her conscious thoughts diffused their roseate charms over her heavenly face, how did my senses beat with the ecstacy of desire? And when you left us alone, how did my imagination glow with all the enthusiasm of the most delicate and tender passion? I again believed my felicity would be perfect; and can you, after such a disappointment, form a conception of the anguish of my tortured and distracted mind?

I shall expect you this evening, or tomorrow morning at farthest, and let me intreat you not to disappoint your wretched friend,

J. ARL——TON

LETTER LI

MR. IL——RAY TO P. P——. ESQ.

Thursday, 2 P.M.

DEAR SIR,

MY friend Capt. Arl——ton crossed over this morning to Clarkeville, and I am obliged to follow him without delay; for some latent cause seems to have distracted his mind, and it appears necessary to administer the offices of a friend, in order to prevent him from falling into some difficulty, as he now is in the Indian country.

I called at your apartments to make an excuse for my abrupt departure; but as I had the misfortune not to find you at home, I hope you will consider this as a sufficient apology, and believe no one is more concerned in the welfare of your friends, than myself; and the moment I return, I shall take every possible step to give proofs of it.

In the mean time if you will do me the honour to correspond with me, you will confer a favour upon me, which it will always be my pride to acknowledge.

Farewell,
G. Il——ray

LETTER LII

P. P—— Esq. to Mr. Il——ray.

Louisville, Thursday Evening.

DEAR SIR,

I Have this moment received your note of this day, and was not more surprized at your sudden departure than I was concerned for the necessity of it.

Permit me to acknowledge how much I feel myself gratified in the thought of that pleasure I shall receive from your communications; and also my gratitude for the interest you take in the happiness of my unfortunate friends; and to assure you at the same time, that I am not insensible of the many favours you have done them.

I have my suspicions of the cause that determined your friend Captain Arl——ton to leave this place with so much precipitation; and I hope in future he will not trifle with a lady under an idea that she is unprotected.[1]

I have the honour to be, dear sir, with the utmost respect, your obedient servant,

P. P——

P. S. As I send a barge purposely with this, I have no doubt but you will receive it before you leave Clarkeville.

LETTER LIII

MR. IL——RAY TO P. P——, ESQ.

Clarkeville, Friday Morning.

DEAR SIR,

I Had the pleasure of receiving your note per express last evening, and I have in reply to say, I communicated the contents to
my friend, who was not a little hurt at the idea, that you or Miss
Caroline T——n, should harbour the most distant suspicion that
he was capable of trifling with any person, much less with an
amiable young lady; and he was very sorry to request me to add,
that it would not be consistent with the sentiments either of a
brave or generous man, to make any comments upon the conclusion of your note, as he is willing to believe the expression was
unguarded; and that while he governs his own conduct, he knows
of no obligation he owes to any person, who has a right, either
to direct or controul his movements; and, that he is constrained
to make these observations, only from that delicate sense of honour, which every gentleman ought to feel.

I hope you will put the most favourable construction upon
these remarks, and while I am discharging the office of a friend,
I also hope you will not doubt the sincerity of my motives; but,
if you should harbour any one sentiment derogatory to the honour
or generosity of my friend, I shall be made most happy on my
return to come to an *eclaircissement* with you upon the subject:[1]
and permit me to assure you, that it is my first wish to promote
a right understanding between you, and in a firm persuasion, that
it is also your wish, I will do myself the pleasure to write to you
from Post St. Vincent.[2]

Commend Captain Arl——ton and myself to all our friends,
and particularly to Miss Caroline.

Farewell.

G. IL——RAY

P. S. Captain Arl——ton begs that I will return you his thanks for recommending to him the young mountaineer,[3] who he finds very useful and alert.

LETTER LIV

P. P——, Esq. to Mr. Il——ray.

Louisville, July.

DEAR SIR,

TO convince you how sincerely I regard your esteem, I embrace an opportunity that has presented itself of doing myself the pleasure of writing to you, without regard to the ceremony of first receiving your letter, which you promised to write me from St. Vincent's.

No sentiments can be more sacred in the estimation of a gentleman, than those of generosity and honour; and I disdain to skreen myself under the allowance, which your friend may suppose he liberally made for me, when he attributed the conclusion of my note to you, touching his conduct, to haste or being off my guard.

If he had felt that delicate sense of honour of which he talks, he would immediately have returned and come to an explanation; for all men who are conscious of having acted in every respect like gentlemen, *always court enquiry and investigation;* and though I will not hastily put any unfavourable construction upon the conduct of a man of whom I have been induced to think well; still I must declare, that I never was more disappointed, than when I found my note had not induced Captain Arl——ton to re-cross the Ohio.

Such are my candid sentiments upon the subject of his conduct, and which I hope when he returns, he will be able to justify; but if he will neither return, or cannot make a justification, I shall be obliged to consider his conduct to Miss Caroline T——n, not only as reprehensible, but I shall think he dared not to have trifled with her, as he has done in two instances, one at Pittsburg, and the other at this place, if he had not supposed that her unprotected situation secured his impunity.[1]

Give me leave to assure you, that you have my most unfeigned wishes, for the enjoyment of every pleasure your excursion can afford.

Your friends have all desired me to assure you of their wishes for your safety and speedy return.

I have the honour to be with the utmost regard, my dear Sir, your most obedient humble servant,

P. P———

LETTER LV

MR. IL———RAY TO P. P———, ESQ.

St. Vincent's, August.

DEAR SIR,

I Had the pleasure of receiving your obliging favour from Louisville two days since, and would have returned an immediate answer, had I not found myself too much indisposed to write.

Whether I took cold, or whether it was from the uneasiness which preyed upon my mind in consequence of the misunderstanding between you and my friend Arl———ton, or whether both conspired, I cannot absolutely say, but I found myself so extremely unwell before I reached this place, that it was with difficulty I could travel; and ever since our arrival, I have been confined to my bed.

Captain Arl———ton, finding that my fever had taken a turn, and that I was out of all danger, and seeing that it would be some time before I could be sufficiently recovered to accompany him, and he being impatient to pursue the object of his journey, while the season continued favourable, set out three days since for St.

Anthony's falls, from which place he purposes to proceed down the Mississippi to Kaskaskia,[1] where I am to meet him about the middle of September, when it is our intention to visit the country upon the Missouri, and when I shall not fail to communicate to him your sentiments respecting his conduct to Miss Caroline T——n.

Men view things differently when they have heard but one side of the question, and with every deference to your good sense and moderation, I must beg leave to assure you, that I think my friend incapable of acting disingenuously by any human being; and if you think he has in any respect trifled with your niece, I will venture to pledge my reputation upon his making the most fair and open acknowledgement.

You must permit me to reserve any opinion I may have formed upon the subject, as the affair is altogether of too delicate a nature for me to promulge a thought upon, without first having consulted my friend: and suffer me to add, that it is impossible for me to entertain one thought derogatory to the delicacy or dignity of the charming Miss Caroline T——n.

It is at present Captain Arl——ton's intention, when we shall have explored the country upon the Missouri, to return to Baltimore by the way of New Orleans, which makes me fear it will not be possible for you and he to have an oral explanation, and thoughts written in most cases of disagreement, I have remarked, tend rather to widen the misunderstanding.

Previous to my leaving this place I shall write to you upon its situation, &c. as I am too weak at present to add any thing more.

Let me desire you to inform my friends, how very sincerely I wish to return to them.

Farewell.
G. IL——RAY

LETTER LVI

P. P—— Esq. to Mr. Il——ray.

Clarkeville, Tuesday, August.

I Am made the most miserable man alive, my dear sir, in the loss of my charming and most affectionate niece Caroline.—

She was carried off this morning by a party of Indians from the heights of Silver Creek.[1]—Every exertion to follow and rescue her has been made, but I have no tidings of their having been overtaken; and as your favour from St. Vincent's dated ————, informs me that you are still at that post, I dispatch a runner with this, in order to request you will send out a party from thence, who may have a chance of intercepting them; for it seems they are some of the remote tribes, as part of them were armed with bows and arrows.[2]

I can give you no instructions how to act upon this emergency, and most melancholy catastrophe; but I know you will make every possible exertion to rescue my lost and unfortunate friend.

It is now seven o'clock in the evening, and General W—— has not returned from the pursuit, who I am waiting to hear from before I dispatch this, and which time I will snatch to inform you how this irreparable accident happened, and which has brought to light a most inhuman and nefarious transaction.

Caroline has been in a most pensive mood ever since your departure, and to amuse her thoughts she crossed this morning into the Indian country, unattended, except by the barge-men, who were to return for her at 3 P.M. and her maid, to view the falls from Silver Creek, where she was when the maid, who was returning back from Clarkeville where she had been for her mistress's glass,[3] that had been left by accident, saw the savages carry her off.—

She instantly by her cries alarmed the inhabitants, who went in pursuit of them, and then recrossed to bring us the unwelcome news. I had gone out in the morning early, otherwise I certainly should have prevented Caroline from going over the river; but I had returned, and was sitting with Miss T——n, when the maid came crying, and said, "That her mistress,—that Miss Caroline was taken by the Indians."—Miss T——n turned pale—I was petrified—Miss T——n threw herself at my feet, and implored my forgiveness, and then with the greatest contrition, acknowledged that she had written a note to Captain Arl——ton which had been the cause of all Caroline's miseries.—

I crossed instantly to Clarkeville, with a mind so agitated that I scarcely knew what I was about; and not untill this moment, am I able to support myself, but from the hope, that the dear girl will be overtaken and restored to us.

It is now nine o'clock, and not one of the parties have returned—I am incapable of making any remarks upon a conduct so unnatural as that of Miss T——n. It was the most ungenerous I yet ever heard—her conscience affected her so powerfully, the moment she heard of poor Caroline's fate, that she could not suppress her compunction.—

Past ten o'clock. I have no news of General W——, and therefore I think it best not to delay another moment dispatching the runner.

I am, dear sir, your much afflicted friend and humble servant.

P. P——

LETTER LVII

MR. IL——RAY TO P. P——, ESQ.

St. Vincent, August.

MY DEAR SIR,

I Received by the bearer within two days after date, the sad accounts of the capture of your lovely niece by the natives.

Never were my feelings more distressed—never were my

senses more confounded—never was my sorrow more poignant —but the moment my recollection would permit me, I started from my bed which I had only occasionally left, and walked to the fort to inform the *commandant* of the circumstance of Caroline's being taken.[1]

In an instant a party was dispatched up the Wabash—and immediately after several others were sent different ways, the return of which I have waited, previous to sending back your runner.

Would God he was the harbinger of good news—not a vestige of an Indian have any one of them discovered—they continued out for four days, by which time, if they had come this way they would have crossed the Wabash.

Unfortunate Caroline! How will her sensible heart palpitate in the agonizing dereliction? How will her tender limbs support the fatigue of being hurried through briary thickets? How will her lovely frame be able to rest, without other covering, than the cloud deformed canopy of the heavens? What will be the sensations of Arl——ton when he hears of the fate of Caroline, and the exposition of the circumstance of the note, which must explain to you the whole apparent inconsistency of his conduct?

We must live in hope—after the effervescence of our passions, our cooler judgment searches for more stable ground to act upon; and it is from the loss we all have sustained, we are bound to demand that Caroline shall be given up; otherwise the whole race of savages, must expiate with their lives the robbery they have committed.

Lay the case before the senate of the state,[2] for I am sure all who have seen Caroline will plead the cause, while the revolution of her beauty will inspire their eloquence with irresistible energy.[3]

Farewell. If you should have any information of her, pray dispatch an express to me.

I am, sincerely your's, &c.
G. IL——RAY

LETTER LVIII

MR. IL——RAY, TO P. P——, ESQ.

St. Vincent's, Sept.

MY DEAR SIR,

I Have this instant received a letter, dated Kaskaskia from my friend Arl——ton, by a runner, who I send forward with it enclosed, as it will save the time of transcribing so much of it as concerns you; and which I hope will convince you of the purity of his motives, and the sincerity of his attachment for your lovely neice.

I am in haste, your's, &c.
G. IL——RAY

LETTER LIX

CAPT. ARL——TON, TO MR. IL——RAY.

Kaskaskia, Sept.

MY DEAR FRIEND,

FROM St. Vincent's we crossed the immense Buffalo plains,[1] and then making our course north-westerly, towards the head waters of the Illinois river, we fell in upon it about one hundred and fifty miles above its mouth, according to the computation of my guide, where we encamped in order to prepare rafts to transport our baggage across the river; and during which time, the hunters would have an opportunity to secure provisions for the party until we should arrive at St. Anthony's falls:[2] As we were falling more into the track of the Indians, I thought it prudent that we should move as compact as possible; and that could not be done in case the hunters should be frequently in pursuit of game: Besides, firing would have been a signal for the savages to discover us; a consideration sufficient to induce me to lay in a plentiful stock before I left the buffalo country, to supply us to the limits of our journey, and, it was my intention after crossing the Illinois, not to suffer a gun to be fired.

It was early in the morning of the 30th ult., that one of my hunters,[3] who had been absent the whole of the preceding day, returned to camp in great haste, and informed me, that morning, immediately after the break of day, as he was watching for Buffalos, at a crossing about ten miles above where we lay, he saw a party of Indians put off from the shore, upon a raft, who appeared to have charge of prisoners; and the moment that he had seen them land upon the opposite bank, he had posted back to the party.

I instantly ordered the baggage to be packed up, when I crossed to the other side of the river, where it was deposited with the provisions we had secured, and then forcing a march to the place where the hunter had seen the Indians land, we took their track, which we followed with all possible celerity;[4] and I think it was about two in the afternoon, when my advanced man returned to inform me, they were then ascending a hill, not distant half a mile.

I halted my party for a moment to instruct them how to act, and desired them to follow about three hundred yards in my rear, and taking with me two men, I went rapidly forward until I obtained sight of them; when I saw their number was double ours, and, that they had only one female prisoner.—

How to rescue the prisoner, without endangering her life, was a difficulty I could not contrive to surmount—at length, I thought the only chance would be to wait until night, and in case they kept no guard, for they were now far removed from an enemy's country, and when they should be sleeping we might retake her, before they would have time to hear, or perceive us.—However that scheme was frustrated by their vigilance; when I devised the following stratagem:—

At the dawn of day I dispatched four of my men, keeping only the mountaineer with me, with orders to advance about one quarter of a mile in front of the Indians, there to discharge their pieces irregularly twice, as quick as possible, and then to make a small circuit, and return with the greatest expedition. The plan succeeded—The Indians were in an instant up, and hastened towards the place where the firing appeared, leaving only two men to guard their prisoner. This was the moment for action—I rushed forward followed by my mountaineer, who had orders to carry off the prisoner in his arms, while I encountered the men, as I expected every instant my people would return to my assistance.

They came—but not until I had knocked one down, and was engaged with the other, who I had aimed a blow at, but my feet slipping, I missed him, when he levelled his piece at me, but it having flashed in the pan,[5] I had recovered myself, and was aiming a second blow when my four men returned and made the two Indians prisoners.

It was my intention not to fire, as had the Indians heard a firing in their rear, they would doubtless have been back upon us, before we could effect our escape with the prisoners.

Fortunately my blows did not prove mortal, or in the least dangerous, and as my men instantly bound the prisoners, we retreated to join my mountaineer, who had fallen back with the rescued captive to the place appointed for our *rendezvous.*[6]

Our peril was not yet over, for the number of Indians being still so much superior to us, it was not only necessary to make a precipitate retreat; but it was an object of the greatest moment to baffle their vigilance in the pursuit, which there was no doubt they would make.

Accordingly I dispatched my guide, with orders to conduct the mountaineer with his captive, by the shortest route, to the place where we had deposited our baggage; who were to prepare the rafts, and put on board the baggage against our arrival, without any regard to any more of the provisions, than would be necessary to last us for a day or two; and then mounted the prisoners behind the two hunters, who had orders to follow the track of the guide, while my brave servant and friend Andrew, who had led the party in the execution of the stratagem, and myself, brought up the rear.

We had travelled in the course of the preceding day upwards of forty miles beyond the Illinois, so that it was nearly 3 P.M. before we regained the bank of the river.

My active guide and mountaineer had embarked the baggage the moment of our arrival, when I first had an opportunity of recognizing our captive.

Ah! Il——ray how did my swelling heart beat with joy, which was instantly succeeded by sorrow, when I first caught a glance from the brilliant eyes of the most divine woman upon earth, torn into shatters by the bushes and briars, with scarcely covering left to hide the transcendency of her beauty, which to be seen by common eyes is a profanation, and it was only by the effulgence of her æthereal looks, that I could have known her?

Caroline has fallen into my hands!—she is at this moment decorating the gardens of this place while I am writing to you, and seems to give enchantment to the whispering breezes that are wafted to my window, and which in their direction as they pass her, collect from her sweets the fragrance of ambrosia, and the exhilirating charms of love itself.

She was sitting upon the bank of the river half harrassed to death when I arrived, which from the horrors of a wilderness was converted into elysium; when I, regardless of every appearance, fell at her feet, and then embracing her, I felt all the transports that the circumstances of our meeting and the divinity of feminine charms can inspire.

I was for a minute regardless of the danger we were still in, when my faithful Andrew came with a *surtoute,*[7] covered Caroline, and then carried and placed her upon a seat which he had prepared upon the raft.

We instantly put off from the shore, when this honest fellow brought us some refreshment, and a bottle of Italian cordial which he carried with him as a *bon bouche.*[8] Neither of us could taste of them, though we had not eat or drank any one thing during the day.

I now believed that we were safe, without ever thinking;—but I was soon roused by the appearance of the Indians, who were arrived upon the shore we had left, before we had fallen a league down the river.[9]

The weather was very fine, and as my rafts were well constructed, I ordered them to be brought along side of each other, and lashed together; in order to render us more compact in case we should be followed: which was not very likely, as it would take them too long to prepare a raft, and it was impossible for them to procure a canoe—but it was not unlikely they would cross and follow down upon the opposite shore, under an idea that we might encamp at night, which would give them an opportunity of coming up with us; for that reason I determined to float the whole night, as it would give us such an advantage, that we should by the morning be out of all danger: accordingly I had a canopy stretched in such a manner as to secure Caroline a place to sleep, who I knew must be much fatigued from our rapid movements, independent of the perils and hardships she must have undergone during her captivity.

Indeed I wondered that she was alive—but she was not only alive, my friend! but she looked more lovely than ever—the lustre of her eyes was like the torch of love—her smiles like the genial hours of May when nature blooms in all its eradiated charms; and though her beauteous face had been lacerated with brambles, still the little loves seemed to vie with each other, as if to prove, which of her features were the most fascinating.

The sun had declined below the horizon, and the bird of Minerva had resumed its nightly vigils,[10] when Andrew told Caroline, that a pallet was prepared for her under the canopy,[11] and that she must retire to rest; for said he, my good mistress, master would keep you up half the night, and I am sure you cannot have spirits or strength to support such fatigue. Andrew was in the right.

When Venus lies sleeping on the couch of night, and one half of the world is cheered by the brilliancy of her charms,[12] so looked my Caroline when Somnus had sealed up her eye-lids;[13] and while Morpheus,[14] his minister of dreams, was agitating her tender heart, her bosom disclosed the temple of bliss, while her lips distilled nectareous sweets.

I was already distracted with the potency of the bewitching joys which I had snatched in my embrace upon the river bank; and while I was constrained to watch as she slept, it was impossible for me to withstand the reflection of the taper, that Andrew had lighted, and which cast its rays upon a bosom more transparent than the effulgence of Aurora,[15] when robed in all her charms, and more lovely than a poetical imagination can paint, when influenced by all its enthusiasm;—and which was now half naked. I was obliged to extinguish the light, to preserve my reason.

> *Oh! how I could for ever her adore,*
> *By tasting sweets new beauties to explore,*
> *Then to entangle in her lovely arms,*
> *And drown ev'ry sense in unrivall'd charms?*

The current had wafted us down by the morning nearly fifty miles from the place we embarked, so that we were secure from all danger from those Indians; and as Caroline had slept very little, and was then awake, I immediately put to shore in order that we might prepare some refreshment for her; after which we proceeded down the river, upon its banks, with an expectation that we might see a batteaux from Cohoes,[16] which I meant to hire to take Caroline and myself to this place, while my men should continue their route by land.

We were fortunate; for it was not yet mid-day when we espied a batteaux with people in it, to whom we made a signal, when they instantly came to us and most readily complied with my wishes.

They were the French of Louissiana, who had been upon a hunting excursion, and as they were well acquainted with the country, and the nature of Indian affairs, I felt my anxiety for Caroline's safety entirely removed.

We arrived that evening about eleven o'clock at Cohoes, and the next morning set out for this place, where we arrived yesterday at four P. M. Here I have been able to procure all the little articles of dress my lovely Caroline you must suppose wanted, after the wonderful journey she had travelled; for according to the best of her recollection, she was taken the twentieth ult.[17] and it must be nearly four hundred miles upon a straight line, from Clarkeville to the place where I overtook her.[18]

What a change has happened in the fortune of your friend?—Every thing conspires to make me the happiest man living—I have been almost three days alone, as it were, with Caroline—She is the most charming woman alive, and as ingenuous as she is lovely—she asked me what I alluded to by the note?—Divine creature! She never knew any thing of the matter.—It must have been a transaction almost equal in blackness to the conduct of S——towards you, in the business of Mr. R——.

Fly to us if you are sufficiently recovered, that you may participate in our happiness, and that we together may return and consummate those joys, which can only be equalled in heaven.

We shall remain here until Caroline has recovered from her fatigue, and if we should set out before you reach us, we shall certainly meet you on the road between this place and St. Vincent's.

I have a thousand little trifles to relate to you, but I must reserve them until we meet, as I am anxious to dispatch a runner to relieve the distress of our friends, and ease the corroding sorrows of Caroline's affectionate and generous uncle; who I reverence for his age and virtues, and esteem for his courage and understanding.

Caroline has this moment entered with a humming bird that a little French lad caught and gave to her;—behold, said she, as she came into the room where I was writing, and look at the little captive, how sad it looks, because it has lost its mate—and was you sad, my Caroline, said I, taking hold of her hand and tenderly pressing it, when you was hurried a prisoner from your friends?

—Her cheek was resting upon my breast—Ah! Il——ray, her murmuring accents, for she could not articulate, expressed the most unutterable things—go thou little innocent thing, said she to the bird, putting her hand out of the window at the same time to facilitate its escape, you shall not be a moment longer confined, for perhaps, already have I robbed thee of joys, which the exertions of my whole life could not repay—Ah! Caroline, said I, and who is to restore to us the rapturous pleasures of which we have been robbed?—or shall we find, my charming girl, a compensation for such a sequestration in our future endearments?— O Il——ray! I dare not repeat another sentence!

Caroline writes with her own hand, her wishes for the immediate restoration of your health, and is very sorry to add, that she has cause to lament your valetudinary habit prevented her from meeting you upon the head branches of the Illinois;[19] which she has been exploring, and hopes when she has the pleasure to meet you, that she shall be able to give you a good account of that delectable region.

Adieu!

J. ARL——TON

LETTER LX

MR. IL——RAY TO P. P——, ESQ.

St. Vincent's, October.

MY DEAR SIR,

I was so overjoyed at the reception of my friend's letter, announcing his having retaken your niece, the charming Caroline, that I was scarcely able to write a line, and which I hope will appear a sufficient excuse for my having written you so crude a letter upon the event.

The instant I dispatched the runner to you with Arl——ton's letter, I posted to Kaskaskia, to assure Caroline and my friend, how very sincerely I participated in the propitious events of their meeting, and the happy developement of the cause of their long and cruel sufferings.

I experienced every sensation that friendship and esteem can inspire, when I first recognized the amiable and affectionate Caroline; she appeared to be recovered from her recent fatigue, though there were still vestiges upon her fair face, of the lacerations she had received in the course of her wonderful journey: But as they were superficial, they are now no longer visible.

Never could she appear to so much advantage. All the sweetness that beauty can give, was heightened by the graces with which she received me, by the cheerfulness of the most ingenuous heart, and which was rendered more delightful, by the ineffable brilliancy of thought, that so peculiarly characterizes her imagination, when she is happy, so that I must leave you to judge, what was my satisfaction, again, to see your affectionate niece, and to find my friend restored to his reason.

After remaining with them a short time at Kaskaskia, we set out together for this place on our return, where we arrived last evening; and here I have induced them to rest for some days, in order that they may see a place, upon which nature has lavished so many favours; and which has been improved by the hospitable French, who are its inhabitants.[1] I was more anxious upon the subject, as I discovered in them both, such an eagerness to return to Louisville, and as I was apprehensive for Caroline's health; for however extraordinary her strength must have been, to have supported her through the rapid and rough journey she was carried by the savages, it was not reasonable to suppose, that she could support such expeditious movement under any other circumstances.

Two things in Caroline's account of her captivity are very extraordinary; they are, that she never felt in the least harrassed, or alarmed for her safety, as she had, from the moment she was captured, a *presentiment* that Arl——ton would retake her; and, that the Indians treated her the whole time with the most distant respect, and scrupulous delicacy.

The first appears to be natural, when we consider the enthusiasm of the human mind when it is in love; and the latter is
corroborated, by the testimony of all decent looking women, who
have been so unfortunate as to fall into their hands. Indeed, I have
been told of instances, where women have been treated with such
tenderness and attention by them, that they have from gratitude
become their wives.[2]

Every thing seemed to be enchantment as we passed the extensive plains of the Illinois country. The zephyrs which had gathered on their way the fragrance of the flowery riches which
bespangle the earth, poured such a torrent of voluptuous sweets
upon the enraptured senses,[3] that my animation was almost overpowered with their delicious and aromatic odours. The fertile and
boundless Savannas were covered with flocks of buffalo, elk, and
deer,[4] which appeared to wanton in the exuberance of their luxurious pastures, and which were sporting in the cool breezes of
the evening; while the sun descending below the horizon was
gilding some remote clumps of trees, it brought to my imagination, the charms of old ocean, when she receives into her bosom
the luminary by which we live,[5] as if to renovate in her prolific
element his exhausted powers. But when the scene was embellished by an image so fair and beauteous as that of Caroline's, we
seemed to have regained Paradise, while all the golden fruits of
autumn hung pending from their shrubs, and seemed to invite the
taste, as though they were jealous of each others delicious sweets.

Yes! my dear sir, we have had the most delectable journey
perhaps that ever was made. The circumstances attending it, and
the season and weather altogether conspired to give us such spirits,
that instead of appearing to be in an uninhabited waste, we seemed
to want only our friends to have determined us, there to have
taken up our residence, for the remainder of our lives.

It is impossible for any country to appear to advantage after
you have seen the Illinois; but still there are a variety of charms
at this place, and could you see the *naiveté* of the inhabitants,
which has united with it, all the sprightliness of the country, from

whom they descended, you would believe you was living in those Arcadian days,[6] when the tuneful shepherd used to compose sonnets to his mistress, and when the charms of love, were propitiated in sequestered groves, and smiling meads.

Here we find all the cheerful idleness that plenty gives; and while the sprightly youth in festive dance, chase away the gloom of the surrounding forests, the neighbouring plantations are cultivated to a perfection, that I have scarcely seen equalled in any part of America; and the hospitality of the inhabitants, who make large quantities of wine, renders it one of the most interesting places I ever knew.—for,

> *Here the well covered board is enrich'd by the vine,*
> *And friendship is season'd with goblets of wine:—*
> *When nectar is sparkling the joys of the bowl,*
> *With rapture inspiring give zest to the soul;*
> *And mirth laughing wit, upon fancy's swift wings,*
> *Bedecks us with myrtle,[7] and endless bliss brings;*
> *While Venus,[8] whose charms most effulgent at night,*
> *Awakes us to reason, when love gives delight.*

I have this instant received a letter from General W——, and as I shall have the pleasure to see you in a few days, I hope you will pardon me for not being more particular. Caroline bids me tell you she has so many things to relate, that she does not know how to begin a letter; besides she thinks they will prove more agreeable to you to be communicated by word of mouth. The truth is, both Caroline and Arl——ton are so totally absorbed in each other, that for either of them to write, is a thing not to be expected.

They both desire me to assure you of their utmost friendship and esteem, and permit me to request that you will believe, I am

> your friend, and most
> obedient Servant,
> G. IL——RAY

LETTER LXI

GEN. W—— TO MR. IL——RAY.

Louisville.

DEAR SIR,

THE incidents that have happened since you left us, are truely momentous; and while I most cordially felicitate myself and friends upon the auspicious event of Miss Caroline T——n's being overtaken, I have to inform you of an other circumstance equally unexpected, which is, the death of Mr. S——.

It was first remarked to me by Mrs. W——, that he drank very copious and potent draughts of brandy and water, of which I began to take notice, and as it appeared not a little extraordinary, that a person remarkable for his sobriety should become suddenly addicted to such a habit, I took the liberty of remonstrating with him upon the pernicious effects of brandy taken in any considerable quantity; but as I observed, that he did not receive my caution, in the manner I expected, I never after appeared to take any notice of it whatever. But I soon observed, he was generally in a state of intoxication; for it seems he has for a length of time past, drank at the rate of three pints per diem:[1]—and Mrs. S——, has informed Mrs. W——, that he commenced the practice shortly after they were married, and that he gradually increased his doses, until they carried him off more suddenly than he expected.

Five days since I was sent for in great haste to visit him, he being thought dangerously ill; and as I entered he asked seemingly with great earnestness for his port folio,[2] but before it could be given him he became insensible; in which state he remained until he died.

It was necessary, that some person should administer upon his effects,[3] and there appeared, considering the connection which

had existed between us, no one so proper as myself, in consequence of which you know his papers went through my hands.

In the port folio, which he was so anxious to have the moment
his reason was leaving him, was a small cabinet that contained
many curious receipts, memorandums, and remarks;—but among
the most extraordinary things in this collection, were a number
of maxims for tricking, This singular collection doubtless was the
cause of his anxiety at the time I entered his apartment, as then
he seemed, by a flash of reason, to have had some idea of his
situation; and he certainly intended to have destroyed it, and
thereby in some degree have prevented the exposition of those
nefarious practices, by which he seems to have risen in the world.

Permit me here to apologize for the manner in which I treated
your communications from Philadelphia touching his character;
and while I feel a pleasure in having an opportunity of making
some atonement for the injustice I did your understanding and
sincerity, to express my warmest admiration for the delicacy of
your behaviour upon the occasion, which I never can sufficiently
admire.

Among his curious memorandums in his diary is the following:

"Miss R—— will most likely be with Mrs. Finbourn to-morrow
about one P. M. and if Patrick leaves town at eleven A. M. he will
arrive with a letter shortly after her; and as the silly old woman
cannot read, it will be natural for her to put my letter into the
hands of Miss R—— to read. But if Miss R——, by any accident
should be prevented from going to-morrow, the old woman from
being desired more particularly to keep the matter a profound
secret, will become more anxious to promulge it, as it will then
be too big for her labouring mind—However, if this should not
succeed, I must take the earliest opportunity to drop the receipts
in some place where Miss R—— will find them, for a foolish
sympathetic heart is never so vulnerable, as when it has undergone
a variety of distresses. I must be in town by nine in the morning.
                              Bristol, White Heart Inn,
                              Tuesday, Eleven P. M."

I have not communicated any of the curiosities which this cabinet contains to Mrs. S——. Indeed I should be very sorry they
should by any means become disseminated through the world; for
in my opinion, they would prove as dangerous as the box of
Pandora,[4] and

> *"Pour the sweet milk of concord into Hell,*
> *Uproar the universal peace, confound*
> *All unity on earth."*[5]

I cannot exactly guess the meaning of the note; but it is very
clear, that he imposed upon Mrs. S—— in making her believe
he was the generous author, who paid her father's debts—However, I have my apprehensions that you are better informed upon
the subject.

When we reflect upon the life of this man, whose character
now it is developed, appears to have been that of a designing
hypocrite, we shall find that the wicked seldom go unpunished;
for his documents not only prove every thing your letter from
Philadelphia to me contained, but they also prove, that he had by
his art, raised himself to no inconsiderable figure in Europe; and
as he by degrees began to be known, he retired farther and farther
from the stage of the great world, until he had reached the utmost
limits where the polished arts are useful to the unprincipled; and
finding that chances were not only conspiring against him, but
that he no longer could find refuge against his former villanies,
he died in the ignominious manner which I have related, without
pity or regard.

It is wonderful how many men there are of his description,
who contrive by mere imposition to pass through life, and who
preserve appearances so well, that they are generally considered
as industrious and useful citizens:—and which was the case
with S——.

I confess I was compleatly duped by his specious manners; and
by the last stroke which gained Mrs. S——, I could not doubt
his being the most friendly and generous man living; while his

secret papers proves him to have been luxurious, voluptuous, false, deceitful, and avaricious,—and his cupidity appears to have been as flagrant as his life has been shameful and wicked: for in the moments of his ruin, and upon the verge of eternity, as it seems that he had previously determined to end his existence, he not only conspired, but he sacrificed innocence and beauty to his concupiscence;[6] first having imposed upon a grateful sensibility by the most atrocious of all frauds, that of contriving by surreptitious means to receive the rewards for an act of benevolence, in which he had no share;—and which was the more cruel, as the person imposed upon, had nothing to give but her person. I hope for the honour of human nature that the case stands without an example.

We are all impatient to see you, your friend Arl——ton, and his fair captive; and we all beg leave to assure Caroline, that we have returned thanks for the joyful event of her deliverance; in which I request that you will inform her, no one is more sincere

Than your most obedient servant,

J—— W——

LETTER LXII

MRS. F—— TO MISS CAROLINE T——N.

London.

MY DEAR SISTER,

I Have experienced every sensation which the strange incidents your several favours contained can produce—

The discovery of our uncle appears miraculous;—and while my wonder was in its full force, I was surprized at the appearance of George in London, whose desertion of our helpless family by his own account is highly ignominious; but when I received your favour that inclosed the history of our uncle's life, and the cruel misfortune which deprived him of his affectionate Juliana and rising family, O Caroline, my blood chills at the recollection of it; and which confirmed my apprehensions, judge what were the horrors of my distressed and indignant mind.

George has met with every neglect that his shameful retreat merited; and though I could not bear to know he was suffering for the common necessaries of life, yet I had no disposition to encourage, in the smallest degree, his prodigality, as I found he was falling into his old habits; and which indulgences in a very short time placed him in the King's-bench prison,[1] where I am afraid he will linger out a miserable existence.

Great God!—How afflicting, my dear Caroline, is it to have a brother so worthless and abandoned? And how impossible is it for a conduct so very reprehensible, to receive any mitigation, even from fraternal considerations?—

I would not be thought hard hearted;—for you know, my sister, that it is not in my nature;—but when I reflect upon the evils which have already been entailed upon us, and figure to my mind, to what a state of degradation and distress, his sacrilegious conduct would have reduced you, if you had not been so fortunate, as to meet our worthy uncle, I confess I can no longer view him in the light of a brother. Let us my dear sister, from regard to ourselves, close the scene for ever.

Assure the friendly exile, how very sincerely I participate in our good fortune, in having recovered so valuable a connection; and that I most anxiously wish to give proofs of it.

You do not know, my Caroline, the ineffable joy I have experienced from a recent event, than which, nothing could have proved more auspicious—I will not anticipate the pleasure you will receive when you see the enclosed.

Mr. F——'s attachment to fashionable life has brought him to the zenith of his ambition, and he is now initiated not only into the clubs of St. James's,[2] but he lives in the first circles in town. How long his fortune will be able to support it, is impossible for me to have any idea;—but I sincerely wish for his own comfort and future happiness, that it may prove competent to his wishes.

God bless you Caroline—pray come instantly to England—I

am more than ever impatient to embrace you—hurry to me for every moment of your absence will increase my anxiety.

I hope you have seen Arl———ton—If you have bring him with you, that I may thank him for his kindness to you.

I am your affectionate, but impatient sister,

ELIZA F———

LETTER LXIII

THE INCLOSED.[1]

SIR THOMAS MOR———LY, BART. TO P. P———, ESQ.[2]

London.

SIR,

I Lament that I have not the honour to be personally known to you; but if you will give me permission, I will assure you that I feel the most lively pleasure, in knowing you are still living; and while I felicitate you upon your having been so fortunately discovered, I have the satisfaction to communicate the substance, which you will find in the inclosed extracts, of the last will and testament of your late uncle the Honourable P. P———;[3] and from which you will learn, that he has left you heir to the whole of his real estate.

As executor to that worthy man, who was my much esteemed, and still lamented friend, I feel a peculiar pleasure in being the instrument of informing you of a circumstance, that must prove, I should suppose, so acceptable to you; and rejoice that in your being restored to your country and friends, I shall have an opportunity of receiving in your society a generous, if not a full compensation for the loss I experienced from the death of your uncle.

I have the honour to be, with sentiments of the utmost esteem and deference, Sir, your most obedient humble servant.

THOMAS MOR———LY

LETTER LXIV

P. P——, Esq. to Sir Thomas Mor——ly Bart.

Louisville, Nov.

SIR,

I Had the pleasure of receiving your polite note, inclosed to Miss Caroline T——n, a few days since, and feel myself highly flattered, by the sentiments therein contained.

While I lament the loss you must have sustained by the death of my much esteemed and honoured relative, I am more sincerely concerned for the causes that must for ever separate me from a man, who I have always regarded as a patron of virtue and benevolence—who had stood firm and unruffled, in opposition to a long but inglorious administration,—and who has given the world a proof, that inflexible integrity affords a lustre to human characters, which the favours of Kings and the wealth of empires cannot equal, when they do not reward the meritorious.

It is painful to me to open wounds that have so often bled for the calamities of my country;—but there are scars which no medical aid can remove, and there are sorrows that will follow us to the grave.

If I had not been banished from the place of my nativity by the grinding hand of injustice, perhaps I now should consider myself happy in knowing I was heir to the estate of my late wealthy relation.

But when I contemplate the disasters that befel my family, which I presume Mrs. F—— has made you acquainted with, reflect upon the causes that led to them, and then compare the happiness of the people who are forming an empire in this remote part of the world, with the vanity and distractions which the depravity of the European manners have made general on your side of the water, I confess I am deterred from venturing again into an element, which is continually ruffled by those contending passions, which have generated under the influence of a system of servility and injustice.

Besides, I have adopted a niece to whom I am attached by every tie that is paternal—whose mind is as unspotted as the radiance of her beauty is lovely—whose heart is formed for social pleasures—and whose disposition is altogether congenial to the uncontaminated pleasures which the virtuous mind may receive in these chaste regions of innocence and joy:—and should I then from considerations of idle grandeur, lead her into the temptations of your great metropolis, which from its overgrown size has become the asylum of the licentious, and the den of the rapacious?

In addition to such considerations, Caroline has formed an attachment for a person of this country, to whom it would be inconvenient to live in Europe—and though I have an heir in my adopted daughter, still I think it ought to be my first object in the appropriation of the estate I inherit, to exonerate the creditors of my unfortunate brother Mr. T——n:—For which purpose I fend a power of attorney for you to settle all his affairs in the most honourable manner.

I cannot form the most distant idea of the sum for which he failed, as I never consulted him upon the business; nor have I a very accurate conception of the value of the estate of my late uncle; but as I have reason to suppose it is very considerable, I have prevailed upon Mr. T——n, my sister, and their eldest daughter Mary, to return to England,[1] as Europe is the only country in which they, from the habits of their lives can be happy.

A man who has forfeited his honour, and rendered himself contemptible in the eyes of the world, must be, provided he has sensibility, the most miserable of human beings; and it is the business of every person who wishes to preserve the dignity of his family, to give them that aid and advice necessary for so precious a security.

It is for such considerations I desire, after you have paid off the debts of Mr. T——n, that you will settle so much upon him and his family, to be paid annually for their lives, as will make them comfortable, not exceeding one hundred and fifty pounds each.[2]

The residue you will please to remit me, which I shall lay out in the purchase of back lands for the benefit of the heirs of my two nieces, Mrs. F—— and Caroline.——

My nephew George, who I understand is confined in London, in the King's-bench Prison,[3] has, I am grieved to hear, given every possible proof of the most abandoned and dissipated disposition. But as it would be needless for me to recapitulate enormities disgraceful to human nature, I shall remark, that while the education of young men continues to be so very loose, it is not in the least surprising that their passions should be ungovernable, and their conduct marked with the most unbridled licentiousness.

There appears to be two species of wickedness, or rather to proceed from different causes. One is the effect of an injudicious education, when it is accompanied with insensibility; and in which case the greatest care ought to be taken to meliorate the natural bias of the temper. The other has for its basis the first inconvenience, and flows from that kind of weakness not uncommon in the characters of young persons, who have long been in the habit of certain irregular indulgencies; and who cannot reject the temptations which are continually thrown into their way.——

Now as it ought to be the object of every society, to correct the bad habits, and make useful citizens of every description of unfortunate persons, *more than to punish them,*——I shall, in contradistinction to the general conduct of the world in such cases as the present, release my nephew from his present wretchedness, for which purpose I beg you will act as my proxy and send him back to this country, where I have no doubt he will reclaim;[4] for I cannot help but thinking the disgrace and sufferings he must have undergone will not only have made him sensible of his former wickedness, but that he must have become so much ashamed of the prominent features of his life, that he will in future endeavour to render himself respectable, by a more ingenuous and manly conduct.

While in England a principal object of the government has been that of the aggrandisement of commerce, every principle of the human heart seems to have been contaminated, and the fordid views of the trader, in many instances, have induced them to encourage a prodigality in the inexperienced, which has ultimately led to the ruin of both parties;—and thus it has happened that the prisons of Great Britain have proved a Tartarus to its citizens.[5]

Was a stranger to contemplate the many benevolent institutions which reflect such a lustre upon the magnanimity of Englishmen, they would suppose the nation the most happy upon the globe, and that there could not, in the whole Island be such a thing as misery, proceeding from want.—But if they were to visit those cells of solitary wretchedness, and there behold the numerous unfortunate debtors who have for years endured every distress that penury and the horrors of a dungeon can inflict, from whence would they not ask, does this contradiction of the national characteristic proceed?

Should such a queston be put to me, I would desire the person who asked it, to look over the English code of laws.

This will be delivered to you by Mr. Il——ray, who I beg leave to recommend to your particular attention. He accompanies my unfortunate relations from motives of pure benevolence. He is the particular friend of the intended husband of my niece Caroline, and the most proper person in the world to take charge of George on his return to this country, and the remittance you may want to make me.

Now permit me to say, that no man more warmly admires your unparalleled worth than myself, and believe me to be, with the most unfeigned regard, your friend.

P. P——

LETTER LXV[1]

Miss Caroline T——n to Mrs. F——.

Louisville, Nov.

THE pangs of disappointed ambition, sometimes seek to be assuaged in the bosom of love, when the charms of oblivious beauty interdicts the sad recollection of misfortunes;—but, my dear Eliza can never be forgotten by her Caroline, who is now as happy as the propitious powers can make her, when absent from her affectionate sister.

Your charming favour which inclosed the note from Sir Thomas Mor——ly came to hand the hour I had returned from a most wonderful journey,—the particulars of which I shall leave to be related by our friend Mr. Il——ray, who has insisted upon attending, thank God, my happy parents, who with Mary, return immediately to England.

I shall only tell you, it produced a confession from Mary, that confirmed our uncle's suspicions regarding the note I mentioned in my last, touching the conduct of Captain Arl——ton.

O Eliza! my felicity would be unbounded could I embrace you while I am relating the ineffable joys which followed the developement of that cruel contrivance.—

It was in the wild regions of the country of the Illinois, where the sweetened breezes attune the soul to love, and nature exuberant, in her extensive lap, folds the joyous meads which enraptured smiled around,[2] and every shrub seemed pregnant with her charms. It was at that hour after we had passed a most perilous day, when the blue expanse appeared in all its æthereal lustre when vivified with the genial rays of glowing Phœbus—and it was at that instant when my recollection was returning,[3] which had left me for several hours, and when I felt an obligation for a deliverance from captivity, that made my high beating heart at the recognition of Arl——ton, almost burst from its confines—Yes, Eliza, he rescued me from the savages.

Wildness seemed to me a heaven, and while the soft gales of nature, which then appeared to unbosom and display her every charm, my senses were ravished with the modulated symphony of the feathered choir.—

Beauty smiled in all its mild effulgence, and when Arl——ton snatched kisses from my lips, all my soul hung lambent to the ambrosial touch.—[4]

Heaven! to what an ecstacy are our feelings brought when they have been wantonly sported with, and thus unexpectedly to taste the rewards of their virtuous struggles?

It is sufficient to have tasted this joy once, to give energy to our actions ever afterwards, as the bounteous recompence over-pays us for all our sufferings.—

But how very cruel is it to suffer and despair—I could only attribute the behaviour of Arl——ton to caprice; and consequently my felicity was so much the higher when I was made fully acquainted with the causes that produced, apparently, in him, so strange and inconsistent a conduct.

The period is approaching when my happiness would be compleat, if you Eliza, was not placed from me so remotely. And what occasions me the more lively sorrow, is, I can perceive by your letters, particularly the last, that you are not happy:—and these feelings are not a little increased by the fears I have of the chagrin you will experience, when you are informed that it is our fate to remain separated.

It is a cruel consideration, and what makes it the more painful to me, is, that your inquietudes appear to be accumulating; and as though fortune was determined there should be no perfect happiness, among us sublunary beings,[5] I find my felicity will be lessened from these corroding reflections.

Whatever has been the indifference with which Mr. F—— may have always treated your wishes, as he was more domestic than at present, you could not feel its influence so powerfully, as you must his neglect; for no doubt his attendance of clubs, must keep him greater part of his time from you, and at all events, it must make your amusements different, which to every woman of sensibility and honour, is the severest of all trials.

I know your inflexible virtue too well, my dear Eliza, to have any apprehensions for the safety of your reputation; but I also know your sensibility is too exquisite, to endure such a situation, without experiencing the most poignant distress.

It has ever been a matter of wonder with me, that there are men, who do not want understanding in some things, nor are destitute of humanity, should give occasion to their wives for uneasiness without having the most distant idea, that they were the only cause, of their unhappiness.

However, there can be no doubt but it proceeds from the habits of life in England; for while it has been next to an impossible thing, for decent and virtuous women to become repudiated, men have found impunity in the exercise of every gross contumely, and the most shameful violations of every cardinal virtue,[6] while beauty and innocence have been victims to the most odious tyranny. Excuse, Eliza, my touching upon this subject; for I am trembling at the thought, of what may be the consequences of Mr. F——'s folly and prodigality.

Our worthy uncle you will find has agreed to settle all my father's debts, and to liberate George, with a view, to endeavour to reclaim him.

O! my sister, how many inconveniences, and how much disgrace do we bring upon ourselves, by the irrational habits of thinking? and to what a degradation have the crude sentiments of the world reduced many amiable families, who wanted nothing but a little salutary advice, to have made them worthy and respectable citizens?

"Never shall it be said," exclaimed our friend and relation, when he had finished reading Sir Thomas Mor——ly's notes "that I am opulent, and my brother's debts unpaid; while many honest creditors, are, perhaps, suffering for want of bread.—No Caroline! nor my friend complain, when I have a guinea in my pocket.[7] We should first be just and then generous. But," said he, taking hold of my hand, while he continued, "it would be impossible for me, ever to be happy in England. However, as I have reason to believe my late uncle's estate is sufficiently ample, to make all my relations, who stand in need of my assistance comfortable, I will make it optional with such of them, as are in this country, to return, or not; and, my friend, however painful it would prove to me to loose you, yet if you wish to return, and finding the mutual attachment between you and Capt. Arl—— ton is perfectly virtuous and sincere, I will make a liberal settlement upon you, to enable you to enjoy that rank in society which you so highly merit. Let your conduct be an act of volition, and do not consider any thing to your own disadvantage; for recollect

I am old, and according to the course of nature cannot expect to live many years; and as the little appropriate knowledge I possess, may be in a degree useful to this infant country, it is a double consideration to determine me here to remain; for, that being, who feels no obligations to society for the benefits it has secured to him, is unworthy to deserve the name of man."

"And if I may be permitted to say one word more," said this good and affectionate man, "and, which I acknowledge has the appearance of proceeding from selfishness, I would recommend you to contrast in your mind, the genial charms of the social pleasures of this hospitable country, with the unnatural customs of the European world;—and then recollect, that you would pass from a state of innocence and joy, into perturbed elements of folly and dissipation, that are as dangerous to youth, as the combustible regions of Ætna are to the verdure of its neighbouring plains."[8]

My grateful heart overflowed at this new instance of his bounty and friendship. I felt a strange mixture of joy and sorrow; and feeling afresh, the obligations I owed to so kind a friend, the duty my love for Arl——ton imposed upon me, and the idea, that I had it in my power again to see my affectionate sister, when every honorary tie, as well as my attachment, obliged me to relinquish without hesitation a prospect which at the first view displayed so many dazzling charms, that it made my agitated heart beat with all the feelings of which it is susceptible.

I assured him there was but two motives that could ever actuate my conduct. The first was affection, and the other was gratitude; and told him I did not hesitate to declare my love for Arl——ton, acted with me superior to every other consideration, and as it was his wish to settle in this country, where we may enjoy, uninterrupted from the busy world all the transports of our reciprocal tenderness, I should not make a merit of saying, I could not think of separating from a friend, whose generosity to our family, and particularly to me, stood without an example, as if to arrest the admiration of mankind. Thus it has happened, my charming sister, that my fate was fixed.

Mr. Il——ray, whose solicitude for the welfare of my dear

Arl——ton, I can never sufficiently applaud, must inform you of every thing which concerns us. I need not I am sure tell you how worthy he is of your confidence; for I am sensible you bear too grateful a recollection of his generous interference for our felicity, when you knew him in Philadelphia. But if he did not deserve my lavish encomiums, I should think his goodness unequalled, as he was the cause of my knowing the only man in the world, who I must always adore.

God bless you, Eliza! O! my sister, could I flatter myself, that you would ever form one of our little society here, I should then have but one more wish to gratify; that of having it realized.

Farewell,
CAROLINE

LETTER LXVI

MR. IL——RAY, TO CAPT. ARL——TON.

London, March.

WE had a passage of fourteen days from Louisville to New Orleans,[1] my dear James, from whence we embarked for Hispaniola, where we arrived the middle of last December, and then took shipping for Cadiz;[2] from which place, after seeing Mr., Mrs. and Miss T——n safe on board a merchant ship bound for London, I set out on my journey through Spain, over the Pyrenees, and so passing the cheerful regions of France to England, which I reached only two days since; having travelled very leisurely through a country, that appeared every where novel to me, and which was the principal cause of my tardy movement, as I apprehended it would be the only opportunity I ever should have of contemplating the characters of a people, whose consequence in the list of nations, form so important a link.

The leading characteristic of this celebrated nation, (I mean the French) appears to be, that of wishing to be thought witty and obliging; and while they are continually saying the most civil things, and proffering the most generous actions, it is obvious they mean nothing more than the practice of what they term good breeding.

It is, perhaps, the only way that a people who have always groaned under the influence of arbitrary power, have of recommending their country to strangers; and while they have fostered the gaiety of the prevailing manners of the country, doubtless they have experienced some alleviation, if not totally forgotten, the sacrilege that has been committed upon their privileges.

And it is only by reflecting upon the influence of their government, that we are enabled to form any distinct idea of the reason for that change in the disposition and temper of the Parisians, between what they were at the period the emperor Julian wintered in that city,[3] and what they are at present. For that philosopher and soldier said "he liked the people of Paris, because they were grave like himself."[4]

Is it not, my dear Arl——ton, a most melancholy truth, that while the priests and courts of Europe, have been in league to subjugate the human mind, that the noble energy of man has degenerated, and the contemptible arts of pleasing by flattery and deception have taken place of that open and ingenuous conduct, that sometimes inspires a degree of admiration in the most depraved. Thus it has happened, that the tyranny of governments has laid the foundation of European depravity.

And is it not a little wonderful at the first view of these idle deceptions, that when once they are detected the authors of them are not treated with contempt? But you have only to know, that practicing them, has become so general, that, to be open and candid is considered as a violation of good manners.

In certain affairs extreme delicacy ought most certainly to accompany our opinions or advice; but it can never be justifiable to say one thing, and mean another; neither is it pardonable when we are asked for our opinion to give it different from our real sentiments, for fear of offending. However, there is no case of so delicate a nature, nor no person so fastidious, but you may, by insinuation, convey your real thoughts.

The talent of insinuation, doubtless, works more efficaciously in nice affairs, than the powers of persuasion; for when we attempt to gain upon a quick sensibility that is interested in the matter, it too often happens, that the least grossness ruffles the smooth current of our passions, and thus the susceptibility of temperament, looses its elegant polish, and is no longer capable of receiving the impression.

This fact S—— appears to have ascertained, for it clearly was more by the plausibility of his manner, than by any real eloquence or good sense, that acquired him so much of the admiration of the world; and while he continued to gild his affability with a suavity of manners, he successfully practiced the arts of deception; and it seems, it was not until his temper was in a degree soured, after having by the extravagance of his desires overleaped the bounds of common prudence, that he ever lost sight of his favourite secret, by which he ingratiated himself into the favour of strangers.

The novelty of his character, and the flagrant outrage he committed upon the ties of confidence, induced me to turn my thoughts upon a subject that appeared to me so inextricable; and I was for a time confounded with the monstrous absurdities of so much folly and wickedness.

In the progress of civilization, manners gradually become polished and refined, and the arts of pleasing have been esteemed more desirable than appropriate and useful talents. But unfortunately for mankind, the basis of the moral system of the world has been materially defective, and has been productive of all the evils of which I complain; for while candour has been considered as rudeness, and honesty as dullness, insincerity has laid the foundation of a general depravity.

I hope, my friend, you will not accuse me of presumption for setting up my opinion in opposition to the established practices of mankind, without recollecting, that society, in every part of the world, is in an infant state; and that it is not so much to be wondered at, that many of its customs are absurd, as it is, that they are not more so.

I am aware that it is a general sentiment among men, that in proportion as they become polished, the greater will be our insincerity.—That is prejudging the subject, and therefore it is necessary we should look up to the very fountain head from whence the evil proceeds.

In almost every country upon the globe splendour and pomp have been substituted in the room of comfort and convenience; and while our artificial wants have been rapidly accumulating, a general commercial spirit has insensibly become unbounded, and has been relevant to the tyranny of courts and the ingenious hypocrisy of priests, in effectually sapping the source of all social pleasures; and which conspired to produce a general venality and adulation in the dispositions of the subordinate orders of men, that is the only ladder, by which they are enabled to climb to the summit of their joys. Indeed it has not stopped here, for its influence has pervaded all orders of men from the lord to the beggar; so that while the dependants of every class have flattered their superiors, or men in power, a degeneracy has spread through all orders of society, and has produced the lamentable criterion of estimating the value of wisdom and integrity by the saving appearances, while degradation is only annexed to the most notorious and atrocious villanies, and unprotected innocence.

It is therefore to be presumed, whenever the rights of man can be clearly ascertained, and equality established, that men will regain their pristine sincerity, and consequently, those base arts that have so often degraded the dignity of man will no longer be known.

The developement of the note you received from Miss T——n at Pittsburg, was the cause of my paying more particular attention to her manners and conversation than I had formerly done: and I could not help remarking, during our passage from Hispaniola to Cadiz, the vivacity she assumed, nor could I forego the propensity I felt to ask her the cause of so sudden a change in her spirits;— particularly, as she had so recently left her amiable sister and worthy uncle, neither of whom she could ever expect to see again.

The answer she returned I thought was extraordinary. "Sir,"

said she with the greatest gaiety, "I am returning to that dear place London, where every thing is enchantment—where every person does as they think proper, without being subject to the wicked comments of the vulgar multitude;—and where they distinguish between good breeding, and *that honest kind of manners* which ever gives me the most distressing *ennui*."

"Pray Miss T——n," said I, "if the conduct of our lives is governed by the rules of decorum and integrity, do you not think the vulgar multitude would be as ready to applaud us for our virtue?"—

I was proceeding, when Miss T——n interrupted me by a "ha, ha, ha,"—and then exclaimed, "virtue was a word of mere sound, without meaning," and that she could have no idea of practising rules or precepts which were violated every day by both the *clergy and legislators, who certainly were the best judges of what was right and what was wrong;* but for her part, she did not know why every person had not a right to do whatever was agreeable to themselves, without any regard to any human being.

"True," said I, "provided it does not injure others." "O Lord!" exclaimed the *sensitive* lady, "if you become metaphysical I shall certainly faint."

I then begged to assure her there could be nothing abstract in a disquisition upon what ought to be the basis of every society; for that nothing could be more simple than the principles which constituted the unalienable rights of man; and then declared to her it was a lamentable consideration, that women who had so great share in influencing the opinions of men, should pay so little attention to a subject in which they were so materially concerned.

Miss T——n replied, "I do not know what is meant by the rights of men, and therefore the subject must be abstract, and which is more distressing to my feelings than metaphysical love; —for it is only realities that can give me pleasure and happiness, and every person has a right to obtain them by every means in their power;—and the most adroit and dexterous in saving appearances, appears not only in my eyes, but in the estimation of the world the most meritorious characters."

"I am not a little astonished," said I, "to hear such sentiments escape the lips of a lady;—forgive the candour, or if you please the rudeness, and attribute my surprize to a want of a knowledge of that politeness, which deems it a breach of good manners to declare an honest sentiment."

"O! my dear Sir, if you are serious," answered Miss T——n, with a tone of voice which proved to me, that she believed she was on the right side of the argument, "does not every man, and those too who are advocates for the rights of men, *violate his conjugal engagements* every day of his life, without paying any regard to the rights of women?—do not the members of the Parliament of Great Britain obtain their seats in the House of Commons by *stratagem, address, and corruption,*[5] *without having any pretensions to wisdom or integrity, while, what you call honest and upright men are mere cyphers in society?*—and are not ministers who have the most dexterously hoodwinked the people, men of the greatest celebrity for talents? And thus has it not happened, that the celebrated Sir Robert Walpole, and the present *premier* of England, are esteemed the two most wise and useful politicians that country ever produced,[6] and who never *seriously said one word about the rights of man, nor puzzled their brains a moment concerning the chimerical idea of virtue?*"

"And is it upon such grounds you estimate the merits of men?" I replied, "without considering the depravity that corrupt and degenerate manners have produced? and would it not be more laudable to analyze the subject, and endeavour to find out the causes of this degeneracy, than implicitly to fall into the error of believing that it is natural."

"I have no talent for analytical speculation," said Miss T——n triumphantly, "But I know the accumulated wisdom of ages has taught us to know, that the most effectual way to obtain respect is by appearances and address—therefore the most wise nations upon the globe have created Kings, crowned them with gold, and decorated them with brilliants, in order to give them a splendour which dazzles the understanding of the vulgar, and makes them believe there is something supernatural belonging to them, while

every person of common sense, knows they are mere men, and
generally not the brightest characters in the world. But was the
veil to be removed, and the minds of the multitude, to be what
you call, in modern language, enlightened, it would destroy every
thing that is beautiful—every thing that is ornamental to the grandeur of empires would decay, and that blandishment which the
subordination of our hearts owes to distinction and power, would be
changed into a rebellious candour, which would at once tarnish
the lustre of that polish, which our glorious and immortal ancestors atchieved with such infinite pains and labour."

"However," said Miss T——n, "as such arguments are un-
answerable, I will not give you the pain to hear any more upon
the subject; but I will illustrate my idea by relating an anecdote,
which I think must give you the utmost delight." I thanked her
for her tender politeness when she began.

"The Honourable H. W——, a young man who possessed the
most perfect address, and whose manners were as accomplished as
his person was graceful and elegant, had lived all his life by his
wits, and so perfectly preserved appearances, that he was considered, not only as the most agreeable man living, but looked upon
as a valuable *subject.*"

"It happened that he had occasion to visit the continent, at a
time when his finances were very low; but that did not in the
least damp his intrepidity and spirit for *finesse.*"[7]

"Accordingly he embarked on board a packet for *Bologne,*[8] having first made himself acquainted with the character of a Mrs.
Knowles, an English woman, who keeps the most genteel *hotel* in
that place."

"Immediately upon his landing a coach attended him, which
he ordered to be driven directly to Mrs. Knowles's, where he
alighted, and was conducted into an apartment suitable to his elegant appearance."

"The first thing he required was to see the kind lady of the
house, who most readily attended him."

" 'My dear madam,' said he, and as Mrs. Knowles entered into
the room, at the same time he arose, and handing her to a seat,

and then placing himself along side of her, 'I have been recommended to your house, where I was assured I should have the best accommodations, and where I should be certain of receiving the most obliging civility and attention; and it is with the greatest satisfaction I acknowledge, that every appearance, *particularly your's,* fully justifies the encomiums my friends lavished upon your superb accommodations, and your more amiable self. But if you will permit me, my dearest madam,' taking hold of her hand at the same instant, 'I must assure you, that I think it is impossible, where ever you preside, should not be all elysium.' Then ringing the bell, he ordered a bottle of champaigne to be brought, and ordering the servant to retire, he poured out a sparkling glass, and handed it to Mrs. Knowles with the most irresistible grace, which she modestly declined accepting;—but with a look of ineffable sweetness, he intreated her to do him the honour to drink only one glass, which so overpowered her, that she yielded to his tender persuasion. 'Now,' exclaimed he, 'I do not envy great Jove the charms of his ambrosial feasts,[9] where the loves and sports frolic as the wanton hours enrapture every sense.' "

"Then suddenly starting, and clapping his hand to his head, as the moisture glistened in his eyes, 'my dear madam,' exclaimed he, 'I am the most miserable man alive! but it is no small alleviation to the pangs I feel, in being sensible, that I have found in you a person so worthy of my confidence—you are superior to your sex, and in that acknowledgment the world has barely done you justice—you are more worthy to be trusted than the famed Portia, whose weakness went near to ruin her loved Brutus.[10]— Yes! my charming woman, I will intrust you with a most melancholy tale. It is not money I want, for I am rich in wealth, which I despise, but I am poor indeed in comfort.' "

"Mrs. Knowles was quite enchanted with his brilliancy, and promised him, that she would preserve the most inviolable secrecy."

"Now with dejected looks; and contrition strongly marked in every feature, he began the relation of his sorrows."

" 'I had dined with my dear friend Lord S——, and after having drank freely, the conversation turned upon different subjects, and as my Lord was heated with wine, he let fall some expressions, of which, as a gentleman, I was obliged to take notice, and accordingly we had a meeting the next morning in Hyde-park,[11] when—*horrid to recollect,* I had the misfortune to wound, I fear mortally, my dearest and best friend; and, consequently I was obliged to escape with the greatest precipitation.' "

"Mrs. Knowles instantly anticipated him; 'Sir,' said she, 'rest satisfied in my confidence, and be assured, no human being shall draw from me the cause of your dejection;—and as I am sure that your flight must have prevented your bringing your wardrobe, you will, I hope give me leave to send for a taylor, hosier, and mercer,[12] in order that you may be supplied with every necessary article; and let me pray that you will consider my credit, and every thing which I possess, entirely at your commands.' "

"The Honourable H. W—— thanked her for such an instance of unparalleled and disinterested generosity, and again assured her that it was not money he wanted, and declared he already experienced a tranquillity of spirits, in consequence of unburthening his overloaded heart, to a person who so highly merited a trust, which, to him, was of so much importance."

While Miss T——n was pausing, for her volubility had nearly taken away her breath, I begged to know, what inference could be drawn from this long story, other than that the Honourable H. W—— was a swindler.

"Give me leave," she replied, as her breath began to return, "to finish my tale."

"The Honourable H. W—— whenever he rose in the morning, enquired with the utmost seeming solicitude and tenderness after the health of Mrs. Knowles, and the moment she appeared, he begged to know how she had rested, and in short treated her with marked attention and respect."

"He continued to appear in the most pensive mood, and as he was a very graceful and elegant man, the eyes of every person were fixed upon him, as he passed through the streets.—Every person was sorry to see an Englishman of his figure and apparent rank so melancholy—every one took an interest in his sorrows, and every one wished to know the latent cause, that spread a gloom over the most benignant face that was ever seen."

"Continual applications were made to Mrs. Knowles for information respecting the accomplished stranger, and the reason why his mind was so much agitated.—"

"She answered by saying she knew every thing;—but as he had intrusted her with a secret of the first importance, she hoped ever to merit the confidence of a man whose manners so peculiarly distinguished his urbanity and superior understanding."

"The taylor, the mercer, and hosier, carried their respective bills in to Mrs. Knowles, all of which she paid with the greatest cheerfulness;—and as the honourable gentleman had discounted bills to the amount of some hundreds upon the credit of the thorough knowledge his kind hostess had of him,[13] he was off in a tangent,[14] and has never since been seen at *Bologne*."

"But what proves the great advantage of address is, that this woman is remarkable for fleecing every person,[15] who has any thing to do with her in business, and is moreover a very plain and disgusting person, and has ever since persisted in saying, that whatever the world may say of him, yet, she is convinced, he was the most accomplished gentleman that ever visited *Bologne*."

"And pray, Miss T——n," said I, "and do you not think he was a most accomplished rascal. However, I hope you have not related this tale to prove the advantages of address; for admitting that such a conduct could be justified, it appears to be a very foolish one, as it must be impossible for a man to continue such practices for any length of time without being brought to punishment. And I wish to know what became of the honourable gentleman after he returned to his own country."

"O Sir," replied Miss T——n, "he continued for a length of time after that æra to live by his address; but an unfortunate affair, something respecting a note, I really do not recollect the particulars, that caused him to be arraigned,[16] and though his friends had frequently saved him, a barbarous jury, and an implacable judge, condemned him to be transported to Botany-bay for seven years;[17] but I assure you that every body pitied him, for he certainly was the most finished gentleman in Europe."

Farewell, my dear Arl——ton, and permit me to assure you, that I prefer the unpolished wilds of America, with the honest affability and good humour of the people, to the refined address of the European world, who have substituted duplicity for candour, and cunning for wisdom. But I flatter myself, the period is hastening when its citizens will be regenerated, and when they must look back with shame at the sacrilege which has been committed.

While you, my friend, have been basking in the radiating charms of your fond and lovely Caroline, was I for some time tossed in the boisterous elements that separates us; at another, in the deserts of Spain, which contains citizens without society, supports a religion without reason, and a government without wisdom, was I cursing the influence of despotism, and the fetters of a superstition, which nothing but time will be able to burst asunder, as they are fastened upon the mind, while a most infernal policy coerces the restraint, and shuts out every ray of light that might be shot to illumine their ignorant minds.[18]

I am anxious to return to you, my dear James, and the moment the business Sir Thomas Mor——ly is transacting for Mr. P—— is adjusted, I shall leave this place to join your delectable society.

Mrs. F—— thinks and talks of nothing but Caroline, her uncle, and you—poor girl she is miserable, and I am unhappy.

God bless you, James.

G. IL——RAY

LETTER LXVII

CAPT. ARL——TON TO MR. IL——RAY.

Louisville, March.

DURING the delirium of my distempered brain, which the violence of my passions, and the circumstances attending my love for Caroline produced, I sometimes forgot, my dear Il——ray, the important duties I owe both to my friends, to myself, and above all to my country.—And it is to your regard for my welfare that I am indebted for the felicity I now enjoy.

The flexible temper of the human mind is capable of being wrought to a polish so elegantly fine, that the most delicate touches makes the most lasting impressions; and perhaps it was owing to the refined and judicious lessons upon morality you have so repeatedly given me, which now makes me feel a glow of gratitude for the benefits I have experienced—and nothing can more effectually prove to me the advantages resulting from a permanent and reciprocal friendship like ours, than a retrospect to the dangers I have escaped, and a view of the gilded prospect by which I am now surrounded.

It was to your active zeal for my honour and health which prevented me from falling a victim to my impetuous disposition and propensity to dissipation, at an early period. It was by your council and advice I learned to distinguish between virtue and vice, which have become so confounded, that it is no difficult task to instruct the understanding of men whose minds have received a false bias—and it was your watchful solicitude for the happiness of Caroline and myself, that led to the unraveling the mystery of our love and unbosomed its sweets in all its blushing charms, which otherwise would have withered, untasted, and unenjoyed.

How can I describe to you our mutual happiness?—The fleeting season seems to have hurried round his course, and has left me the image of a banquet that floats in my imagination, where beauty at rest, lies embraced by love, while the rosy hours are dancing with enchantment to the mellifluous tones of desire.

Every preparation having been adjusted shortly after your departure, that was necessary to the consummation of our wishes, and Caroline's excellent uncle having no objection to our alliance, declared he would never be the cause of procrastinating, by a regard to idle ceremony, the completion of our joys:—and though it was not at that season of which Thompson speaks where he so beautifully describes the glowing charms of the virgin, yet Caroline

> *"Flushed by the spirit of the genial hour*
> *Then from her virgin's cheek a fresher bloom*
> *Shot less, and less, the live carnation round;—*
> *Her lips blush'd deeper sweets; she breath'd of youth;*
> *The shining moisture swell'd into her eyes,*
> *In brighter flow.—Her wishing bosom heav'd,*
> *With palpitations wild;—kind tumult seiz'd*
> *Her veins, and all her yielding soul was love."*[1]

Be so good as to excuse this slight alteration.

When the ruthless hand of barbarous war has in many places desolated the fairest country upon the face of the globe,—a country which Voltaire said "if ever the golden age existed, it was in the middle provinces of America."[2] Who can help feeling an indignation against such gothic practices?

When I recollect the once smiling meads of the gentle Pacaic,[3] which are now untilled—when I reflect upon the plenty that prolific region once produced, which is now a waste; and then figure to my mind the innocent wiles of a growing progeny that used to gladden the fields with the rude songs of the uncultivated bard, which the horrors of a sanguinary warfare have turned into gloom and heaps of ruins,[4] how can I help reprobating a system pregnant with evils the most monstrous?

We can scarcely cast our eyes upon a page of history which is not stained with the relation of some bloody transaction—the sacrifice of innocence—the proscription of the virtuous, or the triumph of a villain; which is sufficient to convince every unprejudiced man, that the greater part of the world has hitherto been governed by barbarians: and which must prove to all men of sentiment and humanity, that it is high time to inquire into the cause which has so often destroyed the repose of the world, and stained the annals of mankind with indelible disgrace.

Such were the considerations, you know my friend, that first induced me to turn my thoughts towards the western territory of this continent, as its infancy affords an opportunity to its citizens of establishing a system conformable to reason and humanity, and thereby extend the blessings of civilization to all orders of men. —And if a circumstance that at first distracted my brain, and debarred me from thinking of living in a country that contained the most lovely woman in the world, but which now affords me such undescribable joy, for a time frustrated my object, and induced me to determine to leave the country; I now assure you that I am more than ever attached to an object interesting to every human being.

I have not the vanity to suppose my exertions will materially tend to effect this important end;—but I have the satisfaction to know I shall be entitled to the reputation of a good, if not a very useful citizen; an honour, in my opinion, that has more real splendour annexed to it than all the inflated eulogiums which have been lavished upon vain and inhuman conquerors, or intriguing and unprincipled ministers of state.

As the government of this district is not organized,[5] it is my intention to form in epitome the model of a society which I conceive ought to form part of the polity of every civilized commonwealth;—for which purpose I have purchased a tract of country lying upon the Ohio from the rapids or Louisville, and extending above Diamond island to a point sixteen miles from its beginning,[6] and running back an equal distance, which will constitute an area of two hundred and fifty-six square miles, or nearly, making an allowance for the bends of the river.

This tract I have laid out into two hundred and fifty-six parcels, upon which I am settling men who served in the late war,[7] giving to each a fee-simple in the soil he occupies,[8] who shall be eligible to a seat in a house of representatives consisting of twenty members, who are to assemble every Sunday in the year,[9] to take into consideration the measures necessary to promote the encouragements of agriculture and all useful arts, as well to discuss upon the science of government and jurisprudence.

Every male being of the age of twenty-one, and sound in his

reason, is intitled to a vote in the nomination of a member to
represent them, and every member is intitled to the rewards and
honours which the institution may think proper to bestow.[10] And
in order that their debates shall be perfectly free and uncontrouled,
the right of electing their president is invested in them also, every
member being eligible to the office; but not to the dignity for
more than one year; and he must then remain out of office for
seven years before he can be eligible again; by which means all
unwarrantable views will be frustrated, and the object of every
member will be limited to the ambition of meriting the thanks of
his country: and thus by the fundamental laws of the society, every
expectation of aggrandizement will fall to the ground, and love,
and harmony, must consequently be productive of every generous
advantage; and the respectability of every citizen be established
upon that broad basis—the dignity of man.

Mr. P—— thinks the object is laudable, and he has promised
to lend his assistance in framing the particular instructions immediately necessary to give order and motion to the machine; and
he has moreover promised, if they will do him the honour to
elect him president, to serve the first year, and give them every
information in his power.

He has also offered to build a house for the assembly with
galleries large and capacious enough to contain all the inhabitants
of the district; for he says, every thing of this sort ought to have
the greatest publicity—and by that means the people will be ed-
ified by hearing what passes, and will also be prevented from lis-
tening to those itinerant preachers who travel about the country
under a pretence of propagating the pure christian religion, but
who are, in truth, the disturbers of domestic felicity,—the har-
bingers of hypocrisy, and whose incoherent sermons are a cloud
of ignorance that too often spreads a gloom over the understanding of the uninformed, which nothing but the rays of reason can
dispel, and which have too long darkened the intellect of mankind, and produced an obscurity of ideas that is truly lamentable.[11]

The plan I am determined shall not be merely theoretical, for
it is in great part already carried into execution.—The land is not

only purchased and parcelled out, but there is upwards of one hundred families settled, and Mr. P—— is making preparations for the public building. Therefore you see, my friend, if I have been folded in the arms of love, I have not been idle as to what ought to be the object of every human being, i. e. promoting the good of his fellow creatures.

Caroline has not either been unemployed for she has paid constant visits to the wives of these brave men, my fellow soldiers, and brothers, and has instructed them in various and useful employments, which must tend not a little to promote their comfort.[12]

Such, you see, is my prospect of happiness after a tempestuous and dangerous conflict that was so near destroying my happiness for ever: and which I have the greater pleasure of repeating as it is a tribute I owe to your unparalleled worth and philanthrophy.

You are too well convinced, I am certain, of the advantages this sort of system will produce, to make it necessary for me to be elaborate upon the subject:—but if you will forgive me, I shall observe that while the embellishment of manners, and the science of politics, have been engrossed by the higher orders of society, the bulk of mankind have been the mere machines of states;— and they have acted with a blind zeal for the promotion of the objects of tyrants, which has often desolated empires, while the once laughing vineyards have been changed into scenes of butchery; and the honest and industrious husbandmen, those supporters of all our wealth and all our comfort, have mourned for the sad havock of their cruel depradations.

The intercourse of men and nations has tended, not a little, to accelerate the advancement of civilization, and I am convinced the only cause why philanthropy is so uncommon a virtue, is owing to the want of a just knowledge of the human heart.

Small societies of this kind established throughout a great community would help to soften the manners of the vulgar, correct their idle and vicious habits—extend their knowledge—ameliorate their judgement—and afford an opportunity to every genius or man of sense of becoming useful to his country, who often lie

obscured, uncultivated, unknown, and their talents unappropri-
ated while the state has suffered: and at the time tyrants would be
effectually prevented from trampling upon the laws of reason and
humanity.

Our society, as one, beg leave to express to you, that they
sincerely wish for your happiness, and to assure you they anxiously
wish for your return. Caroline has the ambition to aspire at a pre-
eminence in your esteem.

Do not omit to mention us affectionately to Mrs. F——, and
inform her, that Caroline will write to her, as soon as we are
settled, which will be in the district I have mentioned.

God bless you my friend. Adieu!

J. ARL——TON

LETTER LXVIII

MR. IL——RAY, TO CAPT. ARL——TON.

London, April.

MY DEAR JAMES,

SUCH have been the advantages of liberty in this country,
while all the rest of the world, for I will leave America out of the
question, has been fettered and groaning under the most diabolical
tyranny, that the extent and variety of its commerce, has tended
to produce an increase of wealth, that is truly wonderful.

Every species of luxury has followed, and in the sumptuous
banquets of the times, the flow of sentiment and the zest of reason,
have been succeeded by sallies of false wit, and the harmonious
sounds of soft music. Effeminacy has triumphed,[1] and while the
sofa has been the pleasurable seat of the lover, the toilet has been
the place where his manliness was displayed.[2]

Nature has its bounds, and vigour is the concomitant of temperance, and exercise, and the charms of fine women can only be
relished by men who have not been enervated by luxury and

debauchery; and thus it has happened in every populous and wealthy city in the world, that the most lovely women have been neglected by men, whose impotence was as disgusting, as their caprices were unbounded.

The novelty to me, exhibited every day upon the great *theatre* of the *world,* was at first matter of surprize and astonishment: for although I had not been inattentive to the opinions of authors and travellers, still I had only an idea in theory of what was called fashionable life; and nothing short of mingling with the world, ever could have given me an adequate idea of its depravity.

The system of governments by securing their own aggrandizement have extended a spirit of venality through every fibre of their organization, while the sinews of their constituent powers, have lost their vigour and elasticity; so that the means of supporting splendour in private life, has become to the generality of the citizens of the great world, of more importance than the reputation for virtue and integrity.

The prostitution of principle has not been limited to political sentiments; but it has extended to the most tender and sacred of all the ties of a gentleman.

It has poisoned the source of delicacy and sentiment, and sapped every principle of honour, at the very moment it was offering an indignity to human nature, too gross and flagrant, not to disgrace the most contemptible reptile, that ever crawled upon the earth.

The embraces of elegant women have been bartered for, and places of *trust* and emolument, have been heaped upon wretches, who have merited the distinction of *singers*.[3]

Yes! my dear Arl——ton my indignation has been roused at a circumstance, that must chill every drop of blood in your veins when I have related it, and I am afraid will harrow up the very soul of Caroline. But while tenderness would silence me, I am actuated by considerations of humanity.

The delicate manner in which Mrs. F—— communicated to Caroline, from time to time, as you informed me, her reflections upon the turn of mind and disposition of Mr. F——, reflects the

highest honour upon her prudence and discretion; but it can afford you no idea of her misery.

F——'s neglect has not been the only cause of her chagrin; for
she has for a length of time, visibly seen, that he was precipitating
his own ruin while she had not the power to retard it.

The habits of his life had compleatly disqualified him for domestic pleasures, and while his vanity was gratified in the *eclat* of
Mrs. F——'s beauty and accomplishments,[4] he was indulging
himself in every extravagance, until his finances became so deranged, that his credit at the gaming clubs, he frequented, was
doubted. However he still flattered himself, that he had a resource
in the charms of Mrs. F——, equal to redeem his ruined fortune,
and give him permanent respectability; and as he had no belief
there could be any dishonour in the proposal he meant to make,
particularly as he had the example of many honourable gentlemen,
he did not hesitate in consequence of an overture made him, by
a nobleman in power, (who had only to charge cash expended in
that way to secret service,) to propose to Mrs. F—— the prostitution of her person.

You have only to know my friend, that the mind of Caroline
is the exact prototype of Mrs. F——'s, to be able to judge of the
horror and indignation with which she received a proposition so
ignominious.

Let me beseech you, James, to use your influence with Caroline, and Mr. P——, to endeavour to prevail upon Mrs. F——
to join them, as I am afraid, it is the only chance she has, of ever
becoming happy: for independent of the mortal wound F——
has given to her regard for him, she pines from being separated
from her sister.

I have given my sentiments upon the subject to Sir Thomas
Mor——ly, who is a worthy and intelligible man, and an ornament to human nature; but he says "it is impossible for Mrs.
F——, to be separated from the bed of her husband, without
bringing an action in Doctors Commons,[5] and as she has not the
power of substantiating any charge against him, it would be highly
inconsiderate, to attempt to sue for a separate maintenance."

I replied, that was not the object, for neither would the disposition of Caroline, or Mr. P——, ever permit her to want, while they were abundantly rich; and indeed, he must recollect, that Mr. P—— meant to settle part of his estate upon the heirs of Mrs. F——; and though it was not very likely, she would ever have any by Mr. F——,[6] still it was reasonable to believe, as Mr. P—— was a rational and considerate man, that he would give Mrs. F——, so much of his property, as he intended to settle upon her children during her life, subject to reversion.[7] But if Mrs. F—— could be compleatly separated, she would then be at liberty to marry again; and certainly it was a cruel circumstance, that the pleasures of her life must be sacrificed, because she had been imposed upon by a man, who most likely the habits of life had rendered impotent; particularly, as, after the flagrant indignity he had offered to her sentiments and honour, it would be impossible for her ever to be connected with him again.

Sir Thomas acknowledged that it was a cruel situation for Mrs. F—— to be in, but said it was impossible to alter the laws respecting matrimony without the utmost danger to the good order of society; and as they now existed, Mrs. F—— could not be intitled to a bill of divorce, without she could either prove Mr. F——'s impotence or infidelity.[8]

"Great God!" said I, "Sir Thomas, how can you or law-makers believe, that a modest woman would ever attempt to prove the debility of her husband? or I should be glad to know how it is possible—for absolute impotence and debilitation are too distinct things, but equally mortifying to women of sensibility; and certainly nothing can be more farcical than to attempt to prove the incontinency of any man in such a place as London, provided he wishes to avoid detection." Sir Thomas made no reply, but shook his head.

Such are the laws and influence of customs in a country celebrated for wisdom and virtue, that from the almost impossibility of married persons being repudiated, the practices of gallantry have totally destroyed conjugal love, and the evils government intended to have prevented, have been extended to a most lamentable pitch of licentiousness.

I have a pleasure my friend, in informing you, in consequence of the request of that good man Mr. P——, George has been liberated from his confinement, and appears perfectly sensible of the absurdities which have marked the conduct of his life, and so often disgraced his character and subjected him to misery and contempt: and I have no doubt, from the signs of compunction which he discovers, that his repentance will be lasting and sincere.

It has been said by a patriot in the British senate that, "there is a degree of wickedness which no reproof or argument can reclaim, as there is a degree of stupidity which no instruction can enlighten!"[9] But you must recollect, this was applied to the most incorrigible and corrupt minister that ever disgraced the government of England.[10] For certainly if a man is not stupidly wicked after he has suffered every disgrace and hardship, which his follies merited, he must endeavour to regain the confidence and esteem of men by a generous acknowledgement of his former errors, and a noble ambition to acquire applause.

Sir Thomas Mor——ly desires I will express to Mr. P——, Caroline, and your self, how very much he is interested in your happiness, and that he will write to Mr. P—— as early as he can adjust the business he has done him the honour to instruct to his care.

Inclosed you have a letter from Mrs. F—— to Caroline.
Farewell,
G. IL——RAY

LETTER LXIX[1]

MRS. F——, TO CAROLINE.

London, April.

I Do not know, my dear Caroline, how to address you, as you only informed me of your perfect happiness, without saying by what date your expected union with Capt. Arl——ton would take place; and it is only from the information I received from Mr. Il———ray, that has convinced me it must have happened some time since; for I cannot draw a syllable from Mary upon the subject.

O Caroline! how did I tremble when Mr. Il———ray related to me the particular and horrid circumstances of your captivity with the savages, and the more wicked one of the note? but the transition of my feelings cannot be described as he proceeded in the narrative of your fortunate escape from barbarian slavery, and eternal melancholy and sorrow, which must have proved to a heart like yours, more gloomy than tedious winter in the arctic regions to the distressed and benighted ship-wrecked crew, who, when surrounded by chaotic frost, often languish unheard, and perish unknown to the world, and to their friends; and the tale of whose sufferings are buried with themselves, while the fond maid has beheld a blank in the creation, and the star that cheered her young imagination, and pointed to the haven of her wishes, has sat, never to rise again.

I have experienced from your affectionate recollection of my situation at a moment so important to yourself, the most unbounded happiness that the feelings of sisterly love can produce; —and it has been no small consolation to me to hear from Mr. Il———ray a relation of things in which you are concerned.

I have not the power to express to you the horror and disgust I have experienced at the late conduct of Mr. F———; and as I have found in Mr. Il———ray that warm benevolence, and delicate sense of dignity and honour which is characteristic of a man of principle, I have not hesitated to communicate to him the circumstances, as I found my existence, as a *woman,* depended upon my finding a refuge against brutality, and I knew not where else to seek for it.

He has written to Capt. Arl———ton upon the subject in order that he may advise with you and our friendly guardian and uncle, whose sentiments and generosity can never be sufficiently admired, in what way it is possible for me to become extricated from a situation the most miserable into which a woman of any feeling can be placed:—and I hope, my dear sister, that you will inform me, as early as possible, of the result of the conference; for I assure you that my situation is too painful to be endured; for while I have been constrained to leave the bed of a man who appears to me in the light of a monster, I am continually receiving insults as gross as they are unmanly.

Express to my dear uncle the exalted sense I entertain of his worth, and promise him that my gratitude for his generous treatment of our family, and particularly his conduct towards George, will be as lasting as it is warm.

Mr. Il——ray has this moment acquainted me with his having written to Capt. Arl——ton respecting our brother—I hope, Caroline, he will continue to conduct himself as he has begun since his emancipation—for I am happy to inform you that he appears quite an altered man. Farewell.

I am your affectionate, but unhappy Sister,

ELIZA

LETTER LXX

Mrs. Arl——ton, to Mrs. F——.

Bellefont, June.

I Had scarcely hurried over your last favour, when I flew with the greatest avidity to my dear Arl——ton to know the particulars of Mr. F——'s behaviour to you, and was petrified with the shocking and degrading injustice offered to your honour.

Not a moment was lost in summonsing our best friend, to know what could be done in order to rescue you from insult and wretchedness—never did he appear to greater advantage—his whole faculties for a moment seemed to have lost their energy: but the next instant, they burst forth into a blaze of manly eloquence which defied all resistance.

"What," said he, "shall an unfeeling wretch, whose excesses in the school of corruption, where the prostitution of principle and the feelings loose their elegant elasticity, and which have destroyed in him, every *manly* sentiment, be suffered, after having offered the most atrocious insult that can be used to a delicate woman, be permitted to continue to treat her with the most aggravating contumely and petulance? shall it be said in a civilized world, beauty and virtue have received every indignity which the most depraved can imagine, and the most callous and abandoned can inflict, and that they cannot find a friend sufficiently rational, and with spirit enough, to protect them against a tyranny more odious than ever was practised by the most contemptible despot that ever tyrannized over a nation? and will it ever be believed by posterity, that in a country renowned for gallantry and honour, and which has given the most glorious proofs of its attachment to freedom, and who have set an example to all the world, of the advantages which its struggles produce, that they should have been insensible spectators of the most inhuman and nefarious oppression that ever disgraced the annals of humanity? Ah! Caroline, I blush for the degeneracy of my countrymen, and while I am confounded at the thoughts of the lowest pitch of infamy to which a being, *for he cannot be a man,* can descend, I weep for the sufferings of the unfortunate fair, who have not friends to chastise the *cowards* who thus insult them with impunity."

Here he paused, and as he held me by one hand, and Arl——ton with his other, "My children! my life!" said he, "has been a series of perils and misfortunes; I have learned in its vicissitudes, how to appriciate its blessings, and I know how to sympathize with the afflicted; but I should deem myself unworthy of being called a man, was my benevolence confined to the effusions of my sensibility; my age and infirmities prevent me from being active, and you my children, have become so dear to me, that if any accident should happen to you in my absence, I never could again resume my spirits; but if you will accompany me, I will return immediately to England, and relieve my dear and virtuous niece from all future uneasiness, and we will bring her with us to this country, where love and joy shall compensate her for past sufferings; and for the loss of the meritricious and unsubstantial pleasures of a court. It will be but a summer's excursion, and our felicity will then remain unruffled, for all our friends will be concentered."

Arl——ton and myself stood for some moments so charmed with the energy of his heroick mind, that we could make no reply until he asked our approbation of his intention.

"It was with the most painful anxiety that I read my friend's letter," replied Arl——ton, which confirmed Caroline's suspicions of Mrs. F——'s wretchedness, "but it remained for me to understand a conduct so unnatural as that of Mr. F——'s to experience the full force of that disgust, which a treatment, to me, so unprecedented and depraved, could not fail to effect; and if you will permit me, I will assure you, that the interest I have taken in the relief of a person whom I consider as a sister, can only be exceeded by your generosity and benevolence, and the merits of a being so amiable and lovely as a woman, whose mind, my friend informs me, is the exact image of the heart of the most charming and delightful of her sex:—But it wanted not this information to have given me the most lively concern for the welfare and happiness of a friend and sister, whom Caroline tenderly loves. However, with every deference to your judgment, I beg leave to submit my opinion to your consideration, respecting the propriety of your undertaking a journey of such extent at your time of life; when it is necessary to take all possible repose, in order to prolong that existence, which is invaluable to your friends, who have barely had time sufficient, in their short knowledge of your talents and virtues, to know your loss would be irreparable: And therefore I beg leave to recommend, that Mrs. F—— may be immediately written to, and requested to put herself under the protection of our friend Il——ray, who I know to be a man of the strictest honour, and as bountiful as he is friendly."

Arl——ton was going to proceed when our dear uncle stopped him by saying:—"My dear friend, I beg your pardon, and Mr. Il——ray's, for not recollecting at the moment I was making my proposition, that our friend was in England:—but as I have the highest reverence and esteem for him, so I have the fullest reliance upon his kindness, and do most readily consent to the adoption of your opinion."

So it has happened, my dear Eliza, that circumstances, the most strange and inhuman, have conspired to produce us a most certain prospect of still living together.

It is this certainty alone, that could give relief to the grief I experienced from the knowledge of the shocking treatment you received from Mr. F——; and I hope you will find a full recompence in our love, and in the innocent charms of this wild country, for the losses you must sustain in leaving the European world.

If persuasion was necessary to prevail upon you, to take this step, I would go fully into a description of its various beauties and amusements, but as I know it is not, I shall only touch upon the subject, so far as to give you some idea of our situation, and the manner in which we live, and pass our time, since we have been settled.

The Ohio has been celebrated by geographers for its beauty, and its country for fertility,[1] but this delightful spot has a combination of charms, that renders it altogether enchanting.

Capt. Arl——ton has purchased a tract of country, sixteen miles square, adjoining to the rapids, which form a stupendous cataract.

This tract is bounded by the Ohio to the west; and here the expansive river displays in varied pride the transparent sheet, that gushing, shoots impetuous over its rocky bed; which, as if in a rebellious hour had risen to oppose its genial current, presents a huge, but divided barrier; and while nature seems to scorn its feeble power, the repercussive thunder proclaims her triumph, and the ethereal hills on the adjacent shore give lustre to the rising moisture, which creeping through the vistas of the groves, the country round, high illumined, in blushing charms its sweets diffuse, and nature shines effulgent to the joyous sight.

The winding river here presents itself in two directions, and on either hand the eye dwells with peculiar delight upon its fair bosom; and while the whispering breezes curl its limpid waters, the azure veins seem to swell, as if they were enraptured with the soft dalliance of their fragrant sweets.

A small island lies in the center of the river immediately in our front, in the shape of a diamond, overspread with sycamore and acar saccharinum,[2] or sugar tree, and with their umbrageous branches, which impend over the river banks, give a deeper hue to the passing waters.

The country gently rises from the banks of the river, for nearly six furlongs,[3] and presents a ridge, that runs parallel with it for several leagues;[4] which elevated prospect affords the expanded beauties of the country a long distance back, and at this genial season, the earth, where Pomona reigns,[5] yields bounteous plenty to all, and every being shares the golden stores that gild the variegated plains.

The country on the opposite shore, over hung with woods, is not less rich in variety; but as it remains yet uninhabited, we have the charms of cultivation contrasted by the beauties of wildness.

This body of land, Arl——ton has parcelled out into a number of lots, which are in part settled, and the remainder are settling, he having reserved six for himself and those friends who may in future wish to join us.[6]

Nearly in the center of one of these lots, is a fountain, I have called *Bellefont*, from whence the name of our seat is taken.

It is in every respect entitled to the distinction; for nothing of the sort can possibly be more beautiful. It gushes from a rock; and when its different pliant rills have joined at its base, they form an oval bason, about three hundred feet diameter, which float over a bed of chrystals, that eradiates its surface, and gives to it a polish more transparent than a mirror of glass.

The water steals off in several directions, and in their meandering course moistens the flowery banks, which, as if to return the loan, spread their blooming sweets on every side, and the soft gales gather their odours as they pass; and while they perfume the ambient air, the wanton hours dancing to the gentle harmony of sweet sounds, which the feathered songsters warble in modulated strains, love seems to have gained absolute and unbounded empire, and here in the couch of elegance and desire, to dally in all the charms of its various joys; to say with the poet,

> —*"And young eyed health exalts,*
> *The whole creation round."*—[7]

Arl——ton's mornings are occupied in laying out his grounds, and planting the several fruits, and other things necessary to the comfort and pleasure of living. He not only attends to this business, but he does great part of it with his own hands, which gives him that exercise so necessary to invigorate the constitution, and to give zest to the hours of relaxation. And when he returns, which is generally at eleven o'clock, he takes some refreshment, and then devotes the remainder of the day to different employments; and after dinner, which is between five and six, we walk into the sugar groves, wherein the gaiety and festivity of our neighbours, who dancing to the rude music of the country seem to have forgotten all their troubles, we pass a few hours perfectly congenial to my sentiments of happiness.

Andrew, a faithful servant and friend of Arl——ton's, and the mountaineer to whom I am equally obliged for his care of me the day I was rescued from the Indians, are generally the promoters of these pleasing entertainments: for most of the settlers are old soldiers, that served under Arl——ton, and whom he regards as his best friends, and the comrades of Andrew.

Their happiness adds not a little to ours, and our uncle seems delighted with our plan of life; for he appears to take peculiar satisfaction in teaching them appropriate knowledge; and it is thus he says, my dear sister, the benefits of society may be extended equally to every description of men.

These are not our only pleasures, for we have a great number of neighbours, independent of our select society, who are sensible and intelligent, and possess all the social virtues in an eminent degree; so that our amusements have all the variety that a rational being can wish. Indeed we seldom dine alone, or at home; for such is the hospitality of the country, and the plenty which every where prevails, that there is no such thing as want.

To a mind formed like yours, replete with sentiment, it is impossible for it not to experience in this way of living, every degree of felicity it could wish.

And it is one of the most singular pleasures of my life, to have it in my power to accompany my wishes with assurances, that your happiness must be compleat, when you shall have joined us. We all shall embrace you with one heart, and will love you with one soul; and you will be protected by the same generous hand from insult, and that tyranny which the caprices of men in the European hemisphere inflict upon unprotected women.

God bless you my dear and fond Eliza. Put yourself under the protection of Mr. Il———ray, and fly immediately from bondage to a land of freedom and love; and here in the bosom of peaceful affection, let the effusions of our hearts drown in oblivion the recollection of former distresses. Fly upon the pinions of the wind,[8] for your uncle and Arl———ton, will be made as happy as myself to receive you; and that the gales which ruffle the ocean that now separates us, may prove propitious to your passage, and waft you safe to its western shores, shall be the constant prayers of,

Your affectionate
CAROLINE

LETTER LXXI

P. P———, ESQ. TO SIR THO. MOR———LY, BART.

Bellefont, June.

MY DEAR SIR,

THE last communications from our friends in London, have given me no little uneasiness, as they have afforded me another proof of the many miseries resulting from the crude policy of the European world.

It is not a time for me to enter into a dissertation of those evils, nor could my troubling you upon the subject, be relevant to removing them.

That you are sensible they exist, and that you have given generous and manly proofs of your abhorence at the cause, I have been well informed. But you must permit me to say, I am apprehensive, that like every other thing, by our growing familiarized with them, they in some degree lose their influence; so it has happened I presume with your opinions upon the important consideration of protecting innocence against the inhuman. However I will not disguise my sentiments upon the business to which I allude.

The conduct of Mr. F—— to my niece, has not only been dishonourable and tyrannic, but it has been brutal; for which reason I have desired that she may be requested to leave him without ceremony, and accompany Mr. Il——ray to this country, provided it is agreeable to her; and if not, I desire that you will give her a suitable establishment on my account.[1]

Give me leave to assure you, that I am with every sentiment of regard,

> Your sincere Friend,
> P. P——

LETTER LXXII

SIR T. MOR——LEY, BART. TO P. P——, ESQ.

London, Sept.

MY DEAR SIR,

I Have had the pleasure of receiving two favours from you since I did myself the honour to inform you of your late relation having adopted you his heir: and the only thing I lament from a circumstance, upon the events of which, I had flattered myself would prove so propitious to my happiness, as well as to yours, is, that I cannot have an opportunity in person, to convince you how very sincerely I reprobate the cause of your misfortunes, and how much at heart I feel the evils of which you so emphatically complain.

I am not insensible of the honour you do me by approving of my parliamentary conduct;[1] and if I have discharged the trust reposed in me with fidelity, and shewn my attachment to the cause of integrity and freedom, I claim no other merit than having acted, to the utmost of my feeble abilities, for the good of mankind in every part of the world.

The baneful effects, the prodigality of the times, and which is the result of the proponderance of servility, that cringing to the power of the crown, which has three millions of money annually at its disposal, is every day marked by some unhappy circumstance, or disgraced by some wanton sacrifice.

I have not been an insensible spectator of the sufferings of your amiable niece Mrs. F———. But to the habits of a desolate life, her late unfortunate husband, added that aspiring folly, which vainly hopes to mount to the summit of glory by the slippery ladder of princely allurements.—

He seems to have commenced his life with error, to have continued it with shame, and to have ended it with infamy.

His attempt to sully the chastity of a virtuous woman, which is too shocking to reflect upon, and to add ignominy to sacrilege, having proved abortive, and consequent poverty having brought upon him the contempt of his associates in vice, he came to a resolution to die as cowardly as he had lived; and by putting a loaded pistol to his head, he fell a victim to those enervating passions, which first lead to the practice of folly, and then prevent the exercise of that bravery necessary to combat the frowns of adversity; and by a feeble effort of unmanly resolution he had the presumption to aim at the reputation of dying like a hero, when he had not spirit to live like a man.

Such, my friend, is the depravity of the manners of which you
so justly complain; that men who are ambitious to live with splendour exceed their income, and when they find their fortunes
ruined, and themselves neglected, which is always the case, they
have recourse to the dastardly practice of putting an end to their
own existence.

Poor Mrs. F—— was so shocked with a series of absurdities
and the atrocious actions of Mr. F——, and particularly at this
last, which happened a short time before your letters came to
hand, that she determined to leave England without delay and
join your society in the western world, where I hope you will
have the wisdom to appropriate useful truths, and thereby interdict the inconveniencies which the state of Europe experience
from evils, that have accumulated under the immaturity of our
establishments.

Mr. Il——ray, who added to the warmest benevolence has an
acute understanding, and almost infallible penetration and judgement, has taken under his care, agreeable to your wish, both Mrs.
F—— and your Nephew, who I hope will continue as he has
begun, to merit the approbation of his friends.

That perfectability which he thinks society may arrive at in the
progression of civilization, is the only thing in which I materially
disagree with him in political sentiments: for I am afraid that the
philosophers of the present day, by aiming at too much, will produce evils equivalent to those they have laboured to remove.[2]

The perverseness of some men, have made it absolutely necessary that government should restrain their licentious habits, and
the executive part of a constitution must have efficiency, otherwise the expected coercion of laws will lose their effect.

When we talk of our privileges we should mention them as
belonging to man in a state of society, such as he is, with his
passions, and not as a perfect being: and we should recollect what
part of them it is necessary to surrender for the greater security
of the remainder;[3] and that when a government preponderates on
the side of the executive branch of the system or on the side of
the people, it is then the wisdom and moderation of the state by

an analysis to bring it back to its original principles; which appears to me, when the constituent parts are radically good, to be the perfection of political science.

The laws of matrimony, which Mr. Il——ray reprobates, as they subject women to hardships, certainly are defective; and it is a cruel consideration, that when a woman of feeling has been imposed upon and insulted, and has taken refuge in the tender solicitude of some friend or lover, and in consequence shall be subject to lose the very fortune she may have carried her husband:[4] and it is also unfeeling and indelicate in us to suffer them in the eye of the laws of this country, to be considered in the light of property,[5] and not as beings to whom we owe every thing, and to whom we are indebted for every felicity worth enjoying.——

But it is at the same time certain, if our laws, in some respects regarding this subject, have the complexion of barbarism and brutality, that no women in Europe enjoy so many privileges, or have so much consequence in the common affairs of life.

The practice of married persons being repudiated for every trifling disagreement, would be productive of endless distractions in families, and which I apprehend would prove more dangerous to the harmony of society than the anarchy of political sentiments.

I am aware that the complication of laws at the advanced age of states will be productive of many inconveniences, and perhaps it is one of the taxes necessarily imposed by the refinement of manners. For in the infancy of every state particular codes and institutions, sometimes of a local nature, must take place, and which doubtless, in many instances, will be destitute of wisdom.

It is from the accumulation of laws and multifarious distinctions that distract the opinions of men, and produce that obscurity of ideas upon the subject of jurisprudence which tends to bewilder the understanding of the most learned; and thus it has happened in common affairs, the perplexity of laws, and the expences attending the administration of justice, which both custom and the practice of our courts have rendered necessary, that peaceable and industrious citizens have continually been the prey of the licentious villain and wealthy miser, while unprotected innocence has been sacrificed to avarice, impotence, and contumely.

The laws of England which are specifically good and wholesome, have multiplied to an enormity that is truly astonishing; and it is to the contradiction of the Judges that we are indebted for that disgraceful proverb the "glorious uncertainty of the law," which is spoken of with as much indifference as though there was no evil annexed to it:—and therefore it has happened that while the form of our government has existed the administration of justice has not only been tardy;—but it has been so heavily taxed that the great bulk of the nation has found security only from the spirit of its citizens;—while partial and cruel violations of our privileges have raised a general clamour against the excellence of our boasted constitution, which is likely to shake it to its very foundation.[6]

There are æras in the progress of civilization favourable to the amelioration of governments, and there are characters sometimes at the head of affairs, who by dispositions unaccountably extravagant and foolish, which excite the disgust of the state, when a general defection never fails to accelerate the removal of abuses or the overthrow of all government.

Such were the characters of Charles the First, and Second, and James the Second, whose follies paved the way for our glorious revolution of 1688[7]—such was the contumely and arrogance of the minions of his present Majesty, that it provoked the people of America to revolt, and ultimately effected a defalcation of that empire from the mother country:[8]—and such I presume will be the obstinacy of the present administration, that by resisting all kind of amendment they will hasten the destruction of the constitution.[9]

I sent you by Mr. Il——ray the whole of the documents respecting the disposal of your different estates, with a statement of the arrangements which I have made for Mr. T——n and his family: but as his departure was very sudden I had not time to write to you so fully as I wished. However, I flatter myself you will consider this a sufficient apology, and do me the honour to continue a correspondence from which I promise myself so much pleasure.

You have inclosed, a statement of the final adjustment of the business confided to my management, with a power to draw upon me for the sum still in my hands.

I beg leave to assure you and your adopted children, and my valuable friend Mr. Il——ray, of my utmost solicitude for their happiness, and to subscribe myself,

Your sincere and faithful friend,
T. Mor——ley

LETTER LXXIII

P. P——, Esq. to Sir Thomas Mor——ly Bart.

Bellefont, July.[1]

MY DEAR SIR,

Mr. Il——ray having made a short delay in Philadelphia in order to adjust his business preparatory to his final settlement with us, necessarily procrastinated our felicity of embracing Mrs. F——, and telling her that we sincerely rejoiced to have it in our power, to prove how tenderly we were interested in all the vicissitudes of her happiness.

The delicacy of her frame, I perceive, has been not a little shattered by the shocks that have been given to her sensibility, and while I was contemplating the animation of her face which so peculiarly expresses the sentiments of a heart pregnant with virtue, moulded with feminine softness, and warm with all the social virtues, I felt the keenest indignation at the cause of her sufferings, and silently reprobated the depredations which unnatural restraint must ever produce.

The change of her situation, and the endearments of her friends, added to the cheerful and joyous pleasures, that spontaneously present themselves to a mind formed like Mrs. F——'s, could not fail to perfect her prospect of happiness, so far as depended upon herself and relations; and which has been compleated by the mutual sympathy, inspired for each other, by her and Mr. Il——ray, and I am happy to inform you, that their union will be, solemnized as early as the rules of decency will permit.

Suffer me to return you my most sincere thanks for the trouble you have taken in the various arrangements that my requisition must have given you; and to assure you, that while I am surrounded by those I love, and feel all the tranquility of mind after a long and boisterous life, which a situation so delectable, as being placed in the center of your friends, and cherished by the cordial interchange of the congeniality of sentiment, must ever afford to a rational being, I am not forgetful of the friendship you have shewn me, by your attention to my unfortunate relations, nor insensible of the honour you do me in requesting a continuance of our correspondence.

The happy effects from changing the situation of my nephew, is every day marked with some new feature, distinguished by manly form; and they now display the renovated energy of a mind naturally good, but which had been long dormant, and like decrepitude in the arms of beauty that views the charms of love through the medium of a palsied frame, and resigns the joys, it has not vigour to attain, was insensible to the pleasures that are obtained by the virtuous exertions of a noble emulation.

Upon his arrival, I requested that he might be formally introduced to me, having previously desired Mr. Il——ray to request of him, never to mention to me his former errors, and only generally to express his gratitude for any favours he might conceive I had done his family; and as I enjoined all our friends to cautiously avoid mentioning to him, any thing that bordered upon the subject of his juvenile absurdities, I soon perceived that my purpose was answered: For in a very short time, he began to shake off his former habits, and having no person to lounge with, he soon followed the example of those with whom he is living.

His understanding has not only been regenerated but his person has already become robust, and he now has more the appearance of an Ancient Briton, than one of those fine fellows, whose nerves require the assistance of harshorn,[2] to enable them to encounter the perils of a hackney coach,[3] or the fatigues of a masquerade.[4]

Among the number of our friends, is a Mrs. S———, whose disposition from being naturally good, has acquired in the cultivation of her mind, all that sweetness, which the qualities of the ingenuous heart, and a lively understanding, produce in such eradiated charms.

This person has not been insensible to the personal accomplishments of George, and I took care to encourage those feelings in him, which her beauty, and the gentleness of her temper, had inspired; and which I was the more anxious of doing, as I thought it the most effectual way to prompt him to the practice of virtue, as it would be making him acquainted with domestic pleasures, resulting from being united with an amiable and sensible woman, and give him a just idea of their superior joys.

Thus you will find my friend, though all my tender hopes were blasted, and all my pleasures mutilated, while my anguish was as corroding, as my losses were severe, I am now surrounded like a Patriarch of old,[5] and with my eyes fixed upon Heaven, where I expect to join my loved Juliana, and fond offspring, I am contented in administering all the good to which the limits of my capacity can extend—and if it is the rewards of my struggles, I confess I am over paid from the alleviation I feel to the pangs of a heart long since overwhelmed with sorrow.

You shall soon have my opinion upon the progress and advantages of philosophy.

Farewell.
P. P———

THE END

EXPLANATORY NOTES

A number of words whose meaning may not be immediately clear to the modern reader—for instance, because the spelling of a word is no longer the same—or whose meaning has changed since the time the novel was written, are given in the Glossary, which follows these notes.

Following the conventions of the discourse of the sentimental novel, Imlay's letter writers frequently use scraps of verse (as well as quotations from a wide array of popular authors of the day) to express their emotions. About half of these verse citations are identified as such by quotation marks (often including the name of the author). The remaining verses, however, are without quotation marks, and, as far as we have been able to ascertain, were written by Imlay himself; hence they are not annotated here.

VOLUME I

PREFACE

1. *my letters regarding the western territory of American received in England:* The reference is to Imlay's *A Topographical Description of the Western Territory of North America*, which had appeared in London in 1792, and which had been widely and favorably reviewed in the British press. Following the example of *Letters from an American Farmer* (London, 1782) by J. Hector St. John de Crèvecoeur (1735–1813), Imlay's text identifies itself on the title page as "a series of letters to a friend in England," a common eighteenth-century convention that was supposed to lend a degree of authenticity and, hence, reliability to the text.

2. *the important political questions now agitated throughout Europe:* Imlay is referring to the spirit of revolutionary radicalism that was sweeping through Western Europe in the early 1790s in the wake of the French Revolution, notably in France and Britain. Among the issues that were being debated were the status of women in society; marriage and divorce laws; education; the separation of state and church; and the relation between natural and civic law.

3. *These important principles have been treated by so many authors of the most consummate penetration and talents:* Among the authors and books Imlay may have had in mind are Jean-Jacques Rousseau (1712–78), author of the educational novel *Émile* (1762) and an influential work of political philosophy, *The Social Contract* (1762); Edmund Burke (1729–97), conservative advocate of British institutions in *Reflections on the French Revolution* (1790); Thomas Paine (1737–1809), author of the radical treatise *The Rights of Man* (1791–92); and Mary Wollstonecraft (1759–97), author of the impassioned reply to Burke, *Vindication of the Rights of Men* (1791) and the feminist tract *Vindication of the Rights of Woman* (1792). Published in the same year as Imlay's novel was what many people now regard as the ultimate manifesto of radical anarchism, *Enquiry Concerning Political Justice* (1793) by William Godwin (1756–1836).

4. *the great difficulty there is in England, of obtaining a divorce:* There were very few grounds for divorce. The system was heavily weighted in favor of men, who could divorce their wives for adultery, but not vice versa. A full divorce required a private bill before Parliament, and was financially far out of the reach of most people. According to Lawrence Stone, "The annual total of court-ordered separations and divorces in the mid-eighteenth century was only about 0.1 percent of all marriages." (*Broken Lives: Separation and Divorce in England, 1660–1875* [Oxford: Oxford University Press, 1993], 120.) The editors' introduction to this work provides further information on this topic.

5. *first minister, in a neighbouring kingdom:* The most likely candidate for the figure referred to here appears to be Charles-Maurice de Talleyrand-Périgord (1754–1838), French statesman and diplomat (though never actually "first minister"). Born into an old, aristocratic family, Talleyrand started his career in the French clergy. Appointed agent general in 1780, he represented the French church in its dealings with the government. He showed great energy in defending the controversial privileges of the church, fighting vigorously for the right of the church to retain all its property and arguing for the continued exemption of the clergy from ordinary taxes. For services rendered, he was appointed Bishop of Autun in 1788, taking possession of his see in March 1789, only months before the Revolution. Elected by the clergy as their representative, Talleyrand soon became an influential member of the post-revolutionary National Assembly. To the astonishment of his fellow bishops, who remembered the zeal with which he had once defended church rights, Talleyrand

urged the repeal of the tithe and the nationalization of French church property. The land thus appropriated was to be used to pay off the state's debts. Talleyrand resigned as Bishop of Autun in January 1791. A year later the French government sent him to London to persuade the British to remain neutral in France's war with Austria. Talleyrand was fêted publicly in Whig and radical circles, and had free access to the highest authorities. His negotiations with the British prime minister William Pitt were concluded successfully during Talleyrand's second mission to London in April–May 1792. However, the overthrow of the monarchy in August and the massacre of the royal prisoners in September made it advisable for Talleyrand to leave France. Arriving in London on September 18 in a private capacity, he resumed talks with the British authorities in an attempt to avert war with France. Imlay's indignation at the British politicians and rulers for welcoming with open arms a person who had so blatantly betrayed the trust put in him by those whose interests he was to defend, was shared by the British statesman Edmund Burke, who, in his *Reflections on the Revolution in France*, denounced Talleyrand for having "pillage[d] his own order."

6. *peculation*: Embezzlement.

INTRODUCTION

1. *obliged him to seek an asylum in America*: Emigration to America was part of the spirit of the age, becoming increasingly popular in the early 1790s. In its issue for May 1793, the *Gentlemen's Magazine* reported that "Several of our periodical publications have of late abounded with essays written to prove the superior felicity of American farmers, and to recommend our husbandmen to quit their native plains, and seek for happiness and plenty in the Transatlantic desarts" (Vol. LXIII [1793], 401). The same periodicals, however, frequently carried essays warning against the dubious activities of British and American land-jobbers, who were trying to tempt potential emigrants to settle in the New World, and sell them land to which they held the rights. Thus, in the September 1793 issue of the *Gentlemen's Magazine* appeared a review of a recent publication entitled *Letters on Emigration, By a Gentleman Lately Returned from America*, which, according to the reviewer, "contain[s] much good admonition to the several classes of men who are disposed to emigrate." Depicting the dire fate of the so-called "redemptioners" (or emigrants

who had returned to Britain destitute and disillusioned), the reviewer can only conclude that "this land of universal promise is the land of general disappointment" (Vol. LXV [1793], 760).

2. *to traverse a region which . . . was inhabited mostly by wild beasts and savages:* When the first census was taken in 1790, the frontier dividing settled land from wilderness ran near the coast of Maine, and included New England (except part of New Hampshire and Vermont), New York along the Hudson River and up the Mohawk to Schenectady, eastern and southern Pennsylvania, Virginia (well across the Shenandoah Valley), the Carolinas, and eastern Georgia. Across the Allegheny Mountains were only small pockets of settled land in Kentucky and Tennessee, which were referred as the back settlements.

3. *querulous:* Here, full of stressful emotion.

4. *the mourners of Adonis surrounding the Queen of Love:* In Greek mythology a beautiful youth, Adonis, was loved by Aphrodite, the goddess of love. He was killed by a boar, and mourned by Aphrodite and her followers.

5. *luctiferous:* Heartrending ("luctiferous" is the adjectival form of "luctation," meaning struggle).

LETTER I
1. *desart:* Desert; a wild uninhabited and uncultivated tract.

2. *Draw upon me:* What Il——ray means is, "You may bring out your weapon against me on sight" (in case he were to break his promise not to divulge their plan).

LETTER II
1. *the mountain:* The term Imlay uses throughout the novel to refer to the Allegheny Mountains, part of the Appalachian system. "The mountain" is actually fifty miles across (as we learn in Letter XI).

LETTER III
1. *Among the gentlemen of the army who have retired to this country:* Officers were granted land rights in the western territories for services rendered in the French and Indian War (1754–63) and the Revolutionary War (1775–83). Especially after the Treaty of Paris in 1783 many veteran

officers (including Imlay) moved across the Allegheny Mountains to claim their land rights.

2. *Mr. W——:* Subsequently referred as "General W——," and probably based on the notorious General James Wilkinson (1757–1825). See the editors' introduction for more information about Wilkinson.

LETTER IV

1. *challenge:* That is, a challenge to fight a duel.

2. *the sublime ideas of ancient cavilliers . . . that heroic institution:* That is, the chivalric code of behavior (which entailed bravery and courtesy) of the chevaliers or knights of feudal times.

3. *Montesquieu says "that among the barbarians . . . none but villains fought on foot":* Imlay's two citations from the *The Spirit of the Laws* (1748) by Montesquieu (1689–1755), the French lawyer, philosopher, and man of letters, are a cross between a loose translation and a paraphrase of the original text, which more properly reads: "The accuser began by declaring before the judge that a certain person had committed a certain act, and the accused would reply that the accuser had lied about it; at this, the judge would order the duel. . . . Gentlemen fought each other on horseback with arms; villeins [*sic*] fought one another on foot and with a staff." Both citations are from chapter 20 ("The origin of the point of honor") of book 28 ("On the origin and revolutions of the civil laws among the French") of part 6 of Montesquieu's work, which is a treatise on the principles and historical origins of law and which analyzes the difference between "natural" (or universal) and "human" (or "positive") law.

4. *assassinate:* To injure or destroy someone's reputation by ridicule.

5. *importuning:* Urgently requesting.

LETTER V

1. *the rout from Philadelphia to this place was through Lancaster:* In his *Topographical Description* Imlay provided detailed travel instructions for European emigrants intending to set out on the journey from the east coast across the Allegheny Mountains to the back settlements—which is not surprising, seeing that it was in his interest as a land-jobber to make the western settlements appear to be less inaccessible than they actually were:

The routes from the different Atlantic States to this country [Kentucky] are various, as may be supposed. From the northern States it is through the upper parts of Pennsylvania to Pittsburg, and then down the river Ohio [this is the route that the T——s take in the novel]. The distance from Philadelphia to Pittsburg is nearly three hundred miles. From Lancaster about two hundred and thirty. The route through Redstone and by Pittsburg, both from Maryland and Virginia, is the most eligible, provided you have much baggage; except you go from the southern and back counties of Virginia; then your best and most expeditious way is through the Wilderness. From Baltimore passing Old Town upon the Potowmac, and by Cumberland Fort, Braddock's road to Redstone Old Fort on the Monongahala, is about two hundred and forty miles; and from Alexandria to the same place by Winchester Old Town, and then the same route across the mountain is about two hundred and twenty miles. This last must be the most eligible for all Europeans who may wish to travel to this country, as the distance by land is shorter, the roads better, and the accommodations good, *i.e.* they are very good to Old Town which is one hundred and forty miles from Alexandria, and thence to Redstone comfortable, and plentifully supplied with provisions of all sorts: the road over the mountain is rather rough, but no where in the least dangerous (Letter VII).

2. *to bait:* To give food and drink to an animal, especially on the road.

3. *sumpter mules:* Mules used as pack animals.

4. *drone:* Lazy, idle fellow.

5. *turnpike roads:* A main (and usually well-maintained) road, for the use of which tolls were collected ("turnpike" refers to the gate at which the tolls had to be paid).

6. *Baron Beilfield:* This is a reference to Jakob Friedrich, Freiherr (or "Baron") von Beilfeld (1717–70). Born in Hamburg, the son of a trader, Beilfeld lived in Leiden, The Netherlands, between 1732 and 1735. During the next few years he made an extensive tour of The Netherlands, France and England, where he was frequently seen in intellectual circles. In 1738 he was presented to Frederick, then prince, later (in 1740) to become Frederick II, King of Prussia. Bielfeld entered Frederick's service in 1739, eventually becoming one of the king's private counselors. He was made Baron Bielfeld in 1748. In his *Lettres familières et autres* (1763) he provides an interesting though romanticized description of his relationship with Frederick II. He is also the author of *Comédies nouvelles*

(1753), *Progrès des Allemands dans les sciences, les belles-lettres* (1752), and *Institutions politiques* (1760). The observation about coaches here attributed to Bielfeld has not been located, although he refers to the relative comforts and discomforts of traveling through the various parts of Europe by coach on several occasions in his *Lettres familères et autres.*

LETTER VI

1. *according to the present system . . . separated from her husband:* This refers to the difficulty, both according to law and moral convention, for a woman to obtain a separation or divorce from her husband.

LETTER VII

1. *"That she was all . . . when they love":* These lines are adapted from the tragic drama *The Fair Penitent* (1703) by the English poet and dramatist Nicholas Rowe (1674–1718). The exact lines read: "Is she not more than painting can express, / Or youthful poets fancy, when they love?" (act 3, scene iii).

2. *Praxillites, or any one of the Grecian Statuarists:* That is, Praxiteles, a fourth century B.C. Athenian sculptor. One of the greatest Greek sculptors, Praxiteles worked in marble and is noted for a relaxed, sensuous style distinct from the idealized forms of Phidias, or the mathematically symmetrical proportions devised by Polycleitus, two of the other Grecian staturists to whom Imlay may be referring here.

3. *"Of whose sweetness . . . gathered from her soul!!":* The source of this quotation has not been located.

4. *the Graces:* In Greek mythology, three sister goddesses—Euphrosyne, Aglaia, and Thalia—who embodied beauty and charm.

5. *tout en semble: Tout ensemble,* the whole.

6. *apropos:* By the way.

7. *en famille:* At home, with the family.

LETTER VIII

1. *Pope . . . his temple of Fame:* The reference is to the poem "The Temple of Fame" (1711), by Alexander Pope (1688–1744), notably the lines,

> O'er the wide prospect as I gazed around,
> Sudden I heard a wild promiscuous sound,
> Like broken thunders that at distance roar,
> Or billows murmuring on the hollow shore:
> Then gazing up, a glorious pile beheld,
> Whose towering summit ambient clouds conceal'd,
> High on a rock of ice the structure lay,
> Steep its ascent, and slippery was the way:
> The wondrous rock like Parian marble shone,
> And seem'd, to distant sight, of solid stone. . . .
> On this foundation Fame's high temple stands;
> Stupendous pile! Not rear'd by mortal hands.
> Whate'er proud Rome or artful Greece beheld,
> Or elder Babylon, its frame excell'd (lines 21–30, 61–64).

2. *packers:* Men who transport goods by means of pack animals.

3. *frequent Indian wars:* There had been more or less chronic hostilities between the Indians and the white settlers in the western territories ever since the end of the Revolutionary War, during which the majority of Indian tribes sided with the British (as they had done with the French during the French and Indian War of 1754–63). According Sydney J. Krause, "The country had a nasty little war in its midst . . . that had been dragging on from around 1784. Outbreaks had ranged over widely scattered areas. On the thinly settled and vulnerable Georgia frontier, for example, even Savannah was not safe; citizens, feeling themselves constantly threatened there, had to mount regular guard details. The district of Kentucky between 1783 and 1790 had lost over 1,500 men, women, and children killed or taken captive, along with the loss of 2,000 horses and other property amounting to at least $5,000 (no insignificant figures for that day). Pennsylvania was no exception." ("Historical Essay," in Charles Brockden Brown, *Edgar Huntly; or, Memoirs of a Sleep-Walker,"* edited by Sydney J. Krause *et al.* [1799; rpt. Kent, Ohio: Kent State University Press, 1984], 381.)

4. *there are not any within two hundred miles of us:* Although land-jobbers like Imlay would have people in Britain believe this, it was obviously not quite in accordance with the truth (see the preceding note, and Letter XIII). Writing less than fifteen years after Imlay's novel appeared, in his *Travels in America, Performed in 1806* (London, 1808), Thomas Ashe (1770–1835) referred with some disgust to the way land-jobbers had

consciously and maliciously misrepresented the state of affairs regarding the relations between Indians and whites, and singles out Imlay for special criticism: "It was whispered abroad that 'the Indian country' was the finest in the world; that Imley's [*sic*] dreams applied to it alone, and that the French, who had visited it from the Canadian border, considered it a paradise of the new world. This was more than sufficient to inspire a disposition to possess this charming territory, and to annihilate its inhabitants" (Vol. I, 195).

5. *Chestnut mountain:* That is, Chestnut Ridge, approximately 40 miles southeast of Pittsburgh.

LETTER IX

1. *Appalachean mountains:* Mountain system in the east of the United States, extending from Vermont down in a southwesterly direction into northern Alabama.

2. *reside at the west end of the town, that is the court end:* The West End was (and is) the fashionable western part of London, which had been growing and changing rapidly during the eighteenth century, and which counts Buckingham Palace, Kensington Palace, and St. James's Palace among its more prominent landmarks. During the reign of King George III (1738–1820, reigned 1760–1820), the West End was the center of courtly life, and many aristocratic families were either rebuilding their homes there or commissioning new ones.

3. *the east of Temple Bar:* Originally a gateway between the City of London and the City of Westminster, now marked by an effigy of a griffin on a pedestal. It was situated opposite the Law Courts, at the junction of Fleet Street and the Strand, near the Temple Church. At one time adorned by a stone gate designed by the English architect Sir Christopher Wren (1632–1723), Temple Bar broadly separated the residences of the wealthy in the west of London from those of the trading class and of the poorer urban population in the eastern part of the town.

4. *Horse Guards:* The cavalry brigade of the British household troops. Aristocrats and upwardly mobile middle-class families would frequently buy a commission for their sons with the Horse Guards for reasons of prestige and social status.

5. *at one time worth ten thousand pounds annually:* £10,000 was the average yearly income of great landlords in the late eighteenth century. Thus, Darcy, the wealthy hero of Jane Austen's novel *Pride and Prejudice,* has an annual income of £10,000.

6. *numerous instances of this sort which disgrace the courts of Great Britain:* The reference is to the rigid sexual double standard, which meant that female infidelity, however provoked, met with no mercy in the British courts. Women were liable to lose the property they brought into the marriage as well as custody of their children. The whole issue was a prominent topic in women's novels of the 1790s; see, for example, Elizabeth Inchbald, *A Simple Story* (1791); Maria Edgeworth, *Letters for Literary Ladies* (1795); and Mary Hays, *The Victim of Prejudice* (1799).

7. *as I have it in agitation:* "As I am seriously considering."

LETTER X
1. *Voltaire was in the right, when he said, that "friendship is a tacid contract . . . Cicero was the friend of Atticus":* The passage is taken from the section on Friendship ("Amité") in the *Philosophical Dictionary* (1764) by Voltaire, pseudonym of François-Marie Arouet (1694–1778). Voltaire's text actually reads:

> [Friendship] is a marriage of the soul, it is a contract between two sensitive and virtuous persons. I say *sensitive* because a monk, a solitary, may not be at all wicked and live without knowing friendship. I say *virtuous* because the wicked have only accomplices, the voluptuous have companions in debauchery, self-seekers have associates, the politic assemble the factions, the typical idler has connections, princes have courtiers. Only the virtuous have friends. Cethegus was the accomplice of Catiline, and Maecenas the courtier of Octavius, but Cicero was the friend of Atticus.

LETTER XI
1. *tutelary guardian:* Protecting guardian.

2. *The fates:* In Greek mythology, the three daughters of Nyx (Night). They controlled the destinies of men. Originally birth goddesses, the Fates came to be represented as three old women who spun the thread of life.

3. *fifty leagues:* Any of various units of distance from about 2.4 to 4.6 statute miles; in general, taken to be about 3 miles. Thus, 50 leagues would be approximately 150 miles.

4. *cavillier:* Cavalier, a gentleman, notably one on horseback.

5. *the spot which was made memorable by the defeat of the gallant Braddock:* The reference is to General Edward Braddock (1695–1755), commander in chief of the British forces in America at the start of the French and Indian War (1754–63). In the fall of 1755 Braddock undertook an extremely arduous wilderness expedition against the French-held Fort Duquesne (later renamed Fort Pitt; see note 7 to Letter XIV). His force had to cut a road westward from Cumberland, Maryland, the first road across the Allegheny Mountains. George Washington, then lieutenant colonel of the Virginia militia, was among the 700 provincials and 1,400 British regulars under Braddock's command. Soon after the British troops had crossed the Monongahela, a forward column of the force was ambushed by the French and Indians in a ravine. Wounded during the ensuing slaughter and riot, Braddock was carried off the field and died four days later.

6. *those beautiful lines out of Tasso, "In vain the spring returns . . . indulge in love":* The reference is to Torquato Tasso (1544–95), the greatest Italian poet of the late Renaissance, whose masterpiece, *Gerusalemme Liberta* (*Jerusalem Delivered*; 1581), reflects the romantically morbid feelings of his melancholy soul. The source of this citation has not been located.

7. *that unfortunate battle:* A reference to General Braddock's disastrous campaign against the French-held Fort Duquesne in the fall of 1755 (see note 5 to this Letter).

8. *when the late unhappy war commenced:* Refers to the start of the American Revolutionary War with armed clashes between British regulars and the minutemen at Lexington and Concord, Massachusetts, in April 1775.

9. *cadet:* Someone in training for a military commission.

10. *dragoons:* Heavily armed cavalrymen.

11. *our journey, which we finished in about fifteen days from the time we left Philadelphia:* In *A Topographical Description*, however, Imlay estimates the duration of the trip from Philadelphia to Pittsburgh as "nearly twenty days" (Letter VII).

12. *habiliments:* Occupational accessories.

LETTER XII

1. *Mrs. W—— to Miss R——:* Erroneously, the text of the first and second editions confuses these characters and superscribes the letter as "*Miss W—— to Mrs. R——.*"

2. *ignis fatuus:* Scientifically, a phosphorescent light that flits over swampy ground at night, perhaps the result of spontaneous combustion of gases; figuratively, any illusive ideal that leads one astray.

3. *Saratoga:* The Battle of Saratoga (1777) is nowadays regarded as the military encounter that turned the War of Independence in favor of the American side. British troops under the command of General John Burgoyne were moving south from the St. Lawrence River to meet the forces of General William Howe along the Hudson River. At Saratoga, New York, Burgoyne's troops were met by 12,000 American troops under General Horatio Gates. There were two engagements, on September 19 and October 7. After incurring heavy losses, Burgoyne surrendered on October 17. The American victory helped induce the French to recognize American independence and to give open military assistance, thus marking a turning point in the uprising and making possible its ultimate success.

4. *Arcadian regions:* According to Virgil, the Greek district of Arcadia was the home of pastoral simplicity and happiness. Figuratively, Arcadia came to represent a simple, rustic life that was idyllic and nobler than a complex urban existence.

5. *the stings of outrageous fortune:* A partial quotation from William Shakespeare's *Hamlet:* "the slings and arrows of outrageous fortune" (act III, scene i, line 58).

6. *necessitous:* Destitute, very poor.

7. *hymeneal:* That is, matrimonial; Hymen was the Greek god of marriage.

LETTER XIII

1. *Pittsburg, Oct.:* The text of the first and second edition of the novel erroneously dates this letter as "Aug."

2. *an expression of the celebrated Rochefoucauld, "That persons . . . to deceive others":* There is no exact match of this quotation in *Reflections or Aph-*

orisms and Moral Maxims, or simply *Maxims* (1665), by François, duc de La Rochefoucauld (1613–80), but Maxim no. 373 seems to be the one Imlay is echoing here: "Often we are taken in ourselves by some of the tears with which we have deceived others."

3. *torrid zone:* The region of the earth between the Tropic of Cancer and the Tropic of Capricorn, i.e., the tropics.

4. *the Goths and Vandals:* The Goths were a Germanic people who over-ran the Roman Empire in the early centuries of the Christian era. The Vandals were another Germanic people who lived in the area south of the Baltic Sea between the Vistula and Oder rivers, and who overran Gaul, Spain, and northern Africa in the fourth and fifth centuries A.D. and who sacked Rome in 455. The terms Goths and Vandals are used to refer in general to barbarians.

5. *Zephyrus:* Greek god of the west wind.

6. *Claud:* That is, Claude Gelée, commonly called Claude Lorraine (1600–82). Well-known French landscape painter who raised the genre from a low standing in the academic hierarchy to a major mode of artistic expression. Born in the Lorraine, he spent most of his painting life in Rome, where he succeeded in giving pictorial form to the nostalgia for a lost Golden Age articulated by the Roman poet Virgil, often illustrating themes from the latter's *Aeneid*.

7. *peregrinations:* Wanderings.

8. *we have been your worst foes in war . . . going to Pittsburg for the purpose of burying the hatchet:* This is another attempt by Imlay to play down the Indian threat in the western territories, where, despite Imlay's claims to the contrary, clashes between Indians and white settlers were numerous in the 1780s and continued long after the end of the Revolutionary War (see also notes 3 and 4 to Letter VIII). As a matter of fact, there was a marked increase of hostilities from 1783 onward (at the time in which the action in the novel takes place), as emigrants began to cross the Allegheny Mountains in great numbers to take up land in the Ohio Valley. Things were bad enough as the whites settled south of the river, but they got decidedly worse when the settlers began to turn toward the north, toward Shawnee country, for the Shawnee chief Tecumseh (1768?–1813) was determined to check the encroachments of the settlers. In 1791 and 1792 Tecumseh fought in many raids on white settlements,

and helped destroy two armies sent out to subdue the Indians, who were fighting for their lands. A peace treaty was signed in 1795 (the Treaty of Greenville) after General Anthony Wayne defeated Tecumseh's forces in the battle at Fallen Timbers near Fort Miami. However, this by no means meant the end of hostilities between the Indians and the settlers.

9. *there was not yet a peace between the Indians and us:* See preceding note.

LETTER XIV

1. *rencontre:* A meeting.

2. *avaunt:* Away, hence.

3. *Ohio, in the Indian language signifies fair:* The name Ohio is derived from an Iroquoian word meaning "fair," "bright," "shining," or "great."

4. *The Allegany is . . . the line between civilization and barbarism:* John Seelye comments on this cultural bifurcation as follows: "Here again we have the theme of two rivers, which from Pownall to Bartram defined the American landscape in disjunctive terms, the savage Allegheny and the civilized Monongahela joining to become the Ohio" (*Beautiful Machine: Rivers and the Republican Plan, 1755–1825* [New York and Oxford: Oxford University Press, 1991], 158).

5. *the dusty rides in Hyde Park:* The reference is probably to the sandy ring along the outer perimeter of Hyde Park (an extensive public park in the west of London) commonly referred to as Rotten Row, first laid out by Charles I as a promenade for the coaches of the wealthy, and especially fashionable in Georgian times.

6. *the state of Great Britain . . . when it was first invaded by the more polished Romans:* The first attempt of the Romans to conquer Britain dates back to the year 55 B.C., when a force of ten thousand men landed in Kent. "Aborigines" refers to the native inhabitants of Britain at the time, notably the Celts.

7. *it was a fort erected previous to the last war by the French called fort Du Quesne . . . during whose administration it was taken:* On the eve of the French and Indian War (1754–63), the French had a firm grip on the North American continent. They occupied both the mouth of the St. Lawrence River in Canada and the mouth of the Mississippi in Louisiana. Their control was secured by a line of fortresses, including Niagara,

Detroit, and Duquesne. It was the erection of this last fort at the confluence of the Monongahela and Allegheny Rivers in 1754 that provoked the war with Britain. Taken by the British in 1755, the fort was
renamed Fort Pitt in honor of English statesman William Pitt the Elder
(1708–78).

8. *Saratoga:* See note 3 to Letter XII.

9. *Cardinal De Retz has given Madam De Longueville; who he said, "had a
great store of natural wit . . . starts of fancy surprizingly fine":* Jean-François-
Paul de Gondi, Cardinal de Retz (1613–79), was a French ecclesiastic
and politician, and one of the leaders of the aristocratic revolt called
the Fronde (1648–53), a rebellion against the government of Anne of
Austria (who was regent for her son, Louis XIV), and her chief minister, Cardinal Mazarin. Retz's *Memoirs* is an account of his life to
1655 and contains a description of his role in the events of the Fronde,
as well as portraits of contemporaries and maxims drawn from his
experiences. One of the people whose involvement in the Fronde he
documents is Anne-Geneviève de Bourbon-Condé, duchesse de
Longueville (1619–79). A princess remembered for her beauty and her
love affairs, she also played a prominent role in the Fronde when she
persuaded many powerful aristocrats to join in opposition to the government.

   The citation is from De Retz's *Memoirs,* and reads in the original:
"Mme de Longueville a naturellement bien du fonds d'esprit, mais elle
en a encore plus le fin et le tour. Sa capacité, qui n'a pas été aidée par
sa paresse, n'est pas allée jusques aux affaires[, dans lesquelles la haine
contre Monsieur le Prince l'a portée, et dans lesquelles la galanterie l'a
maintenue]. Elle avait une langueur dans les manières, qui touchait plus
que le brillant de celles mêmes qui étaient plus belles. Elle en avait une,
même dans l'esprit, qi avait ses charmes, parce qu'elle avait des réveils
lumineux et surprenants."

10. *yeoman:* Small farmer or countryman above the grade of laborer.

LETTER XV
1. *incognitum:* A man unknown, unidentified.

2. *When a sensible heart vibrates . . . the sense of honour?:* The cult
of sensibility agitated the nerves of Europe and America in the mid-

eighteenth century. It touched all literary genres and privileged the qualities of tenderness, compassion, and sympathy. Moral worth and the capacity to feel deeply were signified in the bodily manifestations of tears, fainting fits, and palpitations. The literary and philosophical discourses of sensibility found support in contemporary medical writings, which considered women's bodies particularly susceptible to such feelings. For an illuminating discussion of the phenomenon, see Janet Todd, *Sensibility: An Introduction* (London and New York: Methuen, 1986).

LETTER XVI

1. *the unfortunate African who is torn from his home—from his family— . . . suffering under the most tyrannic and inhuman sacrilege:* The sentimental trope of the disruption of the family is a familiar one in abolitionist writing throughout the eighteenth and nineteenth centuries (culminating perhaps in Harriet Beecher Stowe's *Uncle Tom's Cabin*). For more information on this topic, see Moira Ferguson, *Subject to Others: British Women Writers and Colonial Slavery, 1670–1834* (New York and London: Routledge, 1992).

2. *locquacity:* Talkativeness.

3. *classic:* Someone having received a classical education.

LETTER XVII

1. *dishabille:* Informal dress (i.e., in a private setting, before one is formally dressed for public appearance).

2. *the little wanton deity . . . attendant of beauty:* The reference is to Cupid—in Roman mythology, the god of love, son of Venus and Mercury, and counterpart of the Greek Eros. Cupid is usually represented as an exquisite boy with wings, bearing a bow and quiver of arrows. In later myth he developed into the familiar cherubic but mischievous little boy.

3. *Hebe:* In Greek mythology, goddess of youth and a cupbearer to the gods.

4. *Fell:* Fierce.

5. *Jove:* Another name for Jupiter, the supreme deity of Roman mythology, and corresponding roughly to the Greek Zeus.

6. *in seven days I shall be seven hundred miles distant from the lovely Caroline:* "The common mode of descending the stream [the Ohio River]," Imlay observes in his *Topographical Description*,

> "is in flat-bottomed barges, which may be built from 15 to 500 tons. . . . These boats are built of oak plank. . . . They are covered or not as occasion may require. The object is to build them as cheap as possible, for their unwieldiness prevents the possibility of their returning, and they can only be sold as plank. . . . The distance of descending is in proportion to the height of the water; but the average distance is about eighty miles in twenty-four hours, and from sixty to one hundred are the extremes: so that the mean time of going in a flat-bottomed boat from Pittsburg to the Rapids [of Louisville], is between eight and nine days, and about twenty days more to New Orleans: which will make a passage from Pittsburg to that place nearly a month" (Letter V).

According to Thomas Ashe, who described his trip down the Ohio in his *Travels in America* (see note 4 to Letter VIII), fifteen days would be "a good spring passage" from Pittsburgh to the mouth of the Ohio; in summer, however, "six, eight, and even ten *weeks* are often required to effect the same voyage" (Vol. I, 158).

LETTER XVIII
1. *a celebrated philosopher has said, that the great Prince de Condé "with the most brilliant wit . . . nor weigh things together":* Louis II de Bourbon, fourth Prince de Condé (1621–86), also known as the "Great Condé," was the brother of the duchesse de Longueville (see note 9 to Letter XIV). He was one of the leaders of the second Fronde, and later became one of Louis XIV's greatest generals. A cultivated man and a patron of the arts, Condé had wide intellectual interests, and was known for his uncommonly sound independence of mind. The identity of the "celebrated philosopher" has not been ascertained, nor has the source of the quotation been located.

2. *ruelle:* A reception, normally held in the morning, but here taking place later in the day.

LETTER XIX

1. *Niobe:* In Greek mythology, the wife of Amphion, king of Thebes. Inconsolable after the death of her children, Niobe, at her own request, was turned to stone by Zeus.

2. *the sublime Buffon, or the more accurate Pennant:* Comte Georges Louis Leclerc de Buffon (1707–88), French naturalist who became curator of the Jardin du Roi in 1739. He is best known for his *Histoire naturelle* (36 volumes, 1749–88) and *Epoques de la nature* (1779). Buffon's theories, such as his development of geographic zoology, anticipated those of Lamarck and Darwin. He was attacked by Thomas Jefferson in the latter's *Notes on the State of Virginia* (1781) for his thesis that the animals and aborigines of the New World were smaller and generally degenerated in comparison with their European equivalents. Buffon had attributed this degeneracy to the greater heat and drier climate of America.

Thomas Pennant (1726–98) was a Welsh traveler and naturalist. Author of *History of Quadrupeds* (1781), he was one of the foremost zoologists of his time, and his books were widely read.

LETTER XX

1. *Stoicism . . . contemptible philosophy:* A school of Greek philosophy, founded by Zeno of Citium (*c.* 362–*c.* 264 B.C.) around 308 B.C. The Stoics were austere, advocating freedom from passions and desires. They equated the real with the material and defined the active principle in the universe as a Force of God. They sought to be in harmony with nature and the divine will, and their philosophy was characterized by a detachment from the outside world. Stoicism was highly congenial to the Roman temperament and influenced Roman law.

2. *deviable:* Adjective formed from deviate and meaning liable to change.

3. *Venus:* Roman goddess of love.

4. *Milton has said in pleasant strain, "Come thou Goddess fair and free . . . Jest and youthful Jollity":* These lines occur in "L'Allegro" (1645) by John Milton (1608–74):

> But come thou goddess fair and free,
> in heaven yclept Euphrosyne,
> And by men, heart-easing Mirth,
> Whom lovely Venus at a birth

> *With two sister Graces more*
> *To ivy-crowned Bacchus bore;*
> *. . . Haste thee nymph, and bring with thee*
> *Jest and youthful Jollity"* (lines 11–16 and 25–26).

5. *those eyes which are as brilliant as that torch which led to the illumination of the Grecian world in the destruction of Troy:* The reference is to Helen of Troy—in Greek mythology, daughter of Zeus and wife of Menelaus. Helen's abduction by Paris led to the Trojan war. Throughout literary history, she has been a symbol of womanly beauty and sexual attraction. Imlay is drawing an analogy between the brilliance of Caroline's eyes and the fire that destroyed the city of Troy.

LETTER XXI

1. *If Telemachus wanted a Mentor . . . his father Ulysses:* In classical legend Telemachus was the only son of Odysseus (whose Roman name is Ulysses) and Penelope. When Odysseus had been absent from home nearly twenty years, Telemachus went to Pylos and Sparta to gain information about him, accompanied on his voyage by Athene, the goddess of wisdom, under the form of Mentor, one of his father's friends and a wise counsellor entrusted by Odysseus with the education of his son.

2. *that his object of visiting Louisiana is of the most patriotic kind:* As we have been told before on several occasions, Arl——ton is supposed to have left for Louisville, *not* Louisiana. Either this is a mistake on the part of Imlay, or, since Arl——ton's journey is apparently a "patriotic" one, and since we hear about it through General W—— (the character modeled after the notorious conspirator, General Wilkinson), this may be a covert reference to contemporary French–American plots against the Spanish in Louisiana. See the editors' introduction for more information on this topic.

3. *mal-apropos:* Out of place, improper.

4. *what moral the good archbishop of Cambray . . . when Calypso discovered her tender anxiety:* Refers to François de Salignac de la Mothe, French writer and archbishop of Cambray (1651–1715). He was tutor to the duke of Burgundy, grandson of Louis XIV and presumed eventual heir. Fenelon was the author of *Télémaque* (1699), a didactic romance written for his pupil in which he sharply criticized Louis XIV as a despot who had destroyed the political power of the nobility and ruined France by

his martial and mercantilist policies. Fenelon's story is based on the old legends surrounding the figure of Telemachus, but he adds many incidents, notably Telemachus's love affair with the nymph Calypso, who had been so violently in love with his father, Odysseus.

5. *Thomson has said, "And let the aspiring youth beware of love":* This is a line from "Spring" (1728), one of four blank-verse poems collectively entitled *The Seasons* (1726–30) by the Scottish poet James Thomson (1700–48): "And let the aspiring youth beware of love, / Of the smooth glance beware; for 'tis too late, / When on his heart the torrent-softness pours" (lines 983–85).

LETTER XXII
1. *the ingenuous Fenelon . . . Thomson has cautioned youth:* See notes 4 and 5 to Letter XXI.

2. *coming to an eclaircissement:* Coming to an understanding.

3. *General Wolfe:* James Wolfe (1727–59), British general who was fatally wounded during the French and Indian War (1754–63) at the battle of Quebec in 1759, which ended in a victory of the British over the French troops under General Montcalm. Wolfe's patriotic martyrdom made him the very icon of British colonial heroism.

4. *his Majesty:* Given that P. P—— served under General Wolfe, who died in 1759 at the battle of Quebec (see preceding note), and returned to Britain after his corps was disbanded, the reference is probably to George III (1738–1820), who acceded to the throne in 1760.

5. *contumacy:* Normally, obstinate disobedience or resistance; here referring to P. P——'s resistance to being dependent on others.

6. *Venus:* See note 3 to Letter XX.

LETTER XXIII
1. *to have some fish-ponds drawn:* To have all the fish removed from the ponds by means of nets.

2. *primum mobile:* Mainspring. In medieval astronomy, the outermost of the revolving spheres of the universe, which carried the others around in twenty-four hours.

3. *Rubicon:* A small river separating ancient Italy from Cisalpine Gaul. When Julius Caesar crossed the Rubicon with his army in 49 B.C., he passed beyond the limits of his province, thereby becoming an invader of Italy and precipitating civil war. Hence, "to cross the Rubicon" is to take an irrevocable step.

4. *beauty in distress:* The phrase is an echo of a line in *A Philosophical Enquiry into the Origin of Our Ideas of the Sublime and Beautiful* (1757) by Edmund Burke (1729–97): "Beauty in distress is much the most affecting beauty" (part III, section IX).

LETTER XXIV

1. *your Mercury:* Mercury was the Roman god of commerce, eloquence, travel, cunning, and theft who served as messenger to the other gods.

2. *Cancer:* A northern zodiacal constellation between Gemini and Leo. What Caroline means is, "when summer comes (to the northern hemisphere)."

3. *the Indians are still at war with the low country:* See note 8 to Letter XIII.

VOLUME II

LETTER XXV

1. *sang-froid:* Self-possession, coolness.

2. *humours:* Moods.

3. *bon compagnion:* Good companion.

4. *the Moor of Venice . . . Iago says, "Trifles light as air . . . proofs of holy writ":* The reference is to act 3, scene iii, lines 319–21 of *The Tragedy of Othello, The Moor of Venice,* commonly called *Othello* (c. 1604) by William Shakespeare (1564–1616). Othello is a Moorish general in the service of the state of Venice who is secretly married to Desdemona, daughter of a Venetian senator. Othello's officer Iago is the villain of the play. Iago conspires to make Othello believe that Desdemona is unfaithful to him, and Othello ultimately kills both his wife and himself.

5. *"One brilliant eye-ball . . . beauty charms his sight":* The source of this quotation has not been located.

6. *Minerva:* The Roman goddess of wisdom.

7. *Queen of Beauty:* Venus, in Roman mythology, the goddess of beauty and love.

8. *Frederic II. king of Prussia:* Frederick the Great (1712–86), king of Prussia (1740–86), was an enlightened despot who built up the Prussian state through vast territorial acquisitions and domestic reforms. He was a patron of the arts and a friend of Voltaire. He wrote voluminously, usually in French.

9. *"When the wit is too pert . . . is superior to other men":* The source of this quotation has not been located.

10. *Flora:* In Roman mythology, the goddess of flowers.

11. *"put out the light and then—put out the light":* This is Othello's line from the final scene of the play just before he kills Desdemona (*Othello*, act 5, scene ii, line 7).

12. *curricle:* Two-wheeled chaise usually drawn by two horses.

13. *Don Quixote:* A novel by Miguel de Cervantes Saavedra (1547–1616), published in two parts in 1605 and 1615. It is a satiric picaresque novel about a kindly country gentleman who is so crazed by reading chivalric romances that he feels called upon to redress the wrongs of the world, including fighting windmills that he believes to be giants.

14. *the sun had scarcely passed its meridian:* Literally, the sun had passed its highest point in the sky; that is, noon or midday.

LETTER XXVI

1. *"As to what is called honour . . . the eternal truths of morality":* P. P.——— is presumably quoting here from his own letter to Lord B———, referred to earlier in the present letter.

2. *The first aim of society . . . under the influence of a base jurisprudence:* This issue—that is, the relation between natural laws and what Montesquieu calls "political laws" and "civil laws"—was hotly debated in Europe throughout the eighteenth century, and drew heavily on the work of John Locke (1632–1704), notably his *Two Treatises of Government* (1690). In this work Locke presupposes a state of nature preceding a social contract which was the basis of political society. Locke saw the state of

nature as a peaceful condition in which the laws of Nature and of Reason were spontaneously observed; the idea of the social contract was that it merely provided additional assurance that life and property would be respected. The American *Declaration of Independence*, in particular, echoes his contention that government rests on popular consent and that rebellion is permissible when government subverts the ends—the protection of life, liberty, and property—for which it is established.

3. *"Ye tyrants . . . to think on redress"*: The source of this quotation has not been located.

4. *Emelius*: The reference is to *Émile, ou l'Éducation* (1762), an educational romance by Jean-Jacques Rousseau (1712–78). It describes the upbringing of the boy Émile according to what Rousseau calls the principles of nature. He emphasizes character formation, empirical observation, mastery of useful trades, physical exercise, and hard work. The book was immediately translated into English, and had a notable effect on pedagogical theory in France, Germany, and England.

5. *tergiversation*: Equivocation.

6. *"Mark how spring . . . extracting liquid sweets"*: These lines are adapted from *Adam; Or, The Fatal Disobedience. An Oratorio. Compiled from the "Paradise Lost" of Milton, and Adapted to Music* by the English poet Richard Jago (1715–81). The exact lines read: "mark how spring / Our tended plants, how blows the citron grove, / What drops the myrrh, and what the balmy reed; / How nature paints her colours; how the bee / Sits on the bloom, extracting liquid sweets" (lines 19–23).

LETTER XXVII

1. *when men entered into society, they gave up part of their liberty, the more effectually to secure their more important rights*: Caroline's thoughts here are of the same conservative cast as those of Edmund Burke (1729–97) in his *Reflections on the French Revolution* (1790): "Men cannot enjoy the rights of an uncivil and of a civil state together. That he may obtain justice, he gives up his right of determining what it is in points the most essential to him. That he may secure some liberty, he makes a surrender in trust of the whole of it."

2. *incontinent*: Unchaste; those people who fail to restrain their sexual appetites.

3. *as far as you think education would tend to ameliorate the condition of women, I perfectly agree with you:* Caroline and P. P——— agree in blaming women's faulty education, or lack of education, for their deplorable position in society, as had progressive thinkers for over a century. A notable early demand for women's education is Mary Astell's *Serious Proposal to Ladies* (1694). The appearance of publications on this issue accelerated during the 1790s, including such crucial texts as Catharine Macaulay's *Letters on Education* (1790) and Mary Wollstonecraft's *Vindication of the Rights of Woman* (1792).

4. *blandishment:* Something that tends to coax or cajole.

5. *Rubicon:* See note 3 to Letter XXIII.

LETTER XXVIII
1. *incontinency:* Lack of restraint.

2. *Pittsburgh:* Normally spelled "Pittsburg" throughout the text, but here and on some other occasions Imlay adopts what has become the modern spelling of the name.

LETTER XXIX
1. *anathemas:* Vigorous denuciations, curses.

2. *petit maitres:* Petits *maîtres,* probably a reference to the social radicals of the period, whom Lord B——— and his friends belittle by describing them as fops or dandies.

3. *picquet:* Card game played by two, using thirty-two cards.

4. *I had determined to appeal to his courage:* That is, I had decided to challenge him to a duel.

5. *eradiated:* Shot out like a ray of light.

6. *"through a vista of tears":* The source of this quotation has not been located.

LETTER XXX
1. *fair Aurora:* In Roman mythology, the goddess of dawn.

2. *dies:* Dyes, colors.

3. *to use an idea of Rousseau's . . . lasted an hour:* While no exact source for Rousseau's "idea" has been located, similar sentiments can be found at various points in his *La nouvelle Héloise* (1761), *Confessions* (1781) and *Rêveries d'un promeneur solitaire* (1782).

4. *criminal connection:* Adultery, for which the technical legal term would have been "criminal conversation" or "crim. con."

5. *advocates:* Lawyers.

6. *tissue of Plutus:* In Greek mythology, Plutus was the god of wealth. The phrase refers to the adornments of wealth.

7. *Despots of the east:* The East, and especially Islamic regions such as Turkey, were used as a conventional trope of oppression during the eighteenth century.

8. *St. James's-place:* A fashionable address in London's West End.

9. *brought damages against me . . . that condemned me to live for upwards of ten years in a prison:* The costs of bringing a "crim. con." suit were extensive, and thus the plaintiffs were all rich men. Lawrence Stone notes that

> The number of cases and the amount of damages both rose sharply in the 1790s, when the whole process was given an additional stimulus by the appointment of Lloyd Kenyon as Lord Chief Justice. Inspired by his own brand of Puritanism, reinforced by the moral panic among the élite aroused by the French Revolution, he urged juries to award damages not merely in reparation to the husband for mental suffering and loss of companionship, but also of sufficient size to set an example to the nation, and act as a deterrent to future adulterers. . . . As a result of his influential rhetoric, juries began awarding larger and larger damages running to thousands of pounds. Some awards were for £10,000, £20,000, and even very occasionally £25,000. Damages so far beyond the capacity of the defendent to pay meant, in practice, the condemnation of the latter to a life in prison for debt unless the plaintiff chose to free him.

(*Broken Lives: Separation and Divorce in England, 1660–1857* [Oxford and New York: Oxford University Press, 1993], 24.)

10. *suborning:* Bribing, persuading to commit perjury.

11. *obtained . . . an act of parliament divorcing him from his late Lady:* This is not to say that everybody wanting to separate from their marriage partner went to the length of a parliamentary divorce. There were a number of methods of breaking a marriage: For those with little or no property, desertion, elopement, and wife sale were possible options; for persons of property and standing, the alternatives included separation by private deed, judicial separation from bed and board, and "crim. con." litigation. A parliamentary divorce was necessary in order to gain permission to remarry—an option so expensive that only three or four such divorces were granted a year during the eighteenth century. The procedure entailed three lawsuits, involving an ecclesiastical court, a common-law court (the "crim. con." litigation), and then finally a private bill before Parliament for a full divorce.

12. *King's-bench:* The King's Bench is a division in the English superior court system that hears civil and criminal cases.

13. *jointure:* Property settled on a woman at marriage to be enjoyed upon her husband's death, or, in this case, after a divorce.

14. *unfortunate and distressed objects in such places:* The reference is to other impoverished people also confined within the King's Bench prison.

15. *denying him a character:* By denying him a letter of reference.

16. *getting into place:* Getting new employment.

17. *Land's-end:* Refers to the southwest tip of Cornwall, the extreme west point of England.

18. *Albion:* Ancient name for the island of Great Britain; used poetically in modern times for Great Britain.

19. *gyves:* Fetters, shackles.

20. *during the last war with the French:* The reference is to the French and Indian War of 1754–63.

21. *these back settlements where land is cheap:* In comparison to those areas in the east that had already been fully settled, land in the back settlements was relatively inexpensive at about one dollar an acre (though the land-jobbers, who by the 1790s held most of the land rights, had frequently paid not more than four to six pence per acre). A few years later, however, Thomas Ashe noted in his *Travels in America* (see note 4 to Letter

VIII) that land prices in Kentucky had soared, varying from as much as four hundred dollars for land in the immediate vicinity of Lexington, to five dollars for the poorest land toward the mountains (Vol. II, 95).

22. *a war had commenced between Great Britain and her then Colonies:* That is, the American War of Independence (1775–83).

LETTER XXXI

1. *Venus . . . God of War:* For Venus, see note 3 to Letter XX. In Roman mythology, the god of war was known as Mars.

2. *Jove:* See note 5 to Letter XVII.

LETTER XXXIII

1. *specious knave:* Seemingly reliable rogue.

2. *St. Eustatia:* St. Eustatius, an island in the West Indies (part of the Netherlands Antilles).

3. *a phæton and pair:* A light, four-wheeled carriage drawn (in this case) by two horses.

LETTER XXXIV

1. *"something rotten in Denmark":* This is a partial quote from *The Tragedy of Hamlet, Prince of Denmark* (1600–01) by William Shakespeare (1564– 1616). The complete line reads, "Something is rotten in the state of Denmark" (act I, scene iv, line 90).

2. *captious caprice:* Confusing and unpredictable disposition.

LETTER XXXV

1. *Mrs. F—— to Miss Caroline T——n:* Erroneously, the text of the first edition superscribes the letter as "Mr. F—— to Miss Caroline T——n" (corrected in the Dublin edition of 1794).

2. *our arrival at Falmouth . . . our departure from Sandy-hook:* Falmouth is a port in Cornwall; Sandy Hook is a peninsula near New York Bay.

3. *We hurried up to town:* London.

4. *eclat:* Éclat, distinction.

5. *routs:* Fashionable evening assemblies.

6. *Automatons:* Individuals who act by routine, without real intelligence or consciousness.

7. *"The spider's touch . . . lives along the line":* These lines are adapted from *An Essay on Man* by the English poet Alexander Pope (1688–1744), and read more correctly: "The spider's touch, how exquisitely fine! / Feels at each thread, and lives along the line:" (Epistle I, lines 217–18).

8. *Arcadian regions:* See note 4 to Letter XII.

LETTER XXXVI

1. *hollos:* Shouts to call attention.

2. *Zephyrus:* See note 5 to Letter XIII.

3. *Venus:* See note 3 to Letter XX.

4. *Antipodes:* Parts of the earth diametrically opposite, often used, colloquially, of Australia and New Zealand, considered to be the exact antipodes of London.

5. *factitious:* Artificial, unnatural.

6. *Cato . . . Octavius Cæsar:* Marcus Porcius Cato, known as Cato the Younger (95–46 B.C.), was a Roman statesman who took his own life after the legions of Gaius Julius Caesar (100–44 B.C.), Roman statesman and general, defeated the army of the nobility (which Cato had backed in the dispute with Pompey) in North Africa. Caesar became dictator in Rome, but was assassinated by other patricians, led by Marcus Brutus (*c.* 85–42 B.C.), for overthrowing Roman republican institutions. Mark Antony (*c.* 82–30 B.C.), Roman statesman and general, turned public opinion against the conspirators at his oration at Caesar's funeral, and Brutus and Cassius, another conspirator, fled Rome. Both raised armies, and Antony and Octavius Caesar (63 B.C.–A.D. 14), Caesar's lawful heir (who was later awarded the title of Augustus by the Senate), temporarily suspended their struggle for power and marched against them. Brutus ultimately committed suicide when his forces were surrounded by those of Octavius and Antony at Philippi in 42 B.C.

7. *"A generous friendship . . . and our passions be":* These lines are adapted from the translation (1715–20) of Homer's *Iliad* by Alexander Pope (1688–1744). The exact lines read: "A generous Friendship no cold Me-

dium knows. / Burns with one Love, with one resentment glows; / One should our Int'rests and our Passions be" (lines 725–27).

8. *sycophants:* Self-serving flatterers.

9. *erroneous bias:* Mistaken opinion.

LETTER XXXIX

1. *Princess Matilda, late Queen of Denmark:* The reference is to Queen Caroline Matilda (1751–75), who was the sister of King George III of England. When she was fifteen, she married Christian VII, king of Denmark, who proved to be as deranged as her brother. Matilda became involved with Struensee, the royal physician, and together they effectively controlled the state. They were ousted by enemies at the Danish court, who disliked their reformist regime. While Struensee was arrested and beheaded, Queen Matilda escaped from imprisonment on a British warship. She died at Celle, in Hanover, at the age of twenty-four. Her tragic story captured the imagination of many writers in the latter part of the eighteenth century, notably Mary Wollstonecraft.

2. *the security . . . from the natives:* See note 4 to Letter VIII.

3. *the vapour:* Depression.

LETTER XL

1. *the unfortunate Queen of Denmark:* See note 1 to Letter XXXIX.

2. *religionists:* Persons adhering to a religion, especially, religious zealots.

3. *the æra of protesting against the catholic creed:* A reference to the Reformation, a sixteenth-century movement marked ultimately by the rejection or modification of some Roman Catholic doctrine and practice and the establishment of the Protestant churches.

4. *by statute:* By law.

5. *from the disposition of the faithless and unfortunate James II . . . to protestants:* James II, king of Great Britain and Ireland (1633–1701). He was deposed by Parliament in what was called the Glorious Revolution of 1688, because, as a Catholic, he was threatening the security of the Church of England and at the same time weakening the power of Parliament. He was succeeded by his Protestant daughter, Mary II, in conjunction with her Dutch husband, William III. The fear of a return of

James or of later succession by other Catholics caused further controversy and led to the Act of Settlement of 1701 and later acts which made it impossible for a Catholic to succeed to the throne.

6. *the most lovely woman in the world:* Queen Matilda of Denmark.

7. *illy:* Badly.

8. *mixed government:* The reference is to constitutional monarchy, a system of government whereby a monarch rules in conjunction with a chosen parliament within the parameters of a constitution.

9. *a nugatory attempt:* A futile or unavailing attempt (erroneously appears in the text of the first and second edition as "a nugatory to attempt").

LETTER XLI
1. *Mrs. F—— to Miss Caroline T——n:* Erroneously, the text of the first edition superscribes the letter Mr. F—— to Miss Caroline T——n (corrected in the Dublin edition of 1794).

2. *fluid:* Here, strong emotion.

3. *pathetically:* Touchingly.

4. *if the invitation is not immediately from Mr. F——, and which I know will startle your feelings:* In strict accordance with contemporary rules of decorum, the invitation should have come from Mr. F—— as the head of the household.

LETTER XLII
1. *the impetuosity of your passion . . . the more gentle Monongahala:* Sexual imagery is used frequently throughout the text to describe the western landscape; for a discussion of this feature, see John Seelye, *Beautiful Machine: Rivers and the Republican Plan, 1755–1825* (New York and Oxford: Oxford University Press, 1991), notably 157–60.

2. *to trim a little:* To adjust his behavior as the situation dictates; that is, to ostensibly revise his opinion of Mr. S——.

LETTER XLV
1. *I am suspended as it were between Elysium and Tartarus:* In Greek mythology, Elysium is the abode of the blessed and Tartarus an underworld

of punishment for the dead. Thus, Caroline feels herself suspended between heaven and hell, pleasure and pain.

2. *agreeable to promise:* In accordance with my promise.

3. *an effect upon him, as the unparalled Sterne, said the name of Julia had upon Slawkenbergius, "Harsh and untuneful . . . with sympathetic sway":* These lines occur in *The Life and Opinions of Tristram Shandy, Gentleman* (1759–67) by Laurence Sterne (1713–68), and read more accurately: "Harsh and untuneful are the notes of love, / Unless my Julia strikes the key, / Her hand alone can touch the part, / Whose dulcet movement charms the heart, / And governs all the man with sympathetic sway" (Vol. IV, "Slawkenbergius's Tale"). The character of Hafen Slawkenbergius is an imaginary German scholar, distinguished for the great length of his nose and an equally imaginary treatise on noses. Sterne supposedly translates Slawkenbergius's account of the adventures of the large-nosed Diego and his lover Julia (thus, in fact, the name of Julia affects Slawkenbergius's character, Diego, rather then the imaginary author himself, as Imlay has it).

LETTER XLVI

1. *conspicuous:* Striking.

2. *the sublime philosophy which Pope meant when he said, "Whatever is—is right":* This line occurs in *An Essay on Man* (1733–34) by the English poet Alexander Pope (see note 1 to Letter VIII): "All Nature is but art, unknown to thee / All chance, direction, which thou canst not see; / All discord, harmony not understood; / All partial evil, universal good: / And, spite of pride, in erring reason's spite, / One truth is clear, Whatever is, is right" (Epistle I, lines 289–94).

3. *Diamond Island:* Imlay probably refers to the small island in the Ohio River just north of the falls, off the town of Louisville, called Six Mile Island. If the island was ever referred to as Diamond Island, there is no evidence of this. There is a Diamond Island in the Ohio farther downstream from Louisville, near Henderson, Kentucky. In his *Travels in America*, Thomas Ashe (see note 4 to Letter VIII) described Diamond Island as "by far the finest in the river, and perhaps the most beautiful in the world. It is higher than the adjoining main land, containing twenty thousand acres; and is of the exact form of a diamond, whose angles point directly up and down, and to each side of the expanded river"

(Vol. III, 8). Imlay may well have renamed Six Mile Island after Diamond Island to further add to the appeal and lustre of Louisville.

4. *streamers:* Pennants; that is, nautical flags tapering usually to a point and used for identification or signaling.

LETTER XLVII
1. *From the time we left Pittsburg untill our arrival here [Louisville], which was ten days after our embarkation:* In his *Topographical Description* Imlay estimates the journey to take "between eight and nine days" (Letter V). See also note 6 to Letter XVII.

LETTER XLVIII
1. *entre:* Entree, entrance.

LETTER XLIX
1. *the Rapids:* That is, the falls of the Ohio River at Louisville, a series of rapids where the river drops twenty-six feet in about three miles. The falls were navigable only to lightly laden boats, making Louisville (named in honor of Louis XVI of France for his aid in the American Revolution) the only river port between Pittsburgh and New Orleans where passengers had to disembark and goods had to be put ashore. They were then transported on land around the falls. This lucrative portage business ended in 1830, when a canal around the falls was opened. Visiting the town in 1806, Thomas Ashe (see note 4 to Letter VIII) noted that Louisville, though situated in a picturesque spot near the roaring falls of the Ohio, was a town of only about eighty dwellings, and that its inhabitants were "universally addicted to gambling and drinking" (Vol. II, 267, 269).

2. *an undress:* An informal dress or loose robe, worn in a private setting.

3. *marquee:* A large tent, usually set up for an outside party or reception but here functioning as a type of informal conservatory.

4. *these beautiful lines out of an ode of Thomson's "O mix their beauteous beams . . . all their darts":* These lines are an almost exact quotation from the poem "To Myra" (lines 5–8) by the Scottish poet James Thomson (1700–48).

5. *the azure brightness of a living orb:* That is, the clear sky-blue brightness of his eyes.

VOLUME III

LETTER L

1. *Clarkeville:* Clarksville, Indiana, at the falls of the Ohio, across from Louisville, Kentucky. Writing in 1806, Thomas Ashe (see note 4 to Letter VIII) described Clarksville as "a village of no importance" (Vol. III, 2). The town was named after George Rogers Clark (1752–1818), a general in the Revolutionary army. In 1778, Clark brought 120 soldiers and 20 families of settlers down the Ohio; on a tiny island just above the falls (Corn Island), he set up a base for military operations against British forts in the Illinois country, east of the Mississippi. A few months later, cabins and a fort were built on the mainland. With the help of French settlers in the area, Clark in the summer of 1778 took Kaskaskia and Cahokia (now in Illinois) and Vincennes (now in Indiana). After the revolution, Clark was a member of the board of commissioners allotting lands in the Illinois grant that the state of Virginia had made to his soldiers. In 1786, Clark led an expedition against marauding Wabash Indians, but it failed when most of his men mutinied. Charged by General James Wilkinson (see note 2 to Letter XXI) of, among other things, failing in his campaign because of drunkenness, Clark was shorn of his commission at the age of thirty-five. Wilkinson got his commission, and Clark was left practically penniless. Beginning in 1788, Clark made several vain attempts to recoup his fortunes—by planning a colony in Louisiana and, later, one on the Mississippi, and finally by leading a French force to take Louisiana (see editors' introduction for more details).

2. *half unzoned:* Archaically, a zone was a girdle or belt; here Arl——ton is referring to the informal dress worn by Caroline in the marquee (see note 2 to Letter XLIX) but the phrase also has erotic connotations.

3. *marquee:* See note 3 to Letter XLIX.

LETTER LII

1. *I hope in future he will not trifle with a lady under an idea that she is unprotected:* A woman, usually of the higher social classes, without a male family member to defend her honor, would be considered to be "un-

protected" and hence liable to attract the attention of men who did not necessarily intend to propose marriage.

LETTER LIII

1. *to come to an eclaircissement:* See note 2 to Letter XXII.

2. *Post St. Vincent:* That is, Fort St. Vincent, or Fort Vincennes, a French stronghold founded in 1732. In British hands since the Treaty of Paris of 1763, and in American hands since the Treaty of 1783, the place is marked as Post St. Vincent on the map provided in this edition (see also note 1 to Letter L).

3. *mountaineer:* Here, a native inhabitant of the mountains, who acts as a guide to the company.

LETTER LIV

1. *her unprotected situation secured his impunity:* See note 1 to Letter LII.

LETTER LV

1. *St. Anthony's falls . . . Kaskaskia:* St. Anthony's Falls are situated on the Mississippi River at what is now Minneapolis, and are marked on the map as the Falls of St. Anthony. Kaskaskia is a reference to a former French settlement of that name (see note 1 to Letter L), presumably the place marked on the map as Kaskaskias Village, located near the confluence of the Mississippi and Kaskaskia Rivers. The journey by river between St. Anthony's Falls and Kaskaskia is approximately 800 miles.

LETTER LVI

1. *Silver Creek:* Creek that feeds into the Ohio River from the north at the falls of the Ohio (referred to as the Rapids in the novel).

2. *some of the remote tribes . . . armed with bows and arrows:* P. P—— infers that the tribes are from a distant area because tribes that had been in contact with the British or French were likely to have been in possession of firearms (during the French and Indian War, the French in particular provided their Indian allies with large quantities of arms).

3. *her mistress's glass:* Probably a Claude glass, a slightly convex blackened mirror, popular in the eighteenth century as a device to view landscapes. By turning his or her back on the reflected scene and looking at it in a Claude glass, the Picturesque tourist would see a "composed" image in

finely graduated, harmonizing tones, theoretically reminiscent of the landscape paintings of Claude (see note 6 to Letter XIII).

LETTER LVII

1. *walked to the fort to inform the commandant:* That is, went to inform the commanding officer of the fort at St. Vincent's.

2. *the senate of the state:* Probably a reference to the Virginia legislative assembly, which, until Kentucky achieved statehood in 1792, held jurisdiction over the back settlements in the west. See note 5 to Letter LXVII.

3. *the revolution:* Imlay may mean revelation, or pleasant surprise.

LETTER LIX

1. *St. Vincent's:* See note 2 to Letter LIII and note 1 to Letter LX.

2. *St. Anthony's falls:* See note 1 to Letter LV.

3. *the 30th ult.:* The 30th of last month (ult. is derived from the Latin ultimo, last).

4. *celerity:* Speed.

5. *it having flashed in the pan:* This is a reference to the firing of the priming in the pan of a flintlock musket without discharging the piece.

6. *rendezvous:* Meeting.

7. *surtoute:* Surtout, a man's overcoat.

8. *bon bouche:* A tasty, stimulating beverage.

9. *a league:* See note 3 to Letter XI.

10. *the bird of Minerva:* An owl; in Roman mythology, the emblem of Minerva, the goddess of Wisdom (equivalent of Pallas Athene), was the owl.

11. *pallet:* A small makeshift bed.

12. *Venus:* See note 3 to Letter XX.

13. *Somnus:* In Roman mythology, the god of Sleep, the son of Night (Nox), and the brother of Death (Mors).

14. *Morpheus:* Name given by the Roman poet Ovid (43 B.C.–A.D. 17) to the son of Sleep and the god of Dreams (so called from the Greek word morphe, meaning form, because he gives form to the airy nothings of dreams).

15. *Aurora:* See note 1 to Letter XXX.

16. *a batteaux from Cohoes:* Bateau or batteau (plural forms, bateaux or batteaux), a flat-bottomed boat. Cohoes, also known as Kaoquias but more familiarly as Cahokia (its present-day name), was a small settlement on the eastern shore of the Mississippi River, just south of St. Louis, about eighteen miles below the mouth of the Missouri. At one time held by the French, the settlement became British in 1763 as part of the Treaty of Paris.

17. *the twentieth ult.:* See note 3.

18. *it must be nearly four hundred miles . . . where I overtook her:* This appears to be something of an exaggeration. If, as we are told earlier in this letter, Arl——ton's company came upon the Indians "about one hundred and fifty miles" above the mouth of the Illinois River, the distance referred to is nearer three hundred miles.

19. *your valetudinary habit:* Il——ray's extended bout of ill health (see Letter LV).

LETTER LX
1. *a place, upon which . . . who are its inhabitants:* Fort St. Vincent's, or Fort Vincennes, was a former French stronghold on the Illinois River (see note 2 to Letter LIII and note 1 to Letter L).

2. *Two things in Caroline's account of her captivity . . . from gratitude become their wives:* A concern with the chastity of female captives, on both the part of the captives themselves and the members of their home communities, had been a feature of captivity narratives since the time of *A Narrative of the Captivity and Restauration of Mrs. Mary Rowlandson* (1682) by Mary Rowlandson (1635?–78). Such chastity facilitated the reassimilation of the captive into her former community and guaranteed the continued racial purity (and implicit superiority) of that community. However, especially during the second half of the nineteenth century, white soldiers often pressured redeemed captives to claim that they had been raped in order to justify retaliatory, and imperialistic, action. Imlay

seems quite sympathetic to those women who acculturated and remained with their captors; indeed, as recent criticism has demonstrated, captives often found freedom from the rigid gender roles of white society, which deemed them helpless and sexually vulnerable, and from the prevailing racial ideologies. There are few records of these women's lives, but the accounts of three eighteenth-century captives who went native, those of Eunice Williams, Mary Jemison and Frances Slocum, were well known during the period.

3. *zephyrs:* Breezes from the west; gentle breezes.

4. *Savannas:* The prairie.

5. *when she receives into her bosom the luminary by which we live:* When the sun sets.

6. *those Arcadian days:* See note 4 to Letter XII.

7. *myrtle:* A common evergreen bushy shrub of southern Europe with oval to lance-shaped shiny leaves, fragrant white or rosy flowers, and black berries.

8. *Venus:* See note 3 to Letter XX.

LETTER LXI
1. *per diem:* Latin for "per day."

2. *port folio:* A hinged cover or flexible case for carrying loose papers (especially securities, bonds, and the like), or a collection of such papers.

3. *administer upon his effects:* To manage or supervise the execution of his personal goods.

4. *as dangerous as the box of Pandora:* In Greek myth, Pandora was the first woman; she was sent as a calamity to men by Zeus, who was enraged by the theft of heavenly fire by Prometheus. She was given a box from which escaped and spread all the ills of human life. Some versions of the story blame Pandora's curiosity for this disaster.

5. *"Pour the sweet milk . . . unity on earth":* These lines are a quotation from *The Tragedy of Macbeth* (1605–06) by William Shakespeare (1564–1616); see act 4, scene iii, lines 98–100.

6. *concupiscence:* Voluptuousness, lust.

LETTER LXII

1. *the King's-bench prison:* See notes 12 and 14 to Letter XXX.

2. *clubs of St. James's:* See note 2 to Letter IX, and note 8 to Letter XXX.

LETTER LXIII

1. *The Inclosed:* The text is not quite consistent here; Letter LIX, also an enclosed letter, is not marked as such.

2. *Bart.:* Abbreviation of Baronet, a hereditary title of the minor aristocracy.

3. *Honourable:* Frequently used as a courtesy title.

LETTER LXIV

1. *I have prevailed . . . to return to England:* The transatlantic topography is used to mark the relative moral worth and ideological affiliation of the characters. Those who return to Britain are clearly aligned with the weakness, effeminacy, and corruption ascribed to England, while those who remain, notably Caroline, are identified with the strengths and virtues of the New World.

2. *as will make them comfortable, not exceeding one hundred and fifty pounds each:* Thus, the family, consisting of Mr. and Mrs. T——n and their daughter Mary, will have a combined income of 450 pounds, sufficient for them to live genteelly but not at the level of the minor gentry (which would require an annual income of at least 2,000 pounds). The Dashwood women in Jane Austen's *Sense and Sensibility* move to a cottage in Devonshire with two female and one male servant on 500 pounds a year, while in Mrs. Gomersall's *Elenora* (*c.* 1789) such an income provides a comfortable and elegant lifestyle but with restrictions (her house is small and she keeps no carriage). Much information on the cultural significance of different annual incomes during this period is to be found in Edward Copeland, *Women Writing about Money: Women's Fiction in England, 1790–1820* (Cambridge: Cambridge University Press, 1995), especially 22–33.

3. *the King's-bench Prison:* See notes 12 and 14 to Letter XXX.

4. *he will reclaim:* That is, he will be reclaimed or reformed.

5. *Tartarus:* See note 1 to Letter XLV.

LETTER LXV

1. *Letter LXV:* Erroneously numbered as Letter LXVI in the first edition (corrected in the Dublin edition of 1794). The letter numbering from this point in the text onward is erratic and has been corrected in the present edition. The original sequence is as follows: LXVI; LXIV; LXVIII; LXIX; LXIX; LXX; LXX; LXXI; LXXII. The present edition therefore arrives at a total of 73 letters, whereas the first edition suggests that there were only 72. While correcting the numerical sequence, the Dublin edition, however, introduces another mistake by moving directly from Letter LXVI to LXVIII, the omission of number LXVII thus resulting in a notional total of 74 letters.

2. *meads:* Meadows; that is, rich pasturelands.

3. *Phœbus:* An epithet of Apollo, particularly in his quality as the god of Light. The name often stands for the sun personified.

4. *lambent:* Glowing or softly radiant.

5. *sublunary beings:* Earthly beings.

6. *cardinal virtue:* A quality designated as a major virtue, the four classically defined natural virtues being justice, prudence, temperance, and fortitude, upon which the whole of human nature was supposed to hinge.

7. *a guinea:* An English gold coin issued from 1663 to 1813 and fixed in 1717 at a value of 21 shillings. (Guinea, in Africa, was the supposed source of the gold from which it was made.)

8. *Ætna:* The famous Sicilian volcano.

LETTER LXVI

1. *a passage of fourteen days from Louisville to New Orleans:* In his *Topographical Description* Imlay says that the average time of this journey is about twenty days (Letter V). See note 6 to Letter XVII.

2. *Hispaniola . . . Cadiz:* Hispaniola is an island in the West Indies divided between Haiti on the west and the Dominican Republic on the east. Cadiz is a port in Spain, northwest of Gibraltar.

3. *emperor Julian wintered in that city:* Flavius Claudius Julianus, or Julian, also known as Julian the Apostate (A.D. 331–363), became emperor in

361. He was a nephew of Constantine the Great, and a noted scholar and military leader. In 355 he was proclaimed and invested as caesar (that is, coadjutor and eventual successor) by Emperor Constantius II, who dispatched Julian to Gaul (modern France), where he proved a resolute and successful commander. He defeated and expelled the Alemanni and the Franks. In 360, while Julian was wintering in Paris, the emperor, who was jealous of his military successes, ordered the return of some of his best troops, ostensibly for service in the east, but in reality to weaken Julian. Julian's army hereupon hailed him as the new emperor. Before a clash between Julian's and Constantius's armies could take place, Constantius died, having on his deathbed bequeathed the empire to Julian. Having renounced Christianity when he became emperor, Julian attempted to drive out Christianity and to reinstate a polytheism based on neoplatonic philosophy. He was, however, killed fighting in Persia before he could carry through his plans.

4. *that philosopher and soldier said "he liked the people of Paris, because they were grave like himself"*: The source of this quotation has not been located.

5. *do not the members of the Parliament . . . stratagem, address, and corruption*: At this period, politics in Britain were thoroughly corrupted by various systems of bribery, and Parliament no longer represented the interests of the nation, only those of various sections of the privileged classes.

6. *the celebrated Sir Robert Walpole, and the present premier of England . . . that country ever produced*: The English statesman Sir Robert Walpole (1676–1745) was leader of the Whig party and secretary of war (1708–10), and chancellor of the exchequer. He restored credit after the South Sea Bubble (a stock-jobbing scheme which crashed in 1720) and abolished tariff duties on many articles. An expert in finance and especially commerce, he laid the basis for free trade in England. His ministry fell in 1742 amid charges of corruption and of mismanagement of the war with Spain. William Pitt the Younger (1759–1806) was prime minister from 1783 to 1801, and again from 1804 until 1806. He was famous for his strict integrity. His first ministry was one of cautious reconstruction such as Britain needed for the long wars with France. Politically, he was conservative (Tory), but he was the first political leader to rely on public opinion as expressed in the electoral constituencies instead of on more or less bribed backing among members of Parliament. Miss T——n's

coupling of Walpole and Pitt does not seem to do justice to the latter.

7. *finesse:* Skillful social maneuvering.

8. *Bologne:* Boulogne, city and port in northern France on the English Channel.

9. *Jove:* See note 5 to Letter XVII.

10. *the famed Portia . . . her loved Brutus:* Portia, wife of Marcus Brutus, an ardent supporter of the republican cause, was said to have wounded herself to demonstrate her worthiness to be told of the conspiracy against Julius Caesar (see note 6 of Letter XXXVI). In the play *Julius Caesar* (*c.* 1599) by William Shakespeare (1564–1616) her wifely anxieties prompt her to comment on the weakness of a woman's heart after she has nearly disclosed the secret to her servant, Lucius: "Ah me! How weak a thing / The heart of woman is!" (act 2, scene iv).

11. *Hyde-park:* See note 5 to Letter XIV.

12. *a taylor, hosier, and mercer:* Tailor, or one whose business it was to make outer garments, especially for men; a hosier was a dealer in or maker of hosiery, or knitware, mostly stockings and socks; a mercer was a dealer in expensive textiles and fabrics.

13. *discounted bills:* The reference is probably to a deduction made for interest in advancing money upon a bill not due (i.e., the interest would be deducted from the amount of money that was borrowed).

14. *he was off in a tangent:* He absconded.

15. *fleecing:* Charging exorbitantly for goods or services.

16. *to be arraigned:* Charged or put on trial.

17. *Botany-bay:* A bay in New South Wales, Australia, near Sydney, which Captain Cook claimed for the British crown in 1770. From 1787 (that is, after the historical time of Miss T——n's story, which must be earlier than March 1785, but predating the writing of the novel), convicted criminals sentenced to transportation were sent to Australia. They were not, in fact, sent to Botany Bay, but the name was used in common speech to cover convict settlements in Australia generally.

18. *the deserts of Spain . . . their ignorant minds:* The reference is generally to the repressive ideology of the Catholic Church, which was nowhere more despotic than in Spain, and more particularly to the Spanish Inquisition, a tribunal for suppressing heresy in Spain. Though nominally under papal control, the Inquisition was actually an agency of the crown, and was often used for political purposes. The principal victims of the Inquisition in Spain were the converted Muslims and Jews, but it also investigated crimes against morality. Its procedures were secret, and suspects were accused anonymously, and torture was often used. Penalties ranged from reprimands to being burned at the stake. The Inquisition was suppressed in 1808.

LETTER LXVII

1. *that season of which Thompson speaks . . . "her yielding soul was love":* A reference to "Spring" (1728), one of the four blank-verse poems collectively entitled *The Seasons*, by James Thomson (see note 5 to Letter XXI). As Arl——ton himself indicates, his quotation is not quite accurate. The lines read:

> *Flushed by the spirit of the genial year,*
> *Now from the virgin's cheek a fresher bloom*
> *Shoots, less and less, the live carnation round;*
> *Her lips blush deeper sweets; she breathes of youth;*
> *The shining moisture swells into her eyes*
> *In brighter flow; her wishing bosom heaves*
> *With palpitations wild; kind tumults seize*
> *Her veins, and all her yielding soul is love (lines 963–70).*

2. *Voltaire said "if ever . . . middle provinces of America":* For information on Voltaire, see note 1 to letter X. No exact source of this quotation has been located, so that it is likely that Imlay is quoting from memory. The closest source is a sentence from the fourth letter ("Sur les Quakers") of Voltaire's *Lettres Philosophiques:* "Guillaume Penn pouvait se vanter d'avoir apporté sur la terre l'âge d'or dont on parle tant, et qui n'a vraisemblablement existé qu'en Pennsylvanie" [William Penn could boast of having given the world the golden age which is talked about so much, but which probably never existed but in Pennsylvania"—trans. eds.].

3. *the once smiling meads of the gentle Pacaic:* Imlay is presumably referring to a once thriving Indian tribe; however, no tribe of this name has been identified.

4. *sanguinary warfare:* Bloodthirsty warfare. Probably a reference to the French and Indian War (1754–63), and possibly also to the American War of Independence (1775–83).

5. *As the government of this district is not organized:* At the time the action in the novel takes place (1783–85), the area that now constitutes the state of Kentucky was ruled by the Virginia assembly. However, with thousands of new settlers moving into the Ohio Valley after the end of the Revolutionary War, the need for more effective local government became acute. Between 1784 and 1791, nine conventions were held in Danville, Virginia, to consider the creation of a new state of Kentucky, and Virginia prescribed the terms by which Kentucky should be separated in three enabling acts. Finally, in April 1792 a constitution was drafted, and on June 1, Kentucky was admitted to the Union as the fifteenth state. The first constitution provided for a governor chosen by an electoral college, a bicameral legislature, and a court of three judges. It included an elaborate bill of rights and a provision for manhood suffrage. Slavery was permitted.

6. *Diamond island:* See note 3 to Letter XLVI.

7. *This tract . . . men who served in the late war:* The War of Independence, having started in 1775, had been formally ended with the Treaty of Paris in 1783.

8. *fee-simple:* An unconditional inheritance.

9. *a seat in a house of representatives . . . to assemble every Sunday in the year:* The democratic and utopian government envisaged by Arl——ton has a subversive Jacobin slant, for the "Sunday meeting" would normally have been a religious and not a political one. Arl——ton's utopian plans have more than an antiecclesiastical slant; his proposal to introduce an alternative procedure for the election of a president clearly reveals that what he is in fact proposing here is a secessionist utopia with a government independent of the United States of America.

10. *Every male . . . may think proper to bestow:* Arl——ton extends the right of suffrage of adult males in the mid-1780s—that is, well before such a right was extended in the United States as a whole in the first decade of the nineteenth century. By 1825 every state except Rhode Island, Virginia, and Louisiana had achieved universal white male suffrage. Neither Arl——ton's utopian community nor the historical government of the United States gave voting rights to women or to Native Americans. That the members of the house of representatives of the community of Bellefont are allocated a salary also prefigures the decline of the classical republican conception of government officeholding, which expected public service without compensation.

11. *those itinerant preachers . . . truly lamentable:* From a Jacobin perspective, such preachers fooled the people with tales of religion and led them astray from the path of reason. The itinerant preachers played an important role in whipping up support for the Great Awakening, the religious revivalist movement which swept through the American colonies from the 1730s to the 1750s. It was marked by sensational public repentance and conversion, and prompted a surge of missionary activity. It began in Massachusetts and later spread to the middle colonies. Although its main impetus was over by the time the action of the novel takes place, itinerant preachers were roaming up and down the back settlements of Kentucky and Tennessee, in the lead up to the second wave of religious revivalism that manifested itself in the first decades of the nineteenth century.

12. *Caroline has not either been unemployed . . . promote their comfort:* Caroline and the other women remain firmly in the domestic realm; see the editors' introduction for more information on the gendered division of labor.

LETTER LXVIII

1. *Effeminacy has triumphed:* The novel displaces the prevailing stereotypical cultural dichotomy of effeminate France versus manly Britain and relocates it transatlantically in the New World as a dichotomy between effeminate Britain and manly America.

2. *the toilet:* The dressing table, or the whole dress and appearance of a person.

3. *The embraces of elegant women . . . the distinction of singers:* Another reference to the widespread social and moral corruption in Great Britain. Il——ray is probably complaining about the phenomenon of the marriage of convenience, which was motivated by financial interests rather than by love and trust, and the so-called "marriage market." At the same time, because of the sexual double standard, men could lavish wealth and attention on kept women, here referred to as singers, but more traditionally these were—or were called—actresses, a profession that had long been connected in the public mind with that of prostitution.

4. *eclat:* See note 4 to Letter XXXV.

5. *an action in Doctors Commons:* Name by which the Consistory Court of London was generally known. The Consistory Court, which was the largest canon law court in the south of England and which dominated matrimonial business in the late eighteenth and early nineteenth centuries, was located in Doctors Commons.

6. *though it was not very likely, she would ever have any by Mr. F——:* That Eliza is not likely to have children by Mr. F—— confirms the impotence ascribed to him.

7. *he would give Mrs. F—— . . . subject to reversion:* The property reverts to the original owner on her death.

8. *as they now existed . . . impotence or infidelity:* Impotence would be grounds for an annulment but it was only very rarely invoked as such; male infidelity was not grounds for a divorce during this period in Great Britain. See the editors' introduction for more details.

9. *It has been said by a patriot in the British senate that, "there is . . . can enlighten!":* This person has not been identified, nor has the source of the quotation been located.

10. *the most incorrigible and corrupt minister that ever disgraced the government of England:* This person has not been identified.

LETTER LXIX
1. *Letter LXIX:* This letter is enclosed with the preceding one, but not marked as such in the text.

LETTER LXX

1. *The Ohio has been celebrated by geographers for its beauty, and its country for fertility:* Among the geographers and travelers that had sung the praises of the Ohio River and the surrounding country are John Filson, Thomas Hutchins, and Jedidiah Morse (see editors' introduction). Thomas Ashe spoke for many when he said, in his *Travels in America*, that the Ohio "has been described as beyond competition, the most beautiful river in the universe" (Vol. I, 146; see note 4 to Letter VIII).

2. *acar saccharinum:* That is, *acer saccharum,* botanical name for sugar maple.

3. *six furlongs:* a furlong was a unit of distance equivalent to 220 yards; thus six furlongs is 1,320 yards, or about ¾ of a mile.

4. *several leagues:* See note 3 to Letter XI.

5. *Pomona:* In Roman mythology, goddess of fruit trees, wooed and won by Vertumnus, god of the seasons.

6. *those friends who may in future wish to join us:* This suggests that Arl——ton is motivated by a dream of a utopian community similar to Samuel Coleridge's pantisocracy (see editors' introduction).

7. *to say with the poet, "And young eyed health exalts, / The whole creation round":* The lines are from James Thomson's *The Seasons*, the section on "Spring" (lines 893–94). See note 5 to Letter XXI.

8. *pinions:* Wings.

LETTER LXXI

1. *establishment:* A residence (as well as a settlement to be able to maintain it).

LETTER LXXII

1. *my parliamentary conduct:* It is unclear whether this is a reference to his conduct in Parliament, as the subsequent discussion of British laws and government might suggest, or simply to his decorous handling of the family affairs.

2. *That perfectibility . . . the philosophers of the present day . . . have laboured to remove:* The most prominent philosopher alluded to here would be William Godwin (see note 3 to the preface), who argued the case for

the perfectibility of man in his *Enquiry Concerning Political Justice* (1793). Unlike what Mor——ley seems to be implying here, Godwin in fact emphasizes that when he claims that man is perfectible, he means capable of improvement, rather than capable of attaining a state of absolute perfection.

3. *what part of them it is . . . the greater security of the remainder:* A covert allusion to Edmund Burke's views on the relation between the individual and the state; see note 1 to Letter XXVII.

4. *be subject to lose . . . have carried her husband:* See note 6 to Letter IX.

5. *to be considered in the light of property:* Most married women had no legal existence separate to that of their husband. In his *Commentaries on the Laws of England* (1765–69) William Blackstone notes that "the very being or legal existence of the woman is suspended during the marriage, or at least is incorporated and consolidated into that of the husband" (*Commentaries on the Laws of England*, 4 vols. [Oxford: Clarendon Press, 1765–69], vol. I, 430).

6. *while partial and cruel violations . . . to its very foundation:* Although the plot takes place between 1783 and 1785, the novel was probably written in 1792, and hence the reference may be to the general atmosphere of Jacobin radicalism in the later 1780s and the beginning of the revolutionary decade.

7. *Such were the characters . . . our glorious revolution of 1688:* Charles I (1600–49), king of Great Britain and Ireland in 1625–49, had limited intellectual abilities; the causes of religious and economic conflict were so strong during his reign that it ended in civil war, his defeat, and his execution. Charles II (1630–85) was king of Great Britain and Ireland during 1660–85. The restoration of the monarchy brought him back from exile after the interregnum since the execution of his father, Charles I. Politically unscrupulous and personally immoral, he was nonetheless one of the most intelligent kings in English history, and his court was a center of culture and wit, as well as of moral licentiousness. For James II (1633–1701) and the Glorious Revolution, see note 5 to Letter XL.

8. *the contumely and arrogance . . . the mother country:* Refers to King George III (1738–1820), who reigned from 1760 and who suffered from mental illness from 1788. George III and Lord North exasperated the American colonists with their repeated attempts to impose taxes on

them, and they bear much responsibility for the loss of England's North American colonies. George's obstinacy in dealing with people whom he believed to be rebels in part caused and protracted the war by which the Americans ultimately "effected a defalcation," or separation, from Britain.

9. *obstinacy of the present administration . . . the constitution:* A reference to the Tory government led by William Pitt the Younger (see note 6 to Letter LXVI), and backed by George III, whose policy became one of upholding the established church and state and of opposing liberalism, social reform, and all attempts to curb royal power in favor of increased parliamentary power.

LETTER LXXIII

1. *Bellefont, July:* The letters are dated sequentially by month throughout the novel; since the preceding letter is dated September, it may be that this letter is erroneously superscribed "July," or, alternatively, the novel's two final letters are supposed to have crossed in the post.

2. *harshorn:* Hartshorn, a preparation of ammonia in water, used as smelling salts; originally made from the shavings of a hart's (male deer's) horn.

3. *hackney coach:* A coach kept for hire, especially a four-wheeled carriage drawn by two horses and having seats for six people.

4. *masquerade:* An assembly of people wearing masks and often fantastic costumes, generally at a ball.

5. *like a Patriarch of old:* A reference to one of the scriptural fathers of the human race or of the Hebrew people.

GLOSSARY

Ambrosia: Traditionally, the food of the gods; used in the novel to mean something extremely pleasant to the senses.

Animadversions: Adverse criticism.

Calumniate: To utter maliciously false statements, to slander.

Colloquial: Conversational.

Consanguinity: Blood relationship.

Contumely: Scornful insolence.

Corroding: Debilitating.

Coxcomb: A conceited, foolish person or dandy.

Cypher: Nonentity; a person of no worth.

Dereliction: Abandonment, loss.

Effulgence: Splendor.

Elysium: In Greek mythology, the abode of the blessed; used in the novel to refer to a state of happiness, or to a delightful place.

Encomium: Glowing and warmly enthusiastic praise.

Ennui: Boredom, languor.

Favour: Normally (at the beginning of a letter), refers to a letter.

Immolate: Sacrifice.

Ingenuous: Frank and honorable.

Interdict: Forbid, prohibit.

Je-june: (jejune) Juvenile, puerile.

Lucubrations: Laborious or intensive study protracted late into the night, as well as the product of such study.

Mellifluous: Flowing with honey or sweetness; smooth.

Munificence: Great generosity.

Obloquy: Also appears as "obliquy"; disgrace, bad reputation.

Packet: A vessel plying regularly between one port and another, employed in carrying packets of letters and passengers.

Paltroon: Poltroon, a spiritless coward.

To post: To set off hastily.

Prodigality: Reckless extravagance.

Promulge: Promulgate, make public.

Risque: Rescue.

Schism: Separation.

Sequestration: Seclusion, isolation.

Specious: Deceptively attractive.

Taper: Thin candle.

Venality: Mercenary corruptibility.